If I Can't Have You:

Renaissance Collection

If I Can't Have You:

Renaissance Collection

Dawn Jiles

www.urbanbooks.net

Urban Books, LLC
300 Farmingdale Road, NY-Route 109
Farmingdale, NY 11735

If I Can't Have You: Renaissance Collection

ISBN 13: 978-1-62286-513-0
ISBN 10: 1-62286-513-8

First Trade Paperback Printing April 2018
Printed in the United States of America

10 9 8 7 6 5 4 3 2 1

Distributed by Kensington Publishing Corp.
Submit orders to:
Customer Service
400 Hahn Road
Westminster, MD 21157-4627
Phone: 1-800-733-3000
Fax: 1-800-659-2436

If I Can't Have You:

Renaissance Collection

by

Dawn Jiles

Dedication

I would like to dedicate my first book to my aunts, Patrice and Lashon Goodman. I would also like to dedicate it to my grandmother Mildred Giles. RIP, ladies. I love and really miss the three of you!

To my family and friends, I love you all, and thanks for the support!

Acknowledgments

First and foremost, I want to thank God for the wonderful blessing and opportunity that he has given me.

Secondly, I want to thank Racquel Williams for everything that was done for me to get to this point.

To all my family and friends, I love y'all, and I appreciate all the support.

I want to give a special shout-out to my parents, Kim and Timothy Giles; to my sisters and brother, Shanice Jiles, Tatyana Driver, and Timothy Jiles Jr.; and to my loving and supportive fiancé, Will Jennings. And a big shout-out goes to my granny Bobbie Goodman.

I wish to give my heartfelt thanks to my best friends, Constance Knox, Jenelle Mcglothian, Soliel Green, Chanel Bowers, Chanel Johnson, and Kristen Drew. My spiritual leaders and supporters, I love y'all!

And here's a shout to Milwaukee, Wisconsin, where I was born and raised. Milwaukee, stand up!

Chapter One

Monique

"Monique, wake your butt up and get ready for school. Do not let me have to tell you twice!" my mother screamed from the bottom of the stairs.

I lay on my back and rolled my eyes to the ceiling. I hated school! It was not because I didn't want to be educated; I just really hated the way the other kids made me feel. They'd tease me and call me all types of names. They called me black, fat monkey, and Miss Piggy. I would pinch my nose to stop the tears that formed in my eyes. Although I was alone, I would not give them the satisfaction of a tear.

I climbed out of my bed and headed for my bathroom. I was an only child being raised by both parents. My mom was a nurse, and my father was a lawyer. They gave me everything my heart desired, but I still found myself sad all the time.

Once I was in the bathroom, I stared at myself in the mirror. Yeah, I could stand to lose a few pounds, and I could probably do something different with my hair, but I was really not an ugly girl. I was five feet, four inches tall, with green eyes and long, silky jet-black hair. I had a huge ass, nice-size breasts, and smooth mocha skin. I weighed almost 250 pounds, and I was dark skinned, and that was all people seemed to notice.

I was seventeen years old, and I would be a senior in high school the next year. Thank God this was my last week of my junior year of high school. If it were not for my best friends, Samariah and Bria, I would probably get bullied more often.

I showered, got dressed, and threw on a pink jogging suit from Victoria's Secret. It was early June, but in Milwaukee it still felt like it was winter outside.

I ran out of the house and hopped into my 2011 fire-red Audi coupe, which my parents had got me for my sixteenth birthday. I sped out of the driveway, on my way to school. First, I would pick up Bria and Samariah, Sam for short. My BFFs were two of the most popular girls in school. We had been friends since grade school and had been inseparable since then.

Sam was light skinned, with big breasts and one of the biggest asses I had ever seen. She had a flat tummy and a small waist. She looked like a thicker version of Nicki Minaj. Every guy at our high school wanted her, and all the chicks wanted to be her. Bria had a hazel complexion, with these exotic-looking eyes. She was about five feet tall, with nice, perky breasts. She had absolutely no ass, but you couldn't tell her that. She was slim, and her hair was cut short, like that chick from the show *Empire*.

I picked them up, and we headed to school.

"Bitches!" screamed Sam. "Why has Eric been blowing up my damn phone? He knows I'm with Kevin. Just because I let him eat this good pussy doesn't mean I want his ass." She scrunched up her face and rolled her eyes.

"Why the hell are you scrunching up your face? You knew what you were doing when you allowed him to do that to you," Bria said. "And to top it all off, they are best friends, ho!" Bria was the type to always speak her mind. She didn't bite her tongue for anyone.

"You know Bria is right, Sam. Why would you mess with him, knowing that him and Kevin are best friends?" I asked.

"And turn down great head? That's nonsense!" Sam responded with a straight face.

"You know this ho is a ho. She ain't turning down no nigga," Bria said, shaking her head at Sam and laughing.

Sam had slept with a lot of guys in our school and outside of the school. Everybody seemed to know about it, except her boyfriend, Kevin. They had been together for about two years now, and once he took her virginity, she just couldn't get enough of sex.

"Well, if you two virgin bitches will start fucking somebody, you will understand where I'm coming from. Bria, you and David have been together for years, and you haven't given him any. You better hope he's not getting it from somebody else," Sam said.

"I'll pass, and my man is faithful, but you don't know the meaning of that," Bria said, annoyed.

I thought about sex sometimes and what it would be like, but I had never had a boyfriend, and no one ever seemed to be interested in me. There was this one guy named Corey, who was the star of our basketball team. I had the biggest crush on him. He was so fine, but he didn't even notice me.

We made it to school and rushed to our classes. The day went by quickly. As we headed to my car, after the last bell rang, Kevin ran up behind us and grabbed Sam by the waist.

"What's up, ladies?" he said to Bria and me. Bria and I nodded our heads, and Sam gave him a fat kiss on the lips. "Y'all know I'm throwing an end of the school year bash at my house? It's going to be cracking super hard. Y'all down?" asked Kevin.

"Baby, you know I'm going to be there," Sam said.

"Me too," Bria said.

"I guess I'll be there as well," I said, joining in.

Kevin whispered something in Sam's ear, and she began to blush. "I'll talk to you bitches later. I'm leaving with Kevin," Sam said. She swished that big ole ass as she walked off.

Bria and I got in my car and headed home.

Sam

I was not your average seventeen-year-old. I had the body of a grown woman; I was definitely shaped like the number eight. Couldn't none of these bitches compete with me. With my small waist, big ass, and the face to match, there was no competition. I had all the niggas sweating my shit, and I couldn't blame them. They liked what they saw. I could have any nigga I wanted; I didn't care if he had a girl. If I wanted him, I was getting him.

I loved my boyfriend, Kevin, but he was starting to bore me. It was the same old shit with him. He didn't know how to please my body, which was the very reason I cheated. I know you're thinking, *This ho*, but there was just something about sex. I loved it! I absolutely had to have it. It made me feel good, and I love being wanted.

If I could have sex all day, I would—just not with Kevin's boring ass. I had tried to teach him how to fuck me, but he just didn't get it. That was why when his best friend, Eric, told me that he wanted to taste me, I had to oblige. We did it right there in the girls' bathroom at our school, and it was some of the best head I had ever had. He licked, kissed, and sucked all over my kitty kat. He ate my pussy so good that I wanted to get some of that dick, but the bell rang, and I had to get to class. I might be a ho, but I was going to be an educated ho. Eric kept calling and texting me, telling me that he wanted to finish what we started. I just might take him up on that offer.

I got in the car with Kevin, and we headed to his house. When I was with my BFFs, he had whispered in my ear that he wanted to beat my pussy up, and my kitty kat had started to throb. Although Kevin's sex wasn't that great, I knew how to get myself off when I was with him. Corey was the best sex partner I'd ever had. Yes, I'm talking about the Corey that my best friend Monique is in love with. She had had the biggest crush on him since the ninth grade, but her fat ass had never made a move. Even if she had, that wouldn't stop me. Like I said, I got whomever I wanted, when I wanted them. I didn't care if he was my best friend's man. Just thinking about Corey's fine ass made me want to play with my kitty.

"Baby, let's try something different today. Let's park somewhere secluded and do it in the car," Kevin said.

"Okay. But where will we go?" I said.

Kevin thought he was the only man I had ever been with. Granted he took my virginity, but if he really knew the truth, he would probably beat my ass. I had been fucking different niggas since about a month after we first had sex.

"Let's go to Washington Park. I know a little hidden spot around that way," Kevin said excitedly.

"Let's do it, then," I said.

We headed toward Washington Park and reached our destination. He quickly started to undress me. With Kevin, there was absolutely no foreplay. He always took off my clothes and got right to fucking. Today he surprised me; he took my 40DD titties and put them in his mouth. That shit felt so good, but as soon as it got good, he pulled his six-inch dick out and entered me. He gave me a few good pumps, and it was over in two minutes, tops. Kevin's problems were that his penis wasn't that big and he couldn't hang. I was pissed the fuck off, but I hid my anger. I guessed I'd be taking Eric up on his offer, 'cause this shit here was for the birds.

Bria

I didn't know what was wrong with my best friend Sam. I loved her, but I hated the decisions she made.

I had had a steady boyfriend since the ninth grade. His name was David, and my man was fine. He was light skinned, with black and honey-blond dreads. He was a little on the chunky side, but it was mostly muscle. He was about five-eleven, and he was the star quarterback of our football team. David treated me so good that I couldn't have asked for a better man. I loved him. We were even going to the same college together.

My thoughts drifted off to Mo. I loved my best friend Monique, but she was always so sad. I knew it had a lot do with her weight and them teasing her at school, but when Sam and I were around, we put that shit to a stop.

"I don't know how I feel about going to this party. They are all going to be making fun of me," Monique said.

"Listen, Mo, I'm not going to let none of them bums at school mess with you," I yelled into the phone.

A few days had passed since Kevin invited us to the party, and as you can see, Mo was nervous as hell.

"If I could just lose weight, people wouldn't make fun of me. I hate being big," Mo said.

"Mo, you are beautiful. Big and all, but if you don't like what you see, do something about it. You can always lose the weight, but you have never put forth the effort. You complain to me all the time about how big you are, but you never try to change it," I said.

My girl Monique was so beautiful, but I didn't think she realized how pretty she really was. She had been big since first grade, and she always complained about it but never put forth the effort to change it.

"You know what, Bria? You are absolutely right. I am going to start working on it right away," said Mo.

She sounded serious, so I hoped she did it. "Pull out something nice to wear and get ready for this party tomorrow," I said.

"Is David coming?" Mo asked.

"Girl, you know he is! He never misses a good party," I said. "I've got to go. It's time for dinner." We hung up the phone, and I went downstairs to eat dinner.

"So, how is David? He hasn't been over in a while," my mom said as we sat at the table.

"He's good," I said. My mom thought I was too young to be making plans to be with David. She had been with my dad since high school, so I didn't know why she was riding my back so hard. My mother was a stay-at-home wife and mother. She took good care of my brother and me, but sometimes she got on my damn nerves.

"I still think you're too young to be trying to settle down, even if he's a nice young man."

I didn't respond. I just rolled my eyes and continued to eat my food.

"Honey, leave her alone. If she wants to be with that boy, let her. As long as she keeps getting good grades and goes to college, I'm okay with it," my dad said with a stern face.

"But . . . ," my mom interjected.

"But nothing," my dad said, raising his hands to let my mom know the conversation was over.

We finished eating dinner, and then I rushed off to my room. I started thinking about David. Lately, he had been talking about having sex, but I was scared. Everyone talked about how good it felt, but I was just not sure if I was ready. What if things changed once we had sex? What if he broke up with me afterward? I had a lot of what-ifs. I did know I wanted him to be my first and only, but those what-ifs were holding me back.

It was Friday, and it was our last day of school. Today was also the day of the bash. We had decided to meet up over Sam's house to get dressed and go to the party. When we all arrived at Sam's, my girls and I were looking fly as hell. I had on this red Bebe halter dress with some matching red Bebe six-inch heels. Sam wore some blue jean booty shorts with a white sleeveless blouse and some white six-inch Steve Madden sandals. Her ass was hanging all out of those shorts, but that was how Sam liked it. Mo had on some cut-up skinny jeans and a fitted blazer with some Michael Kors flats. Even though my girl was insecure, she looked good tonight.

We headed out to the party, and we were so geeked.

"I think I'm going to fuck Eric tonight," said Sam.

"Um, you do know you're going to your boyfriend's party?" Mo said.

"So? What he doesn't know ain't going to hurt him. We will be careful with our shit. I does this," Sam said.

All I could do was shake my head. She behaved so recklessly. One day all the shit she did was going to catch up to her. I just didn't know how soon it would be.

Chapter Two

Sam

We entered my man's party, and we were the hottest bitches in there. All eyes were on us, and I could see the envy in their eyes. I started shaking my big ass to one of Lil Wayne's new joints. I turned around, because I felt a pair of eyes on me. Eric was standing there watching me like a hawk. *He is so fucking sexy*, I thought.

He was six-two, dark skinned, with the whitest teeth that I had ever seen. He was dressed fly as hell, and his naturally curly 'fro was lined up perfectly— like Steve Harvey's used to be. Kevin walked up behind me, and I started to dance erotically, the whole time staring directly into Eric's eyes. I knew I had him hooked, and he wanted me just as bad as I wanted him. At first, I had played it off to my girls like I just wanted some head from him, but it was much deeper. I wanted to feel him deep inside of me, and it was going to happen tonight.

Somebody called Kevin's name, so we stopped dancing, and my girls walked over to me.

"Bitch, you think you were staring at Eric hard enough? Anybody with eyes can tell y'all fucking around," Bria said.

"Girl, you're tripping. Wasn't nobody paying attention to us," I said.

"Bitch, please. That's what you think," said Bria.

"What are you going to do when Kevin finds out? You can't keep doing dirt and thinking you won't get caught. I mean, you've slept with so many people, Sam," Mo whispered while shaking her head at me.

"Look, don't worry about me. I do what the fuck I want to do. You tramps are getting on my damn nerves," I said.

"Whatever," Bria said.

I walked away from them in search of Eric. I couldn't find him, so I texted him and told him to meet me in the basement. I snuck downstairs, where Kevin's older brother's room was. His brother was in the army, so no one was ever in there. About two minutes later, Eric's sexy ass walked down the stairs.

He walked up on me in the bedroom and began to kiss me on my lips. His tongue flicked in and out of my mouth like he was a pro. I pushed him on the bed and began to strip out of my clothes. I walked over to him and did the same thing to him. His dick was so hard, and it was big and thick as hell. My mouth began to water. I dropped to my knees, and I kissed the tip of his dick. I began sucking and licking on all ten inches of his beautiful black dick like my life depended on it. I had my eyes on him the entire time. His eyes rolled into the back of his head, and I knew I was giving him pure ecstasy. He picked me up and turned me upside down as he began to suck on my already wet pussy like a pro. I went back to sucking on his shit, and I felt like I was in heaven.

He quickly laid me on the bed, and he entered my hole. I was dripping wet. My walls clamped down on his dick as he filled me up. He began to stroke me at a slow pace. He flipped me over so that my ass was in the air. He entered me from behind and began to beat my pussy up. Just as I was about to cum, the bedroom door flew open.

I pushed Eric off me and covered my body. I immediately began to cry as I stared into Kevin's eyes.

"Aye, man. I'm sorry, bro. I know this is fucked up and hard to believe, but I am," Eric said.

"You know what, bro? I ain't even mad at you. It's this ho that I'm mad at. I guess I ain't enough for you. Everybody was telling me that you were a ho, but I wasn't trying to hear that shit," Kevin snarled.

I ran over to him and began to cry for his forgiveness. "Baby, I'm sorry! I love you so much. I will never cheat on you again. Baby, pl—" I said, but he cut me off.

"Bitch, get out of my face! You and me are done! You will never be my woman again," Kevin said as he pushed me off him. He walked off.

I fell to my knees and began to cry hysterically. Eric put his clothes on hurriedly and walked out the door without a word to me. I put my clothes on and took my ass home. I was so hurt because I had never really thought that my dirt would catch up to me. I really did love Kevin with all my heart, and I had never considered the fact that I could actually get caught. Everything was all messed up, and I didn't know what I was going to do.

Monique

Kevin stormed passed Bria and me, mad as hell.

"I wonder what's wrong with him?" Bria asked, reading my thoughts.

"I was wondering the same thing," I said nervously.

No sooner had I said that than Eric came walking from the same direction, with this guilty-ass look on his face. I could tell that he had just got caught doing something that he wasn't supposed to be doing. He walked out the door and left the party.

"Something isn't right. Did you see the look on his face?" I said, feeling even more nervous.

"Yeah, I saw it, and where is Sam?" Bria asked.

David ran up to us and asked if we had spoken to Sam.

"No," we both said in unison, looking confused.

"Well, y'all need to find her and get her out of here, because Kevin is mad as hell," David shouted.

"What happened, baby?" Bria questioned.

"Kevin said he just caught Sam and Eric having sex."

"Are you fucking serious?" I blurted out. Bria and David looked at me with a shocked expression on their faces. I never really cursed, so it was shocking to them.

"We have to go find her. Come on, Mo," Bria yelled, obviously pissed off. "Baby, I'll call you later," Bria said, then stormed off in search of Sam.

I called Sam's phone several times before she picked up. "Samariah, where the heck are you?" I screamed into the phone.

"I left," she said sadly.

"Where are you going?" I asked.

"Home," she responded.

"Well, we are on the way, so stay put," I said with as much sympathy in my voice as I could muster up. The truth was, I didn't really feel sorry for my friend, because I had warned her. I found Bria and told her what was up with Sam.

We left the party and went to Sam's house. It was just Sam and her mother, who was never at home, by the way. Her father was a known drug dealer, and he took good care of Sam and her mother, but he didn't live with them.

We walked into Sam's room, and she was a mess. I walked over to her to comfort her.

"Bitch, really? In your man's house?" Bria said, without an ounce of sympathy.

"I just couldn't help myself," Sam cried. "What am I going to do?" she asked.

"What do you mean, what are you going to do? You made your bed, now lay in it. We told you it was a bad idea, and you did it, anyway!" Bria yelled at the top of her lungs.

I started to feel bad for Sam, because Bria was giving it to her raw.

"You know I'm not going to sugarcoat shit, because you were wrong, friend. You have to stop sleeping around, or else this will continue to happen," Bria said, with a little bit of sympathy.

"Fuck you, Bria. You know you get on my damn nerves sometimes!" Sam shouted.

"Whatever. It's not my fucking fault you got caught," Bria mumbled while rolling her eyes.

"You know, I have had enough of your ass!" Sam yelled and then jumped up. She was trying to rush Bria, but I jumped up before she got to her. "Let me go!" Sam screamed.

"Yeah, let that bitch go, so I can whup that ass," Bria said as she walked up.

"Enough!" I yelled. "You two are acting like y'all aren't best friends," I said firmly. "Bria, you have to be more sympathetic, and, Sam, she is right, though. You need to pull yourself together, because you were wrong."

Sam flopped down on her bed and rolled her eyes.

"I'm sorry, Samariah. You know how I can get sometimes," Bria said with sincerity.

"You know you can be a real bitch sometimes, but I love you, friend," Sam said.

Bria walked over to her and hugged her. "You know we are going to help you through this."

The next day, I started my diet. I refused to remain big, because I just wasn't happy being that way. On top of that, I was tired of people making fun of me. When I went back for my senior year, it was going to be a new Monique. I was tired of not having a man. I was lonely, and I want to experience love and all the crazy things that came along with it. My mind drifted off to Corey. I wanted him so bad. And you know what? I was going to get him. I was a beautiful girl;

I just need to fix myself up. I thought about what it would be like to walk the halls with his sexy ass. Holding on to his toned, muscular arms, looking into his sexy eyes.

Corey was six-three, with the sexiest body I had ever laid eyes on. He was brown skinned and had a low haircut that had waves rolling through it. His lining stayed on point, and he looked like a taller version of Trey Songz. It was love at first sight. Sometimes I lay in my bed at night and played with myself, thinking about him. Yes, he had that type of effect on me.

The new and improved Monique was in full effect, and she was not taking no shit from anyone anymore. I went to the store and got everything I needed to lose this weight. Come September I was going to be the sexiest bitch at our school. Just wait and see. . . .

Sam

A month had passed since the day I got caught fucking my boyfriend's best friend. Kevin wouldn't talk to my ass for weeks, but after much begging and pleading, he finally gave in and took me back. After popping up at his house one day with tears in my eyes, he finally let me in, and I knew I had him. He led me into his room, and that was wh ere I put on the biggest show ever. I had tears and snot running out of my nose. He looked down at me with forgiving eyes.

I grabbed at his basketball shorts and pulled them down to his ankles. He was hesitant at first, but then he went along with what I wanted to do. I pulled down his boxers and took all of him in my mouth. It was not hard to do, because his dick was not big at all. I put in work that day. I licked and sucked on his balls. I even went as far as to lick his ass, and let me tell you, I had him screaming like a bitch. I didn't try to fuck him that day; I wanted him to know it was all about him. Plus, I had promised Corey that we would meet up later that night. You probably think, *This bitch ain't shit*! Maybe I was not, but a girl had needs, and Corey knew just how to meet them.

Kevin just didn't know how to work this pussy. I loved Kevin, but he was just a horrible lover. Sometimes I didn't even know why I was with him. My man was fine, though. He was dark skinned, with pearly white teeth, muscles popping out everywhere, and his swag was something serious. He looked like Lance Gross, the son from *Tyler Perry's House of Payne*. Whatever the hell his name was, he was fine, and he looked like my man.

I think my problem was that I didn't want him, but I couldn't stand for another bitch to have him. Until I got tired of him, he was all mine.

I met up with Corey that night, and we fucked and sucked the shit out of each other. What I liked most about Corey was that he knew his role. When we saw each other in passing, you would never know we had fucked a few times. He didn't be blowing up my phone and calling my ass all the time, and I loved that.

Eric, on the other hand, was the total opposite. I had let him taste and get a little bit of the pussy, and he had lost his damn mind. He called and texted me all the time. Damn, I couldn't say that I was not interested, because that would be a lie, but I just didn't know when there would be a good time to meet up. Since we had got back together, Kevin had been on my ass like white on rice. I had even had to purchase me a pay-as-you-go phone so that he wouldn't know that I was still cheating on his boring ass. Kevin was so sexy that you would think he had the goods to go along with that sexiness, but he didn't. If we had good sex, I would probably be faithful to him. *Probably* was the key word, because I was a sucker for a good-looking man, and I definitely liked them chocolate.

My father was dark skinned, and he was so handsome. My dad hadn't really been a part of my life as I was growing up. He paid all our bills and kept money in my and my mom's pockets, but I hadn't seen him since I was about five years old. My mom didn't have any pictures of him, and the only thing that I remembered about him was that he was handsome and dark skinned. He would buy me nice things on my birthday, but he had never actually come to any of my birthday parties. Just recently, he had purchased me a 2011 Mercedes E350 for having a 4.0 grade point average, and he wanted me to be riding fly my senior year. I came home one day, and my mom told me that my dad had purchased the car for me.

My mom had never come home with another man. She was madly in love with my dad, but I could tell she was miserable. She was never really at home, and when she was, her ass was drunk and high, so I basically did what the fuck I wanted. I took care of me.

My ringing phone brought me out of my thoughts. It was Eric's thirsty ass.

"Hello," I said in my sexy voice.

"Hey, baby. What are you doing?" Eric said.

"Thinking about you, and what I want to do to you," I said seductively.

"Oh yeah? What you want to do to a nigga?" he asked eagerly.

"Why don't you come over and find out?" I purred into the phone.

"Shit. I'm on my way," he said, then hung up the phone before I got another word in.

I got out of the bed, and my kitty kat was throbbing the whole time. I had not had this pussy beaten up in about a week. Yes, I had had sex with my man, but we all know how that turned out. The last time my pussy was pleased was when I had sex with Corey the night my man and I got back together.

I showered and lotioned my entire body with Japanese Cherry Blossom lotion from Bath & Body Works. I put on a pink Victoria's Secret thong and bra set, and I put on my pink six-inch heels that I got from Aldo. I sprayed my body with my Japanese Cherry Blossom perfume, then sprayed a little extra on my pussy. I made sure I had condoms in the drawer of my nightstand. Last time we had sex, we didn't use a condom, but that shit wouldn't happen this time. Even though I was on birth control, you could never be too careful. Ain't no babies popping out of this good, tight pussy. I didn't know what these niggas walking around with, either, so there would be no more slipups.

I sat on my bed, waiting for him to arrive. It was ten in the morning, and my mom was gone already—not that it would have stopped me from inviting him over and fucking his brains out. I had a movie and dinner date with Kevin tonight, so I wasn't worried about him popping up or anything like that. Plus, he liked to sleep late. Eric and I were definitely about to finish what we had started.

Kevin and Eric were no longer friends, thanks to me, but I really didn't give a fuck. I didn't really think that I cared that he had found us sexing each other down. Obviously, neither did Eric, because he had been blowing my phone up since that day. I had lied to him and told him that I got a new number so that I could have him calling my little private thot phone, as I called it. I think this nigga was whipped, or he really just wanted to bust a nut. Either way, I was going to have him wrapped around my manicured fingers. Just then he texted me and told me that he was at the door. I did a once-over in my floor-length mirror, and I was definitely impressed. I took my bonnet off and fluffed my freshly curled twenty-inch Brazilian hair. Then I went to the door.

I opened the door, and Eric's mouth dropped. "Damn, baby. You are sexy as hell," he said while twirling me around and taking in all my thickness. He kissed me on my lips and slapped me on my ass. He closed and locked the door and followed me into my room.

I lay on the bed with my legs spread and started to play with Miss Kitty. He was watching me with so much lust in his eyes. Wetness was dripping through my lace thong, and I put my fingers in my mouth and licked my juices off them. He walked over to me and took off everything but my six-inch heels.

He pulled me to the edge of my bed and dropped to his knees. He started to kiss up my thighs. Once he got to Miss Kitty, he stuck his tongue inside of my soaking wet honeypot. He proceeded to French-kiss my pussy, and at this point, I was in pure ecstasy. He bit down on my clit and flicked his tongue over my pearl with expert precision. I came hard, and he licked up every drop. He took off all his clothes and tried to go in me raw. I stopped him and placed a condom in his hands. For a minute, I thought he was upset, but he took the condom and put it on. He entered my juice box at a slow, methodical pace. I shifted my hips to match his rhythm. He told me to get on top. I did what I was told.

My feet were planted on either side of him, and my juicy ass was facing his face. I slid down on his thick, juicy chocolate pole and rode that shit at full speed. I watched as his toes curled, and he yelled out like a baby. He was smacking my ass and yelling that he was about to cum. I felt his balls tightening up, so I jumped off him and took the condom off his dick. I took him in my mouth and swallowed all his seeds. He looked as though he was about to pass out once I was finished with him.

I slapped him on the thigh and told him he had to go.

"It's like that, Ma? A nigga can't spend no time with you?" he said.

I was thinking, *Hell yeah, it's like that, nigga. You ain't my man.* But I said, "No, baby. It's not like that. It's just I have some things I need to take care of for my mom."

He nodded his head and got dressed.

As I walked him to the door, he asked, "When will I see you again?"

"I'll let you know," I said with a hint of irritation. Why couldn't niggas get some pussy and go about their business?

"Okay. I'll call you a little later. You are going to be my lady one day. Fuck that nigga, Kevin. He's obviously not fucking you right," he said.

I gave him a weak smile as he walked backward out the door. Once he left, I got in the shower, hoping this nigga wasn't pussy whipped.

Chapter Three

Kevin

I loved my girl, man, but I couldn't believe this bitch had the nerve to be cheating on me, and with my best fucking friend at that. I'd been so heated the night I caught them motherfuckas. I had wanted to dead both of them bitches, but I had played that shit cool, like I wasn't hurt. I had been looking for my girl when I spotted Eric's ass sneaking into my basement. I'd waited, like, ten minutes to see if he was going to come back up. He didn't, so I decided to see what was up. When I made it down the steps, I heard moaning. I thought, *This nigga is in my bro's bed, fucking a bitch.* I was about to turn around when I heard that nigga say, "Shit, Sam. This pussy is super wet." I knew this fucking nigga didn't just say, "Sam," so I crept closer to the door, and that was when I heard the girl I loved, and who was supposed to love me, screaming this nigga's name. I knew it was Sam because she screamed my fucking name the same way.

I ran up the stairs two at a time to go and get my gun, but I stopped once I got to the top of the stairs. I calmed myself down and slowly walked back down the stairs. I told myself that I wasn't going to kill their asses that day, but they were not about to be busting no nuts in my shit. That was when I opened the bedroom door and found my bitch with her ass in the air for another nigga. I'm not going to lie. A nigga was ready to cry like a bitch, but I wouldn't give her or that nigga the satisfaction. I could not let that nigga see me sweat.

I honestly had never cheated on her ass, because I felt like she was the one, but she had me fooled.

Little did she know, I would never marry or be with her ass for the long term. She had messed all that shit up. I absolutely did not trust her, and if I couldn't trust her, there was no future for us. I had bitches throwing the pussy at me, and I was turning hoes down left and right. Well, that shit ended the moment I saw my nigga hitting her ass from the back. I couldn't help but notice that the nigga wasn't even wearing a condom. Now I didn't enter her ass without one.

My parents had never raised me to be no player. My mom and dad didn't play that shit, so it was never in me to be that type of nigga. Even though my parents had split up when I was a youngin', I had always wanted a family for myself, and once Samariah and I graduated, I had planned to marry her and pop a bunch of kids in her ass. Both of my parents had remarried, so I was always around that type of atmosphere. Now a nigga was about to be on one. Yeah, I'd entertain this so-called relationship for a while, especially because my bitch gave good head and her pussy stayed wet and tight, but I planned to fuck off on her ass and leave her for somebody who deserved me.

My mother had always said that there was something about her that wasn't right, but I hadn't tried to hear her, because I was young and in love. I loved her ass, but I was not in love with her. All that "in love" shit had left the moment my nigga hit. Eric thought he had got away scot-free with fucking my bitch, but that nigga had an ass whupping coming his way. Until then, I was going to play my role and wait on my revenge.

Bria

It had been about two months since everything went down with Sam and Kevin. Sam had called Monique and me to let us know that she and Kevin had got back together. She had also informed us that she and Eric had finally finished what they started. I didn't understand how you could get caught cheating with your boyfriend's best friend, beg your man to take you back, and then cheat on him again with the same guy—and even feel bad about it. Sam hadn't always been a bitch. I had noticed a change in her when we were, like, twelve years old. She had gotten worse since she started having sex. I loved her, but I didn't know if we were going to be friends too much longer. I hated how she treated people.

David and I were doing great. Tonight we were going to have a picnic at the lake. I stole a bottle of Moscato from my parents' liquor cabinet and grabbed a blanket out of the linen closet. I put everything in my overnight bag and decided to freshen up. Just as I was finishing up, David texted me to let me know that he was outside. I did a once-over in the mirror, and I loved what I saw. I had on a long white fitted sundress with some white and gold Michael Kors sandals. I wore nothing but a thong underneath. Because my titties were nice and perky, I didn't need a bra. I swished my hips and ass to David's car. I didn't have any ass whatsoever, but you couldn't tell me that. I got in the car and kissed him sweetly on the lips. He pulled out of my driveway, and we headed to our destination.

When we finally arrived at the lakefront, the sun was setting, and it set the perfect mood. We laid our blanket out in a secluded area and enjoyed our view. I looked over at my man, and I just took him in. I could stare at him for days and never get tired. He was so handsome, and he loved me unconditionally. Sometimes I had my fears, but one thing I didn't doubt was his love for me. "How much do you love me?" I asked, resting my head on his shoulder.

"I love you more than all the stars in the sky. I wouldn't trade you for the world," he answered sincerely.

I got up and stood in front of him. Tonight was the night I decided I would give myself to him. I wouldn't want to share my honeypot with any other person but him. I didn't know if it was the wine, but all of sudden, I just felt ready. I untied my dress from around my neck and let it drop to the sand. I walked over to him and kissed him. He broke away from our kiss to take his clothes off. He laid me on the blanket and began to suck on my nipples. He bit down on them softly while playing with my love box. He slowly slid two of his fingers inside my hole. I tensed up a little, but then it started to feel good.

He came back up and began to kiss me on my lips. I sucked on his tongue as he began to ease into my honeypot. I began to feel a lot of pressure once he finally slipped into me. It hurt for a while, but then the pain began to slip away. As he thrust against my clit, I began to feel something that made me shiver all over. I had never experienced anything that felt so good. He began to pick up his pace, and he made a loud grunting nose. He lay on top of me for a second and then began to kiss me all over my face. He pulled out of me and lay beside me. My body felt so good, and I wanted that feeling to never go away. We lay there for a few more minutes before we dressed and headed home.

Later that night, David texted me a thousand times, asking me if I was okay. I told him yes. He was acting like he had shot me or something. I showered and headed to bed.

The next day Sam called and woke me up, talking about Eric's crazy ass. "Friend, what am I going to do? I gave Eric some pussy, and he won't stop calling and texting me. Do you know he had the nerve to pop up at my house unannounced? Kevin had just left minutes before," she said, sounding frustrated.

"I told you to stop messing with him. You have Kevin. That should be enough," I yelled.

"Kevin doesn't know how to treat my body. He just isn't good enough in bed for me. I'll kick Eric to the curb, but I'll have to find someone else to replace him. Someone has to take good care of my pussy," she said seriously.

All I could do was shake my head. She would never change.

I hadn't seen Mo since the day of Kevin's party. She refused to hang out with us because she said she had something she wanted to show us, but we had to wait until school started back up. I hoped my girl wasn't pregnant; that would be devastating. David and I had been sexing each other every chance we got. I could honestly see why Sam liked doing it so much. She didn't need to do it with Kevin and everybody else's man, but I got why she liked to do it. I had been reading a lot of books and watching a lot of videos to build my sex skills, and I couldn't wait to try some of the things I'd learned. When I got done with my man, he was not going to ever want anybody else.

Monique

I finally took Bria's advice and lost the weight. I hadn't seen them all summer, and I was excited to show off my new figure. It took strict discipline and lots of time in the fitness center, but I did it. I was now 150 pounds, and you could see every curve that I had. I already had a big butt and hips, but now they looked really good on me. I lost some off my breasts during the weight loss, but they were a perfect 38C.

I had gone out this weekend and got a whole new wardrobe to go with my new figure. Now I was at school on the first day, getting ready to show the world what I was made of. I hoped that Corey noticed me, because I wanted him so bad. I couldn't wait to have him on my arm. And you know what? I was going to get him. I had decided on some high-waist blue jean shorts with a sleeveless white blouse. I had put on a pair of white sandals that I got from Aldo. My hair was already long, so I had just got some honey-blond highlights added to it. I wore some white diamond hoop earrings with matching bracelets to top off my look.

I walked into the building, and all eyes were on me.

I heard someone say, "Is that the fat girl, Monique? Damn, she looks good."

I tapped Bria on the shoulder, and she turned to face me.

"Monique!" she screamed and hugged me. "You look so good, friend. I'm so proud of you," she said genuinely.

Sam finally spun around to see what all the fuss was about. She hugged me and was happy for me as well. We had first period together, so we headed there. When I walked in, the first person I saw was Corey. He looked up at me but quickly looked down. My heart instantly broke, and I thought that he wasn't interested in me at all.

For the first half of the day, I walked around, sad as hell. When we got to lunch, I expressed to my girls how I felt. "You guys, Corey didn't even look my way," I said sadly.

"Friend, don't be sad. He's not the only guy out here. The person that's for you will come along," Bria said, rubbing my back.

"Fuck him! He's not all that, anyway. You don't want him," Sam said.

Before I could respond, David and Kevin came to sit down with us. I was always the only one who was all alone. Here I was, beautiful as ever, and I still didn't have the man I wanted.

Bria could tell that I was still feeling down, so she said, "He will come around, Mo. You just got your new look, and people still have to get used to it. Besides, he will be a fool not to notice you." That was why I loved my BFF. She knew just what to say to make me feel better.

"I'll be right back. I'm about to go grab a soda," Sam said while walking off.

We started making small talk about nothing in particular, until Kevin abruptly got up and stormed over to the soda machine. We followed him with our eyes, and that was when we noticed Eric and Sam in a heated argument by the soda machine, and neither one of them saw Kevin coming. I knew it was about to go down. Before any of us could do anything, he punched the shit out of Eric. Eric tried to fight back, but it was no use, and Kevin beat the hell out of him. Security was finally able to break it up, and they took the boys in separate directions. Sam ran over to us, smiling.

"I'm about to go check on Kevin," David said, then stood and walked away.

"Did you see them two fighting over me? I'm really that bitch," Sam said excitedly.

"Really, Sam? That shit isn't cute at all. You really disgust me sometimes," Bria snapped.

"Her ass always has an attitude," Sam said before walking off.

I was walking to my car, about to head home, when I heard the sexiest voice call my name. "Monique," Corey yelled out. I spun around, and I was face-to-face with the man of my dreams.

"Hey. W-what's up?" I stuttered.

"Nothing much. Listen, I stopped you because I wanted to ask you out on a date," he said, giving me that sexy smile.

"I would love to go on a date with you," I said, sounding a little too desperate.

He smiled at me again, and we exchanged numbers. My day may have started out badly, but it definitely ended perfectly.

Chapter Four

Corey

I had finally got the balls to ask Monique out. I had been interested in her since the ninth grade, but I had let the fact that she was a little on the big side get in the way of that. I know you're probably thinking that I don't deserve her, but hear me out. For starters, I felt like I had a certain image I needed to uphold, with me being the star of our basketball team, but that was just me being young and dumb. On top of that, I had slept with her best friend a few times, something I was now starting to regret. I had thought about being honest with her, but I felt like I would lose her before we could even get started. David had always encouraged me to be with her if I wanted her. He said I shouldn't care what people think, but I had just been too stupid to step to her.

Today I decided to make things official between us. I took her out to Olive Garden because that was one of her favorite restaurants. We were sitting at the table, chatting it up, when she decided to ask me what had made me ask her out.

"Well, I just figured it was the best time to do it. I couldn't let someone else snatch you up," I said.

She looked at me and chuckled a little.

"So how would you feel about making things official?" I asked.

"What do you mean, official? Like being a couple or something?" she asked eagerly.

"Yes, I want to be with you."

She looked like she was hesitant for a moment, which scared the shit out of me, because I hated rejection. Then, all of a sudden, she gave me the prettiest smile. "I would love to be your girlfriend," she said with a huge grin on her face.

I leaned over the table and kissed her soft lips. That was our first kiss, and I felt like a little kid in a candy store. Just being around her had me feeling some type of way. I felt things that I had never felt before with any woman. I sat back and looked at her, and she became visibly nervous.

"Why are you looking at me like that?" she asked.

"Has anyone ever told you that you look like that chick from *Love & Hip Hop: New York*? I think her name is Yandy."

"Yeah, I have been getting that a lot lately," she said, laughing.

We ended our date, and I went home happy as hell. I had finally got the woman of my dreams, and I didn't plan on ever letting her go. Even though I might not deserve her, I planned to spend the rest of my life making her happy.

Sam

I couldn't believe Eric and Corey were fighting over me. I knew things were going to get ugly when he approached me about sitting with Kevin instead of him. Don't get me wrong. Eric and I still slept around a few times a month, but I could never really see myself in a serious relationship with him. Needless to say, that shit turned me on, knowing that they were fighting because of me. No, I didn't feel bad that I had broken up his and Kevin's friendship, either. Like I always said, I was that bitch, and all the niggas wanted me. Kevin had definitely been pissed at me for a few days after the fight, but he had eventually forgiven me.

Monique called Bria and me on a three-way to invite us out bowling with our men. Monique had a boo now, and she wanted to reveal him to us. I didn't know what was up with her and all these damn surprises and secrets. We all arrived at the bowling alley before her and her date, and when she walked in on Corey's arm, I instantly felt my blood boil. Sure, I was wrong for sleeping with Corey in the first place, because I knew how Mo had felt about him all these years, but I was pissed. To make matters worse, Bria was all excited for them and shit. Although Corey and I had never spoken about being together, I had always told myself that if Kevin and I didn't work out, I would be with Corey. This shit between Corey and Mo had to end today. They came over to greet us, and I tried my best to hide my displeasure.

"Baby, I'm going to head to the bathroom before we get started," Corey said and kissed Mo on the lips. I watched, and when she blushed, I became even angrier. I figured this would be the perfect opportunity to make my move.

"Sweetie, I think I'm going to head to the bathroom as well," I said to Kevin as I rose up.

I walked at a fast pace to catch up with Corey. I finally got to him just before he was about to walk inside the restroom. "Corey, wait. I need to talk to you," I said. I walked up on him and put my arms around his neck. He knocked them away and stared at me with fire in his eyes. I had never seen him like this, and to be honest, it turned me on.

"What the hell are you doing, Sam?" he asked angrily.

"What do you mean, baby?" I said, trying to kiss him on the lips.

"Are you fucking insane? My girl is out there, and so is your boyfriend," he said, pointing toward them. I wasn't worried about them seeing us. The bathroom was all the way on the other side of the bowling alley and quite far from where we were bowling.

"So? I want you, and what I want, I get," I told him. He turned around to walk away, but I grabbed his arm. "Corey, I want you and me to be together. You need to leave her!" I shouted.

"Listen, I'm going to say this as nicely as I possibly can. You and I will never, ever be a couple. You have never expressed interest in me on that level, and neither have I. It was just about the sex. Now that I'm with your girl, you're trying to make it more than what it really is. I'm not having it, so leave me the hell alone," he said heatedly.

"Corey, you mean to tell me that you don't want all of this?" I said, spinning around and showing him my body. "I have the best pussy you have ever had. You can't just walk away from what we shared," I noted, pleading my case.

"You are delusional, and I never told you that your pussy was the best I've ever had," he said with a smirk. "Look, like I said, there will never be a you and me," he added, then walked away.

"I'll tell her!" I shouted.

He stopped dead in his tracks and then turned around and rushed me. He grabbed me by my neck and pushed me against the wall. "Listen, bitch. If you ever tell my girl anything, I will whup your ass. Play with me if you want," he said, gripping my neck a little tighter. He watched as fresh hot tears streamed down my face. He let me go, and I hit the floor. He looked at me one last time before he entered the bathroom. "Crazy bitch," I heard him mumble.

I hurriedly stood up and got myself together. I walked back to the crew and tried to act as normal as possible.

For the rest of the night, Corey and I avoided each other. I would sneak glances at Corey and Mo, and it made me super angry. I started hating a girl who had been my best friend for years.

While I sat on a bench, sulking and waiting my turn to bowl, Bria walked over to me. "Hey, friend. What's wrong with you?" she asked.

"Oh, nothing. I was just thinking," I said.

"Well, you look like you're ready to kill Corey or Mo," she said, sounding suspicious.

"Girl, please. Why would I be mad at them? I'm fine. I was just thinking about Eric's crazy ass," I lied.

"Oh, okay. Well, try to have fun, friend. I know you don't like doing this type of stuff," she said before she walked back over by David.

If Corey thought I was going to sit back and let him be with her ass, he had another thing coming.

Bria

Sam had been acting very strange lately, and I couldn't quite put my finger on it. Maybe dealing with all these different men was starting to get to her. I was so happy that Mo had ended up getting the man she had been in love with since the ninth grade. I knew one thing. He had better treat her right, or I was going to kick his ass.

David's parents were out of town, so I was going to spend the weekend with him. I told my parents that I would be over at Sam's. Her mom was never at home, so I wasn't worried about them catching me in a lie. I packed my overnight bag and waited for David to pick me up. I decided to watch some videos in the meantime to get ready for what I had planned for David tonight. I planned on taking our lovemaking to another level.

I heard David's horn, and I ran out to his car. We made a few stops for food and drinks before we went to his house. We finally made it to his place around nine in the evening. I immediately went to the bathroom so I could change into something sexier. I showered and put lotion on my body, using Twilight Woods from Bath & Body Works. I put on a fire-red matching lace bra and boy short set with some red heels that I had purchased at Aldo.

I stepped out of the bathroom and headed to his bedroom. He had his back to me when I walked in, so I coughed to get his attention. He flopped on his back, and he had to adjust his hardening erection.

"Take off your clothes," I told him, and he did as he was told.

I walked over to him, and I asked him to stand up. I French-kissed him and then slid to my knees. I was super nervous, because I had never done what I was about to do. I planted slow kisses up and down his shaft, and then I added a little tongue to the mix. I slowly took him into my mouth and began to relax my throat. I went farther, and I began to gag, but once I got the hang of it, I went all the way down before I picked up my pace. I looked up at him, and his eyes looked as though they were in the back of his head. I took both of my hands and moved them up and down while twisting them at the same time. I sucked on the tip of his head while using my hands for his shaft.

He suddenly picked me up and tossed me on my back on the bed. He kissed my lips and then trailed off to my breasts and eventually to my honeypot. He stuck his finger inside my hole while French-kissing my clit. He flicked his tongue against my clit, bringing me to an explosive orgasm. He swallowed all my juices as they flowed out of my honeypot. He flipped me over and told me to get on all fours. He entered me from behind and began to drill my pussy. He took his thumb and massaged my clit. I began to cum long and hard, and he was right behind me. He released his seed deep inside of me. He collapsed on top of me, and he just lay there for a while. He rolled off me and took me in his arms.

"Where did you learn to do that at?" he asked me happily.

"I'll never tell my secret," I said, laughing.

"Well, in that case, let's start on round two," he said while lifting my leg and entering me from the side.

We made love all night, and I never wanted it to end.

***

I met up with my girls at the mall so that we could get our outfits for the party that was coming up this weekend. "So, how are things with you and Corey?" I asked Mo.

"Things are good. We are together all the time. I know y'all probably think it's too early for me to say this, but I think I love him," Mo said, cheesing.

Sam frowned up and got an attitude. "You don't love his ass, and I wouldn't go falling for someone who I'm not sure feels the same way," she said with an attitude.

"Sam, that is rude. Who's to say that he doesn't love her already? Mo, you're not wrong for how you feel. The heart wants what it wants," I said. Something definitely wasn't right with Sam. I bet something went down with her and Corey. The night we went bowling, I had noticed that they were both gone for, like, five or ten minutes, and when Sam came back, she looked like she had been crying.

"I'm just saying it's not a good idea," Sam said.

If looks could kill, Sam's ass would be dead, because I definitely gave her the look of death. "Let's just change the subject," I suggested.

"My boo and I have been getting it in something serious. I finally gave him some head, and he loved it," I bragged.

"I want to try it out, but I'm really scared, y'all. I want to make sure we feel the same way before we go to that level," Mo said.

"I think I'm about to drop Eric's ass and find me a new suitor," Sam said.

"How about being faithful to your boyfriend? Do you remember him? His name is Kevin," I said to Sam.

"I love Kevin, but he just don't know how to please me, and Eric's ass is getting too demanding," Sam said.

I refused to even respond, because she was never going to change. We found our outfits and left the mall. We went our separate ways, and I headed home. On the drive there,

I went back over our conversation. Sam was definitely hiding something, and I promised myself that I would find out what it was.

Sam

That bitch, Monique, was pissin' me the hell off! When she said she wanted to have sex with Corey, I nearly lost my damn mind. I wanted to haul off and slap her ass, but I knew I needed to play smart. I had called things off for good with Eric because he was doing too much. He didn't know how to play his role, and although I loved when he was going crazy over me, I couldn't have that going on while I was trying to destroy Mo and Corey's relationship. Kevin and I had been doing okay. We hadn't been having much sex lately, but everything else seemed to be normal.

I started getting dressed for the party. I was on a mission to get my man tonight. I put on a white mesh cutout short-sleeved minidress. It hugged every inch of my body very well. I threw on some white Prada heels to match. My hair was perfectly curled, and I wore some Chanel diamond stud earrings.

I got in my car and headed to the party. When I arrived, I spotted Bria and Monique right away. I swished my ass over to them to see what was up. "Hey, bitches!" I greeted them.

Monique was looking hella good. She wore a black mesh cut-up pencil skirt with a matching crop top. She wore some red six-inch heels with matching red lipstick. I felt jealous as hell. I could see why Corey would want her, but I didn't think she looked better than me. I danced a little with my girls, but then I decided to find what I had come here for.

I found Corey in the kitchen, talking to David. I walked up to him and asked if I could speak with him in private.

He looked like he was unsure about it, but I gave him this look that said, "Nigga, if you don't come with me, I'll act up right here." I would never do it, but I wanted him to think that. We walked into this room that was in the back of the mansion where the party was being held.

"What in the hell do you want, Sam?" he asked, visibly irritated.

"Aw, don't be like that, baby. You know what I want. I want you," I said.

"See, you're on some bullshit. I'm not feeling this shit at all. Why can't you just let a nigga be?" he replied.

"I love you, Corey, and I want us to be together," I said, walking up on him again.

"Sam, that will never happen. What part of that don't you understand?" he said.

"You mean to tell me that you don't miss me?" I asked.

"I love my girl, and she is the only woman I want. I will never be with you. You're not anyone I could take home to my mama. All you were good for was a friendly fuck, and that's it. So if you didn't get it the first twenty times I told your silly ass, I do not want you! Now leave me the hell alone!" he screamed.

I wanted to cry, but I held back my tears. I grabbed at his pants, but he cut me off. He pushed me against the wall, and then he grabbed my hair. He turned me around so that my ass was touching his big dick. He bent me over, pulled up my dress, and ripped off my thong. I heard him unbuckling his pants and pulling down his boxers. My pussy was so wet. He rubbed his dick against my wet clit, and I almost came right then and there.

"Is this what you want? You want Daddy's dick, huh? You want me to stick this big dick deep inside of you?" he said.

"Yes, Daddy, that's exactly what I want," I moaned. All of a sudden, he smashed my face against the wall. My head was hurting so bad.

"Listen, you dirty little whore. I will never stick my dick inside of you again. This dick here belongs to Monique. I won't even let your ass taste it," he spat. "Now, stay the fuck away from me and my girl, or else I'm going to kill yo' ass. Now, do I make myself clear?" he said, smashing my face harder into the wall.

I shook my head rapidly, and he released his hold on me. I fell to the floor, crying hysterically.

He bent down and whispered in my ear, "That wasn't a threat. It was a fucking promise." He stood up and spat on me. He fixed his clothes and walked out the door.

I cried for what seemed like hours before I stood and fixed myself up. I walked out of the room and entered the party. I saw Mo and Corey hugging and kissing in the corner, by a fireplace. I walked out the front door quickly. You would think that after what he just did to me, I would want nothing else to do with him, but I refused to let him be happy with my best friend. If I couldn't have him, no one else would!

Chapter Five

Corey

I didn't know what in the hell was wrong with Sam's ass, but she'd got me fucked all the way up. She was absolutely not getting the picture. I had told her over and over again that we would never be together, but she refused to listen to me. She would text me all day and night, sending me naked pictures. This ho went as far as sending me videos of her playing with herself. I had just recently changed my number. I told Monique that I had changed it because I switched phone companies. It was the weekend, and Mo and I were just coming back from Six Flags Great America. She had decided to spend the night at my house.

My parents were filthy rich, so I didn't want for anything. We had this big-ass house in River Hills. When I'd turned eighteen, my parents moved me into our guesthouse, so I had plenty of privacy. Mo had told her parents that she was spending the weekend with her girlfriends. Once we made it to my house, we got comfortable and watched some movies. She fell asleep on my chest, and she looked so beautiful. I knew right then and there that I could not allow Sam to destroy my relationship. I would have that bitch murdered. My pops was one of the biggest drug dealers in the Milwaukee and Chicago areas. He had retired from the game, but he still had those connections. If that bitch kept fucking with me, I'd definitely be making that call.

Kevin

I really couldn't wait until I got rid of Sam. This was a horrible relationship. I was no longer happy with her, and I hadn't been for a long time. A part of me wished that we were able to fix things and get back to where we used to be, but I knew that could never happen. For starters, I couldn't get over the fact that she had slept with my best friend. Eric and I had been friends since birth. Our pops were best friends, and we were always together. Another reason that it would't work was that I couldn't trust her. I had heard the rumors about her sleeping around, but I hadn't wanted to believe that they were true at the time. So I knew things would never work out between us for those reasons.

I decided to head to the mall to get some gifts for my mother's birthday. She loved Chanel everything, so I decided to get her some perfume, a purse, and some shoes. I didn't need to be spending that much money, because my mom was suspicious of where I got my money. My dad sent me money every month, but I really made my money by selling heroin. If my mom or pops found out, they would kill me. My pops was a drug dealer, but he didn't want me following in his footsteps. Mom deserves what I was about to get her because she worked hard. My mom owned several McDonald's franchises, and she had gone back to school to get her master's degree in business. I really didn't need to be selling heroin, because both of my parents had money. But I just refused to depend on them. I wanted to make my own way.

I headed to Macy's so that I could get my mom's gifts. I got everything I needed and headed to the registers. I got the attention of the woman behind the counter, and when she turned to face me, I was greeted with the prettiest smile I had ever seen. This woman was beautiful. She was about five-two and had smooth dark chocolate skin. She had small breasts that led down to her flat tummy, small waist, and big hips. She had a nice-sized ass too. I normally didn't go for dark-skinned chicks, but I had to have her; she was so beautiful.

"Is this everything, sir?" she asked, showing her pretty white teeth.

I shook my head yes because I was totally speechless. She rang me up and placed all the items in gift bags.

"Thanks for shopping at Macy's. Have a beautiful day," she said.

I stood there, looking at her, and my eyes traced her entire body.

"Can I get you anything else, sir?" she asked sarcastically. She knew that I wanted her, and I could tell by her body language and how she kept smiling at me that she wanted a nigga too.

"What's your name?" I asked.

"Zaria, but everyone calls me Zoe," she said.

"Zoe, I'm Kevin. You should let me take you out sometime," I suggested.

"I would take you up on that offer, but I just got out of something serious. I don't know if it's a good idea to just hop right into something else," she said, sounding somewhat sad.

"Well, how about this? You take down my number, and call me when you're ready," I said.

She put my number in her phone, and I walked out of the store. I'd give her two days, and I bet she would be hitting a nigga up.

It was the day of my mom's party, and the house was super packed with friends and family. David and Bria were here, because his mom and my mom were good friends. Sam's annoying ass was here too. We were standing in the sunroom, talking, when my phone began to ring. I look at my caller ID, but I didn't recognize the number. I thought it was one of my customers, so I answered the phone.

"What's up? Who is this?" I said into the phone.

"Hello. May I speak to Kevin, please?" said the sweetest voice I had ever heard.

"This is Kevin. Can you hold on for a second?" I said. I excused myself and went to my room so that I could talk in private. "Hey, I'm back," I said to her.

"I was calling because I decided to take you up on your offer," she said, sounding sexy as hell.

We set up a date and ended our call. I couldn't wait until I saw her. I walked back into the party, smiling hard as hell.

"Who was that on the phone, and why are you smiling so damn hard?" Sam questioned.

"It's none of your damn business. And a nigga can't smile?" I said, ready to kick her ass to the curb already. It looked like I was going to be getting rid of her ass sooner than I had originally thought, and Zoe would be taking her place.

Monique

My life seemed to be coming together. Corey and I were doing great. We spent so much of our time together. Today he was coming over to meet my parents, and I was sort of nervous. I had never brought a boy over, so I didn't know how they were going to receive him. My mom was in the kitchen, whipping up a good meal, and dad was in the living room, watching TV.

Corey had just texted me and had told me that he was outside. I looked at myself in the mirror one last time and headed for the front door. I opened the door, and my handsome, sexy man was standing there, looking good enough to eat. I gave him a hug, but I was scared to kiss him.

He came in, and I introduced him to my parents. He and my dad sat down and talked while Mom and I finished up the food. Then we sat and ate dinner, and everything went well. My parents ended up loving Corey just like I did. When dinner was over, Corey and I talked in the living room until it was getting late and it was time to send off my sexy face. I walked him to the car because I refused to let him leave without getting a kiss.

The next day I met up with Sam and Bria so we could have some girl time.

"So what's been going on, bitches?" Sam asked.

"Well, Corey met my parents yesterday, and they loved him," I said excitedly.

"That's great," Bria said.

Sam acted like she was mad that he had met my parents or something. I ignored her attitude and kept talking. "He wants to take me out on his dad's yacht. He plans to introduce me to his parents then," I said.

"Why the rush? Y'all haven't even been together that long. Who knows if y'all are going to last?" Sam said.

That made me feel some type of way, and I was about to check her ass, but Bria beat me to the punch.

"Why the hell are you so negative? They love each other, obviously, and they want to be together, so why not? If you would stop hoeing around, maybe your relationship with Kevin would get better," Bria snapped.

I shook my head. Sam and Bria seemed to hate each other nowadays.

"Shut the fuck up, Bria! You always have something to say, and I wasn't even talking to your ass," Sam snapped back.

"Well, I'm talking to *your* ass," Bria said.

"Stop it, you two. Y'all act like y'all hate each other," I said.

"Look, I've got to go. I'll talk to you bitches later," Sam said as she stood up to leave.

"I'm starting to really dislike Samariah for real," Bria said.

"Why? She is your best friend," I said.

"I don't trust her, and I really think she is hiding something," said Bria.

"I think you are just being paranoid," I said.

"Whatever. I have to go as well. I'll call you later," she said and then left.

Bria

I walked away from Mo, thinking that my girl could be so naive at times. I'd been putting some pieces to this puzzle together, and the puzzle was starting to show that Sam was up to no good. Sam was either sleeping with Corey now or she did before Mo and Corey got together. Like I said before, I already had my suspicions when both Sam and Corey disappeared for, like, ten minutes the night we went bowling. Not to mention that anytime Mo said anything about Corey, Sam's whole demeanor changed. I didn't know exactly what was going on, but I planned to find out.

David called, and he wanted me to come over. Every time we were around each other, it was like we couldn't keep our hands off each other. We had been doing it everywhere. He picked me up, and we headed to the movies. On our way home, I decided to start something up. He got on the freeway, because it was the fastest way to my house from the movie theater. I reached over the middle console and started to rub his penis. At my touch, he instantly got hard. I leaned over, unzipped his pants, and pulled his dick out of his boxer shorts. I start rubbing up and down his shaft. I placed my mouth on the head and began licking it in a circular motion. I slowly took all of him in my mouth and gave him the best head he'd ever had.

"Damn, baby. What you are doing to me?" he moaned. I started to go faster and added my hands into the mix. "Shit, baby. I'm about to cum," he yelled in pleasure. He shot his seed down my throat, and I made sure to lick him clean. I fixed his pants and sat back in my seat with a smile.

"You know you're about to give me some of my pussy, right?" he said. He got off the freeway and pulled into the parking lot of a George Webb restaurant. "Go into the restaurant, and go inside the women's bathroom. I'm going to come in a few minutes after you," he ordered.

I did what I was told, and sure enough, he came into the bathroom after me. He picked me up, and I wrapped my legs around his waist. With one hand, he took off his pants and shorts and entered my dripping wet honeypot. He held me firmly by my waist and slid me up and down his pole.

We both were moaning loudly in pleasure, so I was pretty sure the people eating heard our moans. He put me on the floor and told me to put one of my legs on the sink. I did what I was told, and he entered me from behind. He took my leg off the sink and rested it in the crook of his arm, then fucked the shit out of his pussy. We came together, pulled ourselves together, and walked out into the restaurant. People were looking at us like we were crazy, but we didn't care. That shit had just felt too good. When I finally got home, I slept like a baby.

Sam

I was starting to hate Bria as much as I hated Mo now. She always had something smart to say. Our friendship was practically nonexistent, just like the relationship I had with Kevin. We barely saw each other, and when we did, all we did was argue. We didn't have sex at all, and it was not like I didn't try. He just claimed he was always tired.

For some reason, I felt as though he was cheating on me. Like a month or so back, we were at his mom's party when he got that phone call that had him smiling like crazy. If he was not spending his time with me, then who in the hell was he spending it with? Eric's ass would not leave me alone, and Corey was playing hard to get. I had been having a drought, and I need someone to help water me.

I was walking down the hall at school when I spotted someone who would be the perfect suitor. His name was Brian, and he was about five-eleven and sported a low haircut. He has dark skinned and had the cutest dimples. I loved me some chocolate men. He was sexy as hell, and he was about to become a victim of this good pussy. I walked over to him, flashed him my pretty smile. I made sure to put a little extra swish of my hips in my walk.

"Hey, Brian. How are you?" I said.

"I'm good. How about yourself, sexy?" he said, smiling and showing me those dimples.

"Look, I'm not into playing games. You've got something that I want to try," I said, smiling seductively.

"Where's that nigga, Kevin, at? Y'all still together?" he asked.

"Does it really matter?" I said, walking closer to him. I made sure to press my titties up against his chest.

"Fuck that nigga," he said.

"Well, let's exchange numbers, and I'll call you later," I said.

We exchanged numbers, and I walked away, but Miss Kitty didn't want to wait until later. She needed a fix right now. I called his name, and he jogged back to me.

"What's up?" he said.

"How about we go to your truck now?" I said. I rubbed his dick, and it wasn't disappointing.

He grabbed my hand and led the way. We ended up fucking the shit out of each other right there in his truck.

As we exited his truck, we ran into Mo and Corey. Mo grabbed me by my arm, and I could tell she was pissed.

"Why are you getting out of the truck with Brian, and why is your hair all messed up?" she said.

"Mo, we were just talking," I lied.

"Sam, I am not stupid! When are you going to stop with all this mess?" she asked.

I looked over at Corey, and he just shook his head at me. If he had left Monique alone, none of this probably would have happened.

"Mo, I'm grown," was all I said.

"Well, friend, I love you, and you know I'm here for you if you need anything," she said.

Truthfully, for the first time since Mo and Corey got together, I actually felt bad about what I was doing, but not enough to stop me from trying to get Corey for myself. I was on a mission, and I wouldn't give up until I got what I wanted—even if that meant hurting the people I loved.

Chapter Six

Kevin

I had been spending all my spare time with my new boo, Zoe. We hadn't made things official yet, because I hadn't called things off with Sam, but it was definitely in the works. I was surprised she hadn't left me yet. We barely spent time together, and when she called or texted me, I hardly responded to her. I was waiting on the right time to leave her, but I already had this shit planned out. I was horny as hell, though, so I decided to invite Sam's ass over so I could get my dick wet. Zoe and I weren't having sex. Like I said earlier, I refused to have sex with her because I was still with Sam, and I didn't want to do Zoe like that. She didn't deserve it.

She walked into my house, and I must admit, Sam was looking good as hell. She was dressed down, but those leggings she had on hugged her ass and hips perfectly. My little man was standing at full attention just at the sight of her hips. I came up to her and wrapped my arms around her waist. "Let's go into my room," I whispered into her ear. I pushed my dick against her ass and started kissing on her neck. "You feel what you're doing to a nigga?" I said to her.

She turned so that she was face-to-face with me and kissed me on my lips. One thing Sam did right was fuck a nigga, and her pussy was good as hell. That was the only thing I'd probably miss about her ass, but not enough to stay with her.

I picked her up and carried her to my bedroom. We kissed the entire way. I had learned some new tricks. I had had a conversation with Pops, and he had told me how to please a woman properly. At first, a nigga didn't really know how to fuck, and to be honest, I had been with only one woman, Sam, so I really didn't have a whole lot of experience. Tonight I was on a mission. I planned to fuck her brains out, so that when I finally got rid of her ass, she would know what in the hell she was missing. I opened my door, stepped inside my bedroom, and kicked the door shut. I laid her on the bed, then took off all her clothes. I took off mine, and then I climbed between her legs.

I kissed her from her collarbone to her titties. I pushed them together, and I began to suck and twirl my tongue around her nipples. I started making a trail of kisses down her belly until I made it to her juice box. I stuck two fingers in her pussy and began to French-kiss her second pair of lips. Her pussy was so wet, I almost forgot about all the shit she had done to me. I pulled out the vibrator I had purchased earlier just for this occasion. I rubbed it up and down her clit, and her legs began to shake violently. I put my tongue inside of her hole and began to dart it in and out. She came in my mouth, and I swallowed all her juices.

I got up from between her legs and began to kiss her as I stuck my condom-wrapped dick inside of her wet pussy. I slow ground in her pussy, and I could tell she was in pure ecstasy. I started picking up the pace, and she started to match my rhythm. She thrust her hips toward me, and that shit felt so good, but I didn't want to cum yet. I made her stand up and then told her to touch her toes. I entered her from behind, and then I began to drill the shit out of her pussy.

"I'm about to pull this dick out, and I want you to suck my dick and swallow all my nut," I said, slapping her ass.

"Okay, Daddy," she said in this sexy-ass voice.

I was ready to come, so I pulled out of her and took the condom off. She spun around, then started sucking my dick like a pro. I came long and hard in her mouth, and she swallowed all my kids, like she was told. That shit had a nigga weak as hell, and I wanted to go to sleep, but a nigga had something to prove. So I got myself together, got dressed, and walked toward the door.

"I'm about to go. I'll holla at you later," I said. Then I proceeded out the door, without an ounce of remorse. You had to treat a ho like a ho, and that was exactly what Sam was.

Sam

I could not believe that this nigga had just fucked me and walked out the door like I wasn't shit. My feelings were hurt as hell, and to top things off, out of the four years we had been together, he had never eaten my pussy or fucked me so good. He had given me back-to-back orgasms. He had a bitch regretting even cheating on his ass, as he had sexed me so good. I got dressed and grabbed my phone so I could call him and curse his ass out, but when I called, he didn't answer. I was heading for the front door, calling him again, when I heard vibrating on the coffee table. I walked over to the table and noticed that it was Kevin's phone. I picked it up and tried to get into his phone. It took me a few minutes, but I was able to guess the passcode. It was his mom's birthday.

I started looking through his calls and text messages. I noticed that he had been talking to a girl named Zoe every fucking day and all throughout the day. They had been sending each other pictures and all types of shit. I must admit, she was a cute little black bitch, but she didn't have shit on me. I could tell by their conversation that he was actually feeling this girl, and that just made my blood boil.

Who in the hell did this bitch think she was, trying to steal my fucking man and shit? I took a screenshot of Zoe's number and sent that, along with her picture, to my phone. I erased the evidence that I had been in his phone and left his house. I didn't know who this Zoe bitch was, but she was about to feel my wrath.

Bria

I woke up this morning feeling sick as hell. For the past week or so, I had been feeling this way. Since I hadn't gotten any better, I decided I was going to the emergency room. I called up Monique so that she would come along with me. When we arrived at the hospital, they gave me some paperwork. I filled in everything and waited for my name to be called. After about forty-five minutes, they finally called me back. They took my vitals and showed Mo and me to a room. The doctor came in, took blood and urine samples, and then left the room. We waited patiently for the doctor to return. About forty-five minutes later, he entered the room and took a seat next to me.

"So, Ms. Jacobs, we have your test results, and we have figured out why you haven't been feeling well," he said, looking a little nervous.

Now my ass was nervous as hell. I thought he was about to tell me I had a disease or something.

"Well, Ms. Jacobs, congratulations. You are pregnant," he said happily.

Mo's mouth dropped, and I nearly fainted.

"What d-did you just say?" I stuttered.

"I said you are pregnant. You will need to follow up with your primary care doctor to see how far along you are." He gave me my paperwork and prescribed me some pills for the nausea and prenatal vitamins.

My tears started to flow like a flood.

"It's going to be okay, friend. Everything will work out," Mo said, trying to comfort me.

I wasn't on any birth control, and David and I never used condoms. What the hell was I thinking? I was only seventeen years old, and I wouldn't be eighteen for a few more months. How was I going to tell David and both of our parents? I could not believe this was actually happening to me.

Since I found out I was pregnant, I had cried myself to sleep every night and had pretended like everything was normal at school and when I was around my parents. I had made my bed, so now I had to lie in it. My doctor had informed me that I was two months pregnant. I didn't know when I was going to tell my parents. I knew they were going to be pissed off. They probably still thought I was a virgin. Prom was coming up soon, and I had to prepare myself for that. I knew I would eventually have to tell everyone, but until then, I was just going to act like everything was normal. I just hoped that when I did announce that I was pregnant, I didn't lose my man. If he walked away from me because I was pregnant, then I never had him in the first place.

I had been avoiding having sex with David for as long as I could, but tonight I couldn't avoid it. This man knew my cycle better than I did ever since we started having sex, so I was about to give my man what he wanted. I dropped down to my knees and took him deep into my mouth. By now, I had learned to control my gag reflex, so I was taking him deep into my throat at full speed.

He said, "Baby, slow down. I'm about to cum."

He moaned. I didn't stop. Instead, I started fondling his balls and picked up my speed. I went all the way down on his shaft and starting gargling on his dick. When I did that,

I tasted his seed going down my throat, then slid his dick out of my mouth. I felt sort of bad after I swallowed his nut, because I was pregnant, and my baby took in whatever I took in.

I figured after that awesome head he wouldn't want to make love, but I was wrong. He told me to take off my clothes and get on all fours. I did what I was told. He stuck his tongue deep into my honeypot, and I forgot all about my problems as he kissed, sucked, and licked me until my juices flowed into his mouth. He entered my pussy, and instantly, he began to moan.

"Baby, you feel so nice and wet. It's wetter the normal," he whispered in my ear while hitting me from the back. "Shit, I don't know how much more I can take. My pussy feels so good," he said between moans.

I came again, and he was right behind me. He dropped on the bed next to me and then kissed me on my lips.

"I love you so much," he whispered in my ear, looking at me and smiling.

I turned on my other side and then cuddled up close to him. It was moments like this that let me know that everything would be all right.

Corey

Things between Monique and me were going so well. So much so that I could honestly say that I was in love with her. She hadn't even given me the pussy yet, and she had got a nigga whipped. I couldn't see myself without her. Samariah's crazy ass had left me alone. I didn't know if it was because I had changed my number or because she had just came to her senses, but either way, a nigga was happy as hell. This was our last month of high school, and I couldn't say I was going to miss it. We were getting ready for prom and graduation. I was going to throw a huge graduation party the day we walked across the stage.

I had been looking for a place for Mo and me, and I'd finally found the right place. We'd talked a few times about getting a place together, but it was just talk. I was going to make that shit a reality real soon. I planned to surprise her the day after we graduated with keys to our new place. My dad had a lot of properties in nice areas, so I planned to get a two-bedroom through his company. I'd let her decorate everything as soon as I found the place.

I planned to take a year or so off from school because a nigga needed a break from that shit. I know that Mo wanted to go to school in state, so everything would work out. I had talked to my dad about everything, and he supported a nigga wholeheartedly. He and moms had been together since they were sixteen, so he understood how I felt. Pops had told me that I didn't have to pay rent if I didn't want to, so that was good too, because now I could invest all my money into a business I planned to start.

I think that Mo and I were close to having sex, because she had got on birth control a few weeks back. I was thinking that maybe she had something special planned for me, but either way, she was stuck with a nigga forever.

Kevin

It was finally time to get rid of this bitch Sam. I had actually thought this bitch would have changed after getting caught with my best friend, but obviously, she hadn't. Even though I had plans to leave her, I still felt some type of way about finally saying good-bye to someone I gave four years of my life to. All of that changed, however, when I saw her in the car with that nigga Brian. I was taking Mom's car to get it detailed and washed when I pulled up next to her and

Brian in his truck. It looked innocent, until she reached over and stuck her tongue down that nigga's throat. She didn't even see me, and I knew then and there that we were definitely over. I told Zoe all about my relationship with Sam. I knew that Sam wasn't going to take rejection easily, and I didn't want Zoe to find out from someone else. She understood, and because we had never made things official, she didn't get mad at me.

I was headed over to Sam's house now to break the news to her. I had started to dump her ass through a text message, but I'd decided that would be taking the cowardly way out. When I got to her house, I said a little prayer before I knocked on her door. I should fuck her ass one last time and dump her ass right after, but I was not that cruel. She opened the door and greeted me with a kiss and a hug. I didn't stop her, because I knew that this would be the last time she would ever get to kiss me. She put her arms around my neck and stared in my face.

"So, what do you want to talk about?" she asked.

I looked at Sam's face. Man, she was so beautiful, but she was a ho, and I knew she was never going to change. I removed her arm from around my neck, and then I walked inside the house and asked her to sit down so that we could talk. We both took a seat in the living room.

"There isn't an easy way to say this, but you and I are over," I said, a little nervous.

"What do you mean, we are over?" she asked, her voice sounding a little shaky.

"This relationship is over. There is no more you and me. I cannot do this anymore," I said.

She laughed at me and then tried unbuckling my pants. I pushed her away from me and stood up to leave.

"Baby, please don't go. Whatever I've done, I'm sorry. We can fix this," she said, now crying.

"Sam, I am done. When I caught you with my best friend, fucking in my house, I knew then that I could never give you my all again," I told her.

"But I haven't messed with him since then. I haven't been with him or anyone else. I have been faithful to you. I love you so much, Kevin. Please, don't leave," she begged.

I looked at that bitch like she was crazy. "So what were you doing in the car with Brian yesterday?" I said.

"He was giving me a ride home from school. My car was messed up," she lied.

"He was just giving you a ride, huh? So do you tongue kiss everybody that gives you rides?" I asked.

She looked like she wanted to shit on herself. "Who in the fuck is lying on me? I didn't kiss his ass," she lied again.

"So you're trying to tell me that I don't know what I saw? I caught your ass with that nigga, not someone else. You ain't shit but a ho-ass liar, and I will never be with your skank ass. I'm out! Bitch, lose my fucking number," I told her.

She dropped to the floor and wrapped her arms around my legs; snot and tears were all over her face. I kept walking and dragged her ass all the way to the front door.

"Let me go, Sam. You are not going to change my mind," I said.

She wouldn't let go, so I had to force her off me. Once I got out of the house, she ran out behind me.

"Baby, I'm sorry. I promise to do better," she said.

I ignored her pleas and kept walking.

"Fuck you, nigga! I don't need your sorry dick ass, anyway!" she shouted.

"Whatever, bitch. That's why I left your neighborhood-pussy-having ass. Go find that nigga Brian, and whoever else you're fucking, because I'm through with your no-good ass," I spat.

I got in my car. I heard her say, "Fuck you, bitch," when I drove off. It felt good to finally dump that bitch. Now she was the next nigga's headache.

I was so happy to be done with Sam. A few days after I broke things off with her, she began to call my phone all day, every day. I changed my number ASAP. I made things official with Zoe about a week later, and we had been going strong ever since. My life was in a better place, and I couldn't be happier. Zoe and I practically stayed together. Zoe was a year older than me, and she had her own place. She was a freshman at Cardinal Stritch University, and she was very mature for her age. I was starting to fall for this girl, and I was starting to fall very hard.

Corey

I had called David and Kevin up so that we could go and purchase our tuxedos for prom. When we met up at the tuxedo shop, I was happy to see my niggas, because I had a bombshell to drop. Kevin and I hadn't been friends until I started dating Mo, but now that nigga and I were damn near inseparable.

"So, guess what, y'all?" I said to them.

"What?" they asked in unison.

"I'm thinking about proposing to Monique on her birthday."

"Nigga, ain't that in a few weeks? Are you sure you're ready for that?" Kevin asked me.

"Yeah, but I love her, and I know I want to marry her. Why wait to do it?" I asked.

"I love Bria with all my heart, and I want to marry her too, eventually, but I'm not in a rush. When you get married, kids come into the picture. Are you really ready for all that, my nigga?" David said.

"Yes, but just because we're getting married doesn't mean we have to have kids right away. And if we do, that's cool too," I said truthfully.

"Damn. I ain't ready for neither. I will be faithful to Bria, but I'm not about to marry her right now or get her ass pregnant," said David.

"I'm with you on that one, David, but look, man, if you love her, and you really want to marry her, I support you, my dude," Kevin said to me.

"Me too," David said.

"Now, I just have to get her dad's approval. Either way, I'm still going to propose to her," I said matter-of-factly.

We got everything we needed for prom and then went our separate ways. I couldn't wait until everything came together. I couldn't wait to make her the happiest woman in the world.

Chapter Seven

Monique

Bria and I were at the mall, getting some last-minute things for prom. I hadn't heard from Sam in a long time. She never answered calls from me anymore. Bria and Sam weren't even friends anymore. It was crazy because we had been friends since elementary school. Bria didn't trust Sam, and she'd said she didn't want to be around people she couldn't trust. Bria had said that I needed to leave Sam alone, but she hadn't done anything to me, so I was not as willing to let go of our friendship.

"Friend, there is something that I need to tell you," Bria said.

"What is it?" I asked as I browsed through some shoes.

"I think something has happened or is going on between Sam and Corey," she blurted out.

"Why would you say that, Bria?" I asked, a little mad.

"Well, the day that we went bowling, she and Corey both disappeared for about ten minutes. When he came from the bathroom, you could tell he was pissed, and Sam looked like she had been crying. I noticed her staring at you two like she wanted to kill both of y'all. Every time we bring up Corey or he's around, she gets pissed, and on top of that, she never wanted you two to be together," she said.

That was true. He did come back looking pissed that date at the bowling alley, and Sam didn't want me to be with him. "I don't think he's cheating on me," I said.

"Well, maybe he's not cheating, but maybe they slept together," she said.

"But why would they hide something like that from me? Why would my best friend sleep with someone she knew I had had a crush on since the ninth grade?" I said.

"I don't know, friend," she said.

I thought long and hard about what Bria had just told me, and I really didn't know what to believe, but I did know that this better not be true. I wouldn't worry about this, because I knew that what was done in the dark would definitely come to the light.

Bria

I decided to go to Sam's house and question her about my suspicions. I could no longer hide how I was feeling. I knocked on the door, and she let me in. She looked like she had been stressing. She had lost some weight, and her eyes were dark.

"Listen, I just wanted to ask you something. Do you think you can be honest with me?" I said.

"Sure," she said.

"Are you, or have you been, sleeping with Corey?" I asked.

"Seriously, Bria. Why would you ask me that?" Sam said in a shaky voice.

I ran down everything I saw, and I could tell that she knew that she had been caught, but she still insisted on lying. "Bria, don't come up in my shit, accusing me of some bullshit. If I did fuck him, why would that matter to you? He's not your man," she snapped.

"Because Monique is my best fucking friend, and I don't want to see her hurt. Bitch, you're supposed to be her best friend as well. You know damn well she has always wanted to be with Corey," I snapped.

"Fuck you, bitch! I do what the fuck I want to do. I will fuck David if I want to, and your ass can't do shit about it. I'm that bitch, so get the fuck out of my house before I whup your ass," she said, pointing at the door.

I acted as though I was about to walk out the door, but then I spun around and punched the shit out of her. She flew against the wall, and I walked up on her.

"Bitch, if you ever talk to me like that again, I will do more than punch your ass. Bitch, my man will never touch your dirty ass. If I find out that anything happened between you and Corey, I'm coming for your ass. Now, stay the fuck away from me and Monique."

I started walking away, but that bitch tried to grab my hair. I might be little, but I got them hands. I turned around and double punched that bitch, and she fell on the floor. I walked out of her house, pissed as hell. I was fighting and, shit, and I was almost three months pregnant.

On the way home, I broke down crying. I couldn't believe that I had lost one of my best friends. We had been friends for all these years, and now it was all over. Sam was not the same person anymore. She had started to change for the worse when we were about twelve years old. I meant every word I told her. If I found out that anything had happened between them two, I was really going to beat her ass.

Sam

My life had been in bad shape lately. Kevin had broken up with me, and that hurt me so freaking bad. On top of that, Bria had punched the shit out of me three times. I didn't have Corey or Kevin, and this shit was driving me crazy. I honestly hadn't thought that Kevin would ever leave me, and especially not for someone else. I had tried calling him to plead my case, but he had changed his number on me. Every time I stopped by his house, his mom said that he was not there.

One night, I sat at his house all night, waiting on him to come home, but he never showed up. I later found out where his new girlfriend worked through a mutual friend of ours. I also found out that she had her own apartment, so that was probably where he was every night. I hadn't found out where she lived, but I knew I would real soon. I started plotting and planning to get all those fuckers back. I would never let them get away with what they had done to me. I had hurt people before, and I didn't have a problem hurting someone again. I know you're probably thinking, *What is this crazy bitch talking about*? Well, let me catch you up.

When I was twelve years old, I had the biggest crush on this boy named Brent. I would let him kiss me and rub on me, but he wouldn't leave his little girlfriend. One night, I grabbed my bat and some Mace and then followed them to the park. I watched them from a distance to make sure that they were alone. Once I discovered that they were alone, I crept up on them. They were sitting on the swings. I tapped the girl on the shoulder, and she looked behind her to see what was going on. When she did, I sprayed her eyes with the Mace, and she started screaming.

Brent looked back to see what was going on, and I sprayed him in the eyes and hit him in the head with my bat. He hit the ground, and then I hit him a few more times. The girl started to run, but I caught up with her. I swung the bat and hit her in her head from behind as hard as hell. Once she hit the ground, I kicked her in her face and stomach and then took off running. I found out a few days later that Brent had a concussion and the girl was in a coma. She eventually woke up, but the cops never found out that I was the one who did it. I didn't have a problem doing that shit again.

Eric still hadn't given up on him and me being together. He had popped up over at my house the other day and had begged and pleaded with me. He was really starting to make me want to kill his ass. It was his fucking fault that Kevin and I were no longer together, so he was on my hit list as well. Yes, I had a fucking hit list, and I planned to get revenge on everybody who was on it. Eric, Kevin, Corey, Zoe, and Mo had better watch their fucking backs.

Why did these niggas keep leaving me? My daddy didn't want me, so he had left me with my mother. I had never wanted any man to be in my life more than my daddy, but he had let that other bitch take my place. Why couldn't he just love me and be there for me, like a father should? I sat in the middle of my bed, with my legs pulled up to my chest, rocking back and forth. I was crying my eyes out, thinking about all the people who had wronged me, and I vowed to make them pay. They wouldn't get away with this.

Monique

Today was the day that we were going to our senior prom, and I was super excited. We had all decided to ride to prom together in a stretch Hummer limo, so everyone had gathered at my house.

Corey and I had decided to wear peach and white as our colors. I wore a mermaid-style peach-colored dress that hugged every single curve that I had. I had my hair in wand curls, and I wore some Chanel diamond stud earrings and bracelets. Corey had on an all-white Armani tux, with a peach-colored shirt underneath, and a fresh pair of Air Force 1s.

Bria was looking as pretty as ever with a red cut-up lace minidress by BCBG and matching six-inch red pumps. She had let her hair grow out to shoulder length and had it styled in a bob with some red streaks. She was three months now, and even though her stomach was still flat, she definitely had that pregnant woman's glow. David was matching her fly with a black and red Tom Ford suit.

Kevin and his new girl wore white and royal blue, and they were fly as hell too. I was still getting used to having Zoe around instead of Sam. Sam had made her bed, and now she had to lie in it. She still was my girl, though, and I didn't feel as comfortable hanging with Zoe. Bria and Zoe, on the other hand, got along very well. You would think they had been friends all their lives.

When we finally made it to the hotel that was hosting our prom, I was taken aback by how beautifully it was set up. The DJ was playing everything we wanted to hear. After about an hour of us being there, Sam walked in with Brian. She pranced over and greeted us. No one was excited to see her except for me.

"Friend, I'm so happy to see you. Why haven't you returned any of my calls?" I said.

"I was going through something, but I'm better now. Kevin, aren't you going to introduce me to your girlfriend?" Sam said sarcastically.

"I'm going to go to the bathroom, Sam. I'll be back," Brian said, excusing himself. I could tell that he didn't want anything to do with Sam's drama. Kevin looked like he wanted to strangle Sam.

"This is Sam," was all he said.

"Kevin, how rude of you. I'm Samariah, Kevin's ex-girlfriend of four years, to be exact," Sam said with a smirk.

"I'm Zaria, but everyone calls me Zoe, and I'm Kevin's future," Zoe said, not worried about Sam even one bit.

Zoe walked up on Kevin and put her arms around his waist. He bent down and gave her a kiss on the lips. Sam looked like she wanted to kill them both. Bria was smiling so hard; she looked like she was enjoying every bit of Sam's misery. Sam looked over at Corey and me, and then she stormed off.

"You need to leave her alone, friend. She is not to be trusted," Bria said.

"Right," Kevin and Corey said in unison.

"Well, she hasn't given me a reason not to trust her, so until then, y'all need to just drop it," I said with finality.

We continued to dance and chop it up until they announced the prom king and queen.

"Can I please have everyone's attention? We are ready to announce the class of twenty-twelve's prom king and queen. This year's prom king is Corey Anderson, and our prom queen is Samariah Reed."

I wasn't surprised that my sexy face had won prom king, but I was definitely surprised that Sam had won. For starters, no one liked Sam. Well, at least no girls did, because she had either slept with their dude or their dude wanted her, but then again, she was popular. Corey looked so uncomfortable as he walked up on the stage and joined Sam. He looked as though he would rather be anyplace but standing on the stage next to her. Sam looked like she was in heaven. A photographer took pictures of them, but Corey flat out refused to dance with Sam. I had even told him that it was okay, but he had said that he would pass.

Noticing how he interacted with her made me feel a little suspicious. What if everything that Bria had said was true? He definitely hated being around Sam, but why? Either they had messed around before I came into the picture, and now he didn't want anything to do with her, or he didn't like how Sam had done his homeboy. I didn't know, but my gut was telling me something was not right. I hoped that I was wrong. I didn't want to lose two of the people whom I loved the most because of their deceit.

Chapter Eight

Corey

Prom was now over, and we all decided to get rooms at the hotel. Mo's demeanor had changed after they crowned Sam and me prom king and queen. It seemed like she was deep in thought. Once we got to our hotel room, I stripped down to my basketball shorts, got in the bed, and turned on the TV. I was watching some highlights from an old basketball game when Mo came and sat down next to me.

"Baby, we are always honest with each other, right?" she asked me.

"Of course, sweetie," I said.

"You wouldn't hide anything from me, right? You wouldn't cheat on me or anything like that, would you?" she questioned with a serious face.

Mo had never acted even remotely insecure since we started dating, so I was confused by her line of questioning.

"Baby, I would never hide anything from you, nor would I ever cheat on you," I half lied.

"Why would you even think something like that? I have never given you a reason not to trust me."

Truth was, I had never cheated on her, but I had slept with her best friend before we got together. I really regretted that shit. I felt bad hiding this secret from her, but I was more scared of losing her.

"There are some rumors and speculation going around about you and Sam. I could never forgive you if anything ever happened between you two, but I trust you, and I know you wouldn't hide anything from me," she said, smiling at me.

She strutted off to the bathroom, and I felt like shit. Man, I really hated that bitch Sam, and I really hated myself right now for getting involved with her ass.

Mo walked out of the bathroom, interrupting the pity party I was having with myself. She had on nothing but some peach boy shorts and her peach heels. All thoughts about Sam and everything else left my mind the moment I laid eyes on her. She was so fucking beautiful. Her ass and hips were big and toned perfectly, and her titties sat on her chest perfectly. Her tummy was flat, and her hair flowed past her shoulders, making her look even sexier.

"I am giving myself to you. Don't make me regret it," she said sternly.

"I love you, baby. As a matter of fact, I'm in love with you. You are all I need and want," I said truthfully.

"You're in love with me?" she asked, walking toward me.

"Yes," I said.

"I'm in love with you too," she said, then kissed me passionately on the lips. She stuck her tongue in my mouth, and I gladly accepted it. I palmed her ass and pushed her body close to mine. I trailed kisses down her neck and stopped at her titties. I took her left one in my mouth, and then I gently bit down on it. I sucked and twirled my tongue on it while playing with her other nipple with my fingers.

I took her panties off and picked her up. I placed both of her legs over my shoulders and then dove headfirst into her pussy. She had the sweetest-tasting pussy I had ever eaten. I sucked on her clit while taking two fingers and entering her hole. She tightened her legs around my neck, and I knew it was because nothing had ever been inside of it. I laid her on the bed while continuing to lick her pussy. I darted my tongue in and out of her hole while taking my thumb and gently rubbing against her clit. I gave my baby her first orgasm, and she screamed out in pleasure.

I lay between her legs and slowly entered her. She tensed up a little bit, but then she began to relax. Her pussy felt so good; it was warm as hell and, of course, tight. I could lie up in her shit all day and never get tired. I slowly thrust in and out of her while grinding my pelvis into her each time. I flipped her on her side and then entered her that way. I looked down and watched as my dick went in and out of her. That shit was driving me crazy; I was ready to bust just at the sight.

I took my thumb and rubbed on her clit. I felt her walls getting even tighter around my dick. I knew she was about to come, and I was coming right with her. We came, and I just lay there with my dick inside of her. We were both exhausted, so we fell asleep. There was no better feeling in the world than being inside of her. She definitely couldn't find out about me and Sam, or I would definitely lose her.

Kevin

I couldn't believe that I was officially a high school graduate. It had been a week since prom and graduation, and I felt good. People looked at me and how I dressed, and they thought I was just some common thug, but that was far from the truth. Yes, I sold drugs, but it wasn't something I planned on doing for the rest of my life. I had kept a 4.0 grade point average all four years, and I had been one of the star players on the high school basketball team.

Zoe and I practically lived together. I never knew you could fall for someone so easily, but I had. She was so perfect to me. If Samariah had never messed up, I would have never known what true happiness really meant. When I thought about Zoe, I immediately smiled. The sex was off the chain, and she definitely knew how to make her man feel good. Since it was technically her place, we had decided to find a place that we could both call our home. She had said that what was hers was mine, but I would feel better if we just started fresh with a new place.

Lately, strange stuff had been happening. Zoe had told me that she had been getting strange calls and text messages. She'd said someone would call and just breathe into the phone. I immediately thought it was Sam, but how had she got Zoe's number? Then I just assumed it was her ex. Today, though, when I got outside, there was a note left on my windshield, telling me to watch my back. I couldn't front. A nigga was kind of scared. I couldn't figure out for the life of me who in the hell would be threatening me. I had no known enemies, and they had left the note on my car by Zoe's house. None of my friends knew where I was staying, not even David and Corey, but I planned to get to the bottom of this. Until then, we would be moving, and I would always stay strapped up.

Sam had tried to throw shade on prom night by introducing herself as my ex-girlfriend of four years, but my baby had held her own. She hadn't even let that shit bother her at all. Just thinking about how she had handled it made my dick hard.

Zoe

I loved me some Kevin, and I honestly hadn't known I would feel so strongly about him so quickly. We had started out kind of rocking because he was in a relationship most of the time we were dating. Even though he had told me about the relationship, and I hadn't found out through word of mouth, I was still pissed off, but I didn't let him know that, of course. He had given me the rundown on what had happened between him and Sam.

She was a disrespectful ho. Yes, I had class, but that bitch had almost made me lose my cool on their prom night, because she'd been super messy. Don't let this small frame fool you. I could definitely get down with these hands, and I could tell I was going to have to lay them on that bitch. Kevin was mine now, and you could bet your bottom dollar that his ass wasn't going anywhere. He had already been hooked before we had sex, and once we did, that sealed the deal. I knew I had some fantastic pussy, and I gave great head. I gave my man back and foot rubs every night, and I got down in the kitchen.

Sam's ass had messed up, but she refused to let go. I knew that bitch was the one calling my phone, breathing and shit. That was why I was about to meet up with this ho and put an end to this shit, once and for all. After I explained to Bria what had been going on, she gave me Sam's number. I had sent Sam a message, telling her I wanted to meet up. I hadn't told her who I was when I sent the message, but she knew exactly who I was. That just confirmed what I already knew. I did not play these little childish games, and I would hate to let the bitch in me come out, but she had really taken me there.

I pulled up at a Dunkin' Donuts in West Allis, a suburb of Milwaukee. As I walked inside, I spotted her sitting at a table in the corner. I hoped this bitch didn't go running her mouth to Kevin about us meeting up, because I hadn't told him that I was meeting her. I sat down and got straight to the point.

"I'm asking you nicely to stay off my phone and stop playing on my shit. What you and Kevin had is over, and honestly, it had nothing to do with me, so leave me out of it," I said.

"What makes you think it is me that's playing on your phone? How do you know he's not fucking around with someone else?" she said with a smirk.

"I know because my name and pussy juice are written all over his dick, and you are the only simple-ass chick that doesn't want to let go. I know that my man is faithful to me, and if you knew how to keep your legs closed, maybe you would still have him, but you fucked up, and now he's all mine," I said heatedly.

My plan was to come and have a simple conversation with her, but I really disliked this bitch, and not just because she was Kevin's ex, but also because she had a smart-ass mouth.

"Listen here, bitch!" she said, pointing her finger in my face. "You may have Kevin now, but he will always come back to me. And you want to know why? Because I'm his first everything, and I have the best pussy he has ever had. Your little black ass ain't got shit on me. You're just filling the void until I'm ready to take his ass back," she said.

It took everything in me not to haul off and slap the piss out of her.

"Correction. You may have had the best pussy he's ever had, but I'm number one, baby. He whispers that into my ear every night, after I ride the shit out of his dick. You are water under the bridge, baby, and I am definitely not worried about your ho ass taking my place. Now listen up, and you listen very carefully. You may think your ass is crazy, but you haven't seen shit yet. Stay the fuck away from my man and me. This will be my first and last warning," I said. I then picked my purse up and left her sitting there, looking dumb as hell. Next time I wouldn't be as nice. Next time I'd definitely be beating her ass.

Sam

So this bitch Zoe had some balls. She knew it was my ass playing on her phone, but personally, I didn't give a fuck. I also had been leaving notes on Kevin's car, threatening his ass. I really didn't want to hurt Kevin, but I definitely had something in store for his black bitch. I didn't know exactly what I was going to do to her ass, but I planned to hurt her ass real bad. First, I had to handle Eric's ass. He had finally given up on being with my ass, but he had destroyed what Kevin and I had, and for that reason, his ass had to go.

I had the perfect plan. I texted him and told him I wanted to meet up with him tonight so that we could talk. I went to Walmart and purchased a hunter's knife. I had already gotten my gloves the night before. I told Eric to meet me at this secluded area by the park at eight o'clock sharp. When I got to the park, he was already there. I grabbed my purse, climbed out of my car, and headed over to his.

"Hey, baby. I'm so happy to see you," I told Eric once I got in his car. I placed my purse next to me on the seat.

"You sure weren't acting like you missed me. You never returned any of my calls. So, what do you really want, Samariah?" he said, sounding irritated.

"I want you, baby. I know it took me a while to realize it, but I really do love you," I lied.

"You're just saying that because that nigga Kevin left you," he said.

"He didn't leave me! I left his ass," I shouted.

"Whatever," he said.

"Listen, let me just show you how much I really missed you," I told him while rubbing his crotch.

I could see him starting to loosen up. I unbuckled his pants and took him in my mouth. After getting him hard, I climbed over onto his lap and slowly slid down his pole. I clutched my walls around his dick and rode him like a pro.

He closed his eyes and threw his head back against the headrest, and that was when I made my move. I reached behind me to get the knife, which I'd hid in the back part of my bra. Before he knew it, I plunged the knife into his chest and twisted it. He tried to push me off him, but he instantly became weak. I took the knife and stabbed him three more times, and I watched the life leave his body. I took a small plastic bag with a baby wipe inside it out of my pocket, cleaned his dick off with the baby wipe, and then threw the wipe and the knife into the bag. I retrieved my purse, reached inside it, and grabbed the little bear my dad had bought me for my fifth birthday. I held it close to my body, and as I stared at Eric's lifeless body, I began to rock back and forth.

"Daddy, why weren't you around? Why didn't you love me enough to stay with me and Mommy?" I said through snot and tears. "I need you, Daddy!" I screamed.

I grabbed my purse and the plastic bag, got out of the car, and threw the bag, with the knife and the baby wipe still in it, in the Milwaukee River, which ran through the park. I then climbed back in my car and raced home. When I got home, I burned the clothes that I was wearing in the fireplace in my bedroom.

The next day, I heard on the news that the police had found an eighteen-year-old boy stabbed to death in his car. There were no witnesses to the crime, and no visible evidence had been left at the scene. *One down. Four to go*, I thought.

Bria

I had decided that today would be the day that I told our parents and David that I was pregnant. I figured I was a high school graduate and I'd be eighteen next week, so this would be the perfect time to tell them. I asked David and his parents to come over for dinner. We were sitting around the table, eating, when I asked for everyone's attention. I was nervous as hell, but I refused to keep hiding this secret.

"Well, I brought all of us together for a reason. I have something I need to tell you guys," I said nervously.

"What is it, baby? You got accepted to another college?" my dad asked, chuckling.

"No, Dad. I'm afraid it's more serious than that," I said on the brink of tears.

"Let me guess. You're pregnant," David's mom said jokingly.

Everybody laughed—everybody except for me. When they noticed that I wasn't laughing, everyone got quiet.

"You're pregnant!" my mom shouted with anger.

"She didn't say that, Silvia. You didn't say that, right, baby?" my dad said.

I looked in his eyes, and I could tell that he knew the truth. He just didn't want to face it. David and his parents were sitting there, waiting on me to spell it out. David was nervous. I could tell by the way he was looking at me.

"I'm three months pregnant, and I'm due in February," I said, now crying.

My dad put his head down, and my mom started crying too. David's parents were sitting there with their mouths wide open.

"I need to speak to you in private, Bria," David said.

"Hell no! It seems like y'all have been doing enough in private," my mom said.

"Silvia, leave them alone. Let them talk," my dad said, with so much sadness in his voice.

My heart began to break, because I knew I had disappointed my parents. I got up, and David and I walked to my bedroom so that we could talk. I sat down on the bed, but David remained standing.

"How could you do this to me, Bria? Why am I just now finding out about this?" he asked angrily.

"I don't know," I said.

"What do you mean, you don't know? We talk about everything else, and you couldn't tell me this? Then you drop this bomb on me on the same day that you tell our parents. What type of shit is that?" he yelled.

"I was scared, okay! I wasn't ready for this, but it happened, and I told you the best way I knew how," I said through my tears.

"Bria, I'm not ready for a baby. I love you, but I didn't see myself having a baby so soon," he said, on the verge of tears. "This isn't how shit was supposed to play out. We were supposed to go to college, get married, and then have kids. Now shit is all fucked up because of your ass. You are ruining my life!" he screamed.

I looked at him like he had lost his damn mind. How in the hell was this just my fault?

"Wait one minute. You knew exactly what you were doing every time we had sex. Now how dare you blame this on me? With or without your ass, I'm having this baby! And I'll take care of it. We don't need you," I said as I stood up and walked toward the door.

As I was leaving the bedroom, he grabbed my arm and then pulled me back into the room. "I'm sorry, baby. It's just that this is a lot to take in. I'm not ready for a baby, but I don't want to lose you. We will figure everything out. I promise," he said. Then he embraced me and kissed me on my forehead.

I felt much better in his arms, with him reassuring me that everything would work. I knew it would be hard, but it would be okay.

Chapter Nine

David

I almost fell the hell out when Bria told us that she was pregnant. I was definitely not ready for a kid, but she was pregnant. I knew the baby was mine, so I was going to do right by her and my baby. Two weeks after we found out about the pregnancy, Corey's dad hooked us up with a nice three-bedroom condo down by the lake. He gave us a good deal on the rent since we were young and neither one of us had a job.

When Bria turned eighteen a week ago, she received an inheritance check for two million dollars from her grandma, who had died when she was a kid. My parents had set up a trust fund for me, and I would receive money from it once I turned eighteen. It wasn't as much as Bria's, but we wouldn't be hurting for money anytime soon. We went shopping for furniture and stuff for our house, and now we were moving in. Bria's mom was so pissed that she was pregnant that she hadn't spoken to Bria and me since the day Bria announced it. Everybody was at our condo except for her.

Kevin and Corey pulled me to the side so that the three of us could take a little break.

"So how does it feel, man? You're about to be a dad in a few months," Kevin said.

"Man, it is what it is. I really don't know how to feel," I said truthfully.

"Well, man, I know you aren't too happy about things, but is it really worth losing Bria?" Corey asked.

"Why would you ask me that?" I questioned him, confused. "Why would I lose Bria?" I asked.

"Let's go for a walk, man," Corey said.

The three of us left the condo so that we could talk in private.

"Well, Bria told Mo that you have been acting very strange since the day she announced it. Not only that, I was talking to my homeboy, and he told me how you've been entertaining some little chick from his hood. He saw your car over there a few times. If he knows, then so do other people, and I don't want word to get back to your girl, man," Corey said.

It was true. Ever since Bria had told me that she was pregnant, I had been feeling some type of way. I'd even started drinking. One day, I was chilling with one of my boys when this little thick chick walked past. She was smiling at me, so I hollered at her. Under normal circumstances, I would never cheat on my girl, but this pregnancy shit had a nigga in the wrong state of mind.

"I chilled with her a few times, but nothing serious. I didn't fuck ole girl, if that's what y'all thinking," I told them.

"Bro, it's not even in your character to entertain these thots. She's pregnant. So what? That doesn't mean your life ends because you have a baby. Not to mention, you planned on spending the rest of your life with her, anyway," Kevin said.

I loved my girl with all my heart, and I didn't want to lose her, so I was going to get my shit together. "Y'all right, dude. I have to fix this shit," I told them.

"We're here for you, man. We've got your back," Corey said.

We headed back to my place to finish setting everything up. I never in a million years would have thought about cheating on Bria, but now a nigga had that "I don't give a fuck" attitude. I had a vision for my life. I planned to go to college, get married, and then have children. I still wanted to enjoy my life without restrictions. Granted, I planned to do all this with my girl, but with a child in the picture, we would definitely be restricted. Although I felt this way, I still needed to get my shit together, before I lost my little family.

Mo

Bria and I turned eighteen in the same month. Our birthdays were a week apart, so we decided to throw a big birthday bash at this mansion we rented out. Bria was starting to show a little. You still couldn't tell that she was pregnant if you didn't know her, but her stomach had grown a little bit. That didn't stop us from throwing the party of the summer. I decided on an all-white BCBG minidress with some white BCBG sandals with a four-inch heel. Bria decided on an orange pencil skirt by Chanel and a white and orange crop top. Since she was pregnant, David made her wear some flat white Chanel sandals. We were looking fly as shit, and our party was already live.

We had a popular DJ named Stretch, who was from Milwaukee, on the ones and twos. I had invited Sam to the party, but who knew if she was going to show? Her ass had been on some funny shit lately, and quite frankly, I was tired of her bullshit.

Everything was going well until David got on some bullshit. He was dancing with a few other women, and he was drunk as hell. That was something he had been doing a lot of lately. Corey and Kevin kept trying to get him together, but his ass wasn't listening. Plus, he had some nigga named Darrel in his ear, encouraging him to do bullshit. I guessed Bria had had enough, because she went over there and snapped. She slapped him dead in his face. He tried to apologize, but Bria wasn't hearing it. The party ended up shutting down early because of it.

Like, three days after David and Bria moved into their place, Corey surprised me with keys to a place of our own. We moved in, and I completely furnished our place. We had a two-bedroom condo in the same area as Bria and David's, except ours was closer to the water.

I was just about to jump in the shower when Bria called me.

"Hey, girl. What's up with you?" I asked Bria.

"Nothing much, besides the fact that I'm about to leave David," she said with so much sadness in her voice.

"What? Why? I know he was being disrespectful by dancing with those girls, but you don't have to leave him, friend," I said.

"I don't know how much longer I can deal with this. Ever since I told him that I was pregnant, he has changed. Before I told him that I was pregnant, I couldn't get away from him, and believe me, I tried. Now he's gone all damn day, and he comes home late at night. We argue all the time, and all he does is apologize, and then he does the same shit the next day. Mo, you know I don't tolerate that type of foolery," Bria said.

That was true. Bria didn't take shit from anybody. She was quick to drop your ass.

"Bria, just hang in there. Things will get better. Are you coming to the dinner tomorrow?" I said.

"Yes, we are coming," she said.

"Well, I will see you then. I'm about to shower and relax. Love you, and call me if you need me," I told her.

"Love you too, friend, and I will."

We ended our call, and I headed right for the shower. I didn't understand why Corey insisted on going out to dinner tomorrow. We ate out all the time, and I wanted to have a home-cooked meal. I was tired of eating fast food, but he had said there was something special about eating out tomorrow, so I had caved in to his request.

Corey

My baby had no clue what was going on, but I was about to make her one of the happiest women in the world. We had decided to eat at this place called Chops, and I had made sure to invite all our family and friends. I had asked her father two weeks before if I could have her hand in marriage. He had lectured me for about two hours, but he had told me that he would be glad to have me as his son-in-law. Today was the big day, and somehow that bitch Samariah had found out about the dinner and showed up. None of us had heard from her or seen her since graduation, so it was surprising that she showed her face today.

My father had rented the restaurant out for two hours so that everyone was able to sit in one area and chat it up. I was nervous as hell, but I knew this was what I wanted to do. I stood up and asked for everyone's attention. Then I walked over to Mo, and I could tell that she was clueless as to what I was about to do.

"Monique, since the first day I saw you in the ninth grade, I have had the biggest crush on you, but I allowed my own insecurities to get in the way of me being with you. Now that I have you, I don't ever want to let you go. I have never been in love with any woman besides you, and I want to give you the world. You are the air that I breathe, and I need you by my side. With that being said, Monique Peterson, will you please marry me?" I said.

She was crying so hard, but I knew that they were tears of joy. I pulled out a fifteen-carat princess-cut diamond and gold engagement ring.

"Yes, Corey Anderson. I will marry you, baby. I love you so much," she said, then kissed me all over my face.

Everyone came over to congratulate us, and then I decided to step outside to get some air. I felt someone wrap their arms around my waist, and I assumed it was Mo.

"Baby, you didn't have to come out here. I told you I was coming right back," I said as I pulled her in front of me.

When I opened my eyes, I immediately got pissed. I pushed Sam away from me, and for a minute, I almost blacked out. "What in the hell is your problem, and why are you even here?" I asked her.

"Well, I saw Monique's mom at the store, and she invited me here. You know I couldn't pass up the chance to see my boo," she said, trying to touch my face.

I slapped her hands down and began to walk away.

"How could you propose to her, Corey, after what we shared? I love you, and I need you. How could you just walk away from what we had?" she said.

I looked at her like she had just grown two heads. "If I didn't know then, I definitely know now that your ass is crazy. You and I never had a relationship, so get your delusional ass away from here," I said as I walked back into the restaurant.

Sam didn't come back in, so I guessed she had got the picture. We enjoyed the rest of the time at the restaurant, and then everyone headed to their destination of choice. Monique and I made it home, and I made sweet love to my fiancée. I hoped this bitch Sam didn't try to come in and ruin what we had, because if she did, there would be major hell to pay.

Kevin

Bria and I decided to get together and throw Corey and Mo a surprise engagement party. It had been a few months since he proposed to her, but being the party people that we were, we turned everything into a party. Bria and Zoe did the decorating, and I basically paid for everything.

My nigga, David, had gone downhill, and for the first time since he and Bria got together, that nigga was cheating on her. Corey and I tried talking some sense into his ass, but that nigga just wasn't listening. He acted like having a baby was the worst thing in the world. He could still go to college and enjoy life, so I didn't know why he was acting out like this. If Bria found out, we were definitely going to be planning his funeral. Anyway, Zoe and I were doing great. She had even got a nigga thinking about marriage, but I could definitely wait. I was not that nigga Corey. I was not in a rush.

Sam's stupid ass had somehow got my number, and she was up to her same old tricks. She had been calling me all day and night and sending nude pictures of her and that nigga Brian fucking. She was trying to make me jealous, but I honestly didn't give a fuck. I did not want her ass anymore. She had almost caught my ass slipping one time. I thought back on what had happened.

I stopped into Red Robin to pick up some food that I had ordered over the phone for Zoe and me. I headed to the bathroom first, because I had been holding my shit for a while. As I was finishing up, I heard someone come into the bathroom, but I didn't think anything of it until I felt a pair of hands grab at my dick from behind me.

I immediately pushed whoever it was, and then I turned around to see who in the hell was about to get murdered up in Red Robin. It was none other than Sam's ass. I was so shocked to see her that I forgot that my pants and shit were still undone. She walked up on me, dropped to her knees fast as hell, and took me into my mouth. I pushed her off me.

"Sam, what in the hell are you doing?" I asked her.

"Nothing you don't want me to do. It's obvious by how hard you are that she isn't sucking your dick right," she said sarcastically.

Her ass was partially right. I was hard as hell, but shit, I was a nigga. Who wouldn't get hard if some bitch just dropped to her knees and started sucking your dick? Plus, Sam was good at giving head; she was one of the best. But she was wrong, because I thought my baby, Zoe, was just as good as she was. She crawled back over to me and tried to take me in her mouth again, but I stopped that shit ASAP. This time I knew that if I went there with Sam, I would regret it. Her ass was looking good too, but not good enough for me to put my relationship at risk.

"I know you miss me, Daddy. Come back home to me, and I promise to treat you good," she said.

She lifted up her dress and showed me her clean-shaven pussy. My little nigga started to leap in my pants. She took her finger and started to play with her pussy. I suddenly thought about my girl, and I knew that I had to get my ass out of there before I made a mistake. I fixed my clothes and told her ass to stay the fuck away from me. She tried stopping me from leaving the bathroom, but I wasn't going to stay there with her ass. I got my food and got the hell out of Dodge.

She would never catch a nigga slipping like that again. My girl would kill both of our asses.

Sam

I found out that Bria and Kevin were throwing Monique and Corey a surprise engagement party. I figured that this would be the perfect time to destroy their little happiness. I no longer cared about keeping things between Corey and me a secret. If I couldn't be happy with him, Monique wouldn't be, either. Our friendship was over the moment she decided to be with Corey. I didn't care if she didn't know that we had slept together.

I walked into the party, looking sexy as hell, and of course, all eyes were on me. I spotted Bria out of the corner of my eye, and she was looking at me like, "What the fuck is she doing here?" I didn't care how her ass was staring me down. I was on a mission. I knew that they had set aside a time so that everyone could congratulate them, and that was when I had decided to make my move. I walked up to Monique and hugged her tight. I could tell that she was somewhat happy to see me, but that shit wasn't going to last for long. I sat back and waited for the big grand finale, which would be sure to end all this fucking celebrating. Why the fuck should this bitch be happy and celebrating with my man while I sat at home and dreamed about being with him every fucking night? Fuck that bitch. I was about to destroy her ass.

It was almost time for me to go up and speak. I had a group text message prepared, and would be sending it to Corey and Monique. Corey had changed his number on me, but I had sucked his friend Mitch's dick, and he had given me Corey's number. I had scheduled the text message to be sent three minutes from now. Actually, it was a video of Corey and me having sex. The last time Corey and I had sex, I had recorded us doing it. He didn't know about it, and I hadn't planned to use the video against him, because I hadn't even known he had plans to get with Monique. I had recorded it because I loved watching myself fucking, but now this video was about to come in handy. I stood up and grabbed the microphone, and now it was time to put on a show. All eyes were on me, and I was super excited.

"I would like to take the time to congratulate my best friend, Monique, and Corey on their recent engagement. I love you, girl," I said and blew Monique a kiss.

She blew me one back.

"I hate to be the bearer of bad news, but Corey is not who he says his is."

I could tell that Corey was about to shit himself, and Mo looked confused as hell, but her eyes never left mine.

I went on. "Corey and I have slept together on more than one occasion. I want to thank everyone for listening to me, but I just couldn't allow my best friend to marry this liar without her knowing the truth."

As soon as I was finished talking, Corey and Mo received the video. I noticed Mo looking at her phone and then covering her mouth, and that sealed the deal. My work here was done. I walked off the stage, and Bria was coming for me with fire in her eyes. I was tired of this bitch putting her hands on me. This time I would definitely be whupping her ass. Before she got to me, Zoe and David grabbed her.

"You dirty bitch. You're always sleeping with somebody else's man! How could you do that to her?" she shouted, with tears coming down her face.

I just stood there smirking. She tried to break loose, but they stopped her.

"She's not even worth it, Bria. She is nothing but a lonely, scandalous-ass bitch that's not even worth the fight," Zoe said.

"Naw, fuck that! When I have my baby, I'm coming for your no-good ass. You just wait!" Bria said, then stormed off.

I didn't see Corey or Monique, so I left the party, feeling very satisfied. I expected a visit from him sooner or later, and I planned to whip it on him something serious.

Chapter Ten

Monique

I couldn't believe my eyes and ears. I knew that she did not just tell me that she and Corey had slept together. It was one thing for her to admit it in front of everyone, but it was another to see the shit on video. I looked at Corey, and I began to cry.

"Baby, can we please talk?" he whispered in my ear.

I turned to face the man that I had grown to love, and I couldn't even look at him without feeling disgusted.

"Baby, I love you, and it's not what it seems. Baby, ple—"

I slapped the shit out of him before he could even finish his sentence. "You love me? You love me? You don't fucking love me. You don't lie to the people you love," I said.

"Sweetie, I didn't lie to you," he said.

I kicked him in his balls and punched him in his face. I stood over him, and I spoke to him with so much anger. "You better stay the fuck away from me. I hate your ass, and just so that we are clear, we are definitely over!" I said. I threw my ring at him, and it hit him in the face.

I was so pissed with Corey that I forgot the part that Sam had played in all of this. She could have told me in private, but instead, she had decided to embarrass me in front of all our friends and family. This bitch was not about to get away with this shit at all. I drove to her house, but she hadn't made it home yet. I parked a few houses down and waited for her to pull up. She came home about forty-five minutes later, and I was ready for her ass.

I always kept a pair of shoes in my car because I had been wearing heels a lot lately, and I hated to drive in them. I threw my shoes on and then got out of my car. I waited until she got to her door, and then I snuck up behind her. I grabbed that bitch by the back of her hair and slammed her face into the door. Blood started gushing out of a gash on her head, and she fell to the ground.

"Get your ass up, bitch!" I yelled at her.

It took her a second to regain her composure, but then she stood up and rushed me. We fell to the ground, and then we started to tussle with each other. She ended up on top of me, but before she could do anything, I kicked her in her stomach. She rolled off me, and I got on top of her and started punching that ho in her face. I guess her mom heard us fighting outside, because she came out and pulled me off her.

"What in the hell is going on out here?" she said, looking at both of us.

"Ask that ho of a daughter you've got. Samariah, stay the fuck away from me, or the next time, I might kill your ass," I said, and then I headed to my car.

I was so done with both of their asses. I should have listened to Bria when she told me that she had a bad feeling about them. Well, that feeling had just turned into a reality.

Corey

I couldn't believe this bitch Sam had done this to me. It was one thing to tell Mo, but the way she had gone about it was all wrong. I tried to explain to Mo that how Samariah had made it seem wasn't really how it happened. I knew she was going to be hurt once she saw the video, which I didn't know how that bitch had even got. I tried calling Sam so that I could curse her ass out, but she wouldn't answer. I know where that bitch stayed, so I'd be making a stop by there ASAP.

It had been about a week since everything went down, and Monique was not fucking with me at all. Every time I called, I was sent straight to voice mail, or she would pick up the phone and then hang it back up right away. Since she had been gone, my life had been miserable. We were supposed to go see my grandmother the day after the party. I went, but of course, Mo didn't go with me. While I was gone, she came and got the majority of her clothes and stuff from our house.

I was knocked out of my thoughts by my front door being opened. Mo walked in the door, looking as beautiful as ever. She wore a simple outfit—jeans and a shirt with a pair of new Jordans—but she still looked good. She had sadness in her eyes, and my heart broke looking at her.

"I didn't know you were here. I didn't see your car," she said.

"It's in the shop, baby. Can we please talk?" I asked.

"I didn't come here for all that. I just came to get the rest of my things, and I'm heading out," she said.

That was when I noticed the duffel bag that she had in her hand. She headed to our room, but I didn't follow her. About fifteen minutes later, she came out with the rest of her stuff. I stood up and blocked the door so that she couldn't leave.

"Move, Corey, before I kick you in your balls again," she said.

"I'm not moving until you hear what I have to say," I told her. I was dead-ass serious. She was going to hear me out today, whether she liked it or not.

"You've got two minutes, so you better make that shit quick. I don't have all day," she said, sounding irritating.

We sat down on the couch, and I began to tell her what had happened.

"Sam and I did have sex, but it wasn't while you and I were in a relationship. I have never cheated on you," I told her.

"If that is the case, then why didn't you just tell me what happened before we made things official and let me decide if I wanted to stay or go?" she asked.

"Baby, I was so scared of losing you. I know that it was selfish, but I need you, baby. I am so lost without you," I said, on the brink of tears.

"Well, you should have thought about that when you allowed your little whore to tell me what happened instead of you. She humiliated me, and I don't know if I can forgive you or her for that," she said as she stood up.

"Baby, please don't go. I'll spend my life trying to make this up to you," I said.

I kissed her face, then trailed down to her neck. When she didn't stop me, I kissed her on her lips. I picked her up and carried her to our bedroom. I laid her down and took off all her clothes. She began to cry, and I kissed away her tears. I took off all my clothes and began to kiss her from her toes all the way up to her honeypot. I pushed my tongue deep into her opening and flicked my tongue inside of it. I started sucking on her clit like my life depended on it. She came in my mouth, and then I eased into her hole. I long stroked her pussy, and her shit felt so good. She was so tight and wet that the thought of her being with someone else made me mad as hell.

I started kissing her as I pumped in and out of her. I felt her legs shaking, so I knew she was about to cum. I started grinding against her pussy, and she came. I flipped her over on all fours and dove deep inside of her. I picked up my pace when I felt my nut building up. I came inside her, and I fell next to her. I pulled her close to me, and we just lay there. I kissed her on her forehead and told her I loved her. We drifted off to sleep, and I just knew that I had my baby back.

When I woke up the next day, Monique was gone. She had left me a note on the refrigerator, and I almost broke down in tears.

Corey,
I love you so much. I want nothing more than to be able to rewind time, but I just cannot. You hurt me so bad, and I just can't get over it. I do not know what our future holds, but right now, I honestly can't see myself being with you. Let me go, Corey, at least for now. I guess I'll see you around.
Mo

I was about to go strangle that bitch Sam!

Bria

For the past couple of months, David had been on some straight bullshit. He was barely at home, and when he was here, it was like he wasn't. My gut was telling me that he was cheating on me, but I didn't have any proof. I hadn't been insecure in our relationship until the moment I told him that I was pregnant. That was when everything began to change between us. We didn't even have sex anymore.

The other night, when David came home, drunk as usual, I went through his phone. There was no evidence of him cheating, but that didn't prove shit to me, because he could have erased everything. I downloaded this tracking app to his phone so I could track where he was going. I called Mo up and had her ride with me so I could see what was going on.

"I can't believe you've got me out here, stalking David's ass," she said with a slight attitude.

"I need to find out what is going on," I told her.

We pulled up to this bowling alley and waited for him to come out. After about an hour of waiting, his ass finally came out. My heart shattered into a thousand pieces when I saw him holding hands with some little, ugly-ass girl with a big ass. I snapped pictures of them with my phone. I was about to get out and whup both of their asses, but Mo stopped me.

"You are six months pregnant. I am not about to let you out so that you can fight their asses. Let's go," she said.

I looked back one last time, and that was when I saw them kiss. I took another picture. It was a done deal for his ass. We followed him to the girl's house, and I took a photo of them entering the house. Then we went back to the house that David and I shared. I went into the kitchen to get some garbage bags, because his ass had to go. I put every single piece of clothing that he owned into the tub. I grabbed my bleach and poured it all over everything. I grabbed my bat and his PlayStation 4 and beat the shit out of it. I stepped on all his games and put then them back into the cases.

I packed up all his shit, then put it in my car. I made sure to grab my bleach, and we headed back to the girl's house. We unloaded my car and put all his shit on that ho's front porch. I grabbed my bat and bleach, and I busted out every last one of his car windows. I opened one of the doors and poured bleach all over his seats and on the floor. I threw the bleach bottle on his seat. Then I grabbed a screwdriver from my car and wrote, "Stay your cheating ass right here," on the side of his car that faced the house. On the other side, I wrote, "Our son and I don't need you."

Mo and I got back in my car, and I drove home. I called a locksmith and had my locks changed. Mo stayed with me that night because she knew that I was hurt, and so was she. We comforted each other and told each other that we would help each other through this process. I loved my best friend, and I really needed her right now.

David

I walked outside to take my ass home. I had spent the day with this little chick named Meka, my dude Mitch, and his girl. When I opened the door to leave Meka's house and stepped out on the porch, I tripped over a bunch of bags of clothes. The closer I got to my car, the more I realized that I had fucked up big-time. I had definitely gotten caught cheating. Bria had fucked my car all the way up, and I was so pissed. I ran back up on Meka's porch and opened up the bags. My clothes were all bleached, and my PlayStation 4 was broken all up.

I was ready to go home and kill Bria's ass. Now, I knew that she didn't play, but I didn't know she would do all of this. I couldn't believe that I had allowed things to go this far. Things with Meka had started off all innocent, but I had let her suck my dick one day, and that was all she wrote. I didn't love her. As a matter of fact, I had absolutely no feelings for her at all. She was just something to do to help me forget about my problems. Looking at Bria every day reminded me of what I didn't want, and that was why I was never at home. Now I might lose my woman and my baby because of the messed-up decisions I had made. I had got so depressed after finding out that she was pregnant that I had started drinking heavily, and eventually, I had cheated on my girl. I was fucked up about her being pregnant, but I didn't want to lose Bria. I got in my car, and that was when I noticed that her ass had put bleach on my fucking seats as well.

I finally made it home, after sitting on bleach and glass, only to find out that I couldn't get in the damn house. I rang the doorbell several times before Bria decided that she wanted to come to the door. She opened the door, but the chain was on it, so she kept it cracked. Bria rarely showed her emotions, but since she had got pregnant, she cried at the drop of a hat. Tears stained her face, and she looked so fucking sad. My heart broke, as I knew that I was the cause of her pain.

"Baby, why did you change the locks?" I asked.

"Because you are a liar and a cheater, and this is no longer your home," she said.

"What do you mean, this is no longer my home? We both live here, and I'm not cheating on you. Why would you fuck up my car and clothes because you think I'm cheating? You had Mitch and his girl clowning me and shit," I lied to her.

"You fucking liar!" she screamed.

She went into the house, and I heard some shuffling around. I was about to take off, because I knew her ass was crazy, but she came back with her phone. She showed me pictures of Meka and me holding hands and kissing outside of the bowling alley. She also had a picture of us going inside Meka's house. I knew then that I had lost the only woman I had loved.

"You can stop with all the lies. You and I are over. I started to be one of those bitter-ass girls that keep their babies' father away from the children, but I'm not. I will not keep your son from you if you want to be a part of his life," she said sadly.

"I'm having a son?" I asked.

She stepped back inside for something, came back to the door, and handed me an ultrasound photograph. "If you had been home, instead of running around with hoes, you would have known that we were having a son," she said before she closed the door in my face.

I walked away, feeling defeated. I thought about going back to Meka's house, but I knew that would just add salt to the wound, so I headed to Corey's instead. I knocked on the door, and then he let me inside.

"What in the hell happened to your car? And why is there a big-ass bleach stain on the back of your pants? She caught you, didn't she?" he asked.

"Yeah, and she fucked up all my clothes, my games, and my car," I said. "I need to stay . . . just until I can get my shit together, man," I told him.

"Okay. I'll get you a change of clothes," he said, looking at me and shaking his head.

That nigga had his nerve, I thought. He acted like he was not in the same boat that I was in. I was going to get my shit together for Bria, my son, and myself. I just hoped it was not too late.

Chapter Eleven

Sam

I had succeeded in breaking up Corey and Monique, and I didn't feel bad. I still couldn't believe that bitch Monique had had the nerve to come over here to fight. She was normally scared as hell, but I guessed when somebody fucked with your relationship, you grew balls. She had done a number on my ass, because I had a nice-sized gash on my forehead, and she had busted my lip, but I had given her some business, even with my head busted and all.

Corey had finally come to his senses, because he'd asked to come over my crib today. I had hurriedly agreed. I ran to my room and applied my makeup. I wanted to look as natural as possible when he got here. I put on a thong, some black leggings, a black fitted crop top. I wanted to show a little tummy. I made sure to put on a push-up bra so that my titties were sitting pretty. I threw on some Nikes and headed downstairs to wait on him.

The doorbell rang as soon as I made it down the stairs. I opened the door, and there was my boo, standing there and looking fine as hell.

"Are you alone?" he asked with a serious mug on his face.

"Yes. Come in," I told him.

He walked into my house, and I shut the door behind him. As soon as I turned around, he rushed me and pinned me against the door.

"Why the fuck did you pull that stupid-ass stunt? Why did you have to fuck up everything with my girl? What has she ever done to you besides be a good-ass friend to your ho ass?" he asked.

"Corey, I'm sorry. I love you, and I want to be with you. She doesn't deserve you," I told him.

He let me go and just stared at me.

"She doesn't fuck you like I do, baby. I know she's not sucking your dick. Do you want Mama to make you feel good? You know I know exactly what you like," I said as I dropped to my knees and pulled down his jogging pants.

His dick was already hard, and all I did was talk to him. I took him in my mouth and swallowed him whole. I went down his shaft and took his balls and dick into my mouth at the same time. I stood up to take off my clothes, and he watched me with this dazed look in his eyes. He slapped me on my face and told me to bend over. I did what I was told, and he entered me from behind.

"This is all you wanted, huh? You wanted this dick. That's why you're acting all crazy and shit?" he asked while beating the hell out of my pussy.

"Yes, baby, that's what I wanted," I moaned.

"Throw that ass back!" he yelled, slapping my ass.

I threw it back at him, and I felt myself about to cum, but before I could, he pulled out and told me to turn around. He jerked off to finish off his nut and shot his seed all over my face.

"You got what the fuck you wanted. Now stay away from Mo and me." He pulled his pants up and left me sitting by the door, dumbfounded.

Monique wasn't going to take his ass back, so I didn't know why he felt like there was still hope for him. I had made sure of that at their engagement party. She had been embarrassed, and there was no way she was taking his ass back after the show I had put on in front of everybody.

On another note, I had been working out a way to break up Kevin and Zoe. I thought I had the perfect plan. I was going to make sure that bitch regretted the day that she ever became his girlfriend. I didn't understand why both of these niggas insisted on playing with me. I was really trying my best not to hurt them, but they were forcing me to do that. If they really cared about those bitches that they were with, they would let them go. I had fully taken over, and now there was no trace of Samariah. I could still hear her voice slightly, but that bitch wasn't coming back. I had made sure of that the moment I had her stop taking those pills.

She had tried to hide me since she first found out about me when we were twelve. They had found out who hurt Brent and the girl. After talking to the detectives, they had thought it would be best if I was committed to a psychiatric ward to be tested. They had told me that I had multiple personality disorder. Since my father's paper was so long and he knew people in high places, I had got off scot-free. Her mom was so busy chasing after our dad that she hadn't noticed that Samariah wasn't taking her meds. Now that bitch was gone for good, and Sam was in control. Sam got what Sam wanted.

Sam's Mom

I know everyone may think that I was a bad mother, but please, just hear me out. When I got pregnant with Samariah, I had just finished up my last semester of nursing school and her father had just passed the bar exam. Her father and I had been together since we were teenagers, and we were together for about seven years before I got pregnant with her. Everything was great between us. We were engaged to be married, and we had just purchased the house that Sam and I currently stayed in. Not only was her father a lawyer, but he was a big drug dealer as well. We had the perfect little family, but then it abruptly changed. He came to me one day and told me that he was leaving me for someone else and that he had a kid on the way by this other woman.

Months after he left us, I found out that he and the lady that he had left me for had had this huge wedding. I was so hurt; I even had to be committed to the psychiatric ward for a few days because I tried to kill myself. About a year after we broke up, he finally explained to me how he had met this lady. He had met her at the hospital that I worked at, and apparently, she was a nurse there as well. I also found out that our daughters were the same age. He had begun messing with this woman about a week after I had started working at the hospital.

When my baby turned five years old, I enrolled her in elementary school, and while I was at the school, I ran into her father and his new family. I had to stop my daughter from running after her dad. He always used to spend time with Samariah, so she knew who he was, but after that day, he would send us money and gifts only for her birthday and special occasions. Eventually, our daughters became best friends, though they did not know that they were actually sisters. Her father and I still had sex on occasion, but he refused to leave his wife for me—even though I was the one who had him first. I was still in love with him, even though he had told me that he would never be with me and I should find someone else. As long as we met up for sex on occasion, I felt as though there was still some hope for us.

My biggest concern right now was getting our daughter help. She was acting real crazy, like she had when she was twelve. I caught her arguing with herself all the time, and she had become too much to handle.

"Peterson Law Office. How I may direct your call?" the receptionist said into the phone.

"Can I speak with Timothy Peterson please?" I said to her.

"Hold one second while I transfer your call," she said.

"Timothy Peterson speaking. How may I help you today?" he said into the phone, and my panties got wet instantly.

"Hey, Tim. It's Kendra. I'm calling because Samariah is sick again, and it's a lot worse this time," I said.

"Well, get her some help. then!" he shouted into the phone. "And what did I tell you about calling my office? My wife's friend works here," he told me.

"All you ever care about is that bitch that you call a wife and Monique's spoiled ass. Did you know that your daughters were over here, fighting each other? How long do you plan on keeping us a secret?" I cried to him.

"Look, get her some help. Don't call questioning me and shit. As a matter of fact, don't call my fucking office anymore. I warned your ass before," he said sternly.

"Well, I don't know any other way to get your attention. You never answer your cell," I said.

"You heard what the fuck I said. Get my daughter some help, and don't call me back until you do," he said and then hung up in my face.

I sat back and cried. His ass wouldn't be so smart if I told his wife the truth. Maybe that was what I would do. Let's see how smart he was when I destroyed his perfect fucking family!

Kevin

I had just got done playing the game with David's and Corey's sad asses. I had told David that he had to stop cheating on his girl and that he needed to wake up, but he hadn't tried to hear me. But now that Bria had left his ass, he wanted to act right. That nigga had done a complete three-sixty on me. This nigga was even going to church now, but no matter how much he changed, Bria still wasn't fucking with his ass. She had changed her number, and when he stopped by the house, she didn't even open the door. When she did see him out and about, she acted as if that nigga didn't exist.

Mo was giving Corey some act right. I mean, she talked to him on the phone from time to time, but that was about it. I know you're probably wondering why I was not mad at Corey. Well, when Mo and Corey first got together and we started hanging real tough, he took me out to lunch and explained to me what went down. I wasn't even mad at my nigga, because at that point, I knew Sam's ass was a ho. She had fucked my best friend, so I knew she was capable of anything.

Things had actually been peaceful in my household. Sam had been on her best behavior for a few months. I hadn't heard from her or seen her since the day she tried to give a nigga head. Well, that shit came to an end today. When I made it to my house, this bitch was sitting on my front porch, waiting on me.

I hopped out of my car and rushed to the front porch. "What the fuck are you doing here, Sam?" I said, grabbing her by her arm.

My girl was at work, and that was the only reason why Sam's ass was still breathing.

"I need to talk to you, Kevin. It's very important," she said.

"You and I don't have anything to talk about," I said, pointing back and forth between her and me.

"If you don't talk to me, Kevin, I'm going to sit out here all day."

"What do we need to talk about, Sam?" I said.

"Well, can we at least go somewhere and sit down?" she asked.

"Yes. Just hurry up and get off my fucking steps. Let's go to Applebee's," I said while dragging her ass away from my place.

Once we got to Applebee's, we went inside, sat down, and ordered something to drink. I stepped away for a second to use the bathroom, and when I came back, she was still sitting there, looking crazy.

"What do we need to talk about, Sam?" I asked. Then I downed my Coke.

She just sat there and stared at me. All of sudden, I started feeling really light-headed and sleepy.

"I'm not feeling too well all of a sudden," I said. I stood but instantly fell back down.

"Are you okay, baby? Do you need help?" she asked with a smirk on her face.

I couldn't keep my eyes open, and the last thing I remembered was Sam getting up and walking over to me, laughing, before my head hit the table.

Chapter Twelve

Sam

My plan had finally worked. I was able to get Kevin to my house. When he had gone to the bathroom at Applebee's, I had put this special pill that I had in his drink and had mixed it up real well. He'd come back to the table, and he'd gulped down his Coke. I hadn't expected him to drink it so fast, but it had helped my plan move along even quicker.

When I got him to my house, I stripped him down ass naked and started to suck him off, but no matter what I did, I couldn't get an erection out of him. However, I didn't need to have sex with him to accomplish my goal. My plan was to take pictures of us having sex. So, I got naked, lay next to him, and took a bunch of selfies of me lying on his chest and of me kissing him. I waited until, like, midnight, then sent the photos to Zoe and posted them on social media with a caption that said, "I knew he couldn't stay away. My baby loves me. You other bitches ain't got shit on me. Love me some him, but y'all knew that already." The pictures got several likes. I was satisfied with the outcome, so I cuddled up next to my man and then closed my eyes.

I woke up to my doorbell ringing. I ran to the door to see who it was. It was Zoe's crazy ass, and she looked mad as hell. I ran back to my room, put on my sexy little housecoat, and ran to open the door. I opened the door with a smile on my face, and she looked like she wanted to kill me.

"Where in the hell is Kevin, you dirty bitch?" she yelled and pushed past me.

She ran up the stairs and headed to my mom's bedroom first. When she made it to my bedroom, I stood in the doorway and watched as she slapped the shit out of Kevin. He opened his eyes, unaware of where he was.

"What in the hell was that for?" he asked groggily. His eyes finally made contact with mine, and I could tell that he was frustrated as hell.

"I thought you were done with this bitch. You're still fucking her, and you had the nerve not to bring your ass back home. What? You didn't have the balls to break up with me yourself, so you had your ho do it?" she said, pissed.

"Baby, it's not what you think. She drugged me," he told her.

"The proof is in the pictures, Zoe. Why would I need to drug him when I can have him anytime I want? This isn't the first time we've had sex. He told me last night that he was leaving you and that he loves me," I lied.

"That bitch is lying, Zoe. You, of all people, know that I can't stand her ass!" he shouted, running toward me, still naked.

He picked me up by my neck and began to choke the shit out of me. Zoe just stood there and let that nigga choke me. I was not surprised, though. I thought he was going to kill my ass, but then I heard the front door slam. Seconds later Brian ran into the room, grabbed Kevin, and pulled him away from me.

"What in the hell is going on, Sam? Why are there pictures of you and him all over Facebook and Instagram? You're back with him? You weren't woman enough to tell me that you didn't want to be together anymore?" Brian asked.

"Hell no, this bitch and me aren't together. She drugged me!" Kevin shouted. He reached for my neck again, but Brian stopped him.

Brian looked at Kevin like he was crazy.

"If she drugged you like you said, then why were you even alone with her in the first place?" Zoe asked Kevin.

"When I came home yesterday, she was sitting on our front porch, talking about she wasn't leaving until I talked to her. I didn't want to further disrespect you by having her ass at our crib, so I told her I would talk to her at Applebee's," Kevin replied. "I made it up there, and we ordered something to drink. I went to the bathroom, and that must have been when she put something in my drink. I drank it all, and I started feeling drowsy as hell. Next thing I know, I'm waking up to you slapping me. I thought I was at home."

"You were at home, baby," I said to him, not caring that Brian was there. I planned on kicking his ass to the curb, anyway.

"You know what, Kevin? I don't know if I believe anything that you are saying. And you, bitch, I want so badly to bust you in your shit, but I prayed to God on my way over here, and that's the only thing that's saving you from this ass whupping I want to put on your ass. Kevin, don't bring your black ass home," Zoe said. She walked out of the room.

Kevin put on his clothes and ran after her.

"You know, everybody kept telling me that you were a heartless bitch, but I didn't believe them. Stay your crazy ass away from me," Brian said to me.

I didn't even respond; I just watched him leave. Then I lay back on my bed, feeling good about what I had done. I had destroyed two relationships, and now I just had to decide on which guy I really wanted. I knew I couldn't have both of them permanently. I would eventually have to choose. But right now, I was just going to sit back and enjoy my success.

Zoe

I was so pissed and hurt that Kevin would hurt me this way. He had promised me that he would never do that to me. He had said that he would always put a smile on my face, not make me sad. He had followed me home that day and had tried to explain to me what happened, but I really hadn't been trying to hear him.

It had been about two weeks since everything went down, and he hadn't been home since that day. I had allowed him to pack his shit, and then he'd left. My heart had broken into a million pieces as I watched him walk out the door with his things, but I had to do what I had to do. There was no way in hell that I would just forgive him and believe his story. I didn't know if I would ever forgive him. Some days I wanted to call him and tell him to bring his ass home, but on other days, I wanted to kill him and that bitch Sam. I guessed all the guys were bunking at Corey's place, since all three of their asses had got left by their women.

"Girl, you all right?" Bria asked as she and Monique walked through the door.

I immediately started crying and fell into her arms.

"What happened, and where is Kevin?" Bria asked.

I hadn't told her or Mo that Kevin and I were no longer together. I had tried to stay strong and get through this by myself, but I needed my girls to make me feel better. Bria and I had become best friends, and Mo was coming around, since she had realized how big of a snake Sam was.

"Kevin and I broke up," I told them we all took a seat in the living room.

"What do you mean, y'all broke up? What happened?" Mo asked.

"Like, two weeks ago, I came home and Kevin wasn't here. I waited for hours for him to come home, only for Sam to send me pictures of them lying naked in bed, kissing and shit. I immediately went to my safe and got my gun. I was ready to kill both of them bitches, but I had to calm myself down, because I wasn't ready to spend life in prison for double murder," I told them.

They sat there with their mouths wide open. I pulled out my phone and showed them the pictures.

"Wait, why does he look like he's asleep?" Mo asked as she took the phone.

"Right. He doesn't even look like he is kissing her back," Bria said. "Something's not right."

I took the phone from Mo and zoomed in on each picture, and I'd be damned. His ass must have been telling the truth. He did look like he'd been knocked out cold.

"You know, he did tell me that she drugged his ass, but I didn't believe him. A few days later, he also tried to tell me that the doctor said that he had some type of drug in his system, but I was too pissed to listen to him," I told them.

"Kevin hates Sam's ass with a passion, so I believe he was telling the truth. Sam is crazy. You know my dad is a psychiatrist, and I overheard him talking to some man about her beating two kids almost to death, but I couldn't hear why she did it. All I know is that she never got in trouble for it," Bria told us.

"Well, I'm about to get my man back. I have been so miserable without him," I told them.

"I wish it was that easy for me," Mo said sadly.

"It is that easy for you, Mo. He was wrong for not telling you that he slept with Sam before y'all got together, but Sam was wrong because she knew how you felt about Corey. I think you should forgive him," Bria told her.

"Okay, and you should forgive David. He has changed his life for you and his son. If I forgive Corey, you can forgive David. Plus, I've tried, but it's so hard to forgive him," Mo cried.

"Well, my birthday is in a week, and I need y'all to stop all this damn crying and help me celebrate. My homie knows the bouncer at the Six One Eight nightclub, and he can get us all in that Saturday," I told them to lighten the mood.

"I'm down," Mo said eagerly.

"If you two bitches haven't noticed, I'm pregnant as hell. I can't be up in no club," Bria said, laughing.

Bria was eight months pregnant, and she was due next month. Her stomach was still small because she had a small frame, but with the right outfit, she would be able to hide her stomach.

"We are going to get you the perfect outfit so that you can hide that stomach of yours," I told her.

We sat around for a few more hours, pigged out, and then they went home. I sent Kevin a text message, telling him to come home because we needed to talk.

He finally made it home. When I opened the door, I ran into his arms and kissed him all over his face.

"I missed you so much, baby, and I know that you were telling the truth," I told him.

"Baby, I meant every word that I said when I told you that I would never cheat on you or intentionally hurt you. Now, I messed up by trusting her, because I never thought that she would go as far as to drug me, but I will never make that mistake again," he told me.

"I know, baby. Now let's go make love," I told him.

We made love for hours, and he did things to my body that no one had ever done to me. I forgave my man that night, but that bitch Sam had an ass whupping with her name written all over it waiting for her.

Monique

The more Corey and I communicated, the more I wanted to forgive him, but I just felt like it was too soon. We had been apart for months now. My heart ached for him, but I felt like I should see what else was out there besides him. He was the only man that I had ever been with, and maybe he was not the one for me. I guessed it wouldn't hurt to give someone else a try.

I had moved in with Bria after she put David out. She had given me the second bedroom, where I was now getting ready for Zoe's party tonight. I planned to enjoy myself. I looked at myself in the mirror, and I admired my beauty. I had on light makeup, and my hair was curled to perfection. October was cold in Milwaukee, so I wore some high-waisted black leggings and an off-the-shoulder sweater with a red-and-black leopard print on the front. I put on some red leopard-print booties. My stomach showed a little bit, and my ass and hips looked good in my leggings.

I walked into Bria's bedroom and admired her beauty. Ever since she got pregnant, she had let her hair grow out, and now it was as long as hell. She wore her hair like Nicki Minaj with the Chinese bang. She had dyed her hair jet black, and it looked gorgeous against her hazel skin. She wore a pink pants romper with matching heels. She was glowing. David's ass didn't appreciate the woman that he had lost. Bria was stubborn as hell, and she didn't plan on forgiving David at all.

"You ready?" I asked her.

"As ready as I'm going to be." She smiled.

We left the house and headed downtown to the nightclub. The line was long as hell when we finally made it there, but since we were VIP, and Zoe knew the bouncer, we were able to get right in. The club was jumping, but I just wasn't feeling it. I decided to have a few drinks to loosen up. My song came on, so I grabbed my girl Zoe and we headed downstairs to the dance floor. I was shaking my ass to the beat when I felt some strong hands around my waist.

"Hey, Ma. You're sexy as fuck. I've been watching you for a while, and I'm trying to get to know you," the mystery man whispered in my ear.

I turned to face him, and he was sexy as fuck. He was tall and had caramel skin and deep dimples that came out whenever he started talking or smiling. He wore a low hair-cut with deep waves. His body was toned as hell, and he was dressed fly as shit. He came closer to me, and I was dazed by how good he smelled. I wanted to jump up and wrap my legs around his waist and take him down right here in front of everybody. My pussy was wet just looking at him. I hadn't been with a man in a few months, and Miss Kitty was ready to be licked.

"You've been watching me, huh? You like what you see?" I asked, giving him my award-winning smile.

"I definitely like what I see," he said. "So, are you going to let me take you out?" he asked.

Before I could respond, Corey came storming over to us and grabbed my arm. I pulled my arm out of his grasp. I hadn't even known he was here. I looked up at the balcony and noticed that David was here as well.

"What in the hell are you doing, Monique? You're trying to get somebody fucked up in here?" he asked.

"What do you mean, what in the hell am I doing? You have no right to question me. We are not together," I said, then turned around so that I could finish talking to Mr. Sexy.

"Aye, I don't want any drama," Mr. Sexy said. He put his hands in the air in a surrendering motion. He had a big smirk on his face.

"There is no drama." I looked at Corey with a scowl on my face.

"You're not really feeling dude. You know who the fuck you belong to. Don't make me act a fool up in this bitch," Corey said, grabbing my arm once again.

I snatched my arm away from him and slapped the shit out of him.

"Don't you ever touch me," I growled. "You lost that fucking privilege the moment you fucked my so-called best friend and didn't tell me. So move the fuck on, Corey, because I'm done." I walked away, leaving him and Mr. Sexy standing there. I walked to the VIP section and sat down with my friends.

"Corey is fucking blowing me right now," I told them.

I watched as Corey brought his ass back upstairs and sat down a few seats away from us.

"What did he do?" Bria asked. She and Zoe laughed.

"He was just showing his ass while I was dancing with this one guy," I told them.

They started laughing even harder. I didn't find this shit funny at all. A waiter walked up to me and slid me a piece a paper. I opened it up and saw that Mr. Sexy had given me his number. His name was Tremaine. I sent Tremaine a text message to let him know I got his message.

"What are you over there smiling about?" Bria asked me.

I had been texting back and forth with Tremaine since telling him that I had received his message.

"I'm texting the guy that I met on the dance floor. I know this may be wrong, but I'm fucking him tonight. My body needs this," I told Bria.

"You're not wrong. You are single, so why not mingle?" she said.

Corey's ass was getting on my nerves. I mean, I missed the hell out of him, but he didn't own me, and besides, he needed a taste of his own medicine. I wouldn't go as far as fucking one of his best friends, but I damn sure planned to fuck Mr. Sexy, aka Tremaine.

After the club let out, I decided that I would go out to eat with Tremaine. I spotted him standing at his car across the street from the club. I waved and smiled at him while I tried to cross the street. Before I could make it across, Corey stopped me.

"Baby, please don't do this. Come home with me," he said.

"Corey, I need my space. Please just leave me alone," I said as I walked away.

"Monique!" he yelled, but I kept walking.

I got in the car with Tremaine, and I saw Corey standing there, looking pissed as hell.

"I see you've got a lovesick puppy on your hands," Tremaine said while laughing.

"He's just my ex," I said, wanting to change the subject.

I guess he sensed that, because he turned on some music and headed to this restaurant named Michaels. A half an hour later, we were eating and talking about some of everything. But before long I grew tired of talking. I was ready to do some fucking.

"So, do you want to go back to my place?" I asked, staring him directly in the eye.

"Nah, Ma. I don't want you to think that's all I want from you—although a nigga really wants to."

I instantly felt disappointed. After we finished our meals and paid the check, we walked to his car and got in. We didn't say anything during the entire drive to Bria's. Once we got there, he pulled up, and I got out of the car before he could even park. I was mad as hell and embarrassed because I had put myself out there and had gotten rejected. He parked his car and ran after me.

"Wait up!" he yelled.

I slowed down, and he caught up with me.

"I'll come in, Ma, as long as you know what you're getting yourself into," he said.

I opened the front door and grabbed his hand. As soon as we entered the house, we both attacked each other. I kissed his lips hungrily, and he returned the favor. All of a sudden, a light turned on, and we heard someone clearing their throat. Tremaine damn near dropped me on the floor, and I got myself together enough to see who was standing there. I looked at David, and I was confused as hell. What in the hell was he doing here, and why was he half naked at that?

"Oh, um, hi, David," I said, feeling uncomfortable. "This is Tremaine. Tremaine, this is David. He's my best friend's guy."

They nodded their heads at each other, and then we walked past David and went to my bedroom. I knew he was going to tell Corey's ass, but so what? *Let his ass find out*, I thought. He needed to know how it felt, anyway. And Bria definitely had some explaining to do in the morning.

Tremaine and I continued where we had left off as soon as we entered my bedroom. He ripped my clothes off my body, and I did the same to him. He picked me up and tossed me on the bed. He spread my legs wide, then dug in tongue first. He flicked his tongue across my clit with expert precision. He stuck his finger inside my hole while sucking on my pussy.

"Damn, Ma. You taste so good," he moaned against my pussy.

Those words alone had a bitch coming all in his mouth. He climbed between my legs, and I stared at his massive dick. I hadn't gone down on Corey, so I, for damn sure, wasn't going down on him. His dick was fat, long, and juicy. My mouth was watering just looking at it, but it just didn't feel right to go down on him and not the man whom I actually loved. He put a condom on and slowly entered me. He rocked my pussy in slow motion while twisting his hips so that his pubic area was rubbing against my clit. This man was making me feel so good, and I didn't know what to do with myself. He started long stroking me, and then he picked up his speed.

"Damn, Ma. Fuck," he said as he entered me from the back. "This shit is so good. What are you trying to do to a nigga?"

The more he talked, the closer he brought me to my orgasm. I came so hard on his dick, and he filled the condom with his seed. Afterward, he lay next to me and cuddled up close to me. Minutes later, I heard him snoring. I thought about Corey and instantly started crying. I loved that man with all of me. How could he hurt me in such a way? Why hadn't he just been honest from the start? I had given Corey every inch of me. I had given him my virginity, and he had hurt me bad as hell. Tremaine cuddled closer to me and held me. I knew that he didn't know that I was crying, but it felt good being in his arms. I can't lie. I was feeling him, and even though my heart belonged to Corey, it wouldn't hurt to get to know Tremaine. I wiped my tears away and stuck my ass against his dick. I loved sleeping like that.

He woke up and whispered in my ear, "You're trying to start round two, putting that big ole ass on a nigga's dick while I'm trying to sleep." He started kissing my neck.

I laughed at him as he lifted my leg and entered me from the side. Round two was even better, and I went to sleep with a big-ass smile on my face.

Chapter Thirteen

Bria

As we were leaving the club tonight, I asked David to come over. We drove in separate cars, and he beat me to my house. I guessed he was just excited that I was even talking to him. I had one thing on my mind, and that was getting my back beat out. I'd been missing sex, and David was the only person I felt comfortable having sex with, seeing as that I was pregnant and all. I almost told him to leave once we got in my bedroom. I still had feelings for David, and I didn't need those feelings clouding my judgment. I was not sure if I could have sex with him without getting back together with him. My heart was telling me one thing, but my body was screaming another. I took off everything and walked over to him.

"You look so beautiful, pregnant with my baby," he whispered in my ear as I wrapped my arms around his neck.

I didn't say anything; I just gently kissed him on the lips. He took off his clothes, and then we went to work. We went at it three times in a row, and if I wasn't already pregnant, I damn sure would be now. After the last session, we lay there in the bed, catching our breath. He got out of the bed and put on his boxer shorts and left the room. He came back moments later, with a confused look on his face.

"Mo is in there with that dude from the club. Corey is going to be pissed," he said.

"It's time for you to go, David," I told him seriously.

"What did you say?" he asked, looking confused.

"I said it's time for you to go. You can't stay here overnight," I told him.

He looked like he wanted to choke my ass. "I thought this meant that we were getting back together and working on being a family," he said.

"I tried being a family with you, David, but you ruined the chance of that ever happening the moment you cheated on me," I said, on the verge of tears.

I tried to hold them back, but I couldn't. I just let the tears flow. "David, I gave you everything you could possibly want, and when things got a little tough for us, because I got pregnant, you left me high and dry," I cried. "I can't trust you to be there for me when we hit rough patches. How do I know that if I take you back, you won't just walk out on me and cheat with these ratchet-ass hoes? You left me when I needed you the most, and for that reason, you have to go."

"I'm sorry, Bria. I would never do any of those things to you again. My mind wasn't in the right place. Baby, please forgive me. I want to come home to you and my son every night. I want to hold you in my arms and never let you go. I know you were the best thing that ever happened to me. Baby, please. I need you. You can't just have sex with me and then put me out." He dropped to his knees to plead his case.

I really wanted to believe him, and I felt myself on the verge of taking him back, but deep in my heart, I felt as though it just wasn't the right time. "The only reason you're here is that I'm pregnant, and I didn't feel comfortable having sex with someone else," I told him.

"Are you serious, Bria? You can't be that heartless," he told me.

He started crying. I looked into his eyes, and I could see that he was really sorry for what he had done. Unfortunately, the damage was already done, and there was no changing that for now. I couldn't get back with David and pretend like I was happy and not still hurt.

"David, please get your things and go," I told him as I walked out my bedroom door.

I locked myself in my bathroom and cried for what seemed like hours. I heard the front door open and then shut, so I knew he was gone. I went to lock the front door and then returned to my bedroom and got in my bed. I closed my eyes to get some rest. My son was kicking me, so I knew he was tired of Mommy stressing.

I woke up to a pair of eyes staring down at me.

"What the hell you looking at, Mo? Can a sista get some sleep?" I said, already knowing what she wanted to talk about.

"No, chick, so wake up, because I'm not going nowhere. I'm going to sit here in this comfortable-ass La-Z-Boy recliner until you get up," she said, smiling. I knew her ass was serious too.

I turned over to face her and stuck my middle finger up at her. Then I ran down every detail of last night to Mo.

"You don't think you were a little harsh?" Mo asked me when I was done.

"No, I don't. He did this to us—not the other way around," I told her.

"You know you love him, Bria. You talk a good game, but I know you want him back. You tell me all the time how you want to be a family with him. Why won't you just forgive him?" she said.

"Why won't you forgive Corey?" I asked her.

"I will someday, but right now, I choose to have a little fun. Mr. Sexy, aka Tremaine, is just the right person for the job," she laughed.

"Whatever," I said, rolling my eyes at her.

"How would you feel if David gave up on trying to work things out with you?" Mo asked me.

I thought long and hard about the question. I would honestly be hurt, but could I really expect him to wait on me forever?

"You know, at some point they will get tired of chasing after us and will move on with their lives," Mo said.

"I would be hurt, but I would get over it, just like I had to get over the fact that he cheated on me," I said.

"I honestly don't want to see Corey happy with someone else. It would probably kill me," Mo admitted.

I would feel the same way if I knew that David was happy with someone else. Even though he had cheated, I knew that he wasn't happy with ole girl. It was just something to do so he wouldn't have to face his reality, and it was ultimately that decision that had us split up. Maybe one day I'd forgive him and take him back, but right now just wasn't that time.

Corey

I was pissed as hell the night that Mo left the club with that weak-ass nigga. I didn't think that she would actually have sex with him, until David confirmed otherwise. He said he caught them in the living room, practically sexing each other down by the front damn door. I was so heated that I wanted to kill this nigga and Mo's ass too. How could she give my pussy to another nigga? She knew that she belonged to me. Her ass could keep playing hard to get if she wanted to, but she was bringing her ass home sooner than later. She was really giving this nigga time too; I had seen her and this nigga together more than a few times since Zoe's party. That was why when I saw this nigga at the gas station, I had to stop and holla at him.

I jogged over to him as he was coming out of the station. "Yo, my man, let me holla at you for a second," I called.

"What do you need to talk to me about, my dude?" he asked cockily.

I started to knock his ass out right then and there, but I had something I needed to say to his ass.

"Look, man, Mo is my woman. Now you've had your fun with her, and now it's time for you to move on," I said, looking him right in his eyes so he would know that I meant business.

"What's your name?" he asked me.

"Corey," I told him.

"I'm Tremaine. Look, Corey, man, Mo chose me. It is obvious that you didn't know how to treat her, or else she wouldn't be spreading her legs for me every night," he said with a smirk on his face.

I was two seconds from deading this nigga, but I kept my cool.

"Like I said nigga, you've had your fun. Now walk away, before we have some problems," I told him as I walked closer to him.

My father had started training me at an early age to be a killer. I could kill a nigga with my bare hands, but I wouldn't waste all that energy on this nigga. I'd just push a few hot ones in him.

"We will let Mo choose, and we all know how that's going to end up for you. She chose me a few weeks ago at the club, and she is still choosing a nigga. I lay up in that tight, wet, tasty-ass pussy every night, my nigga. She doesn't want you. That's my bitch now, and if you knew what was best, you would back the fuck off," he said, then walked away, like he was putting fear in my heart.

Now, I was fucked up after hearing him describe how good and wet my bitch's pussy was. I almost shot that nigga right then and there, but there was a time and a place for everything.

"I'll be seeing you, nigga," I told him.

"Yeah whatever, nigga," he said, then sped off.

I'd definitely be seeing that nigga later. Didn't nobody talk to me like that and get away with it. I could already see that this nigga was going to be a big pain in the ass.

I called Mo, and she sent me to voice mail, like her ass had been doing for the past two weeks. I hopped in my car and headed to Bria's. When I arrived, I rang the doorbell and waited for one of them to answer. Bria came to the door, looking like her stomach was about to burst.

"Can I help you, sir?" she asked.

"Where's Mo's ass at?" I said, walking in without an invitation.

"Um, how rude of you, but she's in her room," she said, rolling her eyes at me. She closed the door and then went in her bedroom.

I burst into Mo's room, ready to tear some shit up.

"Why in the hell aren't you answering your fucking phone, and why in the fuck do you keep sending me to voice mail?" I snapped.

"First of all, don't come up in here acting like your ass is running shit. Secondly, I don't want to talk to your ass, and that's why I don't answer when you call!" she yelled at me.

"Naw, fuck that shit. Pack all your shit. It's time to come home. I tried letting you have your space. I tried being Mr. Nice Guy, but you're playing too many fucking games. One minute you're telling me that you love me and you miss me, and the next minute you hate a nigga. On top of that, you're fucking this nigga Tremaine. You're giving my pussy away to this lame-ass nigga. You know what? Fuck you, Monique. I don't want your ass, anyway," I said, then headed for the front door.

"Naw, fuck you, nigga! Did you forget that you were fucking my best friend and didn't fucking tell me about it? I do love you, but you hurt me, Corey," she cried.

She had me about to say fuck her ass for real. Just the thought of this nigga fucking her pissed me the hell off.

When I saw her tears, my heart softened for her. I walked over to her and hugged her.

"I love you too, Mo. I will never stop loving you," I told her.

She grabbed my hand and led me to her bedroom. We made love, and we spent the rest of the day together. We didn't officially say that we were back together, but since she had given a nigga some, I figured we were making progress. She was definitely bringing her ass back home, whether she liked it or not.

Sam

Ever since things went down with Kevin, I'd been lying low, trying to figure out how to make him mine again. I had decided that Kevin was the one I really wanted. He reminded me of my daddy the most. Well, what I could remember of him. I had decided that I'd leave Corey and Mo alone for now because I needed to put all my energy into getting my man back. Kevin and I had so much history together, and I was not willing to let it go, even if I had to kill Zoe's ass. If that didn't work . . . Well, you know the saying. "If I can't have him, no one else will."

I was out and about, doing some shopping late one night, when I spotted Bria wobbling to her car. I really hated that bitch with a passion, and I thought it was time for me to get some payback. I ran to my car and waited for her to get in hers. She drove off, and I decided to follow her. I had my handy-dandy bat with me, and I was about to fuck her ass up.

She had gotten away with hitting me a few times, and it was time for me to get her ass back. I watched as she parked her car at her place and got out. She walked around to her trunk and then started gathering her bags. I got out of my car, snuck up behind her, and hit her once in the back with my bat. She screamed out in pain. I punched her super hard in her mouth, and it immediately started bleeding. I punched her again, and she instantly hit the ground. That was when I noticed how big her stomach was, but that didn't stop me. I kicked her a few times all over her body and then took off running to my car. That ought to teach that bitch not to fuck with me anymore, I thought.

I drove to Zoe's house, because I was in the mood to fuck some shit up. When I pulled up to her house, I saw her and Kevin walking into the house, holding hands. I wanted to get out of the car and kill both of their asses right then and there, but I decided I would wait.

I grabbed my pocketknife from the glove compartment, climbed out of my car, and crept across the street. I slashed the tires on both of their cars and threw a brick threw a window of Zoe's car. I ran back to my car and grabbed my lipstick, and then I dashed back to Zoe's car. I wrote, "He's mine, bitch," on the hood of her car. I ran back to my car once more, climbed in, and headed back home. I couldn't believe she had taken him back; I was sure that she was done with his ass. I started crying. *Why can't I just have the man I really want? Why do I have to fight all these bitches over my man?* I wondered.

As I drove, my thoughts drifted to my dad. I wished I could remember exactly what he looked like. Mo's dad was the closest person to a dad that I had ever had, but it wasn't the same. "Why didn't he want me?" I asked aloud as I began to rock back and forth in my seat. All my mom would ever tell me was that he loved me, but he had another family that he had to take care of. I was his family too. How could he just exclude me like that? Once I found out who my dad was, I was going to kill the woman and the kids who had stolen him away from me. I refused to continue to let them live happily ever after, when my mom and I had to suffer. Then, once I killed them, I would be happy with my daddy.

Samariah

I had been fighting this sickness for a very long time. I was not nearly as ruthless as Sam was. I was actually a nice girl. I didn't like having sex with all these different guys, but Sam made me do it. I had been trying to fight her back, but she was too strong now. I had first realized that someone else was living with me the last time I saw my daddy. I was five years old at the time, but she lay dormant until I turned twelve. That was when she attacked those people. I didn't even like Brent like that, but Sam just had to have him. They put me on these pills, but they weren't strong enough and she started to take over everything. Now she had taken over fully, and I didn't know how to get myself out of this mess. She was killing and hurting all my friends. I had to find a way to get back in charge before she killed someone else.

Chapter Fourteen

Monique

I heard someone screaming, so I threw some pants on and then went to my front window to see what was going on. That was when I noticed Bria on the ground and a figure running away. When I made it outside, a car was turning the corner, and Bria was lying on the ground, unconscious. I pulled out my phone and dialed the police. They made it in, like, two minutes, and they rushed her to the hospital. I called her parents, David, and Corey, and they met us at the hospital. I was so distraught that I thought I was going to have a nervous breakdown. I couldn't afford to lose my best friend. They rushed Bria to the emergency room.

"What happened to my baby?" her mom asked me when she and Bria's dad found me in the waiting room.

"Someone attacked her. There was blood everywhere, so I couldn't tell where it was coming from," I told them.

"My baby has got to pull through. I never got a chance to apologize for treating her so badly when she got pregnant," her mom cried.

"She's strong, honey. She's going to pull through," Bria's dad said.

We sat in the waiting room for hours before the doctor finally came out to talk to us. "Jacobs family," the doctor called out. He was a thin white man with gray hair.

"We are here," her dad said. "What's going on with my baby?"

"We finally have her stabilized. She has a few bruises on her face and throughout her body. It looks like whoever attacked her hit her in the back with some type of object, causing her to go into early labor. We are about to perform an emergency C-section, because the baby is in distress. I came out to see if the father of the baby and one other person would like to be with her."

David quickly stood up. "I want to be in the room when you bring my baby into this world," he said.

"I'll let my wife go back with him," her dad said.

"Okay. You two can follow me," the doctor instructed.

I couldn't believe that someone would hurt my friend. She didn't have any enemies except for Sam, but she wouldn't hurt Bria, would she? Maybe it was just a robbery gone wrong. Bria did have a smart mouth, and I couldn't see her just handing someone her stuff.

"You okay, baby? You are shaking," Corey said, putting his arms around me.

Corey and I had been spending a lot of time together. I had never told him that we were back together, but we had been acting like it. I was still fucking Tremaine too. He wasn't better in bed than Corey. I just wasn't quite ready to commit to either one of them yet. It was hard trying to juggle two men, but I didn't plan on stopping anytime soon.

Bria's mom interrupted my thoughts.

"He's here. Everybody come back!" she yelled with excitement.

We walked back to the room, and I immediately went to Bria's bedside. She was sleeping right now. She didn't look as bad as I thought she would look. Her lips were super swollen, and she had a few scratches on her body. It looked like there was a footprint on her arm. I rubbed her hair and gave her a kiss on her forehead.

"I knew you would pull through this. You are strong," I told her.

As soon as I said that, her body began to shake violently.

"Help! Somebody help her! Something is wrong!" I yelled.

Two doctors ran into the room and pushed us all out. I cried my eyes out until one of the doctors came back out with an update.

"We got Ms. Jacobs stabilized, and she's doing well. Her blood pressure dropped, and she had a seizure. Her body has gone through more than she could handle. We have to ask everyone to leave and come back in the morning. She needs her rest."

We all did as we were told, except David. He refused to leave, so the doctor said that it was okay for him to stay.

Once I made it home, I took a shower and cuddled up with Corey. I was so scared for my friend that I couldn't sleep. Corey held me close and told me that she would be fine. Hearing those words allowed me to sleep for a few hours. But the police had to find out who did this. I wouldn't feel safe until they did.

David

I had never been more scared in my life than I was now. Seeing Bria like this had roused my anger, and I had a fear of losing her. I needed her to pull through this, because I loved her. I changed my son's first diaper, and it was the greatest feeling I had ever experienced. I knew that this little boy was mine, because he looked just like me. He didn't look anything at all like Bria.

"David Jr." I said out loud.

I walked over to Bria's bed with my son and kissed her on her swollen lips. The doctors were keeping her heavily sedated until the morning came. I laid my baby back in his bassinet and cuddled up next to Bria. I loved this girl so much, and I hoped that she finally forgave me for what

I had done to her. I planned to fight for my family by any means necessary, and when I found out who did this to her, they were going to be six feet under.

Bria

I woke up in so much pain, and I was confused about where the hell I was. I looked around the room, and that was when I noticed that I was in the hospital. I tried talking, but my throat was so dry that it felt like it was about to crack. I moved a little bit, and that was when David jumped up and scared the shit out of me. I didn't even realize that he had been lying next to me all this time.

"I'm going to get the nurse," he said, then ran out of the room.

I rubbed my stomach, like I did every morning out of habit, and that was when I noticed it was soft. I instantly went into panic mode. What happened to my baby? I remembered getting attacked last night, but I didn't see who it was. I did know that it was a girl. I could tell by her legs once I hit the ground. The nurse came into the room and began to check my vitals. She gave me some water to drink so that it would feel better when I tried to talk. She also gave me some painkillers to help with the pain.

"Where is my baby?" I asked the nurse.

Before she could get the words out, David came over to me. He was holding the most beautiful baby that I had ever seen. I reached for my son, and he gave him to me.

"Hello, Mama's baby," I cooed at him.

This little boy looked just like his daddy, and that was a damn shame because I was still pissed at him.

"So what are we going to name him? David Jr., I hope," David said.

"I guess we can name him David Smith Jr.," I said, looking up at David and smiling.

"Friend, I'm so glad you are okay," Mo said as she rushed through the door like she hadn't seen me in ages. Corey was right behind her. She ran over to me and then kissed me all over my face.

"Get off me. Dang!" I laughed at her.

"Sorry. I just thought that I was going to lose my best friend." She laughed and cried at the same time.

"I'm not going anywhere. I've got this handsome little man to live for. Say hi to your auntie Monique, DJ," I said to my handsome son.

Mo picked him up and cooed at him.

"He looks just like David," Corey said as he and Mo played with the baby.

My mom and dad made it out to the hospital. My mom finally apologized for how she had treated me throughout my pregnancy. She wanted me to move back home so that she could help me with my baby, but that wasn't happening.

The police came and took my statement. They told me that they had collected some evidence from where I was attacked, and that they would keep me updated on the case. I didn't care what they did. I was moving somewhere else before I left this hospital. David and I needed to talk about a few things, but right now, I was just going to enjoy being alive and being with all the people I loved and cared about. I wasn't going to worry about anything else for now.

Chapter Fifteen

Sam

I jumped up out of my sleep because I thought I heard someone moving around in my house. I knew that it wasn't my mom, because she had gone to visit my grandmother in St. Louis. I thought that maybe I was being paranoid, so I went back to sleep. All of a sudden, the covers were snatched off my body, and I was smacked in my face with the butt of a gun. I couldn't see who it was, because it was dark in my room and blood was now dripping in my eyes.

"Please, don't hurt me," I begged the intruder.

"Shut the fuck up before I kill your ass right now," the man said. The voice sounded so familiar, but I just couldn't place it right now. He grabbed me by my hair and pulled me out of my bed. "Take off everything," the intruder ordered.

"Sir, please don't make me do this. I'll give you anything you want. Just please don't hurt me," I cried. I tried to run past him, but he caught me by my hair and slapped the shit out of me.

"Now listen here, bitch. The next time, I'm not going to slap your ass. I'm going to kill you. Now do what the fuck I told you and strip!" he yelled.

I slowly took off my pajamas and stood there in my bra and panties.

"Take every fucking thing off," he warned.

I did as I was told as tears streamed down my face.

"Now, sit down on the bed and put both of your hands together in front of you," he told me.

I did as I was told. He wrapped tape around my wrists, and I began to cry even harder. The intruder dropped to his knees, and just as he was about to tape my legs together, I kicked him as hard as I could in the face. He fell backward, and I took off running. I ran down the stairs, but I lost my balance and fell down hard. I hit my head on the last step. I felt really dizzy, and I tried to get up, but I couldn't. I crawled to the front door to make my escape. I reached up to open the door, and that was when I felt him pulling me by my legs. He picked me up and carried me back up the stairs. He threw me on the bed and hit me in my face again with the gun.

I jumped, thinking that I had just had the worst dream. My head was spinning, and I had trouble adjusting my eyes to the darkness. I tried moving my legs, but I couldn't. That was when I realized that it wasn't a dream, after all. Someone really had me taped up in my own home.

"I'm glad your ass finally decided to wake up. I couldn't have you knocked the fuck out. I need you to feel all the pain that I'm about to bring your way," he told me.

He cut the tape on my legs and spread them wide. It was still dark in the room, but I could tell that he was ass naked except for the ski mask that he had over his face. "I'm going to make you feel real good before I kill your ho ass," he said to me.

He started eating my pussy. I tried not to enjoy it, because this bastard was raping me, but I was Sam, and this shit was hard not to feel. He ate the shit out of my pussy, and there was something very familiar about the way that he did it. He climbed between my legs and fucked the shit out of me. It was pain and pleasure at the same time. He finally came, and he stood up and got dressed. He turned on the lights and then stood at the foot of my bed. He took his ski mask off, and I couldn't believe my eyes.

"Surprise, bitch!" he said. I almost pissed my pants when I saw the man who stood before me. "Did you really think I would let you get away with what you did to me?" Eric said.

"I killed you! You are supposed to be dead," I cried.

"Well, when you stabbed me in my chest, you almost killed me, but the doctors were able to save me. They reported to the news that I was dead so that my killer would think so. I spent months in the hospital because of what you did to me!" he shouted. He jumped on top of me and grabbed hair. "You know the cops questioned me day and night about what happened to me and if I knew who did it," he said, with this creepy look on his face. "You know what I told them?" he asked.

I didn't say anything. I just listened to him rant.

"I told them I didn't know who did this to me, because ever since the day I woke up, I have been plotting my revenge," Eric said while laughing.

I really got scared when he began to laugh.

"Look at what you did to me. You see this scar? I have to live with this for the rest of my life because of your dirty ass," he yelled and slapped me with the butt of the gun.

"Eric, please, don't hurt me, I am sorry for what I did to you. We can move forward from this," I lied. *If I get out of this, I'm going to make sure I kill his ass this time,* I thought.

"You know what? I thought about keeping you around so that I could fuck you, because you do have some of the best pussy I have ever had," he said, licking his lips at me. "But I won't fall for your lies this time, and unlike you, I'm going to make sure your ass is dead. You are nothing but an evil, deceitful bitch, and you deserve what I'm about to give to your ass," he told me as he raised the gun and pointed it directly at me. "Bye, bitch." He shot me three times in my chest.

Bria

It had been a week since my attack, and I had my baby
boy. After holding my baby in my arms and after almost
losing my life, I decided to give David a second chance since
God had given me one. I wanted to be a family with David
and our son. I had not told him yet, but when he picked me
up from the hospital in a few, we would sit and talk about
it. My mother wanted me to move back home with them
so that she could help me with the baby, but I refused to.
Corey's dad had hooked us up with another place that was
on the same block as Corey and Mo's place.

David finally arrived at the hospital to pick me and Junior
up. We rode home in silence, and I had a lot on my mind.
We arrived at our new place, and he parked in the under-
ground parking. He grabbed the baby, I grabbed the bags,
and he led me to our place. He handed me my keys so that
I could unlock the door. I walked inside and flicked on the
light.

"Surprise!" my family and friends shouted. I was so happy
to see everyone, and I was even happier to see that our place
was already furnished, and that the baby room was already
set up with the things David and I had bought him when we
were at our old place.

"Friend, I'm so happy you're home," Zoe and Mo said in
unison as they walked up to me and hugged me tight.

"I'm happy to be home. It's time to party. I am not pregnant anymore, so no excuses," I told them.

I entertained my guests for a few hours. My mom, Zoe,
and Mo stayed a little longer to help me clean the house up.
When they finally departed, I was left alone with David and
the baby.

"Okay, Bria. I'll be back in the morning to check on you
and my son," David said as he headed to the door.

"David, don't go. Can we talk please?" I urged.

"Sure," he said, with this unsure look on his face. We sat down on the couch and just looked at each other for a moment.

"Listen, you hurt me really bad, but I really want us to have a family," I said.

"I want that too, but not just because I want a family. I love you, Bria, and I want to be with you because I love you and I want to spend the rest of my life with you. It's not just because I want a family for my son, though it seems like that's what you are trying to say," he said.

"David, just listen, because this is really hard for me to say. When you cheated on me, you hurt me like I have never been hurt before, and a big part of me is scared to take you back because I don't know what you are capable of anymore. Once upon a time, throughout our relationship together, I thought you would never cheat on me or hurt me like you did," I said, fighting back my tears.

"I admit that I was really wrong for hurting you, but I can honestly say that I have learned my lesson and I will never cheat on you again. And that is a promise," he said.

"I love you too, David, and I really want to be with you and have a family with our son, but if you mess up again, I will leave your ass without a second thought," I told him, and I meant every word I said. I was not forgiving him if he cheated on me or if he even looked like he wanted to mess around on me. It would be over, and I would absolutely be moving on with my life.

"Well, let's go check on the baby and have makeup sex," he said, smiling at me.

I laughed at him. "We have to wait six weeks, baby, and I will be getting on birth control before you stick that thing in me again," I said truthfully.

"You know you want to have more of my babies," he said, slapping my ass.

"Not going to happen," I laughed.

"I see my son did you some good. You got a little ass and hips now," he said, hitting me on my ass again.

It was true. My baby did give me some ass and hips. I didn't have them before the pregnancy. I was so glad I had chosen to forgive David and to work on our relationship. I felt ten times lighter now.

Mo

I had decided to move back in with Corey because I was ready to take my man back. I was still communicating with Tremaine, but my heart was with Corey. I wanted to keep Tremaine around because I wasn't sure if I could fully trust Corey. I hadn't told Tremaine that Corey and I were back together, either, and it was partially because I didn't know how. I had moved back in with Corey the day after Bria's attack, and we had officially said we were a couple again. What Corey did was wrong, but I felt like Sam was more in the wrong because she was my best friend since grade school, and it had been her responsibility to tell me when it first went down. But that was in the past, and we were working on our future.

Tremaine had been blowing up my phone, trying to see me, so I had decided I was going to meet up with him today to break things off with him. He asked me to meet me at his house. I pulled in his driveway, got out of my car, and rang the doorbell. He answered the door and let me in. He pulled me close to him and kissed me on the lips. I should have stopped him right then and there, but when he started to caress my breasts, I instantly caved in to his advances.

"Damn, I miss your sexy ass," he said as he kissed my neck.

I didn't respond; I just continued to enjoy the pleasure he was giving me. He pulled my shirt over my head, then went to work on my breasts. He took off the rest of my clothes and all of his. He sat me on the couch and pulled me to the edge. He got on his knees and took Miss Kitty in his mouth. I laid my head back on the couch as orgasm after orgasm flooded his mouth. He lay on the couch and ran his hand up and down his shaft.

"I want you to ride Daddy," he said with this sexy-ass look on his face that drove me crazy.

I slid down his pole and rode him like crazy. I turned around so that my ass was facing his face and continued to ride that big fucker. He toes began to curl, so I knew he was about to cum. He gripped my waist so that he could hold me in place as he spilled his seed deep inside of me. I fell on the couch beside him and began to catch my breath. My phone began to ring, and Corey instantly popped in my mind. I felt nothing but regret for even coming over to see Tremaine. I retrieved my phone and saw that it was my father calling me.

"Hello," I said into the phone.

"Hey, baby, you need to get to the hospital. Sam is here. She's been shot," he said.

My body immediately went numb, and I could not believe what my father had just told me. Even though Sam had hurt me, I would never wish death upon her, nor would I want her to be hurt this badly.

"Monique! Monique!" my dad yelled into the phone. "Do you hear me?"

"Yes, I heard you. I'm on my way," I said, in complete shock.

"Hurry. They said they don't know if she's going to make it," my dad said right before he hung up the phone.

I grabbed my things and put them on hurriedly.

"What wrong?" Tremaine asked.

"My friend is hurt, and I have to go," I told him.

"Do you want me to come with you?"

"No, I'm good," I told him, and then I dashed out the door.

I called Bria on the way to the hospital and let her know what was going on. When I arrived, my parents and Sam's mom were already there. Bria, Corey, David, and even Kevin pulled up right after I did. I was surprised any of my friends had shown up, but I guessed they all felt how I felt. Sam had made every last one of our lives a living hell over the past year, but we were all there to support her.

"What's going on? What did the doctors say?" I asked my parents.

"She is in surgery now. We won't know anything until she comes out," my dad said.

I sat next to my parents, and that was when I noticed Sam's mother, Kendra, giving us the look of death. She looked like she wanted to come over to where we were sitting and kill all of us. *What the hell is her problem*? I thought. I knew she couldn't be mad at me because I had whupped Sam ass. After all, Sam had deserved that shit. We sat around for another hour or so before the doctor came out with an update on Sam. He approached Kendra, and we all gathered around her.

"Your daughter is a fighter. We were able to save her life, but unfortunately, we were not able to save the baby," the doctor said.

"Wait. My daughter was pregnant?" Kendra asked.

"Yes, she was maybe about two months pregnant, but we are not exactly sure about that. But what we do know is that she was indeed pregnant. We also noticed that she has been using cocaine," the doctor said with a concerned look on his face.

My dad looked at Kendra like he wanted to kill her. I was confused as ever at this point, because as far as I knew, they barely knew each other. They were connected only because Sam and I were best friends. Now that I thought about it, I wondered how my parents had found out before me what was going on with Sam. *Is there something I'm missing here*? My thoughts were interrupted by the doctor.

"She is a strong girl, so she will make a full recovery. She will need months of therapy, and we recommend that you enroll her in rehab as well. She is highly sedated because she is in a lot of pain right now, so no visitors tonight, but you are more than welcome to come back tomorrow, during visiting hours," the doctor said.

"I can't believe Sam was using drugs," Bria said.

"Me neither," I said.

"Hold up. You two little bitches better keep my baby's name out of your mouths before I beat your asses!" Sam's mother yelled.

"Who are you talking to like that? If you had been a better mother, your daughter wouldn't be so fucked up!" Bria yelled.

"That's enough Bria!" my dad yelled.

"Naw, fuck that, Mr. and Mrs. Peterson, excuse my language, but she was never at home with Sam. Sam did not have her mom and dad there guiding her. That's why Sam is going through what she's going through. And you want to get mad at us when it's your fault that she in here? Sam has been running around, reckless as hell, because you never tried to be a mother to her!" Bria snapped.

"Fuck you, you little bitch," Kendra said as she tried to run up on Bria. My dad grabbed her before she could.

"Don't get mad at us because you were too busy running behind Sam's dad, whoever he may be, to focus on your child," Bria yelled as David held her back.

"Take her home, David," my dad said.

David immediately dragged Bria out of the hospital. We all know Bria's crazy ass didn't care about whupping Kendra's old ass. I had never seen or heard Kendra talk or act like this. Every time I was around her, she was so nice and sweet. Everyone left with Bria and David except for Corey and my parents.

"Kendra, don't you ever speak to my daughter like that again!" my dad snapped.

Kendra stared at my father long and hard. "The way I feel right now, I have no problem letting the world know your little secrets!" she snapped. She walked closer to him. She had this deranged look on her face.

"Bitch, not today. You get out of my husband's face before I show you a side you been dying to see," my mom said as she stepped in front of my dad.

"Um, what's going on here? You all barely know each other, and you are arguing like y'all have known each other for a lifetime. And what secret is she talking about?" I asked.

"Monique and Sharon, let's go," my dad said, staring Kendra down.

"Ask your dad what I'm talking about," Kendra said as we were walking off.

"Get your daughter some help," my dad yelled.

"My daughter!" Kendra yelled and started to laugh hysterically.

We walked outside, and I stopped my parents. "What is she talking about, y'all?" I asked my parents.

My mom looked at my dad, unsure of what she should say.

"Nothing, baby. That lady is just crazy. Leave it alone," my dad said before he kissed me on my forehead. He and my mom then headed to their car.

Corey and I walked to my car, and he got behind the wheel. He knew I was in no condition to drive. Something wasn't right, and I would get to the bottom of it. I was tired of the people I loved hiding shit.

Chapter Sixteen

Timothy

I was going to give that bitch Kendra a piece of my mind. I know y'all may think I was a horrible-ass father, but what was holding me back from completely being in Samariah's life was Monique. She still didn't know that the two of them were sisters, and I knew that once she found out, she was going to be hurt. At first, I had tried to hide the fact that I had a whole other family from my wife, but I had eventually told her the truth. Samariah was five years old when I did that. Sharon was mad at me for a few months, but she eventually got over it.

I used to fuck Kendra every now and then, when I needed a stress reliever from my wife, but we had stopped soon after the girls turned six, and I had been faithful to my wife ever since. But Kendra's ass refused to move on. She hadn't been with another man for over twentysomething years, and she had it in her mind that there was still hope for me and her. I would never take Kendra as back. For starters, she was crazy as hell; that was why we had broken up in the first place. She had it in her mind that Sharon had stolen me from her, but that wasn't the truth.

Yes, I had bought Kendra a house, but it wasn't for us to stay in. We had already been apart for six months when I purchased the house for her. She had gone around telling everybody that everything was all good and we had bought our first house together so we could be a family with our new addition, but that had been far from the truth. Now, granted, I was still fucking her at the time, and I should not have been, because I had known I would not be getting back with her, but she had some good pussy and she could suck a mean dick.

When Kendra got pregnant, that was when I decided to purchase a house for her and my daughter to stay in. Kendra and I broke up because when we were together, her ass would still be stalking me, as if I didn't come home to her every night and do everything for her. She would show up whenever I was hanging with my guys, and she would call me all fucking day if I was away from her. She would beg me to sit in the house all day with her, and if I left, we would always get into an argument. She accused me of fucking my own sister; she said we were too close. The straw that broke the camel's back was when she showed up at one of my business meetings once, acting a straight ass, talking about I wasn't answering my phone, because I was in there trying to fuck these bitches. I was done with her crazy ass after that.

I had met Sharon a few months before I called it quits with Kendra. It had been like love at first sight. When Sharon was younger, she had looked just like Monique did now. Sharon had been, and still was, the most beautiful chocolate woman I had ever laid eyes, and I had just known back then that I had to make her mine. Sharon got pregnant with Monique a few months after Kendra found out she was pregnant with Samariah. I didn't know how to tell Sharon about Kendra and my baby, and I was scared to lose her, but I did finally come clean to my wife.

Now I had to figure out how I was going to tell my girls about this. The way Kendra kept trying to go about it all was not cool at all. She kept threatening to expose me and shit like that. She probably knew now that my wife knew what was going on by the way my wife had reacted when

Kendra was talking shit. What my wife didn't know was that Kendra called my ass excessively, begging me to be with her.

I dropped my wife off at home and headed straight to Kendra's house. I walked in after opening the front door with the key I still had, and her crazy ass was sitting on the couch, with her knees pulled to her chest, crying and rocking back and forth.

"What was that stunt you pulled at the hospital?" I snapped.

She didn't respond; she just stood up and looked me square in the eyes. She had tears mixed with snot running down her face. All of sudden, she started punching me. She was swinging wildly at me, and it was hard for me to control her. I finally got ahold of her arms, and she calmed down.

"I'm sick of doing this all by myself just because you don't want to hurt Monique or your wife's feelings. What about me and Samariah? We need you in our lives too," she cried.

"I may not be there physically for my daughter, but I'm there the best way I know how to be right now, and my wife knows about Samariah. I'm scared to hurt Monique and Samariah because we hid this from them for so long," I told her.

"You don't give a fuck about Samariah. All you care about is Monique's little spoiled ass. And what type of wife wants to keep you away from your child?" she said.

"First of all, my wife has told me for years that I need to tell the girls the truth, so don't try to make her seem like she's the bad person. Secondly, your ass is scaring me. You almost told Monique the truth, and the way you trying to go about it is all wrong. I need to be the one to tell both my girls the truth," I said.

"Well, someone needs to say something, because your black ass sure ain't. So when are you coming home to be with your real family?" she said, walking up on me.

"See? That's why I don't deal with your ass, because you always be on that bullshit. I don't want your ass. I keep telling you to move on with your fucking life. I love my wife more than any other woman in this world. God created her for me, so you need to face the fucking facts," I snapped.

"Baby, you don't mean that shit. Why else would you be over here? Why else would you keep a key to our house if you don't plan on coming back? You love me, Tim. I know you do," she said as she grabbed at my belt buckle.

When she tried to pull down my pants, I pushed her off me, and she fell back on the couch. I took the key off my key chain and threw it at her. She instantly started crying hysterically.

"You don't love me or your fucking daughter. You don't care if my baby dies!" she screamed.

"I love you as a person, but I don't love you in that way, Kendra. I love my wife, and I definitely love my daughter. I would not be able to live with myself if my daughter died," I said.

"You got a funny way of showing it!" she snapped.

Now I tried to be cool, but this bitch had pushed all my buttons. She was acting like her ass was a saint.

"You know what, bitch? I tried to be semi nice to your ass, but you have taken me there," I snarled. "You need to get your shit together, because from my understanding, your bitch ass is never here to take care of my fucking daughter, which I don't understand, because yo' ass has not worked in years. I don't know if you have forgotten, but I pay all the bills in this bitch, and I send my daughter and your ass money every two weeks."

I went on. "On top of that, our daughter is on drugs because yo' neglectful ass wasn't doing your job. I know one thing, your ass better get your shit together right now and start taking care of my daughter, or we going to have some problems. You better go find a job, because I'm giving your ass one year, and then I'm done taking care of you. I'll always be there for my child, but I'm done with your ass. This house is paid for, so you will be good as far as that is concerned." I turned to walk out the door.

She ran up on me and began to punch me in the back of my head and in my back. I turned to push her ass off me, and she fell to floor, crying like somebody had murder her mama.

"Fuck you, Tim. I hate your ass!" she yelled.

I ignored her ass and continued to walk out the door. She got up and ran behind me, then grabbed one of my legs.

"Tim, don't go. I need you, and I didn't mean it when I said I hate you. I love you so much. Please don't go, baby," she cried as I dragged her ass out the door, since she wouldn't let go of my leg.

"Kendra, pull yourself together. We haven't been together for over twentysomething years. I have told you a million times that there will never be you and me again. Wake the fuck up. It's over," I said as I pulled her arms from around my leg.

I jogged to my car so she couldn't pull anything else. I hoped this bitch got the picture, because I was tired of her ass.

Corey

I almost jumped out of my skin when the doctor said Sam was pregnant, as I remembered that time she and I had had sex. I couldn't say I was not excited when the doctor said she had lost the baby. Even though I knew that, most likely, I was not the father, because I had shot my seed all over her face, you still could not be too careful. It was sad to know that she had got shot and was in the hospital, because no matter how much trouble she had caused me, I would never really want to see her dead. I knew I was a trained killer, but I would use those skills only if I really needed too.

Mo and I were back together, and I was happy as shit. Mo was in the kitchen, with just her bra and panties on, cooking us breakfast. Her phone, which was in the living room, began to ring, but of course, she didn't answer it. She was doing her thing in the kitchen with her headphones on, listening to music on her iPod. Practically naked, my baby looked so sexy as she shook her ass and cooked. Her phone rang again, and my curiosity got the best of me. I picked up her phone and noticed that she had a few missed calls and some text messages from Tremaine. I opened the latest text message and instantly got heated. I saw I was going to have to hurt this nigga, because either he was not getting the picture or she hadn't told him that we were back together. I walked into the kitchen and spun her around.

"Oh, hey, baby. What's up?" she asked as she took off her Beats headphones. She smiled at me, then tried to kiss me on my lips, but I moved out of the way. She frowned up at me, then gave me this confused look. "What's your problem?" she asked.

"You still fucking that nigga Tremaine?" I asked.

She started looking nervous, which heightened my suspicion. "Why would you ask me that, Corey? I'm with you," she said as she turned around to finish cooking.

"Turn that shit off. We need to talk," I said, then walked back into the living room.

She turned everything off, then came and sat down next to me, with this somber-ass look on her face.

"Why is this nigga saying he wants to see you and taste you again?" I asked.

"Corey, I don't know. I have not talked to him," she said, on the verge of tears.

"You still fucking that nigga, aren't you? Why did you let that nigga have my pussy in the first place?" I said heatedly.

"I said no, Corey. Damn. And did you forget you and I were broken up when Tremaine was in the picture!" she snapped.

"Then why the fuck is this nigga still texting you, talking about he misses you and shit like that? What? You didn't tell him that we were back together?" I asked.

She got quiet as hell, so I got my answer. I was done playing games with her ass.

"I'm done with your ass, Monique. You can have that nigga Tremaine, because I'm tired of playing games with you. It's obvious you still feeling that nigga if you haven't shut shit down with his weak ass. I'm going to leave now, before I murder his ass and fuck you up," I said. I turned and headed to our room. I would never put my hands on Mo. I was just talking shit because I was mad, but that nigga Tremaine? I might just kill his ass because he fucked my girl, and I didn't want his ass to live to talk about it. Mo ran behind me, and I could hear her crying.

"Where you going, Corey? I'm sorry. I'll do whatever you want me to do. I love you, not him. I want to be with you, not him. Don't go, baby, please," she cried. When we got to the bedroom, she sat on the bed and looked at me with pleading eyes.

"Tell that nigga right now what it is," I said as I handed her the phone.

"What you want me to do?" she asked, acting dumb.

"Tell that nigga that y'all are done," I said.

She immediately opened her phone, then sent him a text message, letting him know that she didn't want to see him anymore and that she was done. Satisfied with what she had done, I packed a small bag, because I needed to teach her spoiled ass a lesson.

"I thought you were not leaving, Corey," she cried. I hated to see her cry, so I almost changed my mind, but I had a point to prove to her ass.

I didn't respond to her; I just grabbed my keys and headed out the door. She immediately began to blow up my phone, but I didn't answer. I checked into the hotel that was not far from our house for two nights. I missed my baby already, and I hadn't even been gone two hours, so I knew this was going to be hard to do.

She texted me the next day, letting me know she had got a new number and begging me to come home. I went home two days later, and she said that she loved me and that I had better not leave her like that again. She said she wanted only me. I bet that her ass had learned a lesson.

Kevin

It'd been a month since Sam was rushed to the hospital after being shot. She'd been healing well, but then she ended up slipping into a coma. Zoe had tried to act like she wasn't upset when we all went to the hospital the night Sam got shot, but I knew she felt some type of way. As a matter of fact, Zoe had changed a lot since we got back together. We argued all the time, and she picked arguments with me for no reason. She was also very distant, and right about now I was tired of these women. I would rather be single than deal with this shit. It was like she picked an argument with me, left, and didn't come back for hours. And when I asked her where she had been, she would always say she had just drived around. I didn't believe that shit at all. I was starting to think she didn't want to be with me anymore. Why else would she be acting like this?

Anyway, I planned to get to the bottom of this, because I was sick of dealing with the drama with these women. I just hoped she was not on the same shit Sam was on, because I didn't know if my heart could take any more heartbreak. Women were always screaming that they wanted a good man who was faithful, but when they got one, they didn't know how to act. When Corey, David, and I met for lunch at a local pizza joint, I decided to tell my guys what had been going on with Zoe and me.

"Maybe she is still upset with you because of the things that went down with Sam," Corey said through a mouthful of food.

"Yeah, you know women can hold a grudge forever," David said before sipping on his soda.

"Why would she take me back and say she believed me if she really didn't?" I asked.

"I have learned that you will never understand these crazy-ass women," David said.

"Maybe she has someone else, or maybe she's not happy," I said.

"I don't get that vibe from her, but maybe it's true. Why don't you just ask her what's wrong? That's the best approach," Corey said.

He was right. I should just talk to the woman whom I said I loved about our problems. It was just that every conversation turned into an argument. My mind had been on Sam a lot lately. I remembered all the good times we once had together. We used to do everything together. Then, all of a sudden, that changed. I couldn't lie. I missed the good times, but she had done more damage than good, and for that reason, I could never see myself being with her again. I wished that things hadn't changed so drastically between us, because I actual had had plans for us, but that was old news.

I thought Zoe was my future, but it was not looking so good for us right now. I had really thought this girl was different, but I was starting to think otherwise. When we first started dating, she was so sweet and nice. She was very caring, and she went out of her way to make sure I was happy. We had been together for less than a year, and already she didn't do all the things she used to do. She did not put any effort into our relationship whatsoever.

I was starting to think something was wrong with me. Maybe I was the problem, and not these women I had been dealing with. Maybe I was missing something. All I knew was I had to get to the bottom of things, because a nigga was just trying to be happy, without all the extra drama. If I found out that Zoe was cheating, I was done being faithful to these hoes. I was going to fuck them and leave them. I refused to keep putting my heart into them when their asses didn't appreciate shit.

Chapter Seventeen

Zoe

Things between Kevin and me were definitely not at their best, and that was because I was hiding something from him. About a week after Kevin and I got back together, I ran into my ex-boyfriend Dontae. Dontae and I had been together for two years before he went off to college and left me here. We hadn't ended on bad terms. He hadn't cheated on me or anything like that. We'd just thought it would be best that we separated instead of doing the long-distance thing. I really had been in love with Dontae, and I really had seen myself being with him long term.

When I met Kevin, I had really thought I was over Dontae, but seeing him had brought back these old feelings. I loved Kevin too, so I was so torn that I really didn't know what to do. Dontae didn't know about Kevin, and of course, Kevin didn't know about him. Dontae was back home for good. We had been texting every day and talking every chance we got. I had not told any of my friends about what I was going through right now, because honestly, I didn't feel like being judged.

I was on my way to this diner downtown to meet up with Dontae. He had said he had something he wanted to tell me. I couldn't say I was not happy about seeing him, because that would be a lie, but I was nervous about what he had to tell me. I pulled up to the diner, then parked my car. I walked inside, and there he was, sitting in the corner, looking as sexy as he could possibly be. Dontae was a mix of Puerto Rican and black, and he had a curly 'fro. He had gray eyes and some big pink lips. He was about five feet nine inches tall and had a toned, muscular build. He was so fucking irresistible that it was hard for me to keep my hands to myself. I sat down in front of him and gave him a big smile.

"I'm so happy you came to see me," he said, smiling at me.

"I'm happy to be here," I said, smiling back.

"Well, I asked you here for a reason. You know I love you, Zoe. I have never loved another woman like I love you. You know, all the time we spent apart has not changed anything for me," he said.

I didn't know what to say. I thought about Kevin and how I would feel if the shoe were on the other foot. I knew Kevin loved me, and I was starting to feel bad about even being here with Dontae. And hearing him say he loved me put me more on edge. I loved Kevin, and he treated me like a queen, but I also loved this man sitting in front of me. *Is it possible to be in love with two men*? I thought.

"That's so sweet, Dontae," I said.

"Well, Zoe, I want us to be back together. I love you so much, and I can't see myself being with anyone else. It was a big mistake to leave you in the first place. You are all I thought about when I was in Minnesota, and if you have another nigga in your life, drop his ass, because you spend all your time texting and talking to me, so obviously that nigga is already history," he said.

That statement was true as hell. When I was with Kevin, I found myself thinking about Dontae, and me being here showed me what I really thought about my relationship with Kevin.

"I don't know what to say," I told him, blushing.

"Say you want to be with me as well. I know you love me, Zoe. I can see it all over your face. We could get a place together when your lease is up, and who knows? Maybe start a family," he said. This man was speaking to my soul, and it was like he was saying everything I wanted to hear. At this point, Kevin was not even a thought, so I said the first thing that came to my mind.

"I love you too, Dontae, and I want nothing more than to be with you," I said as I reached over the table and kissed him on the lips. We sat at the table, ate, and talked for hours about our life goals and plans for each other.

When I left the restaurant and headed home, that was the first time I thought about Kevin in hours. I started to feel so bad about what I had done. I had just committed to being with another man, and I was still in a relationship with someone I claimed I loved. I had never been the type to cheat.

What the hell am I going to do? I wondered.

Monique

When Corey walked out our door, I felt like my heart was being ripped out of my chest. I knew right then and there that Corey was the only man I wanted. I knew for a fact that if it was Tremaine, I would not feel the same way. I didn't regret telling Tremaine it was over between us, but I did regret not telling him to his face. When I sent him that message, he immediately got to calling me. I didn't answer the first few times he called, but I figured the least I could do was talk to him. He wanted to know why I wanted to end things with him, and I just told him I had too much going on right now and just wanted to be alone. I didn't know why I lied. I guessed I just didn't want to hurt his feelings.

I decided to go to the hospital to check on Sam since I hadn't been there since she first got shot, which was over a month ago now. When I walked in her room, Eric was there, holding a pillow. I was shocked as hell because, for starters, Eric was supposed to be dead.

"Hey, Eric. What you doing here? I thought you was dead. You were all over the news and stuff," I said. I must have scared the shit out of him, because he almost jumped out of his skin when he heard my voice.

"Oh, I, um, the cops were just telling everyone that so that the person who tried to kill me would think so. I am just here visiting her. I know we didn't end on the best of terms, but I don't want to see her like this," he said as he fluffed the pillow in his hands and then placed it behind Sam's head. He stood there and stared at her for a while.

I took a seat in one of the chairs.

"I'll see you around, Monique," Eric said suddenly, then rushed out of Sam's room. Shit around here was getting crazier by the minute. We had gone to this boy's funeral. His mom and other family members had been extremely emotional, and it had looked real.

"Sam, I know we are not on the best of terms, but I wish you would wake up," I told her.

I sat with Sam for a few hours, and then I stopped by Bria's to pick her up. We decided to go for a walk by the lake just to chat and catch up. We drove to the lake, got out of the car, and walked along the path that circle the water. We were in deep conversation when, out of the corner of my eye, I spotted Zoe walking down the street—and she wasn't with Kevin.

"Is that Zoe over there, across the street?" I asked Bria. She looked in the direction I was pointing and brought her hand to her mouth.

"Girl, yes. That's her. Who is that dude she is with?" Bria said. Then she hurriedly left the path and headed toward the street.

"What are you doing?" I asked when I caught up with her.

"I'm about to find out who that is," she said, with a serious look on her face.

I didn't object, because, hell, I wanted to know too.

"Hey, Zoe girl," Bria said as we crossed the street.

Zoe looked like she saw a ghost when she saw us walking up to her. "Give us a minute," she told the guy. He was sexy as hell too. Zoe met us on the sidewalk.

"Who is that?" Bria asked, getting straight to the point.

"Um, he's a friend," Zoe lied. I could tell her ass was lying, and apparently, so could Bria.

"Girl, who the hell you think you are fooling? We are your friends. You can be honest with us," Bria said.

Zoe looked hesitant at first, but then she began to spill the beans. "Dontae is my ex-boyfriend. I recently reconnected with him. We are actually back together," she said.

"What about Kevin? Y'all broke up?" I asked.

Zoe looked very uneasy at this point. "We are still together," she said, looking away from us.

"What!" Bria and I both shouted at the same time.

"You are playing with fire right about now," Bria said.

"I know, but I love them both, and I don't know who to choose. Look, I got to go. I will call you two later," Zoe said, then hurried off.

"When Kevin finds out, it's going to be some drama, and he is going to be hurt," I said. "And it looks like she already chose who she wants to be with," I added.

Bria didn't say anything; she just shook her head. We ended our walk early, then headed home.

When I walked inside my house after I dropped Bria off, Corey, Kevin, and David were playing the game. I instantly felt bad for Kevin. I walked past them, and Corey smacked me on my ass. Corey had been holding out on me since the day Tremaine had sent those text messages. When he smacked me on the ass, that shit turned me on. Whether he liked it or not, he was giving me some of that dick tonight, even if I had to take it.

Bria

I decided to take my baby for a walk in the park. I was tired of sitting in the house. I was strolling through the park, minding my own business, when I noticed three girls pointing at me and laughing. I decided to keep walking and ignore those bitches, because I had my baby and I was outnumbered. I didn't have any enemies, so I didn't know what their problem could be. They got up and started walking behind me, and they were talking plenty of shit indirectly. If I didn't have my child, I would have fought all those bitches, but God was on their side today. One of the chicks looked real familiar, but I could not place her face.

"Yeah, that nigga left me, talking about he wants to work things out with his baby mama. I know I look way better than that bitch," one of the girls said.

Now things were starting to make sense. That was the bitch that David was fucking around with. I stopped dead in my tracks, because I was about to give that bitch what she wanted. I had never been a punk about mine, and I wasn't going to start now.

"Um, excuse us," that ugly-ass bitch said. The only thing that bitch had that I didn't have was a big ass, but I looked way better than that ho, and my body did too.

"You got something you want to tell me?" I got straight to the point.

"As a matter of fact, I do. For starters, I don't appreciate you coming to my house a while back and dropping off David's shit. How did you know where I live, anyway?" she said, making this ugly face.

"Well, I decided to let you borrow him since his ass was misbehaving, and he needed to see what he was walking out on," I smirked.

"Borrowed honey? If I really wanted David, I could have him. I figured I'd send him back to you for a while. I don't appreciate you coming to my house, and I honestly don't see what he sees in you any fucking way. You don't have shit on me," she said.

"Bitch, please. I'm class, and your ass is trash. And I was never in danger of him leaving me for your ratchet ass. You are not wifey material. You probably just a good fuck, if that," I said. "What? You mad because he decided to be with his family? Bitch, he will always choose me and his son. You are not even an option. What's crazy is you over here trying to treat me like I'm the side bitch. I'll always be number one, and your ass will always just be fucking somebody else's nigga. I got better things to do than sit around and go back and forth with you." I turned around, then headed toward my car.

"Bitch, he will be back. You just wait and see. I know how to treat a man," she said.

I stopped in my tracks and faced her. "I am not worried or pressed about shit you are saying right now, because I know it will never be you and him. Let me get home to my man and fuck the shit out of him. You hoes have a nice day." I turned back around and walked in the direction of my car. When I reached it, I placed the baby in the car seat, loaded the stroller, and got behind the wheel. Then I drove off.

That ho had really pissed me off, but I would never give her the satisfaction of knowing that. Why the hell did David even mess with a ho as ratchet as she was? If I saw that bitch again, and I didn't have my baby with me, it was on. I had never had drama with a female over my man. This was the first time, and it for damn sure better be the last. I felt like going home and giving him a piece of my mind, but I didn't want to bring the past into our future. However, I was going to let him know that I had run into her ass today.

When I got home, David was lying in bed, watching sports. I put my baby in his crib, then headed back into our bedroom.

"I ran into that chick you was messing with at the park today," I said.

"So, I don't mess with that girl no more," he said nonchalantly. David hated confrontation, and he really hated to argue, so his response didn't surprise me.

"Oh, I know, but she decided she wanted to confront me," I told him.

"I see I'm going to have to check her ass. I can't have her messing with my baby," he said as he pulled me on top of him. He started kissing me on my neck. I knew he was doing that to change the subject, and that was cool, because I still planned to beat that bitch's ass whether he liked it or not. I hated when women came for me when I didn't send for their ass.

"You need to let me hit this. Them six weeks are up," he said, smacking me on the ass.

I straddled him, then smiled at him. "We have to hurry up. The baby might wake up," I said, then kissed his lips passionately.

"The baby will sleep for a while. We don't have to rush," he said as he flipped me onto the bed and got on top of me.

He pulled off my dress and bra. He didn't have to worry about my panties, because I didn't have any on. He kissed my lips and neck while caressing my nipples and breasts with his hands. He was rubbing his hard dick against my kitty, and that drove me crazy.

"Um, I missed this," I moaned as he trailed kisses down to my breasts, then to my tummy.

He spread my legs and began to kiss my inner thighs. He pushed both of my legs toward me, then dove headfirst into

Miss Kitty. He sucked and licked her until I exploded inside his mouth. I wanted to return the favor, but he wouldn't let me. He took off the rest of his clothes, then pulled me to the edge of the bed. He cradled both of my legs in the crook of his arms, then entered me. My walls clutched his dick tightly, and I felt like I was in heaven.

"Shit, Bria. You feel so good, baby," he whispered in my ear.

He had me lie flat on my tummy, and then he entered me. He was pounding Miss Kitty until we both came. He lay on top of me for a while, until we heard DJ crying through the baby monitor. He stood up, threw on his shorts, and then rushed to the baby's room.

Thank God I had got on birth control yesterday, when I had my six-week checkup. Otherwise, we would probably be pregnant with baby number two.

Kevin

I was on my way to check up on my mom when I thought I saw Zoe inside this restaurant. I wanted to be sure, so I made a U-turn and then parked in front. I looked through the restaurant window, and I saw her sitting by herself. I figured I would go in and have a bite to eat with my baby, since I was hungry and I needed to eat, anyway. I walked inside, and as soon as I got close to her, some light-skinned dude walked up, kissed her on the lips, and sat down in the seat in front of her. My heart instantly broke, because I had not expected anything like this from her. I had known something was wrong because of all the arguing for no reason and the distance I felt between us.

I stood there and watched her for a second, and I could tell she was happy with this nigga. I started to turn around and leave, but the hostess walked up to me and asked me if

I wanted to be seated. Zoe turned around to see what was going on, and her mouth hit the floor. I walked up to her and decided to confront her.

"So this is how you do me? You could not come talk to me and break things off the right way? I had to catch you up here fucking off on me?" I said.

"Kevin, I am so sorry. I didn't mean to hurt you. I just didn't know how to approach this situation," she said, then began to cry.

"You cheating on me? After I told you all the bullshit I went through with Sam, you turn around and do the same thing? You are just like her. And your ass don't have no problems talking to me about anything else, so that's bullshit you spitting out of your mouth," I said, getting closer in her face.

"I am nothing like Sam. Just please let me explain," she said.

"Zoe, who is this guy?" the dude asked her as he stood up.

"Dontae, can you please give me a second? I will explain everything to you once I'm done talking to him," she said as she stood up. I knew right then that our relationship was definitely over.

"Naw, I'm not going anywhere with you. You out here in public with this nigga, so obviously, you don't have nothing to hide. I'm Kevin, by the way, and we been in a relationship for about a year. You don't have to explain shit to me, because I stood here and watched how you interacted with this dude, so I have seen enough to know that I'm done," I told her and dude. He looked just confused as I did.

"Kevin, I am sorry. It was hard for me to choose between you two, because I love you both. He is my ex, and I told you how I felt about him. He came back home, and we rekindled things, but I never meant to hurt you," she said.

"You better tell this nigga it's over between y'all two, or I'm out," Dontae said.

Zoe started to cry harder. "Please don't make me do this," she said.

"You bitches is all the same. I don't know what made me think yo' ass would be any different than the rest of these hoes out here. You don't have to tell me shit, because I'm done fucking with yo' ho ass," I said, then turned to walk out.

When I was almost to the door, she ran up behind me and started punching me in my back. I guessed she didn't like what I had said to her. I pushed her off me, then continued to walk toward the door.

"Aye, nigga, you better watch your fucking mouth and keep your hands off my girl," Dontae called.

"Or what, nigga? What yo' ass going to do?" I said as I turned around, then headed toward him, with Zoe on my heels. When I reached him, the manager of the restaurant got between us before I could get in that nigga's face.

"I'll see you around," he said.

"Fuck you and this bitch. I am not worried about neither one of y'all," I said, then turned to walk back to the door.

That nigga swung his arm over the manager in an effort to hit me, but he missed. I was going to turn around and give that nigga what he was asking for, but I just left the restaurant. I went to the house and packed all my clothes. Then I went to the hospital to visit Sam. I said my good-byes to her, jumped in my car, and got on the freeway.

I didn't know where I was going, but I needed to get away from Milwaukee for a while. I was tired of the bullshit. Maybe I'd go and start a life somewhere else.

Chapter Eighteen

Sam

I opened my eyes, and they were heavy as hell. I must have snorted too much, because I felt drowsy as ever. I looked around my room, and nothing seemed familiar. I looked to my right, and that was when I noticed all the machines and realized I was in the hospital. *What the hell am I doing in the hospital*? I thought to myself. I instantly began to panic, because I had no idea what had happened to me. I pressed the call button and waited for someone to come. The nurse finally came into my room, and I guessed she was surprised to see me awake.

"Samariah, you are awake," she said excitedly. She paged the doctor, then began to check all my vitals.

"What am I doing in the hospital?" I asked her.

"You were shot three times, sweetie, about two months ago. I am Tasha, by the way, and I have been taking care of you since you got here," she said.

When the words *you were shot* left her mouth, I instantly remembered everything that had happened that horrible night. I couldn't believe that Eric was still alive, and that he had raped me and tried to kill my ass.

"Can you call my mom please?" I asked the nurse.

Forty-five minutes later my mom rushed through the door to my room, in tears. She ran over to my bed and kissed me all over my face.

"I'm so happy you are awake, baby. I will never leave your side. And I am going to be a better mother to you," she said as she picked up my hand, then kissed it. "Did the doctor update you on your condition and everything you went through up until this point?"

"Yes, pretty much," I told her.

"Even about the baby?" she asked.

"What baby?" I asked her, confused as ever.

"Samariah, honey, you were pregnant when you were shot," my mom told me, tears streaming down her face.

"I was pregnant?" I asked my mom, not believing what I had just heard. In the months leading up to my shooting, I had become careless. I used to take my birth control pills faithfully, but once I started using drugs to dull all the emotional pain I was experiencing, I would take them whenever I remembered. There was no telling who the father of my child was. I had slept with at least four or five dudes. I had slept with Brian the most, though. Although he had said he was breaking up with me when he caught Kevin in my bed, he could not get enough of my pussy and had come crawling back weeks later.

"Has Brian been out here to visit me?" I asked my mother.

"That boy is here every day, all day. He was devastated to learn that you were pregnant with his baby and lost it," my mom said.

I cried over the loss of my baby, but maybe it was a good thing, because I had no clue who could have possibly been the father. It was obvious that Brian thought he was the only person I had slept with, but if he only knew the truth . . .

"Your so-called sister, I mean friend, has been out here to see you as well, with her spoiled ass," my mother said.

"Who? Mo?" I asked. How the hell did my mom mistake Mo for my sister when I didn't have any siblings, at least none that I knew of?

"Yes, her and that little bitch Bria," my mother said. Now, I could see Mo coming to visit me, but Bria was a whole other story. Her ass was probably just here to make sure I never woke up. Even though I hated both of those bitches' guts, I was glad they cared enough to make sure I was all right.

"I have something I need to talk to you about," my mother said.

"What's that?" I asked.

"You have to start back taking your pills, Samariah. It's not an option. I noticed how crazy you were acting, and if you don't take those pills, they are going to lock you up," she said.

I refused to take those fucking pills. I didn't need to change. I was fine being just who I was. I agreed with her, just because I didn't want to discuss the shit any further. I was grown, and I was going to do what the fuck I wanted to do.

Just then, Mo and Bria walked in the door, and they look surprised to see me awake. My mother gave them the evil eye, then walked out of the room. Mo came to my side of the bed, but Bria stayed closer to the door.

"I'm happy you are awake, Sam," Mo said as she sat down next to me. I could not help but notice that she was wearing that expensive-ass engagement ring that Corey had bought her.

So I guess I didn't do enough to split their ass up, I thought.

"I'm happy to be awake, and I'm glad y'all are here to see me," I said, nodding toward Bria. "Look, I am sorry for everything I did to hurt you and Bria. This was a life-changing moment for me, and I realize that I was a horrible friend to both of you. If you forgive me and accept me as your friend again, I will do everything in my power to show you two that I have changed." Tears were streaming down my cheeks.

Bria looked like she wasn't buying it, but Mo's ass was crying, so I knew she had fallen for everything I said.

"It's okay. We can work on our friendship. Isn't that right, Bria?" Mo said.

I gave Bria the saddest eyes I could muster up, and she came to the other side of the bed and grabbed my hand.

"I forgive you, and we will just take things one day at a time," Bria said.

Maybe I will take our friendships seriously. Who knows? I thought. I might actually change. Only time would tell, but I knew one fucking thing—when I found Eric's ass, he would be one dead fucker, and I would make sure of it this time. As far as these two were concerned, I'd play nice for now.

Zoe

I could not believe Kevin had caught me with Dontae. I was having so much fun with him that I was practically spending all my time with him. I would lie to Kevin and tell him I was working or working late. Other times, I would tell him I was spending time with my parents, which was far from the truth. Dontae and I had even started having sex again. I wouldn't let Kevin touch me; I would always come up with some type of excuse as to why we could not have sex, or I would start an argument. Kevin's sex was just as good as Dontae's, if not better, but I just felt like my heart belonged to Dontae.

I was so hurt when Kevin found out I was cheating on him, because I had never been that type of girl. I wished I had handled things the right way, because the way things ended between us, I knew he would never talk to me again. My heart was really telling me that it belonged to Dontae, so things just got out of hand. Sam had already torn his heart out and stepped on it, and I did the exact same thing.

I really did feel like a ho when Kevin called me all those names. I might have gone about things the wrong way, but I thought he took it a little too far when he began to call me out of my name. I must admit that I really missed him. I had tried calling him a few times but he would never answer, and after a while he just changed his number. Bria told me he had moved out of town and he'd been gone for about a month now. She also told me that bitch Sam woke up, but I could care less if she did or didn't.

Things between Dontae and I were just okay. When we first started off, they were great, but now he had become very overprotective. If I was not with him, he would call me every hour on the hour to see what I was doing or where I was at. At first I had thought it was cute, but now it was getting out of hand. If I was going anywhere besides work or my parents' house, he had to come with me. Otherwise, he just wanted to sit in the house and have sex all day. Not that I didn't like sex, but that was not all I want to spend my life doing.

When he found out Kevin had moved out of our place, Dontae moved in without even asking me. One day he just showed up with all his things, and we had been living together since then. One good thing about him was that he payed all the bills; I didn't have to pay for anything. Dontae was a manager at a bank in downtown Milwaukee, so he made good money. When I was with Kevin, he was so attentive to my needs. He took me out all the time and showed me that he really loved me, and I was starting to miss that feeling, but I wouldn't live in regret, because I loved Dontae and I had made my choice. I just hoped it was the right one.

Bria and David had asked us to come out to dinner with them since they had a babysitter for the weekend and they wanted to get out of the house. When we arrived at the restaurant, Bria and David were already seated. Dontae was in a sour mood because he didn't know them and he really hadn't wanted to go, but he had caved in after I worked my magic with my tongue and mouth on him. We sat down, looked at the menu, and placed our order. David tried to make conversation with Dontae, but it was like pulling teeth to get anything out of him, and when he did answer, his replies were very dry. David didn't even have to try to make conversation with him, because Kevin was his best friend, but Dontae was just stubborn. I excused myself so that I could go to the restroom, and Bria was right on my heels.

"What the hell is wrong with your man's attitude?" Bria asked as soon as we made it inside the restroom.

"I think he just tired," I lied.

"Yeah, whatever," Bria said as she walked into a stall. We used the restroom, then went back out to our table.

The waiter placed our bill on the table, and I slid it over to Dontae, but he slid it back over to me.

"I'm not paying for this shit. I didn't like the food, anyway," he said to me.

I was pissed as hell and embarrassed, but I didn't show it, and though he did not like the food, he sure as hell cleaned his plate. I paid the bill, stood up, and said my good-byes. Dontae and I left the restaurant and hopped in the car.

I don't know what the hell I have gotten myself into, was my thought as I sped in the direction of our house.

Sam

I was finally able to go home a month after I woke up, and I was happy as hell. I had the doctor give me an IUD, because I was not trying to get pregnant again. My father had rented us out a new place since I refused to go back to the house we used to stay in. The funny thing about all this was my father had not come to see me one time since I had been awake. My mother had said he was there the night I was brought in, but that was about it. It made me sad that he could buy me all these things and never once show his face. I wanted to be able to hold him and tell him I loved him, things normal kids got to do with their dad. Mr. Peterson and his wife came to see me several times, but not my own fucking father. Thinking about that shit had me wanting to snort a line, but I hadn't had it in months and I was trying to stay away from it.

A week after I woke up, Brian and I were having sex right in my hospital bed. You know I stayed horny, so I had him spend the night with me every night so that I could get some whenever I felt like it. The first time we tried to have sex, it was a little painful, so Brian ate the shit out of my pussy and brought me to a fast orgasm. I was really starting to like Brian, but I still loved Kevin. I was happy to hear he had come to see how I was doing a few times, because that meant there may still be hope for us, after all. I had convinced Monique to get Kevin's number for me; I had told her I wanted to apologize to him. Surprisingly, when I called, he agreed to meet up with me, since he happened to be in town.

We decided to meet at the TGI Fridays that was in Miller Park to grab a bite. When I arrived there, he was already seated at a table, looking at his phone. He looked up and waved me over to him. I walked over to him, and he stood up and embraced me tightly. That also shocked the hell out of me, because I wasn't expecting that, either.

"I'm happy you pulled through, Sam. What do you want to talk to me about?" he asked, giving me a big smile.

"I wanted to talk to you about everything I put you through before. I want to apologize for my behavior and let you know it will never happen again," I lied, because I knew if taken there, I would do the same thing again, but maybe even worse the next time around. I wanted to make him feel like I had really changed, so I began to cry and continued to confess how sorry I was. All of sudden, his eyes left mine, and his entire attitude changed. I followed his gaze, and that was when I laid eyes on Zoe and some light-skinned guy. I was very shocked because, for starters, I had no clue what Zoe would be doing here with another man when she was supposed to be with Kevin. I stared at her, and I could not believe this was the bitch he had left me for.

"I don't mean to get in your business, but what is she doing here with another guy?" I asked Kevin, interrupting his thoughts.

"We are not together," was all he said before giving me his undivided attention again. "I forgive you for all the shit you pulled, just don't pull that shit again." He smiled.

The way he kept smiling at me, and the fact that he was no longer with Zoe, was giving me hope for us. I was wondering why he had moved out of town, and now I had got my answer. It pissed me off that he had left me for that bitch and she had ended up hurting his ass too. Zoe and her man walked by us, and the look on her face was priceless. She was shocked to see Kevin, but even more shocked to see him with me. She gripped dude's arm tighter, then sped up her pace. I grabbed Kevin's face and kissed the shit out of him, and to my surprise, he went along with me. When we finally came up for air, Zoe was staring a hole through both of us. She looked like she wanted to murder us both, and I felt like I had accomplished my job.

"Let's get out of here," Kevin said before we could order food or anything. He stood up, grabbed my hand, and then we walked out of the restaurant. I made sure to put a little something extra in my step.

We went back to my house, and we fucked all day and night. When I woke up in the morning, there was a note on the nightstand, telling me he had enjoyed himself and he would hit me up later. I didn't know how to feel, because I had made myself believe that we were going to get back together, but now it seemed like it was just a friendly fuck.

Mo

Corey and I went to a restaurant in Brookfield to grab a bite to eat. We had not been able to do things like this recently since he had been working with his father on some project that was supposed to bring in a lot of money for the two of them. Once we were done with our food, I decided that we should walk around Brookfield Square, the mall, so that we could find me something nice to wear. My parents had decided they wanted to throw Corey and me another engagement party, since the first one had been a disaster. I had told them to keep it small, because I was not sure if I was ready to face all those people again. Just before we were about to enter the mall, I felt someone grab my arm hard as hell.

"So this is the real reason why your trifling ass broke up with me," Tremaine said. I instantly got scared, because I knew Corey was about to go crazy.

"Nigga, you really tried it, coming over to her straight disrespectful," Corey said while pushing Tremaine in his chest.

I jumped in front of them to prevent any further fighting.

"Naw, bitch-ass nigga, I just don't appreciate her ass lying to me. You had me think your ass was over this nigga, but you right back with his bitch ass," Tremaine spat, pushing me out of the way, then jumping in Corey's face.

"I am not going to be too many more of your bitches, you ho-ass niggas. I'm trying to save your ass the embarrassment of whupping your ass," Corey spat.

"Man, fuck you. You don't put no fear in my heart," Tremaine said, pushing Corey. And that was when everything went from bad to worse. Corey punched Tremaine right in his face, and that was all she wrote. I tried my hardest to break them up, but my little ass couldn't do it.

"Corey, stop! Get off him," I yelled. "That's enough!" But my pleas went unheard.

Finally, mall security broke them up. Corey had beat the shit out of Tremaine by then, but Tremaine had held his own. He had got a few swings in on him, enough to slightly bust Corey's lips. Tremaine's entire face was bloody. I knew Corey had hated him from the time he saw Tremaine and me talking at the club that night.

"Now, bitch-ass nigga, that should teach your weak ass to listen to what you have been told," Corey said heatedly.

"That didn't teach me shit. Her ass will be back. We was just fucking not to long before she ended things with me. She loves daddy's dick. She told me that all the time when she was riding this big motherfucker!" Tremaine said, smiling, with blood all on his teeth.

My heart nearly dropped to the pit of my stomach. I just knew Corey was going to be done with me after that comment. Corey didn't know about the fact that I had slept with Tremaine the day Sam got shot, and I was hoping to take that to my grave.

"Corey, let's go. You two are scaring me, and you are bleeding. Let's just go home," I said.

"Man, fuck you. Your ass see who she with, and she is going to continue to be with me, homeboy. If you come anywhere near my fiancée again, I will kill your ass and make sure they will never find your body, you hear me? Let's go, Monique," Corey said, grabbing my arm.

"Fiancée," Tremaine said, then laughed out loud. Before Tremaine and I broke up, I had never told him that Corey and I were engaged, so he never knew that. I felt so bad because Corey had beat that boy's ass. He hadn't shown him any mercy, and I was scared as hell because I didn't know what he was going to say to me.

"Get your ass in the car, Mo. You got me out here fighting these weak-ass niggas over you. If you had never given my pussy to another nigga, we wouldn't even be having this conversation right now," he said as he got in the car and slammed the door. He shut it so hard that the glass cracked.

I got in the car and didn't say a word.

"You better stay away from that nigga before you get him hurt, and your ass is definitely cut off. I am not giving you no sex," he said. I hated that when he got mad at me, he wanted to withhold sex. I was going to start treating his ass like that.

"I'm sorry, Corey. You acting like I knew he was going to be at the mall," I said.

"I don't even want to talk about it anymore. All I know is if you want to be with me and you value our relationship, you better stay away from that nigga, point-blank, period," he said with finality.

I had never been in so much drama in my life. This past year had been full of good times, but it had mostly been bad times. I just hoped that things began to change for the better. I loved Corey, and he had made his mistakes too, but I had just chosen to forgive him. He needed to do the same for me with this Tremaine situation. Otherwise, we were not going to make it.

Chapter Nineteen

Zoe

When I'd seen Kevin with Sam, I immediately got pissed as hell, and when they'd kissed, I knew he no longer cared about me or even thought about me like I thought about him. I still wanted to beat that ho's ass, and now that they may be back together, my hate for her grew even more. Things with Dontae had gone from bad to worse. When we'd got home from the restaurant, we'd got into a heated argument. I still remembered what happened as clear as day, and it had been a month since everything went down.

We walked in the house, and Dontae immediately got to snapping on me.

"Your ass still want that nigga. I saw how you was looking at him," he said.

"Baby, I love you, and I don't want him," I said, trying to kiss him on his lips to reassure him that it was him I wanted. He pushed me out of the way, and I landed on my ass. I was so shocked that I actually sat on the floor, trying to compose myself.

"Don't try to kiss on me and shit when I know you was thinking about kissing that nigga," he said, staring down at me.

I looked at Dontae with pleading eyes. I really did love this man, but I felt like I had become weak since I had gotten back with him. Before, there was no way anyone would have gotten away with pushing me without my snapping.

"Baby, I love you. I don't know why you acting crazy right now, because I'm all about you," I said.

All of a sudden, he snatched me off the floor by my hair, then smacked me in my face. I stood there, shocked, for a minute, because I could not believe he had put his hands on me.

"Bitch, who the fuck you think your ass is talking to like that, huh? Who you calling crazy?" he said, walking into my face.

I slapped the shit out of him and began to rain punches all over his body. He grabbed me by my hair again, then dragged me into our bedroom. I could feel strands of my hair being pulled out by the roots. Once inside the bedroom, he threw me on the bed, then jumped on top of me. He slapped me repeatedly on my face, then began to rip off my clothes. By this time, I was crying my eyes out, and I couldn't fight back. He took off his clothes, then lay between my legs.

"Baby, I am sorry. I just get so angry when I think of another man trying to take you from me. I'll never put my hands on you again," he said, then placed kisses all over my face and neck.

He stared into my face and asked me if I would forgive him. I shook my head yes, and then he kissed me on my lips. He placed his dick against my opening and began to rub it up and down my clit while sucking on my nipples. I tried my hardest not to feel anything for him, but I loved this man. He entered my wet hole and began to pound in and out of me, bringing me to a fast orgasm. He flipped me over so that I was lying on my stomach, and then he came inside of me shortly after. He held me close to him for the rest of the night and would let me up only to go to the bathroom.

I believed Dontae when he said he would never put his hands on me again, and so far so good.

***

Here I was, leaving the doctor's office with a prescription for prenatal vitamins. The doctor had told me I was six weeks pregnant. I was happy to hear the news, because I really wanted a baby, and maybe this would help Dontae be more secure in our relationship. I couldn't wait to give him the news. I went to Walgreens to fill my prescription, then headed home to make dinner. I had decided to make his favorite tonight for dinner, when I dropped the good news on him. I made fried pork chops, macaroni and cheese, and corn on the cob. I lit the candles on our dinner table, and that was when Dontae walked in the door. I greeted him with a kiss and a hug, then led him to the dinner table after we washed our hands. We both took a seat and filled our plates.

"Hey, baby. How was work?" I said, making conversation as we ate.

"It was great. It was a good day. We met our quota for this month, so that's always a good thing," he said and gave me a huge smile.

I decided this would be a good time to give him the good news.

"So I went to the doctor today for my yearly checkup, and the doctor gave me some good news," I said.

"What's that?" he said, taking a big bite out of his pork chop.

"I'm pregnant, baby," I said, smiling sweetly.

He frowned and was quiet.

"Are you okay, honey? I thought you would be happy. . . . We talked about starting a family early," I said.

"Whose baby is it?" he asked.

I looked at him like he had lost his damn mind, because he knew I had been only with his stinky ass. I stood up from the dinner table and ran into our bedroom. *The nerve of his ass!* I thought. I had left a very good man for him, and he had the nerve to question my loyalty? I began to cry. He walked into our bedroom, got on his knees in front of me, and began to apologize.

"I'm sorry, baby. I know you are pregnant with my child. I don't know what came over me. I am happy that you are pregnant with our baby," he said, then kissed my stomach and my lips.

Dontae needed to get his shit together, because I didn't know how much I could take of this bipolar-ass shit.

Monique

It was the night of our engagement party, and Corey and I were on our way to the hotel that was hosting our party. I was nervous as ever, because I didn't know what people would think of me accepting Corey back after I'd been embarrassed at our first engagement party. To make matters worse, Sam would be at this party too, but I had warned her that she better not start no mess. We had been hanging out a lot lately, and it felt like old times. It actually felt good being around her again. She seemed to be on the straight and narrow, so I guessed I didn't have anything to worry about as far as she was concerned.

When we entered the hotel ballroom, it was packed as ever. I should have known my parents couldn't do anything small. I spotted David and Bria on the dance floor, dry fucking. She was glowing, and I could tell she was happy to have her David back. No matter where we went with them two, it was like they could not keep their hands off each other. If she was not on birth control, she would definitely be knocked up with baby number two before long.

As we walked through the door, the DJ announced our arrival. Zoe and her man walked up to us, and she hugged me tight. I looked in her face, and she had definitely lost that glow she used to have with Kevin, and if I was not mistaken, there was a small cut above her eye. *I wonder what happened to her*, I thought. Corey nodded at Dontae, but that was all Dontae was going get. Kevin had told Corey what happened between them, and you know Corey's loyalty was to Kevin.

As soon as Zoe and I got done embracing, Kevin walked in with some thick chick. She was pretty and dark skinned, and she almost gave Zoe a run for her money. Zoe looked at Kevin for a second, then at Dontae. She entangled her arms with Dontae's, then told us she would see us a little later. She and Dontae disappeared into the crowd. Kevin embraced me, then gave Corey a brotherly hug. I had not seen Kevin in about three months. He came up here all the time, but he hadn't visited Corey and me. He introduced us to the chick he was with, and her name was Imani. Corey, Kevin, and his girl—whom he referred to as his friend, by the way—walked off.

Samariah walked up to me with Brian and her mom. I knew she was going to be upset, because she had told me that she and Kevin had been having sex a lot lately. She had said she had been driving up north, to where he was staying, and spending weekends with him. She had told me she felt strongly that he was going to make things official between them. And she had also told me he said he was moving back home in about a week or so. He had been staying with his dad's brother for a while. She pulled me to the side so that we could converse in private.

"I can't believe he showed up here with some chick. He told me he was not fucking nobody but me, but you know he is fucking that girl," Sam said, looking hurt.

"Sam, you are here with Brian, so you really cannot be this upset over what Kevin is doing. Plus, y'all are not together," I said.

"Kevin knows about Brian, and I told him I would stop seeing him whenever he decides to make things official with me," she said.

I was about to respond, but my dad got on the stage and called Corey and me up front. I walked up on the stage and grabbed my man's hand and stood there, feeling nervous as hell.

"I would like to take this time to congratulate my beautiful daughter on her engagement to her awesome fiancé, Corey. I am so happy for her, and I am very proud to say she's my child. I would move the moon and stars for her, and I could not ask for a better daughter. I love you, baby, with all my heart," my father said.

A waiter came over and handed my father, Corey, and me glasses of champagne.

"Cheers to you two," my father said, then raised his glass. At the same time, he sat the microphone down, and everyone said, "Cheers." As soon as we took our drink, I watched Sam's mom storm onto the stage and grab the mic.

"Your tired ass act as if you only have one fucking daughter, and that's this spoiled little bitch right there," she said as she pointed at me.

This was the second time this old bitch had come for me, and I was tired of her shit. *Wait. Did she just say that he acts as if I'm his only child? I am his only child. What is she talking about?* I thought.

My father tried to take the mic out of her hand, but she had a death grip on it.

"Naw, let me the fuck go. I can't hide this shit anymore. Samariah is your fucking daughter too, and I am tired of you acting like she isn't. My baby has not spent time with you since she was five years old, and she does not deserve this, but that all ends today. For those of you who are still confused, the two girls, who have been best friends for all these years, are actually sisters. They share the same daddy, which is this sorry motherfucker right here," she said, pointing at my dad. "I just thought it was time to let the cat out of the bag."

I looked at my father, then collapsed on the floor. I knew we couldn't have a party without some type of drama, was my thought as everything faded to black.

Samariah

I could not believe my ears. Did she just say that Mr. Peterson was my father? I had so many emotions going on, and I did not know how to feel. Brian grabbed my hand tightly, and then the tears began to pour out of my eyes.

How could this man be my father and never really acknowledge me? I wondered. I had spent so many nights over at his house, with Mo, and he had never once mentioned that he was my dad. How could he be there for Mo and not for me? What made her so much better than me? Why didn't he want me? I hated Monique's ass! She had stolen the life I should have had with my father. I really had to get rid of that little bitch now. She always got whatever she wanted. She had taken everything from me.

My thoughts were interrupted by the commotion on the stage. Mrs. Sharon ran on the stage and punched the shit out of my mother. My mom instantly hit the floor. I ran up on the stage to get my mother. I was pissed at her too, but at the moment she needed my help. My dad, or Mr. Peterson or whatever, grabbed his wife and pulled her off the stage. The security escorted everyone out except for Monique and Mr. Peterson and me. They were able to wake Mo up after her dumb ass fainted on the stage. Once everyone was out, it was just Mo and I with our father.

We all took a seat and sat in silence, not knowing what to say. I looked over at Mo, and she was crying her eyes out. I really hated her now—I mean really hated her—and I was going to show her how much sooner than later.

"Girls, I am so sorry you two had to find out this way. I had planned to sit you two down and discuss this in private, but Kendra took it upon herself to do things the wrong way," he said.

I looked at my father real hard, and I realized I looked just like him. The only real difference was I was light skinned and he wasn't. How had I never noticed the resemblance?

"Dad, how could you lie to us all this time? I don't know if I can ever forgive you for this. We have been friends since we were five years old, she has spent nights over at our house, we have done some of everything together, and you never once mentioned that she was my sister," Monique said.

"Look, I am sorry, baby. I love you both, and I never meant to hurt either one of you," he said.

"What did you think was going to happen with you lying to us for all these years? Did you think we would be jumping for joy? I really don't have nothing else to say to you or mom. I am tired of everyone around me keeping secrets from me and shit. I'm done with everybody at this point. I can't even deal," Monique said as she stood up to leave.

"Monique, sit your ass down, and you better watch your mouth. You are not that grown. I will still whip your ass," our dad yelled.

She didn't listen to him; she just kept walking toward the door. He just stared at me, and you could tell he was searching for the right words to say. But it did not even matter, because I finally had my father, and that was all I had ever wanted.

"I am sorry, sweetie. I really am. I know I haven't been much of a father to you, but I would like to start being a better one, starting now. Can you please forgive me, Samariah?" my dad said to me, on the verge of tears.

"I forgive you, Dad. I'm just happy to finally know who you are. When I was little, all I could remember about you was that you were dark skinned. Can you please just promise you will never leave me again?"

He stood up, and so did I. He hugged me tight, then kissed me on my forehead. "I will never leave you again, baby girl," he said. "Come on. Let's get out of here. Your sister is probably pissed that her engagement party was ruined once again, and I know she is upset with me."

I did not respond, because honestly, I didn't give a shit about her feelings, and as soon as I got the chance, I was going to get rid of that bitch for good. I was tired of her taking everything from me—first, Corey, and now my dad. Oh yeah, she definitely had to go.

Chapter Twenty

Samariah

When I finally made it home that night, I found my mother in her bedroom with a bottle of Hennessy. She was drunk as hell. I know you are probably thinking, why did she forgive her dad? But hear me out. All I ever wanted was my dad around. I would see my friends and relatives doing things with their fathers, and I wanted to do those things too. I remember not going to the father-daughter dances, because my daddy was never around. I remember Mo bragging about how she would go with her father and they would have so much fun. She was the reason I could never go to those dances.

"Mom, why are you in here getting drunk?" I asked, startling her. She was so drunk that she didn't even know I had been standing in the doorway all this time.

"Baby, I am so sorry you had to find out who your father was that way. I was getting sick to my stomach hearing him brag about Monique like he didn't have another daughter. That shit just pushed me over the edge," she said, taking a swig from her bottle.

"I don't understand how you and my father could hide something so important from me for this long. Mom, you should have told me. It's always been me and you," I cried.

"I wanted to tell you, Samariah, but your father made me promise not to tell. All his ass cares about is that bitch Sharon, who I plan to fuck up next time I see her ass, and your sister," she said.

"When did y'all even date? I mean, how did this happen?" I asked.

My mom told me everything that had happened between her and my father. Knowing that my mother had him first pissed me off even more, because if Sharon had never stolen my dad from my mother, I would be his only child. Now I had to hurt Sharon's ass too. I refused to let her old ass get away with hurting my mom, so now her ass was on my list too.

"Mom, how did you just let her steal your man? You look better than her!" I shouted. "You need to get up and get your man. Why are you sitting here drunk and shit? You need to be figuring out how you're going to get my damn daddy back."

My mother looked at me like I had lost my mind.

"Why you sitting there looking at me? We got work to do! We are going to get revenge on both of those bitches for taking our lives. We cannot let them get away with what they did," I said.

"Sam, watch your fucking mouth. I am still your mother, so do not talk to me that way. But I am down with revenge, so what are we going to do?" my mother asked.

"Sorry, Mom, but this is serious. You have to get your stuff together," I told her.

She looked at me and began to cry. "I love you so much, Samariah, and I never meant to hurt you. I love your father with everything in me, but he refuses to even look my way. I gave that man everything in me, and he allowed that bitch to just steal him away from me. All I ever wanted was for us three to be a family. Let's do whatever it takes to get him back," she said, smiling.

My mother was very beautiful, but she had let herself go over the years. She was light skinned and had the sexiest body ever. She had a big ass and a small waist, and she had small, perky breasts that sat nice on her chest. She had hazel eyes and small pouty lips. She kind of put you in mind of Vanessa Williams, but she was much shapelier.

"Mom, you are very beautiful, but you have let yourself go over the years. Look at these big-ass clothes you got on, and look at your hair. You wear that same dirty-ass ponytail. We have to get you made over. Get yourself some rest, and the first thing tomorrow morning we are getting you some clothes, and we are going to the nail and hair shop," I said. I kissed my mom on the forehead and then went to bed.

The next day we did everything I said we would, and my mom looked sexy as hell. Now it was time to make our move.

Kendra

I could not believe my daughter was talking to me the way she was, but she was absolutely right about everything she said. I needed to get my shit together if I wanted my man back. I got my hair washed and curled in some loose body curls with some brown and blond highlights. Over the years, I had saved up a lot of money. When I was working at the hospital, I had saved every last one of my checks because Tim had taken care of everything, so I didn't have to spend any money. He would put six thousand dollars in my account every two weeks to take care of me and Sam. I would put three thousand dollars in Sam's checking account and keep the rest for myself, so I was pretty set. That was why it was easy for me to get a whole new wardrobe.

Tim sent me a message letting me know he was on his way so that we could talk. I threw on a formfitting, leopard-print halter pencil dress with some red Chanel heels. I put on a gold diamond tennis bracelet and matching earrings, and I topped it off with some red lipstick. I made sure to wear nothing but a thong, because I knew he loved the way my ass jiggled when I was wearing one.

I strutted to the door when I heard the doorbell ring. Sam was in her room with Kevin, but I knew she was wondering what was going to happen. She knew her dad was on the way. I looked through the peephole, and there Tim was, standing there, looking as sexy as could be. Tim was dark as hell and had pearly white teeth. He had his hair cut like Usher had his cut, in a Mohawk, but he had naturally curly hair, so it looked even better. Muscles were popping out everywhere; he definitely resembled Idris Elba's fine ass.

I looked past him to his car, and I noticed Sharon sitting in the car. She looked pissed as hell. Well, by the time he left here, I was going to give her a reason to be mad. I opened the door wide as hell so that she would notice me, and just like I expected, she looked right at me. I smirked, then turned to walk back in my house. I had definitely noticed how Tim's mouth dropped when I opened the door. He had expected the old Kendra to open that door, but her ass was gone, the new and improved Kendra was here, and she definitely had something to prove. She was getting her man back. He closed the door, and I turned to face him. His eyes were roaming all over my body, and then they landed on my breasts, which were popping out of my halter dress at the moment.

"What do you need to talk about, Tim? I have somewhere to be," I lied while adjusting the top part of my dress. I made sure to expose some of one of my nipples while fixing it.

"I, um, I need to talk to you about the stunt you pulled yesterday," he said, adjusting his pants.

"What about it? My daughter deserved to know who her father is. We held this from her long enough, don't you think?" I said, smiling, as I walked into the living room. He followed. We both took a seat on the couch.

"I agree, but that was not the way to go about it. That was totally out of line, and you started some bullshit. Do you know Monique refuses to talk to me or her mother because of the shit you pulled?" he said, growing angry.

"Look, she would have been pissed either way. I am sorry she had to find out the way she did, but the damage is done, so what the hell do you want me to do about it?" I snapped, growing impatient.

"You know what? I don't know what made me think that your ignorant ass would actually feel bad for hurting my fucking daughter. You have always been a selfish bitch," he said as he stood up to leave.

"Look, Tim, I do feel bad, but there is nothing I can do about it now. The damage is already done," I said as I walked behind him, then placed my arms around his waist. He smelled so good; he still wore that same cologne by Armani that he had worn all those years ago. He turned to face me, but he didn't remove my hands from around his waist. I looked into his eyes, and we just stared at each other for what seemed like forever. The more we looked at each other, the wetter my pussy got.

"Look, Kendra, that shit was out of line, and you owe Monique and my wife an apology for showing out the way you did," he said.

I kissed him on the cheek, then on his neck. I began to caress his dick, and he did not stop me. I was about to kiss him on the lips, but his wife blew the horn. He immediately pulled himself together, then walked to the door. He turned to look at me again, his eyes roaming my body once more.

"Tell my daughter to call me," he said, then walked out the door.

I locked the door, then headed to my room with a big smile on my face, because I knew I had just started some shit. I knew he would be back to me sooner or later to get a taste of me. It was always hard for Tim to resist me when I was on my shit.

Tim

I got in the car, and I knew my wife was pissed at me. She had been feeling some type of way since the incident at the hospital. She had refused to give me any pussy. And last night had really pushed her over the edge.

"What took you so long? You were supposed to go in there and put her ass in her place and that's it. You was in there for ten minutes!" she snapped.

"I know, baby. You know how Kendra can be sometimes," I said, trying to get my mind off Kendra's body.

Like I said, my wife had been holding out on me for months, and I must admit that Kendra was looking sexy as hell. I had almost forgot my wife was outside in the car. I was definitely ready to go up in her ass. I knew for a fact that Kendra got some good pussy, and she knew how to suck dick. My thoughts were interrupted by a hard smack on the side of my face. I pulled the car over, then looked at my wife. I almost forgot who she was and hit her ass back.

"What the hell are you putting your hands on me for?" I snapped, looking her dead in her face.

"What the fuck is red lip prints doing on your face and neck!" my wife said, smacking me again. I couldn't believe that bitch had left her lip prints on me. I had forgot she had on lipstick, because I was thinking with my dick and not my head.

"Sam kissed me," I lied.

"Who the fuck do you are think you are talking to? Your black ass is lying," she yelled as she began to swing wildly. My wife could fight her ass off. That was why I hated when her ass got mad. She was like a mini Tyson. I finally was able to get control of her hands.

"Baby, calm down. Why would I be messing with Kendra when I know you are right outside? That don't even make sense," I said, looking at my wife. I knew for a fact that she didn't believe me. I was one of the best lawyers in the Midwest, but I could never get one over on my wife. It was like she saw right through my ass.

"Take me home, and your ass better find somewhere to go tonight, because you better not think about bringing your ass home. You can go back to that bitch, for all I care," she said. I could see the hurt and pain in her eyes, and I knew she was tired of dealing with my shit. When we finally made it to our home, Sharon damn near hopped out of the car before I stopped. I climbed out quickly and followed her. She ran to the door and tried to shut it in my face.

"I was not playing with your ass when I said you need to find a place to stay tonight. You and I absolutely cannot be in the same house tonight, because my temper is out of control right now and it's taking everything I have not to punch you dead in your shit right now. So I'm asking you nicely to please get the hell out of our house," she said. Then she stormed off to our bedroom and slammed the door.

I stood there for a while before I left out of the house. I drove aimlessly for hours before I ended up in front of Kendra's house. I knew this might get me in deeper trouble, but I was thinking with my little man instead of my head right now. I had needs that she was willing to meet for me. I parked inside of her garage, then entered the house from there. I made my way into her bedroom, and she was lying in the bed with nothing on but them red heels she had on earlier.

She licked her fingers, then began to play with her pussy. My dick instantly sprang to life and was at full attention. She began to pat her clit, and her eyes rolled to the back of her head. I took off all my clothes, then walked over to her. I pulled her to the edge of her bed, then dove headfirst into her pussy. I sucked on her clit while inserting two fingers inside of her pussy. I continued to run laps on her clit with my tongue as she pushed my face deeper into her pussy.

She moaned out my name as she came inside my mouth. I was ready to just fuck the shit out of her, but she had other plans.

She pushed me up against the wall, then squatted in front of me. She took me in her mouth and then played with her pussy with her left hand. Kendra was the freak of all freaks; sex with her was almost better than with my wife. My wife had the best pussy ever, but Kendra knew how to please a man in the bedroom. She was freaky as hell and always into it. Her pussy stayed wet the entire time. She took all ten inches of me into her mouth, then began to smack her lips down my shaft. She repeated the process again, and I nearly exploded in her mouth.

I pulled her up, had her get on all fours on the bed. I entered her soaking wet hole; I began to long stroke her. She threw that pussy back at me, and then we began to pick up our pace. She clutched her pussy walls down on my dick, and I nearly lost my mind. If I didn't love my wife so fucking much, I would definitely wife Kendra because of the way her ass was making me feel right now. She told me to lie on the bed; then she got on top and slid down on my pole. She rode my dick, and I felt myself about to come.

"Oh, shit. I'm about to come, baby!" I yelled.

She jumped from on top of me, then took me in her mouth. I shot my seed down her throat. She went into the bathroom, cleaned herself off, and then did the same for me. We got under the covers, then went to sleep. A few hours later, I was awakened by her warm mouth on my pole. I lost count of the many times we had sex that night. I loved my wife, but a nigga had needs. I'd figure out how to make shit up to my wife in the morning, but tonight I was going to enjoy this warm, tight pussy Kendra was offering up.

Zoe

Dontae didn't say much to me after we ran into Kevin at the engagement party. He was obviously pissed at me, and I didn't even do anything. I was so tired of him taking his anger out on me. He thought that I still wanted Kevin, which I didn't at first, but now I knew for sure I had made the wrong decision. Kevin was all I seemed to think about nowadays. He treated me so good, and I gave it all up because I thought I was in love with Dontae. It was crazy seeing him with all these different women: first, Sam and now some other girl.

When we made it home, I stripped down to my birthday suit and quickly got in the shower. I cried a little bit and thought about my life and where it was heading. I was pregnant with Dontae's baby, and I was not sure that we were going to be together. There was a knock on our bathroom door; then it opened. Dontae pulled the shower curtain back and stepped in with me. He stood behind me—I guessed he was staring at my body—and began to caress my breasts and ass. I wanted so badly not to be turned on, but he knew how to make my body do what my brain didn't want to do.

He dropped down to his knees and placed my leg over his shoulder. He placed his mouth on my kitty, then began to bring me so much pleasure. Moans escaped my mouth as my fluids mixed with the shower water and slid down his throat. He entered me from behind; he quickly brought both of us to an orgasm. We washed our bodies and got in bed. It was moments like this that made me so confused when it came to Dontae. I loved him so much, but I really hated how bipolar he got sometimes.

We drifted off to sleep, with him holding me tightly. A little later I jumped out of my sleep because it felt like someone was watching me. When I sat up, Dontae was standing over me, staring down at me. I got nervous because he had this crazed look in his eyes.

"Baby, what's wrong?" I asked nervously.

He didn't respond right away. He just continued to stare at me with a look I had never seen before. "You want to leave me, don't you?" he finally asked.

"What are you talking about, baby? I am here with you, so why would you ask me that? I don't want to leave you," I said as I began to caress his arms to make him feel comfortable.

"Don't touch me! You want to be back with that nigga Kevin. You want to leave me and raise my baby with that nigga, don't you?" he asked, getting in my face.

"Sweetie, please, calm down. I want to raise our child only with you. Where is this coming from?" I said to him.

"Don't tell me to calm down. I seen how you kept staring at him at the party. You want him back. I know you do," he said and slapped me in my face.

I sat there for a moment, in shock. This was the second time this man had put his hands on me, and there for damn sure was not about to be a third time. I jumped out of the bed and slapped his ass back.

"Don't you ever put your fucking hands on me again! I am not that bitch that will just allow a man to whip my ass. You got the wrong one, nigga. You have to go!" I shouted, then headed straight for the front closet, where his luggage was. He was right on my heels, mumbling some shit under his breath. I didn't care what his crazy ass was saying, but he was getting the hell out of my house today. I stormed back in the bedroom and began to pull his shit out of the drawers. "You have to get the hell out of my house right the hell now! I will not allow you to put your hands on me again!" I snapped.

He ran up behind me, then grabbed me by my hair and threw me on the bed. He immediately jumped on top of me so I could not move. He slapped me three more times on both sides of my face. I felt dizzy as ever at this point.

"I am not going anywhere, bitch. You got me fucked up! I love you, and until I get tired of being with you, your ass is mines," he said, then threw me on the floor. I slid into the corner of the dresser and felt a sharp pain shoot from my back through my stomach. He ran over to me, then kicked me in my stomach twice. "You want me to leave so you could have that nigga in my shit, taking care of my baby, and fucking on my pussy. That shit is not going to happen. You belong to me," he said, bending down to where I was.

By this time, I was crying hysterically because I was in so much pain.

"Shut the fuck up and get in the bed," he said, pulling me up by my hair.

I limped over to my bed, but then something in me clicked. I refused to let this nigga beat my ass without my fighting back. I spun around, then began to rain punch after punch all over his body. He tried to gain control of me, but I was moving too quick for his ass. All of a sudden, he kicked me so hard in my stomach that I flew across the room and hit my head on the wall. The next thing I knew, everything went black.

When I woke up about an hour later, I was in so much pain and the bedroom was a mess, but I didn't see Dontae anywhere in sight. I pulled the covers back, and that was when I noticed all the blood. I knew immediately something was wrong with my baby. I ran into the living room, and Dontae was sitting on the couch, and it looked like he had been crying. He looked up at me and was about to apologize until he saw all the blood on me. We both sprang into action, and we rushed to the hospital.

When I arrived at the hospital, they immediately admitted me, then checked my cervix and gave me an ultrasound. I had miscarried, and that became the worst day of my life. When the doctor told me the news, I turned my back to him and began to cry my eyes out.

"It is okay, baby. We can get pregnant again," Dontae said.

I looked at Dontae like he was crazy as hell. I would never take his ass back.

"Go away! And don't you ever bring your ass back around me. We are done! Do you hear me? Done!" I snapped at Dontae. The only reason he complied was that the doctor and a nurse were in the room.

The doctor gave me an X-ray because I kept complaining of pain in my ribs. It was later found that Dontae had cracked one. I couldn't believe I had stooped so low. The doctor told me I would have to stay in the hospital for a while. That afternoon I was questioned by the police, because the doctor had told them he thought I was experiencing domestic violence. I denied the allegation. I thought Dontae should pay for what he did, but I didn't want to see him in jail.

When I woke up in the hospital the next day, I had a room full of flowers and balloons, all sent by Dontae's sorry ass. Kevin and the crew walked in shortly after. I had spoken to Bria last night to let her know I had had a miscarriage, but I hadn't told her how it happened. I was actually happy to see Kevin's face. I had missed him like crazy. I chopped it up with everyone for a while before they left Kevin and me by ourselves.

"So you got pregnant by dude and you letting him beat your ass?" Kevin questioned me.

"Why would you say that? He doesn't hit me," I lied.

"Zoe, you have bruises on the side of your face, and I overheard the nurse talking about how you have a cracked rib. I know you, Zoe, and I know every inch of your face. Just because you are dark, you can barely see the bruises, but I noticed them," he said, and I began to cry.

"I should have never left you, Kevin. I miss you so much," I said truthfully.

"Honestly, Zoe, I miss you too. I don't know if we could ever be together, but I am here for you," he said, then kissed me on my forehead. "You need to get your shit together and leave dude's ass alone," he said.

"Trust me, I'm done with him. I just hope that one day you can find it in your heart to forgive me and take me back," I told him.

I had decided to put myself out there because at this point I really didn't want to be alone, and I really did miss Kevin. And I definitely hated seeing him with Sam. I loved Dontae—he was my first love—but I couldn't see myself being with him, because he was abusive. I had never seen signs of him being this way before; I didn't see them until we got back together.

"I forgive you, Zoe," he said, then walked out of the room.

I fought back the tears that were threatening to slip from my eyes. Kevin didn't want me anymore. The crew all came back to say their good-byes, then left the hospital. A few hours passed; then Dontae came to see me.

"Can we talk?" he asked.

I was hesitant at first, but I guessed I could hear him out.

Kevin

It had been about six months since everything went down with Zoe and her visit to the hospital, and since Sam's mom had dropped that secret on everybody. That shit had been crazy as ever, because I would have never guessed that Mr. Peterson was Sam's dad. Now that I saw Sam and Mr. Peterson together all the time, I could help but notice their very strong resemblance. Speaking of Sam, I had been spending a lot of time with her. It was nothing serious. We just fucked all the time, but that was all I wanted from her. She kept pressing the issue of us getting back together, but that shit would never happen. I just couldn't trust her. Initially, I had thought I missed her. I had even entertained the thought of us being together, but when we started having sex again, I'd realized that was the only thing I missed about her.

Sam was still stuck on being on that high school shit, and we were all about to be twenty years old this year. I was on my grown man shit, and I needed a woman who was on the same thing. Plus, I had started to notice that something was not quite right with her. There had been more than one time that I had caught her having a serious argument with herself, and when I had asked her what was going on, she just brushed that shit off. I had stepped back some after that. And so had she, because she couldn't have sex for long without being in a relationship.

Imani was different. She loved to have fun with no strings attached, and that was what I was looking for right now, because obviously, being a good, faithful nigga was not good for me. Imani had a lot going for her. For starters, she was in college and was studying nursing, and she was already a medical assistant. She wanted to settle down eventually, but right now she wanted to have just a casual relationship, because she didn't want anything to get in the way of her finishing school. Both of the women I chose had cheated on me, and that shit had me feeling some type of way.

I had been talking with and texting Zoe since the day I left the hospital. I was actually still in love with her and missed her ass like crazy. I mean, I had really thought that she was the one for me, and I actually still kind of did. I just thought she had made a mistake. I had thought about taking her back and trying to work things out with her, but right now my heart wouldn't allow me to do that. She had taken that nigga back after a month of being away from him.

She claimed it was because I didn't want her and she didn't want to be alone, but I didn't know if I believed that bullshit. About a month ago I had finally moved into my own place. I still hadn't told Sam where I was staying, and I didn't plan to, either. I didn't need her ass popping up and acting crazy and shit.

I decided to get up and grab some food for Imani and me. She was coming down for a few days to visit me, and I was happy because I needed to get my dick wet. I had been occupying my time with Corey and his dad. We were about to open up a shopping plaza, and Corey's dad wanted Corey and me to run it, so we were constantly in business meetings. We were trying to get David to go into business with us, but he was talking about how he wanted to finish college first and play football. That nigga loved him some football. Corey's dad had been teaching us how to successfully run a business without us having to be there all fucking day, every day.

I decided to go grab some Chinese food from this joint called William Ho's. On my way out of the restaurant with my takeout, I spotted Zoe's bitch-ass nigga Dontae walking out of the fitness center. My blood instantly began to boil, because his bitch ass was a woman beater. Even though Zoe continued to deny everything, I knew what I saw and she had multiple bruises on her face that day. And why else would she cry when I told her what I saw? I put my food in the car and then jogged over to him.

"So your weak ass like hitting women, huh?" I said as I walked up to him.

"Nigga, get out my fucking face with that bullshit. What goes on between me and my woman don't concern you," he said, trying to walk around me.

"Now, nigga, what you do to Zoe definitely concerns me, especially you putting your weak-ass hands on her," I snapped.

"Nigga, you heard what the fuck I said, and I'm not going to repeat myself. Zoe is my bitch, not yours. Are you mad she chose me?" he said, laughing like some shit was funny. I wanted to beat his ass right then and there, but I held my composure.

"Yeah, whatever. You put your hands on her again, yo' ass going to see me, no doubt," I said, and I walked off.

I should beat that nigga's ass right now, I thought. The only thing that saved that ass was the fact that she was still with the nigga, but I thought I would bring that shit to an end real soon. I missed her, and she truly had my heart.

Part 2

Chapter Twenty-one

Mo

I had not spoken to my father in almost nine months. Every time he came over, I ignored his ass completely. I had not talked to my mom for a while, either, but I had ended up forgiving her because it had not been her responsibility to tell us what was going on. It had been my dad's place. My mom had told me everything that went down, but I still felt like my father was wrong. No matter how much he claimed he didn't want to hurt me and Sam, he should have told us when we were children. I had always wanted a brother or a sister, and to know that I had had one all these years but hadn't known it pissed me off. I could not understand for the life of me how they'd been able to hide a secret this big for so long.

Sam and I had gotten even closer since finding out we were sisters. She always talked about all the time she and our dad spent together. I was happy for her, because she was now getting to experience all the things I did when I was younger. When I was a child, and up until the day my father's secret was exposed, I thought my dad was the best man in the world. Now I saw he was just like all these no-good niggas out here.

My mom and dad had been on bad terms for about three months. He hadn't even stayed at the house, but they had eventually got their shit together, and now they were stronger than ever. Corey and I had been trying to figure out what type of wedding to have. At first, I had wanted this extravagant wedding, with my father walking me down the aisle. Now I just wanted to fly out to Vegas with my best friend and sister. Corey was not feeling that, because he wanted all our family and friends to be able to attend and see us get married, but right now, I was not feeling my father, so it was not looking too good for that scenario.

Somehow, Tremaine had got my number, and he had been blowing me up. The way he had acted before I stopped seeing him, I would have thought his ass would let go without a problem, but he had had me fooled. He kept asking me to meet with him so we could talk, so I decided to finally meet up with him and see what the hell he wanted. I pulled up in the parking area of McGovern Park and walked over to his brand-new Lexus. He got out of the car and then tried to hug me, but I stepped back. Corey was very possessive, and I didn't need to give him a reason to act up.

"Why did you need to see me, Tremaine, and how did you even get my number?" I said with much irritation.

I regretted messing with Tremaine. For starters, we had not messed around that long, and yet he refused to let go; and on top of that, messing with him was totally out of character for me. I was not the type of woman who would sleep with somebody like that. I knew that my heart belonged to Corey, but I had just wanted to make him feel the hurt I had felt when I found out about him and Sam, so I had basically used Tremaine. I hadn't known his sex was going to be that damn good—otherwise, it would have been a one-night thing—but at the time I could not get enough of him.

"Aw, baby girl, don't be like that. I can't get a hug?" he asked.

"Tremaine, get to the point, or I am leaving now," I said, rolling my eyes at him.

"I want you back, Mo. How could you just drop me for a nigga that slept with your sister?"

When those words left his mouth, they hit me hard, because I knew something was up.

"First of all, Corey and I were not together when he and Sam did what they did, and for that reason, I chose to forgive him, not that it is any of your business, anyway. How did you know that the girl he slept with was my sister? I never told you that, because at the time I didn't know she was my sister. So who you talking to that's telling you all my fucking business?" I snapped.

"Fuck all that bullshit. That nigga don't deserve you, point-blank, period," he said as he walked up on me and tried to kiss me. He grabbed both of my arms and pinned me against the car. "It's only a matter of time before I have you again. I know that little nigga don't make your body feel like I make it feel," he said as he rubbed his hard erection against my stomach. "You see what your sexy ass do to me?" He licked my ear, then trailed kisses down my neck. "I miss you, girl," he said, staring down at me.

I pushed him away from me, and he had this shocked-ass look on his face.

"Look, you stay your ass away from me. I guess that ass whupping Corey gave you was not enough. And whoever the bitch is that is feeding you information, that's who you should be with, because there is absolutely no hope for me and your ass. If you call me again, I will get a restraining order put on your ass for stalking. My father is a lawyer, and he would do whatever it takes to get rid of your ass," I said, then stormed over to my car.

"Whatever. Your ass will be begging to come back to me," he yelled after me.

I got in my car and immediately put his ass on the block list. One of these bitches in my circle was on some foul shit, and I bet I could just about guess who the hell it was. I knew for sure that Bria would never cross me like that, so that left only Sam and Zoe. When I found out who the hell it was, they would be cut off, because I was tired of playing nice.

Sam

I had been spending a lot of time with my father since I had found out who he was, and I could not be happier. My mom had been doing her best to hook my dad. He had been spending a lot of nights with my mom, until he decided he wanted to go back to his wife. That shit wouldn't last for long if I had my way. Mom and I were still working on a way to ruin their marriage, and a way to get rid of Monique for good. We had finally decided to just get rid of both of those bitches permanently.

I had been spending a lot of time with Kevin. We had had so much sex that I had lost count. I had completely gotten rid of Brian, because I wanted to show Kevin that I was able to be with one man. I really loved that man with everything in me, and if I had to change to get him, then so be it. I couldn't believe how much his sex had changed. Kevin knew exactly how to please every inch of my body. If he had been doing that shit from the start, we probably would have never had any of the problems we had. I gave it to my man however he wanted it, wherever he wanted it, and whatever hole he wanted to stick it in. I didn't want him to have to go anywhere else to get anything. I wanted to show him that I could be everything he wanted me to be.

I had finally gotten Kevin to take me somewhere other than my bed. We had decided to go to the Cheesecake Factory to get some dinner. I met him up there, and we walked in together. When we were walking to our seats, we walked past a table that had four dudes sitting at it. One of the dudes and Kevin exchanged head nods, and of course my nosy ass wanted to know who he was.

"Who was that?" I asked.

"That is the nigga Mo was messing with when she and Corey split up. His name is Tremaine," he said.

That bitch could definitely pull her a sexy-ass man. I needed to speak with Tremaine to see where his head was, because I could definitely use him as a pawn to make Mo's life a living hell. See, first I wanted her and her mother to suffer; then hopefully, both of those bitches would just kill themselves. I had to get Tremaine alone so that I could hook his ass. We ordered drinks and an appetizer, and then the waiter walked off.

"So are we going to your place or mine tonight?" I asked, hoping he would say his. I was trying to do things the right way, so I hadn't followed him to find out where he was staying, but if he kept playing, I'd have to take matters into my own hands.

"Your place, but I can't stay all night. I got some shit I need to do early in the morning," he said.

"What does that mean? And why can't I just come to your place?" I asked.

"I'm not ready for all that yet, Samariah," he said.

I knew he was getting frustrated, because that was the only time he said my full name. I dropped the subject because I didn't want to piss him off. He had already gotten a little distant, but ever since I started sucking his balls and dick at the same time, he had started to spend more time with me. We finished our food, then paid the bill. Tremaine and his friends were leaving at the same time. I noticed that Tremaine was heading to the bathroom, while his friends were walking toward the exit.

"Hey, baby, I'm going to head to the bathroom. Then I'll be leaving. You can just meet me at my place," I told Kevin, hoping he would fall for it, because I needed to talk to Tremaine tonight. Kevin agreed, then walked off. I waited until Kevin was out the door before I headed to the bathrooms. Before I could make it back there, Tremaine was coming out. I was pretending to look for something in my purse when I ran into him. He said, "Excuse me," then gave me this sexy-ass smile. I smiled back, then asked him what his name was, and he told me. I decided to get straight to the point, because I had to get back to my man.

"I think you are very sexy, Tremaine. Do you have a girlfriend?" I asked.

"No, but it looks like you got a nigga. I saw you with that nigga Kevin," he said.

"That's not my man. We are just friends. But that don't mean I don't have room for more," I said seductively. "You know you like what you see," I added, and I modeled in front of him.

We exchanged numbers, and he told me to contact him whenever I was free. I definitely planned to, because I had shit I needed to get done, and I planned to use his ass to help me.

Chapter Twenty-two

Sam

I contacted Tremaine a week after we first met, and we decided to meet up the following day. I made sure to put on an outfit the screamed "I wanted to fuck." Although I didn't want Tremaine like that, it was still not a bad idea to try him out. I wanted to see what Monique had let go. I made sure everything was together, and then I walked out of the house. I hadn't heard from Kevin since the night he left my house, and I was not feeling that shit at all. He wasn't responding to any of my text messages, either, which pissed me off. He had made me fall deeper in love with him, and I refused to let him be with anyone else.

I pulled up to Tremaine's place and texted him to let him know I was outside. He opened the door and waved at me. He was looking good as hell, and I was ready to jump on his ass right now, but I had a plan I needed to stick to. I hadn't had sex since I last saw Kevin, and Brian really was done with my ass. He said I played too many games.

Tremaine's caramel skin complexion was smooth, and his hair was lined up to perfection. I couldn't lie. He was giving Kevin a run for his money. I might just keep him all to myself. I greeted him with a tight hug, making sure my breasts pressed firmly against his chest. He smelled so good. This man was making it hard for me to stay focused right now, and you know Miss Kitty was just acting a fool. She was screaming to be touched. When I entered the house, I instantly smelled food.

"I made us some dinner, so I hope you are hungry," he said, giving me an award-winning smile as we walked into the kitchen.

I wanted to say, "Yes, I'm hungry for some of that dick."

"Yes, I can definitely eat," I said. I had lost a lot of weight during the months that I was in the hospital, but I had gained that all back. My body was perfect again, and I even had a six-pack now. I had been working out to control my anger, because if not, somebody would have been dead by now—particularly Mo or her mom. Speaking of dead, I still had not found Eric's bitch ass, but when I did, that ass was mine.

Tremaine motioned for me to have a seat at the table. "You look very good, Ms. Sam," he told me, checking out my body while placing some pan-seared salmon with risotto and asparagus in front of me. He grabbed a cool bottle of white zinfandel and poured us each a glass. Then he sat down. I could tell he was a little older than I was by the way he carried himself.

"So are you dating anyone right now?" I asked him.

He cleared his throat. "Um, no, I'm not anymore. It ended badly," he said. He tried to hide the irritation in his voice, but I still noticed it.

"Sorry to hear that," I said, not wanting to press the issue. I knew sooner or later I would get it all out of him.

We ate our dinner and talked about a bunch of bullshit that I didn't care to talk about anymore. Once we were done eating, he cleared the table, and then we sat down in the living room to watch a movie. Tremaine's house was very nice and clean. It looked like a woman had helped him decorate, because although it was a bachelor pad, it had its share of femininity to it. I decided not to play any games with him and got straight to the point. I was horny as hell, and I needed my fix. I just hoped he was able to meet the challenge.

I placed my hand on the crotch of his pants and began to caress it, and to my surprise, he was already hard. It was nice to know we were thinking the same thing. I stood up and dropped between his legs, then unbuckled and unzipped his pants. He stood up and pulled them off, and his pole was the most beautiful thing I had ever seen. It was as big as hell, and you could see the veins popping out, he was so hard. I took all of him in my mouth, and the rest was history. We sucked and fucked each other for about two hours; then I fell asleep in his arms.

After about two weeks of me spending time with Tremaine, he spilled the beans on everything that had happened between him and Mo. Also, told me that he had beat Corey's ass. I eventually told him who I was, and he told me he would help me destroy their relationship—not because he wanted Mo back, not because his ass was all into me now, but because he hated Corey and he didn't want to see that nigga happy. With the three of us against those bitches, they didn't stand a chance.

Bria

David and I decided to go to Olive Garden, which was one of our favorite places to eat. We were back to the old couple we used to be, but even stronger. It turned out that our little man happened to bring us closer together, after all. David loved that little boy with everything in him, and he looked more and more like David as he got older. My baby didn't look like me at all. He was eight months now, and he was the cutest, chubbiest baby ever. David's parents had him for a week. They had taken him down South to visit some of their relatives. We had a little vacation time since he was gone, so we had decided to make the best of it.

I excused myself so that I could go to the bathroom. When I was walking back to the table, I heard some ghetto-ass girl cursing some nigga out. *Bitches just don't know how to act*, I thought. When I got closer to my table, I realized it was my man who was arguing with some bitch. I instantly got pissed and was ready to tear some shit up. I couldn't see who the girl was, but I was for damn sure about to find out.

"You all up in Olive Garden, eating good and shit, but you can't return none of my phone calls. You back with your ugly-ass baby mama, and now you don't know a bitch," the girl snapped.

"Bitch, get the fuck out of my face before I embarrass your ass in this bitch. You just mad because I don't want your bum ass," David said, clearly irritated.

"What the hell is going on over here?" I asked. David looked like he was about to piss on himself, and that ugly-ass bitch David had cheated on me with was standing there with a smirk on her ugly-ass face. I was ready to beat that bitch's ass, because for one, the bitch was talking mad shit when I had my baby, and for two, this ho obviously didn't know how to let go.

"Oh, I am glad baby mama is here so that I can share the good news with her as well," she said, with this ugly-ass look on her face.

"David, what the hell does this rat want? You better get her ass in check, because you know my patience is very thin," I said, trying with everything in me not to punch the shit out of her.

"I was just about to tell David that he needs to come see his son, who is three months old, by the way. My son has not seen his father yet. You need to come sign this birth certificate and come be with your real family," she announced.

My heart instantly broke, because I knew there was a chance that her baby could actually be his. The crazy thing was when I saw her at the park months back, she had a little stomach, but I thought it was because she was a little chubby. He had told me that he slept with this rat a few times after we split up, but he had also told me he used protection each time.

"David, you better pray to the good Lord above that her baby is not yours," I snapped.

"Oh, baby, my son is definitely his, honey. You are the one he needs to be getting a test for," she said.

All I saw was red when she said that, because I knew for a fact that we shared a son. After all, he was the only man I had ever been with; he was my first everything. I had gone through hell and back and had still found the courage to take him back after he hurt me so badly. I hated bitches like her. She didn't have any class about herself. She did this shit in public, and she absolutely did not care. Well, I was about to stoop to the ho's level, because right now she had embarrassed me, and she was trying to break up the family that we had worked so hard to build.

I picked up the bottle of wine off the table next to us and slapped that bitch on the side of her head with it before anyone could protest. She hit the floor, and I jumped on top of her and began to throw blow after blow. I took all my anger and hurt out on her. I literally blacked out. I thought about all the nights I had cried over David when we were split up. I thought about how lonely I had felt, and how bad my heart had ached over him. It was not her fault that David had chosen to step out on me, but she felt my wrath because of him. It was not until that very moment that I realized I was holding on to all the pain that our breakup had caused me.

David and the restaurant manager were finally able to pull me off her. She was not dead, but she was lying there like she was. David threw me over his shoulder and rushed me out of the restaurant. He put me in the passenger seat of the car and strapped me in with my seat belt. I was still in a daze at this point.

"Bria, do you hear me?" David asked me after he had climbed behind the wheel and was pulling out of the parking lot.

"No," I said as tears started to pour out of my eyes. I never in a million years thought this was where our relationship would be. I thought we had that one-of-a-kind love, the perfect little relationship, but I was dead wrong.

"I said you can't be letting people get you that upset. You could have been arrested behind this shit. And you hit her with a bottle! You went too far, Bria," he said.

I looked at him like he had lost his damn mind. Why did he even care how badly I had hurt that bitch?

"What? You still want to be with her? I guess you already knew that the ho was pregnant. You just didn't tell me. This shit is all your fucking fault. You wanted to be out here, slinging your dick all over Milwaukee," I said as I got mad all over again. I punched his ass in the side of his face.

He pulled over, and I unhooked my seat belt and began to punch his ass all over his body. He was finally able to restrain me.

"Calm your little ass down. And you better keep your damn hands to yourself, before I knock your little ass out. Now, I know you're mad, but you haven't even given me a chance to explain anything to you!" he snapped.

"Explain what, David? How you cheated on me, and now she's claiming you got a three-month-old baby? How you was still fucking this ho when you was claiming you wanted to be back with me? Or how you have broken my heart once again and you want to tell me a lie so I won't leave your sorry ass?" I said. "Well, I am done, because I absolutely cannot go through the baby mama drama with you and your weak-ass baby mama." I got out of the car and slammed the door. He got out and ran behind me.

"Baby, she does not have my baby, and I honestly didn't know she was even pregnant. When we got back together, I cut all ties with her," he said, and I believed him. It was just that right then I wasn't in the right frame of mind, and I felt like killing him and his little bitch, so I needed to get away before I did something I would regret. I flagged down a cab, and he stopped right in front of us. David grabbed my arm.

"David, please let me go. I need some time to myself," I said as I snatched my arm from him, then dashed to the cab. He tried to stop me, but it was too late.

Through tears, I told the driver to take me to my parents' house. I cried the entire way. It was late when I made it to their house, so I used my key and went straight to my bedroom. I cried my eyes out until I fell asleep. I guessed there was no such thing as happy endings.

Kevin

Zoe called me and asked me to pick her up the night I left Sam's house. She was crying and sounded like she was in trouble. When I got to the gas station, she was hiding in the bathroom, with nothing on but a wife beater. I ran over to her, picked her up, and put her in my car. I walked over to the driver's side and got in. I inspected her face and body. She had blood pouring out of a cut above her eye, and her neck had scratches all over it. I also noticed that she had bite marks all over her breasts and chest area.

"Zoe, baby, what happened to you?" I asked as I pulled her onto my lap.

She calmed herself down enough so that she could tell me what happened. "He beat me because of you. He always beats me because of you," she cried. She had finally admitted that this nigga had been putting his hands on her.

"What do you mean, because of me?" I asked.

"He would always accuse me of still wanting to be with you. He thought I wanted to leave him for you. I was asleep, and he went through my phone and found the messages between me and you," she cried.

She told me that he had pulled the covers off her, raped her, and beat until she was unconscious. When she'd woken up, he was lying next to her, asleep, and with a bottle of Remy in his hand. She said she had then grabbed her phone and ran out of the house and called me. We drove to my house in silence; the only thing you could hear was her faint sniffles. When we entered my house, I immediately turned on the shower and told her to get in. I got in with her and washed all the blood off her face. Next, I washed her body, then gave her a towel so that she could dry off. I led her into my bedroom and gave her a T-shirt to sleep in. We got in bed, and I held her close. She cried for a while; then she eventually fell asleep.

Once I was sure she was sleeping well, I threw on some sweats and a shirt, grabbed my keys, and climbed into my car. I made sure my gun was under my seat and then headed to the house Zoe and I had once shared. This nigga was about to die tonight. Once I got to the house, I grabbed my gun and headed to the door. I still had my key from when we lived together, so I let myself in, then crept to the bedroom. I slowly opened the door, but he was not in the bedroom. I checked the rest of the house, but he was nowhere in sight. This nigga definitely had God on his side, because he was definitely about to lose his life tonight. I drove back to my house. When I walked in the bedroom, Zoe was rocking back and forth in the bed and crying.

"What's wrong, bae? Why are you crying?" I asked as I walked over to her, then sat down and rubbed her back soothingly.

"What did you do, Kevin? Did you hurt him? Did you kill him?" she said as she looked into my eyes.

"No, I didn't. I wanted to, because that nigga deserves it for what he did to you," I snapped.

"Kevin, I can't lose you, baby. Please promise me you will never leave. I can't live without you," she said as she cried into my chest.

"I won't leave you, Zoe. I promise. I love you too much," I said truthfully.

"How could you love me after what I did to you?" she said.

"The heart wants what it wants. I can't explain it," I said to her.

"I would never hurt you again, nor would I ever leave you or cheat on you. I am not ashamed to say that I have made a mistake, and I will spend the rest of my life making it up to you if I have to," she cried.

I believed her, and I know y'all might think I'm a dumb nigga, but I wanted to be with her just as bad as she wanted me right then. I'd been sleeping around with these other women, trying to fill the void that only Zoe could fill. I already felt whole, just having her in my presence right then. I honestly believed that she would never step out on me again. I had never felt complete with anyone but her. Not even with Sam. She had come in and stolen my heart like no other. I loved everything about her, and if I could forgive Sam for sleeping with my best friend, I could forgive Zoe for what she did.

"Let me make something clear. Just because I love you don't mean that I am going to keep taking you back. If you even look like you want to cheat, I am leaving you for good, Zoe. I am looking for somebody to build a life with. I don't have time for games. I got plans for us, and I need you to be on board. If you know you aren't ready to be with me, then let's just remain friends. But if you know that you are ready, then we can move forward. But be honest with yourself before you answer that question," I said.

"I knew a long time ago what I wanted. I just went chasing after the wrong man because I was confused about my feelings at the time. My heart was always with you. That's why he tried to beat it out of me. I love you, and with you is where I want to be," she said, then kissed my lips. I didn't think I had ever loved anyone as much as I loved Zoe. I was still a little on edge about taking her back, but I was willing to take the risk.

"I'm not letting this nigga get away with what he did to you, and that's a promise," I told her.

She didn't say anything; she just snuggled up close to me. I was going to kill that nigga when I saw him, and I meant that shit with everything in me.

The following day, Corey, David, and I went over to Zoe's house, packed up all her things, and brought them to my house. We threw her furniture and stuff out because I had completely furnished my place with all brand-new stuff and her stuff was old. We left that bum-ass nigga's shit right at the house. I started to burn all his shit up, but I felt that was being petty. Now I needed to let Sam know that things between her and me were over. I just didn't know how she going to take it.

Chapter Twenty-three

Corey

Mo and I were lying in the bed, chilling for the remainder of the night. I had been at the Plaza all day, signing contracts with business owners who were looking to rent out some of the space we had available. All I had wanted to do was come home, eat, and lie up with my lady. When I made it home, she had made us some fried chicken, macaroni and cheese, and a side salad. That shit had been fire; my baby knew how to get down in the kitchen. Now I was watching TV, and she was reading some book on her Kindle. My phone had alerted me, so I grabbed it to see what was going on. I had a message from an unknown number. When I opened it, a picture popped up. My blood instantly began to boil. I looked over at Mo, and she was just in her own little world, not realizing that shit had just got real.

"We need to talk," I said, snatching the Kindle out of her hand.

"What the hell is your problem? Don't be snatching my shit out of my hand. If you want to talk, just say that, but don't be rude about it," she snapped at me, then rolled her eyes. I wanted to smack her damn eyes out of her head, but she was lucky I didn't hit women.

"You still fucking with that nigga? You trying to send me to jail, aren't you?" I asked, getting in her face.

"What nigga?" she asked, looking clueless and pushing me back some.

"What you mean, what nigga? You got that many you don't know who I'm talking about? You just became a little ho when we broke up, huh?" I asked. When those words left my mouth, I instantly regretted them.

She slapped spit out of my mouth. "Corey, if you ever in your fucking life call me a ho again, we are definitely going to have some problems," she said, on the verge of tears. I could tell that had really hurt her.

"I'm sorry, Monique. That was really disrespectful. I need to know if you are still messing with that nigga, though," I said.

"Corey, you are being really fucking irritating right now. You know damn well that you are the only person I am with. I don't know what your problem is, but you need to just spill it out, because this shit you doing right now isn't cool at all," she said.

"Explain this shit here, then," I said, showing her the picture. Someone had sent me a picture of Tremaine and Mo, and he was all up on her.

Her face dropped when she saw the picture, and she looked guilty as hell.

"You better not say that shit is old, because you were wearing that pink jogging suit from Victoria's Secret that I just recently bought you," I said, staring directly in her eyes.

She remained silent.

"What? The cat got your tongue? You don't know how to speak now?" I asked.

"Corey, I can explain. That is not what it seems. I can promise you that," she said.

"I think I seen all I need to see right about now. You still want that nigga, so I am just going to let you have him. I am tired of fighting over you. There is no explanation good enough that's going to explain this. Why are you even alone with this nigga? Why is anyone able to take a picture of you two together when y'all are not supposed to be around each other?" I said. I stood up to leave.

"Corey, I am not with him. Somehow he got my number, and he was blowing me up. I blocked him, and he would just call me from other numbers. I met up with him to tell him to leave me alone. He got up in my face, talking shit, so I snapped on him and left," she said.

"Why would you even go meet with that nigga? You should have changed your number again, or you could have told me so I could have handled that nigga myself. I think you wanted to see that nigga," I snapped.

"That's not true. I love you. I don't want him. I am tired of changing my number. I am tired of all this damn drama. I just want peace in my life, but it seems like I can never get it," she said through tears.

"Yo, I need some time to think about things, so I'm out," I said. As I headed toward the door, she begged and pleaded with me, but I left.

It really bothered me that Mo could be so damn naive at times. I loved her and I believed her story, but it was frustrating, because she should not have been with that nigga in the first place. It bothered me that someone else knew how good my baby's pussy was. It bothered me that she had kissed this nigga and he had touched all over her body. Thinking about that shit drove me crazy. It made me want to go kill a nigga right now. I had proposed to this girl because I really did love her and wanted to spend a lifetime with her, but her being with that nigga had really put a damper on our relationship. It was harder than I had thought to move past that shit, and obviously, somebody didn't want us to, because they had sent me this picture. I knew eventually I was going to take my ass home, because I still had a skeleton in my closet. I had fucked Sam after Mo and I broke up, and Mo still didn't know about that. I prayed her ass never found out.

She had changed me so much, because I was honestly faithful to her ass. I had never cheated on her. Now, I had done some fucked-up shit, but it had never been when we were together. When I was in high school, I had had plenty of hoes, but I had settled down once I got with her. I was going to have to really get rid of this nigga Tremaine, because he was causing too many problems for me. I decided to go over to Kevin's house to play the game before I took my ass back home. I knew my girl was probably tripping.

Mo

I was so tired of all this fucking drama. It was like a never-ending cycle of bullshit. I was tired of being mad at folks; I just wanted some happiness in my life. Corey had come back home that night, and we had sat and talked about everything and had been able to move forward. Somebody was trying to make my life a living hell, and I was tired of sitting around and letting them.

I had decided to call my father so that we could make up. I was tired of being angry with him, and this was the longest I had ever gone without talking to him. It'd been about nine months that I had been avoiding him. We had agreed that I would stop by to talk. I pulled up to my parents' house and walked to the door. Before I could stick my key in, the door swung open. I fell into my father's arms and just cried for, like, ten minutes straight without saying a word. We went into the house and sat down; then he handed me some tissue.

"Baby girl, I am so sorry for lying to you all these years. Please find it in your heart to forgive me," he said, with much pain in his voice. I knew that not being able to talk to me for all these months had taken a toll on him.

"I forgive you, Daddy, and I am tired of walking around with all this anger. I just want to put all of this behind us and move forward, as long as you promise not to keep anymore secrets," I said.

"I promise," my dad said.

I sat around with him and watched some movies for a few hours before I left to meet up with Bria. She hadn't been back home with David in a few weeks. Honestly, I didn't think that baby was David's, but I guessed only time would tell. When I got to Bria's place, I climbed out of my car. I knocked on Bria's door, and she let me in. She was holding my chubby godson, so I took him from her. She led me into her bedroom, and I sat down on the lounge chair she had in her room.

"So what's been going on, *chica*?" Bria said.

"Nothing much. Just left from seeing my dad," I told her.

"I'm glad you finally made up with him. Your ass should have forgiven him sooner. Everybody makes mistakes," she said.

"You really got your nerve, Bria. Look where you are at. You are back with your parents because David may have gotten someone else pregnant while y'all were broken up. You left him, and you don't even know if the bitch was telling the truth about even having a baby. In my opinion, you are handing your family right to her," I said.

"First of all, I left David because I didn't want to deal with baby mama drama. I can honestly see myself beating her ass every time I see her, because that ho got a smart-ass mouth, and I cannot deal with that," Bria said.

"But you don't even know if the girl actually even had a baby. She could have made that shit up to get on your nerves. And even if she *did* have a baby, who is it to say that it's David's? You need to take your ass home and fight for your family. You give up too easy," I told her.

"You are right, but my heart still feels very broken. I don't know how to let it go," she said, on the verge of tears.

"You let it go the first time, so you can do it this time," I said.

I stayed over there for a few hours, then went home to my man. Whoever that bitch or nigga was who had tried to break us up needed to give it up, because I was not going anywhere and neither was Corey. And when I found out who was behind the bullshit, someone was going to have an ass whupping coming their way, because I was sick of the bullshit.

Bria

I had decided to take my stubborn butt home and make up with David. He had told me that the girl indeed did have a baby, and that he had gone to see the child. He'd taken a picture of the little boy, but when he'd shown it to me, I honestly couldn't tell if the baby was his or not. The baby didn't look like David or the girl, whose name was Meka, by the way. I refused to allow David to spend time with the baby until he got a paternity test. That bitch was not to be trusted, and I honestly thought she just wanted to be with David. He had also told me that she had slept with several men. That was the main reason he had slept with her; he had just wanted an easy fuck, without all the pressure. David was being honest with me now, and even if it hurt my feelings, but I would rather know the truth instead of being lied to.

David was still sleep at the moment, but I was wide awake, because we had some shit to take care of today.

"Baby, get up," I said as I shook him out of his sleep.

"Why are you waking me up? The baby is not here, and we don't have no place to be," he said as he rolled over on his other side.

"We do have somewhere to be, so get dressed and meet me in the living room," I told him.

Ten minutes later, he finally got his yellow ass up and headed to our bathroom. About thirty minutes later, he came downstairs, fully dressed.

"Where are we going?" he asked, obviously irritated and still sleepy.

I pulled out a paternity test and handed it to him. He had this shocked look on his face. I refused to wait months before he got a paternity test; we were about to do this shit right now.

"Really, Bria? This couldn't wait?" he said.

"Hell no, this can't wait. You are going to get a paternity test so that we can move forward with our lives. You acting like you don't want to know if this baby is yours or not," I said, with much attitude.

"Of course I want to know if he is mine. I just don't feel like dealing with all this damn drama," he said.

"Me neither, but it needs to be done, so move your ass and let's go," I said as I stood up.

We walked out to his car. Once in the car, we drove to Meka's house in complete silence. I knew the bitch was at home, because her ass was on W2, and she didn't have shit else to do. I honestly didn't know what the hell David saw in her, because she was not cute and she had absolutely nothing going for her at all. The bitch did have a body, though. I would give her that, but that was about it.

When we finally arrived at her house, I stayed in the car, because I didn't want to be held responsible for what I might do if her ass tried me again. David walked up to the porch and rang the doorbell. His friend Mitch answered the door, with nothing on but some boxers and socks. I shook my head, because this ho had slept with his friend. I didn't know what the two of them said, but a minute later, Mitch disappeared and David remained standing on her porch. Moments later, Miss Rat came to the door.

"What you doing here, David? And why did you bring that ho to my house?" Meka said, loud enough for me to hear.

I just ignored her ass, because I was not trying to go to jail today.

"Look, don't worry about all that. I came to swab little man so I could send this test off to see if he's mine," David said.

"Oh, hell naw. You didn't get a test with that bitch, but you over here trying to test my baby? He is yours, and you are about to be on child support, so you better start paying up," she said, popping some damn gum.

"Look, I am not giving you shit until you take the damn test. I know that DJ is mine, but you just a ho. You over here with one of my friends, and I am supposed to believe little dude is mines? Shit. For all I know, he could be Mitch's baby," David said.

"Fuck you, David. My baby ain't taking shit, and you best believe your ass is going to pay up," she said, and then she slammed the door in his face. I had a feeling this ratchet-ass ho was going to be on that bullshit. We were twenty years old; we should be able to handle shit like this without all the drama.

"Now what?" David said as he got back in the car.

"Look, we tried. If her ass don't want to get a test, then that's her problem," I said.

"I just hope I am making the right decision. I don't want to miss out on my son's life if he is indeed mine," he said.

Hearing those words saddened me, but I sucked it up because I had decided to stay with him. But I refused to play stepmom to a child I didn't even know was my man's baby, and I refused to let David take care of a child he didn't even know was his. Either the bitch got the test or she had better find her another dummy to play Daddy, because this one right here belonged to me. I was not about to play games with that ratchet bitch.

Chapter Twenty-four

Kendra

Tim had practically stayed with Sam and me for three months, until he decided he wanted to go back home to his wife. I knew she didn't have any idea that he had stayed with us, or that Tim and I had been fucking that entire time, but she was about to find out. Sam had come up to me one day and had told me to record Tim and me having sex, and I had done that shit. Now I had proof that we had slept together. I had another surprise for that ass too, but I was not ready to reveal that just yet.

I hadn't heard from Tim since the day he went back to Sharon's black ass, but I bet when she left his ass, he was going to crawl right back to me, and I would be waiting with open arms. I had never loved another man as much as I loved Tim, and I refused to just let him continue to live the life we were supposed to be living together with someone else. I had not even slept with another man in all these years. I had been faithful to him the entire time, and you would think he would appreciate that.

Sam was able to get Sharon's e-mail address out of Monique's phone. Right now I was heading to Tim's office, because I had something to tell him that I could not tell him over the phone. When I walked into his office and asked to speak with Tim, I lied and told the receptionist that I needed to speak with a lawyer about something and that I was referred to Tim by one of his clients. She told me to have a seat and handed me a bottle of water. About ten minutes later, Tim walked out into the lobby, and you would have sworn he saw a ghost. He gave me a fake smile and told me to come into his office. He shut the door and immediately got on my ass.

"What the hell are you doing here, Kendra? I told you my wife's best friend works here!" he snapped. I guessed the receptionist was his wife's best friend.

"Well, you wouldn't answer any of my phone calls. How else was I supposed to get you to talk to me?" I said.

"We have nothing to talk about, unless it concerns my daughter, and since she is twenty years old, there is nothing we have to discuss," he said.

"What you mean, we have nothing to discuss? You can't just pretend like nothing ever happened between us recently," I said.

"What exactly happened between y'all recently?" Sharon said, startling both me and Tim.

I hadn't even heard the door open, and apparently, Tim hadn't, either. I figured I might as well spill the beans to her, since she had shown up. I wasn't expecting to tell her this way. I was just going to send her the video and call it a day, but this was going to be even better. Once I got done telling everything, I knew for sure she was going to leave his ass. I was tired of hiding this secret, and she should know exactly how her man felt about me. When Tim and I made love, he would tell me that he loved me and missed me, so I knew there were some feelings still there for me, and Mrs. Sharon should know.

"Baby, I have no clue what's she talking about, and I have no clue why she's even here. I was just telling her that since our daughter is twenty, we no longer have anything to discuss as far as she is concerned," he said nervously.

"Tim, don't try to stand there and play me. Tell your wife how you were practically staying at my house when you and her split up this last time. Oh, and tell her how you was fucking me and eating my pussy every night the entire time y'all was split up," I said.

"Baby, she is lying. You know I wouldn't do that to you," he said with a straight face.

The receptionist came in just then. I guessed we had gotten too loud. "Sharon, so this must be that bitch who told Mo about Tim's little secret," she said, looking like she wanted to kill me.

"Yeah, that's her, but apparently, my husband still wants this bitch, because according to her, they are still fucking," Sharon said, pissed as hell and looking like she wanted to beat my ass.

"Like I said, she is lying, Sharon. And, Kim, go back out there and do your job. This doesn't concern you," Tim said heatedly. Sharon was about to walk up on me, but Tim stopped her.

"Oh, I'm lying?" I said. "You was all in my bed, telling me you loved me and missed me, and when your wife decided to take you back, now all those feelings conveniently went away? You did not mention Sharon the entire time you was staying with us. Don't try to front like you wasn't happy when you was with me and Sam. We was even going out to eat and things like that as family."

Sharon remained quiet this time; she was just staring at Tim with a look on her face that was so serious that if looks could kill, he would definitely be dead. I decided to push her further. I wanted to get everything out.

"This bitch is dirty," Kim said, shaking her head. I could tell she was there to support her friend, and I knew if anything popped off, she was going to help her friend whup my ass.

"Oh, and just so you know, we are expecting another child, a boy this time," I said as I slammed the sonogram on the table.

Yes, my old ass was six months pregnant, and that was half of the reason I had enough courage to spill everything. I knew that once they realized I was pregnant, they wouldn't put their hands on me. Sharon, Kim, and Tim all looked at my stomach. I wasn't that big, but you could tell I was pregnant.

"The day you decided to go back to your wife is the day you got me pregnant," I said with a smirk.

"Honey, she is lying. I did not get her pregnant, nor did I have sex with her," Tim lied. This man was a good liar. The way he was acting, if I didn't have proof of my pregnancy, I would believe him my damn self.

"You know what, Tim? I am so tired of dealing with this bitch right here and your trifling lying ass. I have stuck by your side for all these years, when you lied about having a baby and everything else your tired ass lied about. Well, I am done. You can go stay with this dirty bitch and spend the rest of your life with her, because I'm done for good," Sharon said. "Oh, and, bitch, don't think for one second that when you drop that baby, I am not whupping that ass, because I am. The only reason you are not getting that ass whipped today is that you are pregnant. Oh, but I am going to do this." She slapped me dead in my face. She then threw the bag she had been holding the entire time at Tim. She stormed out of the office, and he ran right behind her.

I left that office feeling I had accomplished something, because if there was one thing I knew about Tim, it was that he was definitely going to come see me. And when he did, I was going to be ready, because he could never turn down this good pussy. I started to call the police and report that Sharon had slapped me, but I figured I had caused enough problems for the day. Once I got to my car, I sent Sharon the e-mail with the video of me and Tim fucking. I knew for sure that she would be divorcing his ass once she saw that video, and then he would be all mine.

Sharon

I had felt in my heart something was not right the moment Tim and I got back together, but I had ignored my intuition, thinking I was just being paranoid. However, his little bitch had confirmed everything. When she told me she was pregnant by him, my heart had literally been ripped out of my chest. After we had Monique, Tim and I had tried having another baby, but I hadn't been able to get pregnant. We had seen all types of doctors, but when they'd run tests on both of us, everything had come back normal. The doctors couldn't explain to me why I couldn't get pregnant. Maybe it was just God's plan for us to have only one child.

It had been a week since everything went down at Tim's office, and I had been miserable as hell. I had come home that night, had packed up everything that belonged to him, and had sat it in front of our garage. Of course, he had followed me home and had tried to talk me out of leaving him, but at the time I had really been done with him. When he came home the next day, all his shit was still outside and the locks had been changed. I was so torn, because I wanted to file for divorce, but I couldn't find the strength to do so. I had been with this man for twenty-plus years, and it was really hard for me to let go.

The last time we split up, I had reconnected with an old friend of mine who had always wanted to be with me. We would text each other from time to time, just checking on each other, but it was nothing serious. I felt bad about doing even that, but my husband was out doing way more than that. My friend had been really lifting me up this past week, because I had been really sad and I hadn't eaten anything. I had to block Tim's calls, because he would blow my phone up all day and night, and that wasn't doing anything but making me feel worse. I really missed him and wanted to answer his calls. However, he definitely wouldn't learn a damn thing if I took him back this soon.

I really hated that bitch Kendra's guts; she had always been a pain in my ass. I would see all the calls and messages she would send Tim, asking him to come back home or asking him for sex. I had dealt with that shit long enough, and I was honestly tired of it. I had drawn the conclusion that as long as she was in the picture, I could never truly be happy with him.

I knew there was a very strong possibility that the baby was Tim's once I saw that video of them having sex. I had actually believed that there was a possibility that she was lying about them having sex, until I saw with my own eyes that they had. Tim may be a good liar to most people, but he wasn't always that great of a liar to me. I could see right through most of his lies. I honestly hadn't thought he would actually cheat on me with her. Yes, I still considered it cheating even though we were separated. We were separated, not divorced, so his ass had cheated.

I didn't know if I could ever get over the fact that he might possibly have another baby with her. If he had got her pregnant, you could definitely consider us divorced. Until then, I was going to pull myself together and explore my options with my friend, and with whomever else I decided to see. Hell, why not? He didn't have a problem fucking Kendra, so why should I have a problem seeing someone else?

Chapter Twenty-five

Sam

For the first time in a very long time, my mother had finally done something right—she had succeeded in breaking Sharon and my dad up. It'd been about two months since everything went down with them. My mother was eight months pregnant now, and my dad had been around. He never stayed overnight, but he did take her to her doctor's appointments and things like that. He had told me he was excited about having a boy. I believed that once he saw his son, he would definitely make things work with my mother.

Kevin had called me and asked me to meet up. He had been ignoring my calls for about a week straight, but he had started to come around again. We had barely spent time together, but he had still fucked me, and I would suck his dick on random occasions. I felt like today was the day he was going to ask me to make things official with him. Shit, he'd probably even ask me to move in with him. Who wouldn't want to be with me? I looked damn good, and my body was off the chain. My pussy and head game were the best.

I was going to have to break things off with Tremaine, though, and I was actually starting to feel him. He was a great lover, and he did whatever I told him to do. I could tell at first he was still stuck on Mo, but now I had him eating out of the palm of my hand. I had had him bug Mo until she finally met up with him. I had hidden in the car that was facing them and had taken pictures of them talking. When he had got close to her and had been all over her, I knew we had something.

I had sent the pictures to Corey days later, but that shit obviously hadn't worked. Corey loved that girl, and he was not letting her go. I still planned to fuck her life up the best way I could, because I was so tired of her getting whatever she wanted. I knew that she was my sister, but I could not get over the fact that she had had the childhood I always wanted. I also couldn't get over the fact that Corey loved her the way he did, and I wanted someone to love me like that. It seemed like everybody loved her, while I was just pushed to the side.

Kevin finally walked into the café we had decided to meet at. I stood up and gave him a hug. I tried to kiss him, but he kind of sneak blocked it. We sat down, and he had this serious look on his face, so I knew the discussion we were about to have was serious.

"Hey, Sam, I brought you here because I need to talk to you about something serious," he said.

"What's that?" I smiled and grabbed his hand.

"Sam, I have been having so much fun with you lately, and honestly, I never thought that we would reconnect like we did," he said.

"Well, I am glad we did. I have fallen deeper in love with you, and I can honestly see us spending a lifetime together," I said, gripping his hand tighter. I could see his demeanor changing, almost like he was uncomfortable or something.

"Sam, I love you, but I don't love you like that. I love you as a friend," he said.

"Well, you can learn to love me like that. You did once before, and you can do it again," I said.

"Sam, I don't want to be with you on that level. Zoe and I are back together, and we are going to work on improving our relationship. I brought you here so that I could call things off with you. I am committing to my girl," he said.

Tears poured out of my eyes. "You don't mean that, Kevin. You love me. You want to be with me. We could make this work. I'll do whatever you want me to do," I said in between sobs.

"I'm sorry that I led you on this far, Sam. I never had any intentions of being with you like that. I can't help how I feel about her. I really love that girl, Sam, and she is who I want to be with," he said.

"But what about me? What does she have that I don't?" I asked.

"She has my heart. I have to go, Sam, and again, I am very sorry," he said as he stood.

"Kevin, please, don't do this to me again. I love you. I can't live or breathe without you," I said.

"Sam, you are going to be all right. You are a beautiful woman. Someone is going to make you happy, but that someone is just not me," he said before he walked out the door.

I walked into the bathroom and cried my eyes out. I had really thought we had something. I had thought we were going to be together. How could he leave me for that bitch Zoe once again? I had changed for him, and he had still left me high and dry. Words could not express how I felt right now. If she was gone, I bet he would be with me. I called Tremaine and told him I was coming over. I needed someone to help me release some of my stress, and he was the perfect person for the job.

Tim

My life had been a living hell since Kendra had decided she wanted to air all our dirty laundry to my wife. Sharon was absolutely not fucking with me at all. She didn't

answer any of my phone calls, nor did she open the door
when I came by. I had been staying at this condo I had
that I used to rent out, because I wanted to show my wife
that I was sorry and that I would never sleep with Kendra
again. I couldn't say that I was not happy that Kendra
was pregnant with my son. I knew for a fact that the baby
was mine, because Kendra had not slept with another
man in all the years that we were separated. I wished my
wife were the one who was pregnant, but the fact was that
she was not able to make that happen. We had been trying for years, but she had never got pregnant. I hadn't
even been trying with Kendra, and her ass had ended up
pregnant.

Every time I went to the doctor's appointments with
Kendra, she tried to have sex with me. It was very tempting,
because Kendra was fine as hell and she was even more
beautiful since she was pregnant with my baby, but my
heart was with my wife, and I didn't even want to risk her
thinking that Kendra and I were back together. I really just
wanted to be there for my son. I knew this was going to hurt
my wife, but she would just have to accept it.

I refused to give up on my wife. I knew she was pissed
off at me, and I'd let her be that way for a while, but I was
eventually taking my ass home, whether she liked it or not. I
had sat with Monique and had told her about the baby and
about what was going on with her mom and me, and she
had been pretty understanding. She was upset that I had
hurt her mom, but she didn't push me away. She called and
checked on me every day.

I was hungry as hell, so I decided to go to Bar Louie to
grab a bite to eat and a drink. I'd been doing a lot of drinking lately, ever since my wife left me. I had really been sick
since the day everything went down. Normally, when my
wife was mad, she would still text me or communicate with
me somehow, but this time her ass was not fucking with me,
not even a little bit.

I walked into the restaurant and sat down. A pretty little waitress walked up to me and took my order. I ordered a Henny and Coke, with one of the tasty-ass burgers. The waitress came back with my drink right away, then left me with my thoughts. I downed my first drink and had her get me another one. I was just about to take a sip of my second drink when I heard someone laughing. I knew that laughter; I had heard it every day for twentysomething years. I got up and followed the laughter to the other side of the room. There I saw my wife having a good ole time with some nigga. I immediately lost every bit of my mind. I ran over to the table and snatched her ass right up.

"Aye, man, get your hands off her," the guy said as he stood up, ready to fight me if he needed too.

"Nigga, back the fuck off! This is my fucking wife, and her ass don't have no business up in this bitch with you, laughing and shit," I said. I kept my hand on Sharon's arm and tried to lead her to the door, but she refused to budge.

"Tim, you better let me go, before I embarrass your ass in here. We are not together, so I can do whatever the hell I want," she said. I really almost lost my mind when she said that.

"I don't give a fuck if we are separated! Yo' ass belongs to me. I got paper on that ass, so get your shit and let's go," I said.

"Look, man, she obviously is not trying to go with you, so accept it like a man and let it go," dude said.

I let my wife's arm go, walked over to dude, and punched him right in his fucking face. He stumbled back, then looked at me like I was crazy.

"Nigga, don't you ever tell me how to handle my wife," I said.

My wife ran over to the dude with a napkin and began to wipe the blood off his lip. "Are you crazy, Tim? Why would you put your hands on him? I cannot believe you," she said as she continued to help dude out.

"Oh, so you stupid enough to help this nigga. You are my wife. You supposed to have my back," I said, hurt as hell.

She whispered something in the guy's ear, then pulled me outside with her. Once we were somewhere private enough, she began to snap. "Tim, what you need to understand is we are no longer together. You don't own me. Now you brought your ass in that place, showing your ass," she said.

"I'm not trying to hear none of that shit you are talking. You are still my wife, and your ass is not going anywhere. I refuse to watch you be with another man. Who the hell do you think I am? You know damn well I don't play that shit. I'm coming home, and we are going to work out our marriage. End of story," I said.

"I don't want to be with you. You have absolutely no clue how to keep your dick in your pants, and on top of that, you are about to have a baby by someone else. And still you up in here, trying to fight over me. You need to go be with her, and don't worry about what I am doing," she said.

"You heard what I said, Sharon," I said.

"I heard what you said, but that means absolutely nothing to me at this point. I am seriously done with you, and I hope I am making myself clear when I tell you I want a divorce," she said, staring me dead in my eyes. Those words had never left her mouth before, and I could not believe what she had just said.

"You don't mean that," I said, trying to laugh it off.

"Oh, but I do mean that. I am done with you this time, Tim. I have given you the best years of my life, and you showed me your appreciation by getting your baby mama pregnant again. I refuse to keep allowing you to run over me and treat me any way you want. I am not Kendra. I refuse to wait on your ass for twenty years. I don't think you will ever change. You got her pregnant, and y'all are having a boy, something we tried to have for years. I'm done, Tim. Good night," she said, then turned to walk away.

"I know you not like Kendra. At least she know how to wait on a nigga," I said and instantly regretted letting those words leave my mouth. I didn't mean it; I just wanted her to hurt like I was right now.

Sharon stopped in her tracks and turned back around. "Just so we are very clear, I am divorcing your sorry ass," she said. Then she stormed off.

I felt like shit. I might actually lose my wife, and I didn't know if I could live with that reality.

Bria

So the bitch Meka refused to take a paternity test but was constantly calling David, asking him for money. She would come by our house and leave notes on the car, telling him to pay. It got so bad that I was ready to go over to her house and beat her ass again. This ho even had the nerve to egg David's car. I didn't know how much of this shit I could take; this was exactly the type of shit I was trying to avoid. I did not want to deal with this shit, but I loved David, so I was going to stick it out. But something had to give, and I mean ASAP.

I had decided to go to the nail shop to get my fingernails and toes done as a way to relax and get things off my mind. David and the baby had left the house early, so I had got up, cleaned the house, and then left. On my way to the nail shop, I decided to stop at McDonald's to grab a quick bite to eat because I was starving. I decided to go inside because the drive-through was backed up. I placed my order, then went to fill my drink cup. Out of the corner of my eye, I spotted somebody who looked real familiar, so I walked up to get a closer look. That was when I saw Meka holding her son, and she was chowing down. I decided to try to talk to her without all the anger, just so we could try to resolve all this. I grabbed my food and walked toward the back, where the play area was.

When I walked back there, I absolutely could not believe my eyes. David and my son were sitting across from her, and they were eating. David looked up, and our eyes met. He knew there was about to be some drama. He jumped up and ran over to me.

"Baby, it is not what you think," he said.

I looked at Meka, and she was just staring at us with this ugly-ass smirk on her face. If she didn't have that baby in her arms, I would smack the smirk right off her face.

"What am I thinking, David? That you are in here with this bitch, having a good time, when you are not supposed to be?" I said, trying with everything I had to hold in my tears.

"Baby, I promise you that I am not here on a date or anything like that with her. I asked her to meet me here so that the boys could meet and so that I could get her to take the test. That is it," he said, and I believed him. Surprisingly, that ugly bitch remained quiet while we talked.

"Why couldn't you tell me that before you got caught here with her? We told each other that we would not keep secrets from each other," I told him.

"I didn't tell you, because I knew you would go off, like you always do. I'm just trying to figure this shit out because I don't want this to ruin what we have," he said.

I grabbed my baby from his arms. "Well, you better figure it out, because I am tired of the games. I'll see you when you get home." I stepped closer to David and tongued his ass down. When we finally came up for air, she was staring at me with a look that would have killed me if looks could kill.

As I turned to walk off, David slapped me on the ass. That bitch needed to know that she would never be me and that she would never take my place. She was not even on my level. That would teach her ass to mess with somebody whose heart belonged to someone else.

Chapter Twenty-six

Corey

So the couples had decided to go to Red Lobster for dinner. It was Mo and I, Kevin and Zoe, and David and Bria. We all had been going through a lot lately, so this was a much-needed break and time for us to unwind. The girls were talking about DJ's party, which was coming up soon, since he was about to be a year old in two weeks. Kevin and I were telling David about how things were going with business when I spotted something strange out of the corner of my eye.

"Is that Sam?" I said out loud, even though I had intended to say it to myself.

"Where?" Mo said.

I knew she would be pissed when she saw Sam, because she was not alone. She was with Tremaine.

"What the hell is she doing with him?" Mo said as loud as hell. "I knew that bitch was the one who was trying to break us up. I guess that first ass beating I gave her ass wasn't enough." Mo stood up to confront her. Before I could stop her, she was halfway to Sam, with Zoe and Bria hot on her heels.

"Bring your ass here," Mo said as she grabbed Sam by the arm like she was a little child.

You could tell Sam had been caught off guard. Tremaine was standing there, smiling and shit, like something was funny. The guys and I didn't interfere, but we remained nearby just in case something went down.

Mo

I was sick and tired of Sam and her shit. I kept giving her ass chance after chance, and she continued to find a way to piss me off. I was not mad that she was with Tremaine, because this was the type of shit she did. What made me mad was the fact that I knew it was she who had tried to break Corey and me up.

"You are always on some bullshit, Sam. You are my fucking sister, and you are always trying to find a way to hurt me. What have I ever done to you, besides be there for your ungrateful ass?" I said to her as Bria and Zoe flanked me.

"Mo, what are you talking about? I haven't done anything," she said, but I could tell her ass was lying, and it took everything in me not to slap the dog shit out of her.

"You know exactly what I am talking about," I said. "You was the one sending Corey them bogus-ass pictures of me and Tremaine, trying to break us up. Not that I give a fuck about Tremaine, but now you with him and I used to fuck with him. You don't have no respect for me. You don't give a damn that I am your sister."

"I didn't send any pictures, and I had no idea that you knew Tremaine," she said, lying.

"You are a fucking liar. This shit has your name written all over it. What? You want to be me? You want my life, don't you? That's why you tried to break Corey and me up, and when that didn't work, you went after Tremaine. You wish you was me, don't you?" I said. I could see her mood visibly change.

"You know what, Mo? You are right. I hate your ass. You stole my dad and Corey, and your ass think you are all that, but you don't got shit on me. I got my daddy now, and I got Tremaine. Your ass don't deserve to be happy. That's why I tried to break you and Corey up. I am tired of you living the life I should be living," Sam said, getting in my face.

Bria shook her head. "Sam, you sound crazy as hell. This is your sister. How could you do anything to hurt her?" she said.

"This bitch is not no sister of mines. Fuck her!" Sam said.

I slapped her ass so hard, I thought her head would spin around on her neck. Corey and all the guys ran over and grabbed us.

I stepped up to Tremaine, and I spat right in his face. "You better stay your ass away from me, because next time I just might kill your ass," I growled. "You dirty bastard!"

I stormed out of the Red Lobster and found my way to our car. Corey appeared a second later, and once we were inside the car, I cried on my fiancé's chest. "Why does she keep trying to hurt me? I don't get it. I have not done anything but show her love, but she hates my guts," I said as I sobbed on him.

"Sam is all about herself. She doesn't know how to love people, because her heart is full of hate," he said.

"But toward me? We have been in each other's lives since we were small kids. We should be better than that. And we are sisters, so that should have made us bond even more, but it has only made us worse," I said.

"I know that's your sister, but you have to leave her crazy ass alone," he said, and he was right.

I was done with her ass, and if she came near me again, I was going to beat the hell out of her.

Kevin

Sam really almost had my ass completely fooled, but I now knew her conniving ass was not going to ever change. If you could do your own sister that way, you wouldn't have a problem doing that to anyone else. She had backstabbed me when she slept with my best friend. I had had to change my number once again, because Sam would call me all damn day, would leave voice mail after voice mail, and would send my ass a text message every freaking second.

Zoe and I were just leaving her parents' house when I spotted Dontae sitting across the street in his car. When he saw us coming out, he got out of his car and headed toward us. Zoe began to shake visibly.

"It's okay, baby. I won't let anything happen to you," I said. I had my gun with me too, so this nigga was about to lose his life.

"Zoe, I don't want to hurt you. I just want to talk to you for a minute," Dontae said when he reached us.

"We have nothing to talk about, Dontae," she said.

"Step off, homeboy, before you lose your life right now," I said.

"Nigga, I'm not scared of you. And like I said, I'm here to talk to Zoe, and I'm not leaving until she hears me out," he said.

I wanted to dead that nigga right there, but I didn't want to scare my lady.

"Whatever you have to say, just say it, Dontae, and leave please," Zoe said.

"Can we talk alone?" he asked.

"Hell no!" Zoe and I both said at the same time.

"Look, I just wanted to apologize for what I did, and I want you to take me back," he said, like I wasn't even standing here.

"Dontae, that will never happen. You were right. I love Kevin, and I always have loved Kevin, so any hopes of you and I getting back together are over, just like this conversation. Come on, baby. Let's go," she said, then grabbed my hand.

I looked at his bitch ass, then smirked. He tried to grab Zoe, but I pulled my gun out and held it to that nigga's head before he could get to her.

"Look, nigga, the only reason your bitch ass is not on the ground, bleeding, is that Zoe is right here, and I don't want to put her through that trauma. But trust me, your days are numbered. Now back your weak ass up and leave," I said.

He did as I told him. "I'm going to see you again, nigga," he said before walking back to his car.

"I'll be waiting," I said.

Zoe wrapped her arm around me tight, and I led her to the car. It was a quiet ride home; we both were in our thoughts. I pulled up to the house, and Zoe hopped out and ran across the street to grab something out of her car. I headed to our condo to open the door. All of a sudden I heard some tires screech, so I spun around to see what was going on.

"Zoe, watch out!" I screamed as I ran toward her, but it was too late. A black car with heavily tinted windows hit Zoe, then sped off. I ran over to her in a panic. "Baby, get up! Please get up," I cried, but she was unresponsive. I grabbed my phone, then called the police. "Baby, please get up. I need you," I said as I cradled her in my arms.

I rocked back and forth with her in my arms. I kept repeating, "Baby, wake up," until the ambulance took her away. I was going to kill that bitch-ass nigga Dontae. I couldn't see if that was him in that car, but who else would hurt Zoe?

Chapter Twenty-seven

Mo

We were all at the hospital, waiting to hear what the doctors had to say about Zoe. All we knew at this point was that she was in critical condition. Kevin was a mess right now, and there was nothing any of us could say or do to change that. He was comforting Zoe's parents while he was in pain himself. The paramedics burst through the door, and it shifted everyone's attention toward them. Kendra's old ass was on the stretcher, and I guessed she was in labor. Sam and Tremaine walked in moments after they brought Kendra in, and so did my dad. I rolled my eyes at Sam and then pulled my dad to the side.

"What's going on?" I asked my dad.

"Kendra is in labor, but it's kind of early. She's only eight months," he said.

"Well, I hope the baby is okay," I said.

"I'm sure he will be," my dad said.

I walked back over to my friends and sat down. I'd go check on Kendra later. Even though I couldn't stand her ass, I wanted to make sure my little brother was okay.

I couldn't believe we were going through all this shit right now; it really was always something. My thoughts were interrupted by Dontae running into the hospital, screaming, "Where is Zoe?" Kevin stood up, and I knew there was about to be a problem. Without saying a word, Kevin ran at full speed and tackled Dontae.

"How are you going to bring your ass in here, looking for my girl, when you did this to her!" Kevin said. Kevin was beating that boy so bad that it took Corey, David, and Zoe's dad to get him off Dontae.

"Naw, let me go. He did this to Zoe!" Kevin said through tears.

"Kevin, baby, calm down. It wasn't him," Zoe's mom said.

"Yes, it was. He's the only person who has been stalking her," Kevin said.

"He was at our house, trying to convince us to get Zoe to talk to him," Zoe's mom said.

Kevin looked defeated as hell and worn out. Bria and I were standing there, shocked. Kevin ran out the door, and David and Corey followed behind him. Zoe's mom helped Dontae clean his face up, and then we all sat back down and waited for the doctor.

I went to look for my dad in the labor and delivery wing of the hospital to see how things were going with Kendra. They were prepping her for an emergency C-section because the baby was in distress. I glanced over at Sam and Tremaine, and the way they were all over each other, you would have sworn that they had known each other for years. I really couldn't stand Sam, because she was nothing but a ho—she and her mom. They would do anything to get what they wanted, no matter who got hurt in the process. Truth be told, it was probably her ass who had hit Zoe. We all knew how crazy her ass was about Kevin.

I walked back over to where Zoe's mom and everyone else was sitting. About thirty minutes later, the boys came back in, and then the doctor came from the back with some news. We all crowded around Kevin and Zoe's mom. The doctor began to speak, and Kevin dropped to his knees. I couldn't believe this was happening.

Sam

It felt good to hit that bitch Zoe with Tremaine's car. Like I said before, if I couldn't have him, no one else would, either. I had given that man all of me, and he had chosen to give his love to someone else. Well, he wouldn't be loving her ass soon; I had made sure of that. I had left Tremaine at his house and had told him I needed to run to the store. My plan had been to cut the brake line on Zoe's car, but when I turned the corner and saw her getting something out of her car, I figured I could just run her ass over. As she was about to cross the street, I placed my foot all the way down on the gas pedal, and the car jerked forward. I hit her before she could move out of the way. I started to reverse and run her ass over again, but I figured that at the speed I was going, I had probably killed her already. I lied and told Tremaine that I had hit a deer, and he believed me. Just when I was about to get comfortable, my mom called and said she was going into early labor. I met her and my dad at the hospital, and that was when we saw Kevin and his crew. I wanted so badly to comfort him, but I knew now was not the time to make my move.

The doctor came out and informed us that the baby wasn't doing well and that his cord was wrapped around his neck. I started to panic, because we needed this baby to be born; that was the only for sure way that I could get my mom and dad back together officially. They were already prepping my mom for an emergency C-section, and they allowed my father to go in the room with my mom. Tremaine and I sat and waited. Ten minutes later, I decided to walk over to where Kevin and Mo were, and that was when I saw Kevin on his knees, crying. Next to him was Zoe's mom, or at least I assumed it was her mom. She was on her knees and was holding Kevin. I could tell by the looks on everyone's faces that I had succeeded at doing my job.

I walked back over to where Tremaine was sitting and pulled him into the nearest bathroom. It was time to celebrate because I had finally got rid of that bitch. Once in the bathroom, I dropped to my knees and began to suck Tremaine's dick. I played with his balls as I began to lick up and down his shaft. He picked me up and sat me on the counter and then began to suck on my already wet clit. He spread my lips so that he could get better access to my pearl. He stood, picked me up, and slid me up and down his shaft. I threw my head back, and my pussy walls clamped around his dick. We came long and hard and then pulled ourselves together.

As soon as we walked back into the waiting area, my dad walked out from the back with a somber look on his face.

Lord, please let my brother be alive. If he wasn't, maybe God was punishing us for all the wrong we'd done. If my brother died, then everything would be ruined. . . .

Zoe

I woke up to a bunch of machines beeping and my family and friends surrounding my bed, crying hard. My body felt really heavy, and I could barely move anything.

"Somebody get the doctors. She's awake," I heard my mom scream.

I looked over at Kevin, and he had a shocked look on his face. I could tell he had been crying, because his eyes were bloodshot.

"Baby, can you hear me?" Kevin said, rushing over and grabbing my hands.

"Yes, I can hear you. Why are y'all crying, and what happened to me? Why am I in the hospital?" I asked, confused. The last thing I remembered was Kevin and I getting out of his car in front of our house.

"You don't remember what happened?" my mom asked.

Before I could respond, the doctors were pushing everyone out of the room. Then they poked me everywhere and checked all kinds of stuff.

"Ms. Jones, you are one lucky woman. There aren't too many people that die and wake back up," one of the doctors said. I was shocked as hell to hear him say that I had died and woken back up.

"What happened to me?" I asked.

"You were hit by a car. We thought that the impact from the hit had killed you, but I see how wrong we were. We are going to run some tests to make sure there isn't any brain damage or anything else of concern. Until then, you are still considered critical," he said, then walked out of the room.

A car? Who would hit me? What was I doing when I was hit? I thought.

Everybody came back into the room and asked me a thousand questions. I told them that I didn't remember ever being hit and that my body was really sore. I told them that I just wanted to be alone with Kevin, and that I would answer their questions tomorrow. My mom refused to leave, so I told her to give Kevin and me some time alone and then to come back.

"Are you feeling okay, baby?" Kevin asked once everyone had left my room. He lay down next to me in my bed and spooned me.

"I am really sore, but other than that, I feel okay," I said. Surprisingly, I didn't have any broken bones, but I did have a huge knot on the back of my head from hitting the concrete so hard.

"I thought I lost you. I don't know what I would have done if you were actually gone," he said, holding me tightly.

"I'm not going anywhere. You can't get rid of me that easy," I said weakly.

"Well, get some rest, baby. I will be here with you when you wake up," he said as he got off the bed.

I closed my eyes and no longer resisted the sleepiness that had long ago overtaken my body. I was just thankful that I was still alive.

Chapter Twenty-eight

Kendra

I couldn't believe I had just given birth to my son. Things had got complicated very fast. So, what y'all don't know was that even though Tim had talked all that shit about loving Sharon and trying to get her back, he had been in my bed every chance he got. Although he had claimed he would be staying away from me, that was a damn lie. We seemed to mess around even more. He had told me that if I said something to Sharon again, we would be done for good. I had kept quiet for this long, but I couldn't say that if he pissed me off, I wouldn't spill the beans again.

Before I went to the hospital, we had been in my bedroom, and I had been on top of him, riding the hell out of his pole. I had been bouncing up and down on him as if I wasn't eight months pregnant when I felt a sharp pain rip through my stomach.

"Damn, baby. You ain't never came that hard. You're wet as hell," Tim had said.

"I didn't cum. I think . . . I think my water just broke," I'd said.

His eyes shot open. We both looked down, and that was when we noticed some fluid and blood mixed together. He damn near pushed me on the floor, then got up and started gathering everything we needed for our son. Although it was too early for me to be in labor, I was somewhat glad that I might be having my baby, because I was tired of being pregnant. He helped me get cleaned up as best as I could, and then we made a call to Sam to let her know what was going on.

After they got me situated at the hospital, they checked me out, and it was then that I found out that my baby's cord was wrapped around his neck and that I had to have a C-section. My baby wasn't breathing when he came out, but the doctors were able to save him, and now he was healthier than ever. I wondered how that bitch must feel, knowing that I had given Tim the one thing that she wasn't able to give him. I knew for certain that real soon, I would be marrying Tim, and we would finally be a family. When I became Mrs. Peterson, I was going to make sure that I flaunted that shit all in that whore's face.

Monique

Two years later . . .

Bria, Zoe, a bunch of girls I was cool with in high school, and I were all out celebrating. In a few days, I would officially be Mrs. Corey Anderson. At twenty-two years old, I would become a married woman, and I almost couldn't believe it. Zoe had ended up pulling through after her accident. They never found out who did it, but I had my own suspicions about who did it. Of course, I hadn't spoken to that bitch Sam since the day we left the hospital. My dad was in my ear every time he saw me about us making up, but he didn't know all the messed-up shit that she had done to me.

"Girl, what you over here thinking about? You are supposed to be getting drunk and having a good time," Bria yelled over the music.

"I *am* having a good time," I said.

Just as those words left my mouth, two sexy-ass male strippers came into our VIP section. My friend placed a sash around my body that said BRIDE TO BE, and then one of the male dancers picked me up and placed me on a chair. He began dancing between my legs and doing all types of crazy stuff as my girls cheered him on. About an hour later, the strippers left, and my girls and I headed to the dance floor. We were dancing our asses off and having a good time, until I heard a familiar voice.

"These bitches have no class about themselves. Hoes out here, looking a hot-ass mess," Sam said.

Lord knows I ain't trying to get into it with these messy bitches on the night of my bachelorette party, but I could already see that ho Sam was on one. She had come into the club with a group of bitches I didn't know—except for one girl. She had all of a sudden became best friends with David's so-called baby mama.

"Look at them hoes," Bria whispered in my ear.

"Forget them. Don't nobody got time for them ratchet hoes. Let them do what they do best," I said and then started dancing again. That group of bitches came onto the dance floor right next to us. Sam bumped into me once, but I let that shit slide. If it happened again, it was going down.

"I don't know what Corey sees in that black bitch. He didn't want her until her fat ass lost weight," Sam said, and that was all I needed to hear to go and speak my mind to this bitch.

"You got something to say? I hear your messy ass talking shit about me, but you ain't woman enough to say the shit to my face," I said after I walked up on her.

"Bitch, get out of my face before I whip that ass," Sam said and then muffed the shit out of me. Just when I was about to punch that bitch in her face, security grabbed me. Sam had grown some balls over the past two years, because she had always been a known shit talker, but she had never before thrown the first punch.

"Bitch, I'm going to see your scary ass, you better believe that. And when I do, it's going down," I said heatedly.

"Bitch, shut up. That's why I fucked your so-called man first, and I bet if I see his ass, I can fuck him again," she yelled.

"Whatever, ho. That's all your tired ass is good for. All you do is lay on your back for whatever nigga that wants to fuck," I said. I grabbed my shit and stormed out of the club. This bitch always found some type of way to ruin shit for me.

"Let's go somewhere else. This bitch ain't about to stop nothing," Zoe said as she followed me outside.

I was down for that because I definitely needed a drink after dealing with that silly ho.

Chapter Twenty-nine

Sam

I really could not stand Monique's simple ass. She really made me sick. I wished I had done more than muffed her, but security had interfered. I had to take a break from all the drama that was going on, because I had become a mommy. Yes, I, Sam, was a mother now to a little boy named Tremaine Mitchell, Jr. I had never known I was capable of loving anyone more than I loved my dad—and myself, of course—until I had my son.

A few months after my mom gave birth to my little brother, I had found out I was pregnant. I hadn't been opposed to having my son, because I had known for a fact that Tremaine was the father of my baby, and he had just happened to be at the doctor's office when I found out. I must admit, I had had thoughts of aborting my baby, but Tremaine had been on me like white on rice, refusing to leave my side, so I had decided against it. I had also been pissed off because I'd been on birth control and still got pregnant. My baby looked like my father and Tremaine. He was so handsome. He had a caramel complexion, curly hair, and the deepest dimples I had ever seen. He had light brown eyes, and he was bowlegged as ever.

Tremaine didn't go anywhere without my baby. Things between Tremaine and me were very serious. For starters, we had stayed together, and he had asked me to marry him several times. At first, I had kept telling him that I wasn't ready, but after the third time he asked me, I'd said yes. He'd been an absolute gentleman about it too. He'd gone to my father and asked for my hand in marriage before he even proposed to me. At first, I had messed with Tremaine to get back at Mo, and it had been the same for him, but somewhere down the line, we had both fallen in love with each other. Now he didn't give a damn about Mo or Corey; his main focus was his son and me. He had told me that I should let go of whatever ill feelings I had toward Mo and just move forward with my life, and as far as he knew, I had, but I couldn't let go of how much I hated her and how I felt like she had stolen my life from me.

I still loved Kevin and always would, but my love for Tremaine was starting to grow stronger. My feelings for Kevin were what had been holding me back from marrying Tremaine, because I had been feeling like there was hope for me if that bitch Zoe was out of the picture. Imagine my surprise when I had found out that her family was crying tears of joy instead of tears of sorrow at the hospital. I had got word that she had actually died but then had somehow woken back up. I had been sure that the ho was dead, but I guessed I didn't hit her ass hard enough.

Even though I had agreed to marry Tremaine, right now, I had mixed feelings. Whenever I saw Kevin, I questioned my love for Tremaine, but whenever I was with Tremaine, which was every damn day, I hardly thought of Kevin. I loved Tremaine, and I really didn't want to lose him, but I knew in my heart that I still loved Kevin. Or maybe I just didn't want him to be with Zoe's ass. It could be both. I didn't know. Either way, I felt stuck right now.

"Damn, babe. What are you in there doing? You've been in there forever," Tremaine said as he poked his head inside our bathroom door. After I had left the club, I'd come home and run a hot bath so that I could gather my thoughts.

"I'm getting out now. What? You waiting on me?" I asked while smiling seductively.

"Hell yeah. I've been waiting on your sexy ass to get home all night. I knew that once you walked out that door with them heels and that sexy dress, I would be waiting up for you so I can taste that," he said, licking his lips.

Miss Kitty began to moisten, and she was ready for Daddy's tongue to make her purr.

"Okay, baby. Let me finish up, and I'll be right out to take care of you," I said.

I finished my bath, and I didn't worry about putting on any clothes. My man wanted me badly, so I had to oblige him. I dried my body off and walked into our bedroom. When I made it to the bed, I found Tremaine lying down, buck naked, his pole standing at attention. I straddled him, grabbed his pole, and slid down on it. I rode him long enough for my wetness to coat him. I hopped off him, then took him in my mouth and made sure I licked and sucked everything off. I played with his balls as I continued to suck up and down his shaft. His balls began to tighten up, so I knew he was about to cum. I stopped what I was doing and then straddled him again. I rode him until we both exploded. Minutes later, he was sleeping like a baby.

I was extremely happy that my brother had pulled through. My mom had had complications during his birth, but my brother had come out healthy and my mom had recovered. I was so happy because without my little brother, I didn't see any chance of getting back my family, which Mo and her black-ass mother had stolen.

I know you're probably wondering how I ended up being friends with David's baby mama. I was at the mall a few months after I had my son, picking up some clothes for my fat man, when I overheard some girl talking about how she had to check that bitch Bria for making David question whether he was the father of her son or not. Now, Milwaukee was small, so I knew for sure that she was talking about the same Bria and David that I knew. The most shocking part of all of that was that I had no idea that David had had a baby with Bria, and I was shocked as hell that Bria was still with him, as I knew that Bria didn't play that shit at all. Now, I had been around her baby many times, because our sons played together all the time, and I thought the baby looked just like Meka, but that didn't mean he wasn't the father. Bria had told me she was positive that he was, and I believed her. So, anyway, being the bold bitch that I was, I walked up to her and introduced myself, and the rest was history. So, not only were my mom and I looking to make these bitches' lives miserable, but Meka was too, and we were going to do everything in our power to make sure it happened.

Sharon

I had taken my husband back once again after his ass did some dumb shit and got that bitch Kendra pregnant. My main reason for taking him back was that I didn't want her to have him, and of course, I still loved my husband, but I regretted the decision every time I look into that little boy's face. He looked nothing like my husband, but he looked every bit like that whore of a mother he had. Even though he didn't look like my husband, I was positive Tim was the father, because Kendra's dumb ass had been faithful to a married man all this time.

Tim did everything for that little boy. He was about to be three years old, and he had everything a teenage boy would have. Tim had him all the time, and when the boy was not here, Kendra was calling Tim every five minutes. She was always claiming that the baby wanted to see him, was sick, or wanted to talk to him. She'd say that the baby needed more clothes or needed to go to the doctor, which was a bunch of bullshit, and every time she called, he would run to do something for her. Between work and being with his son, he didn't have a spare moment, and we barely spend time together. I was honestly fed up with this shit.

If he weren't so far up Kendra's ass, Tim would have noticed the distance that had grown farther between us. When we initially got back together, things had been strained, but now they were even worse. I thought my little secret had a lot to do with why things were strained. I would be a damn fool to go back to Tim and not have some candy on the side. Since his time was all taken up, I had been occupying myself elsewhere. I had met a few guys during the year that Tim and I were separated, and when we got back together, I had placed my friends on standby.

Things were really serious with one of my friends in particular. He really wanted to be with me, and to be honest, I kind of wanted to be with him too, but my husband somehow still had a hold on me. No matter how much he did me wrong, I couldn't seem to shake him. I still loved him, and there was hope that he would change, but I had made a commitment to myself that I would never be faithful to him again unless I felt for sure that he was serious about us. I knew that was not the best way to go about things, but I felt like this was the best way to protect my heart.

My friend had been trying to see me, so I decided that I'd go to his place and hang out with him. His name was Cameron, and he was so sexy. He owned several businesses, and he carried himself in such a professional manner. He was not what I usually went for, because, for starters, he was white. I had never dated a white man, nor had I thought I would ever be this attracted to one, but when I met him, he stole my heart. He had a dark tan, dark hair, and ice-blue eyes, and he was tall, with a muscular build. He looked like Eddie Cibrian, the guy who played Nia Long's boyfriend in *The Best Man Holiday*.

He greeted me at his door with twelve long-stemmed roses and a kiss. I walked in, and he led me to the dining room. He had me take a seat at the table, and then he served dinner. We ate steak and potatoes and talked for hours while sipping on wine. Everything was fine until the conversation shifted to us being together.

"So, when are you going to walk away from this marriage that you are obviously not happy in?" he asked. I had been up front and honest with Cameron when my husband and I got back together. He respected my wishes, but we couldn't stay away from each other.

"Cam, it's not that easy, and you know it," I said.

"But it *is* that easy. You are not happy, and he has no idea how to treat you. Sharon, I have been in your shoes. You know my ex-wife cheated on me, and I took her back, thinking she would change. I got slapped in the face when I caught her bouncing up and down on my best friend's face," he said. Cameron was a good man, and I knew he would be perfect for me. It was just hard for me to let my husband go.

"I really hate when you put all this pressure on me. You have to let me make this decision when I'm ready," I said.

"Listen, I want to be able to show you how a man is really supposed to treat a woman. I shouldn't be here with you. When he let you go, because of his foolish mistake, he allowed a real man to creep in and steal you. I promise, if given the opportunity, I will introduce you to a world that you never thought was possible," he said, smiling that sexy smile.

"I hear you," I said, smiling back.

"That's what your mouth says, but your actions are saying something else. I have already given you my heart, and I am risking it because I'm hoping that you will see that with me is where you belong. I won't press the issue any longer. I'll let it go for now," he said.

I was glad. The conversation was making me uncomfortable because I wasn't ready to make a decision just yet. Not to mention my husband didn't even know that he could possibly lose me. I was tired of thinking about my problems, and I just wanted to unwind and enjoy the time I was spending with Cameron. I stood, walked over to him, straddled him, and covered his lips with mine, and you know what happened next.

Bria

Things between David and me were just okay. Our love was still strong, but this bitch Meka was still on her bullshit, which was making things harder between us two. We still didn't know if David had fathered her son, Caiden, or not, because she never let Caiden come over, and she let David see him only if I was not around and if she was with them. I knew David was helping her financially, because the bitch had moved out of the hood, and she was living in a really nice area. David really believed the baby was his, and that was fine, but I wouldn't believe that shit until the DNA results said so, and since it was on my mind, I decided to speak about it.

"I am really tired of having this conversation with you, but you really need to find out if that baby is yours," I said after we had finished having sex. I was lying with him, wrapped in his arms.

"Bria, I really wish you would just drop this mess. I really feel like Caiden is mine. We just made love. Why do you have to ruin the moment with this bull?" he said.

"Really? Our son looks just like you, but Caiden doesn't look anything like you. I feel like you're being soft when it comes to her," I said, pulling away from him.

"Bria, I am just tired of all the drama between you and Meka. Caiden is mine, and I'm not going to tell you that shit again. You and Meka better start getting along, for our kids' sake, and I mean that shit," he said, looking at me crazily.

"You have really lost your mind if you think for one second that I would ever get along with her. I don't ever pop off until that bitch says something to me. I think your ass is being naive at this point, because you believe anything her messy ass tells you," I said.

"Whatever, Bria. You're looking for an argument, and I am not about to give you one. I am tired. I just wanted to come home to a hot meal and some warm pussy, but you just had to be extra tonight," he said.

"I'm just saying I don't think it's cool that you're taking care of a child that you don't know is yours," I said.

"Well, you don't think Junior is mine, and you tell me that I should get a test done for him. I haven't done it, but I take care of my son, so I'm doing the same with Meka. Meka said she is positive that I am the father, and that's all that matters to me. I really don't have any choice but to believe what she says at this point," he said.

I hopped out of the bed so fast and stared at him with the look of death. "It's nice to know that you two are having personal conversations and shit, when the only thing you should be talking about is your so-called son. Unlike her son, my baby looks exactly like your trifling ass, so I guess you're back fucking with that bitch, since you two are all personal and shit. I was your fool once. I won't be it twice. I am getting a paternity test done, so you can know for sure that my baby is yours. When you and I are over, you can go play house with that ratchet ho, and if you really wanted to find out if Caiden is yours, you could take her ass to court and make her get a test done," I said as I walked over to the closet to find something to put on.

"Bria, where are you going? You know damn well that I'm not messing with Meka on that level. I'm just saying, she be in my ear, spitting the same shit that you're spitting, but I don't listen to her ass. I love you with all my heart, and I know my son is mine," he said, getting up and wrapping his arms around my waist.

I knew he was not messing with Meka, but the way he was defending her was pissing me off. I knew one other thing: I was getting that paternity test just so a bitch could never say that David was not the father of my baby. I gave in to his kisses, which he was placing all over my neck and back, and I made love to my man, putting all thoughts of our problems to rest for the time being.

Chapter Thirty

Tim

Things in my life were finally coming together. I finally had my son, and my wife had taken my butt back. She hadn't been playing when she said she was divorcing me. She had actually had the papers drawn up and sent to me. When they were delivered to me, I'd initially been shocked and very pissed, because I'd felt like she was taking things too far. So, I'd gone into overdrive, begging her to accept my apology and take me back, and she finally had. I had never been in danger of her not taking me back, because if I didn't know anything else, I knew my wife loved me. She would never leave me, and I refused to let anyone else have her. I knew I did some messed-up shit sometimes, but I really did love my wife, and the thought of another nigga being inside of her made me want to kill somebody. My wife had the best pussy in this world, and I just couldn't give that up. It was not just about the sex; she just fit me perfectly. She was ride or die, and she knew how to really treat a man.

Things between us were going perfectly until I allowed Kendra back into the picture. I must admit, I had always had a soft spot for Kendra, and if she had kept herself up all those years ago, I would have probably continued to sleep with her. I had tried being faithful, and I had been for a while, but I would always see some chick whom I just had to have. I was an ass man, and when I saw a perfectly round one, it was hard for me to pass that up.

These women were not making it hard for me. Any chick I messed with made it easy for me to hit. I never lied to any of these women and told them I was single. The only one I lied to was my wife. Case in point, this woman named Madison, who was currently going through a divorce, came into my office, crying about how her husband had cheated on her and had done her so wrong. I became her lawyer and her fuck buddy. Her husband wanted to work things out, but now she was trying to be with me. I had no intentions of ever being in a relationship with her, but she was sexy as hell, and she was a good fuck. I knew I shouldn't play with this woman's emotions, but shit, I felt like I was young and in my prime, so why not? Not to mention that she knew I was with my wife.

I loved my wife to death, and there was nothing that she was doing wrong. I just liked variety. Truth be told, I had been cheating on my wife for most of our relationship, but the only person she knew about was Kendra. Even if she did find out about the other women, she would just leave for a little while and come right back. Sometimes, I was very serious about changing for my wife, but I felt like I had a problem, because I just couldn't reform myself.

In fact, I was with Madison at this very moment.

"Baby, I am really ready for this divorce to be final so that we can be together in public," Madison said.

I didn't respond. I just grabbed her head and pushed it back down on my dick. I knew I couldn't keep doing shit like this and get away with it, but I felt like I couldn't help myself. I was mad that this bitch had fallen in love with me, because this was only temporary, and when I got done with her, I'd hand her over to the next nigga so that she could be somebody else's headache.

Kendra

Life for me couldn't be better. For starters, I had given Tim something that Sharon couldn't, and that was a son. I knew Tim had always wanted a son, and when we started back sleeping together, he would tell me that he wanted me to have his baby and give him a son. After I gave birth to his son, he had told me that it was just sex talk because we were in the moment, but I honestly believed that deep down inside, he had tried to get me pregnant, and I didn't have a problem with that. I would give him anything that he wanted, because I really wanted my man back, and I would do whatever it took. He was not living with me yet, but we were still having sex almost every day. He was even telling me that he loved me, and I knew he meant it. He ate dinner with me most nights, and he always took my son and me on out-of-town business trips.

The only problem we were having was that he wouldn't leave his wife. At this point, I didn't even care, because I would take him any way that I could get him, because I loved him that much. Sam had said that if I got pregnant by him again, that would seal the deal. The only problem with that was that my pregnancy with my son had been bad, and because of that, I had ended up getting an IUD so that I could avoid getting pregnant again. Sharon had to know something wasn't right. After all, with all the time he spent with his son and me, he was definitely not spending a lot of time with her. I'd be glad when she was finally out of the picture and I had him all to myself.

I had lost all the weight I gained during the pregnancy. I had even gone to the gym to tighten my stomach, so that it was like it used to be. So I was looking and feeling good. Tim got so upset when we were out and men stared at me or tried to hit on me. One time, he got pissed and cursed me out because some man was staring at me for too long. That was how I know that things between us were getting serious, and that sooner rather than later, he would leave Sharon and come and be with his real family.

"You know I love you, right?" I asked Tim as he ran his fingers through my hair.

"Yeah, I know, and I love you too," he said.

"Then why won't you move in with me and your son? I know Sam would love that too, especially since you were absent for most of her life," I said. I knew he had a soft spot for his kids, so I used them to get my point across.

"I know, Kendra, but it's not that easy, and you knew what you were getting into when we started back sleeping together. Don't get me wrong. I love you, but I just ain't ready to leave my wife yet . . . if ever," he said.

"You're not ready to leave her, but you are here every day— eating, sleeping, and shitting. But I'm not good enough for you to leave your wife. It's obvious you belong here with me. She doesn't treat you like I do, and she can't love you like I do," I said, pleading my case.

"Whatever, Kendra. I don't feel like dealing with this shit with you right now. Go in there and cook me some food so I can take my ass home," he said.

I did what I was told, but his ass wouldn't be going home tonight. I cooked his favorite meal and poured him a glass of Hennessy to wash it down with. Before I gave him his drink, I crushed two sleeping pills and then placed them in his drink. I stirred it up and gave it to him. Then I gave him his food. He tossed the drink back and told me to make him another one, and I did what I was told. He ate his food, and as soon as he was done, he lay down on the bed. I could tell that the meds had kicked in, because it was hard for him to keep his eyes open.

"I'm going to take a nap. Wake me up in about an hour," he said.

I told him that I would, but we all know that was a lie. Moments later, he was out for the count. I had no plans to wake him up, and when Sharon realized that he wasn't bringing his ass home tonight, there would be trouble in paradise.

Zoe

Things between Kevin and me had been good up until recently, when I discovered he was still talking to that chick Imani, the one he was messing around with when we were separated. I got real insecure when he took me back because of how bad I had done him when Dontae was in the picture. Now I went through his phone every chance I got. I hadn't found anything until recently. It was not that he was saying anything inappropriate; it was she who was doing too much. She was saying how much she missed what they had had and just how she missed him in general. She kept saying she wanted to meet up with him and things like that, but for the most part, he didn't respond. When he did, he would just say that he couldn't mess with her on that level and that they could only be friends, but I was not okay with that. I wanted so badly to say something to him, but I couldn't, because I wasn't supposed to go through his phone.

"Baby, are you happy with me?" I asked.

"Yes, I am happy with you. Why do you keep asking me that?" he said.

"I just want to know. You don't tell me those types of things," I said.

"That's because I show you. My actions should tell you that I am happy," he said.

"And you don't want to be with no one else, right?" I asked, sounding really insecure.

"No, I don't want to be with anyone else. I wouldn't be with you if I did," he said.

I decided to ask him about Imani without letting on that I had actually gone through his phone. "The other day, when you were taking a shower, your phone beeped, and I saw a message from Imani. Y'all still keep in contact?" I said, looking him dead in his eyes.

He chuckled, and then he finally answered my question. "I see what this is. You are insecure for some reason, but I guess I will feed into it. She texts me every now and then, but I don't talk to her like that. Look, I'm with you, not her. I don't even want to be with her, so you can stop thinking whatever you are thinking, because it is not like that at all," he said.

I felt a little better, but not much. I couldn't shake the fact that he might just up and leave me like I did him. No matter how much he said he loved me, there was a strong possibility that he would leave me, and I was just not ready to lose him. I loved this man with every ounce of my being, and I knew I had made some mistakes. I just hoped he had forgiven me like he said he had.

"I don't feel comfortable with you texting her, and I think you should let her know that," I said. He looked at me like I was crazy, but I was dead serious. I was not okay with my man's ex-girlfriend texting him.

"All right, Zaria. I'll tell her, but don't come at me again with your insecure bullshit," he said, turning on his side so that his back was facing me.

I hoped I had done the right thing by telling him how I felt. Only time would tell.

Chapter Thirty-one

Kevin

I met up with the guys at a local bar because I had some shit I needed to get off my chest. Things with Zoe and me had been good on my end until she came to me with that insecure bullshit. I knew it was because she thought that I was sweating the shit from the past, but honestly, I was not even thinking about what she did. Everyone made mistakes, and I had decided to forgive her, so I had let that shit go. Plus, I knew she was not really that type of girl. I loved her, and I had plans to spend my life with her. She needed to forgive herself, because she was the only one who had a problem.

"So, what's up, man?" David asked while sipping on his beer.

"Man, nothing much. Having woman problems, as usual," I said.

"Tell me about," Corey and David said in unison.

"What type of problems are y'all having? It seems like we are all going through it lately," I said.

"Mo's mad at me about some shit Sam said when she saw her at the club. I don't understand why she is pissed at me about some old shit that we have moved past," Corey said.

"She's still marrying your ass, so y'all good. Me, on the other hand, I got big nigga problems. For starters, I've got Bria and Meka in my ear, talking shit about each other on the daily. Bria feels like I should get a blood test on Caiden to make sure he's mines before I go claiming him, and Meka feels the same way about Junior," David said.

"Man, you're not sleeping with Meka's ho ass again, are you?" Corey asked, taking the words right out of my mouth.

"Man, hell naw. I learned my lesson the first time Bria left my ass. A nigga was sick as hell. I'm super faithful to her ass, and Meka hates that shit. She just feels like if I test Caiden, I should test Junior too, but I feel like little man is mine, though," David said, sounding slow as hell.

"Man, listen, Bria is your woman, and you know for sure that Junior is yours. He looks just like your ass. Plus, we know that Bria's crazy ass has only been with you. Now, Meka, she is a known ho. You need to test that little nigga, and low key, he looks like your boy Mitch, in all honesty," I said.

"Right. Why would you take care of a kid that may not be yours? I mean, you're dealing with extra drama when you might not have to. I know you are a standup guy, but damn," Corey said, then downed his glass of vodka.

"Y'all niggas are right, but I feel like it's going to cause more drama if I get the test," David said as he continued to sip on his beer.

"You sound crazy. Test that little nigga, and if he's yours, put that ho in her place and take care of your shorty. But if he's not, kick her ass to the curb and let her go find her real baby's father. She has no business with you if you are not the father," Corey said.

"Man, I called you two niggas here so I could talk and fix my problems, not to fix y'all problems," I said, laughing at them.

"Oh, yeah. You're right. So what's up with you?" Corey said.

"Yeah, let's drop this conversation, because this is stressing me the hell out," David said with a stressed look on his face.

Corey and I just laughed at his crazy ass.

"So, y'all remember that chick Imani I was messing with when Zoe and I were going through our shit?" I asked, and they nodded their head yes. "Well, she has been texting and calling me, talking about 'she misses me and wants to be with me' type shit. I haven't talked to her since a few months after Zoe and I got back together, and that's been a few years ago. Now, all of a sudden, she wants to be with me. She said she has been feeling this way for the longest, and she just decided to reach out now," I said.

"Man, don't fall for it. Zoe has been through enough already. Just look at what David's going through. You don't need those problems," Corey said, and then he chuckled at David.

"Shut up, Corey. But he's right, man. You love Zoe. Don't fall for that bullshit. Side chicks are problems you don't need," David said.

"Well, that's not even the worst part. The worst part is she is talking about moving down here to be with me," I said.

"Why would she do that if you told her that you ain't looking for that? You sure you are not sleeping with this girl?" Corey said.

"Man, I am positive. I barely even text the girl back when she texts me, and I definitely don't answer none of her phone calls. I don't know, man. I just hope she doesn't move here. I don't need the extra drama," I said.

"You got another crazy-ass girl on your hands. It seems like you only attract the crazy ones," David said, laughing.

"Right, Sam's ass needs to be on some pills or something. That ho is beyond crazy, and low-key Zoe is a little crazy too," Corey said, laughing hard as hell. I wanted to punch his ass right off the bar stool with the way he was laughing.

"Man, fuck y'all. Let's take some shots," I said, putting Imani out of my mind.

Monique

Today was my big day, and I couldn't be happier. Corey and I had been through so much over the past years, and we had made it through all of that.

"Girl, why are you sitting over there looking like you're about to cry?" Zoe asked.

"I'm just sitting here thinking about everything we have been through, and where we are at now. It's almost too good to be true," I said, pushing back my tears so I wouldn't mess up my makeup.

Moments later, there was a knock on the door. My mother walked in. She looked like she had been crying, but she was still stunning in her peach cocktail-style dress. My mother looked like a slightly older version of me. She was so beautiful, with her shoulder-length jet-black hair and those same green eyes that I had. She was very curvaceous, but petite at the same time.

"Can I have a moment alone with my daughter?" my mom asked.

No one said a word; they just left the room.

"You look so beautiful, honey," she said, cupping my face in her hands.

"Thanks, Mommy. So do you," I said.

"I know this might catch you off guard, but as your mother, I have to ask you these types of questions. Are you sure you want to do this?" she said, kind of shocking me.

"Yes, I want to do this. Why would you ask me that?" I wanted to know.

"Never mind that. Do you really love Corey, and do you feel like he's going to treat you like you deserve to be treated, to be faithful to you, and really hold true to the vows he's about to take?" she said.

"Of course, Mom. I wouldn't be here if I didn't believe he was going to be true to me. Mom, what's going on? Why are you asking me these questions?" I said.

"I'm just making sure. I don't want you to make the same mistakes that I did," she said.

I knew that she and my dad had been going through some things, but I didn't know she felt like their marriage was a mistake. When I looked deeper into her eyes, I could see all the hurt and anger she was holding in.

"I'm sure Corey is the man for me. Mom, why do you feel like marrying my dad was a mistake?" I said.

"Monique, I am going to be honest with you, because you are my daughter, my only child. The day your father and I got married, I felt deep in my heart that something wasn't right and that maybe I shouldn't be marrying him, but I was so blinded by the love I had for him that I ignored the signs and married him, anyway. Your father is a cheater, and he has always been a cheater. Kendra is not the only woman your father has cheated on me with. There have been several women. I just overlooked things because I felt like we were young and he would change. I'm not saying that all men are the same, because there are some good men out there. Your father is a good dad, but he is a horrible excuse for a husband," she said.

"Wow, Mom. You seem so unhappy. Why do you stay if you feel this way?" I said, fighting back my tears.

"Don't worry about me, baby. I've got this. I just want to make sure that you are happy and you really want to do this," she said.

"I really do. I love him, and I feel in my heart that he is for me. I know we had a rocky start, but things have never been better between us. He's my first and only love," I said, meaning every word. I loved the hell out of my future husband, and he had my heart completely.

"Well, good. Just remember not to lose yourself. You are so young, and there is still so much life to live. Just because you are getting married doesn't mean you have to stop living. You can still pursue your dreams," she said and then hugged me tightly.

Our moment was interrupted by no other than Sam's silly ass. I was pissed because I damn sure hadn't invited Sam. Our ceremony was small, and we hadn't invited anyone but our parents and close friends. We had come all the way to Puerto Rico to get away from everybody, and this bitch had still found a way to be here.

"Mom, excuse my language, but, Sam, what the hell are you doing here?" I said, balling up my fists.

She laughed at me and stared at me like I was some type of joke. This bitch just had to ruin my day; she couldn't just ever let me be happy. "I'm just here to support my sister. My dad said I needed to be here, so he flew Tremaine and me out here so that we can support you. You know Dad wants us to get over our differences and support one another," she said sarcastically.

Just then, Zoe and Bria walked in the room. They gave Sam the look of death.

"Look, bitch. The problem is you don't know how to be real. You are not capable of loving anybody but yourself," I snapped. "I don't believe for one minute that you came here to support me. You came here so that you could start some more shit, but let me tell you something. You pull that shit today, and today you will take the last breath your pathetic ass ever takes. Now get out!"

"Yes, get out, bitch, before that ass gets beat. I refuse to let you mess up my best friend's big day, like you have everything else. You pull that shit today, and your ass will be flying back to the States on a stretcher," Bria said, and I knew she meant every word.

"Try me, and I will hurt you, like I did before," Sam said, getting in Bria's face and then blowing her a kiss and smiling.

This bitch was crazy, but she knew Bria was crazier. And what the hell did she mean, like she hurt Bria before? As far as I knew, Bria had done all the hurting when they had that little altercation. Something in my heart didn't feel right about what she had said. Bria reached back and was about to smack the hell out of Sam, but my mom grabbed her arm.

"Calm down, babies. Don't let this upset you," my mom said, looking at Bria and me. "Sam, let's go," she said as she grabbed Sam's hand. She led Sam out of the room. The entire time Sam was leaving, she was staring me down with this big-ass smile on her face.

"That bitch is very lucky it's your wedding day, or else I would have beat the tramp's ass," Zoe said.

"Right," Bria said, obviously pissed off. "This ho really knows how to push all my buttons."

"I'm good. Her ass is just jealous, but I am about to marry my man and enjoy my wedding. I'm going to act like her ass doesn't exist," I said.

"Well, come on. It's time," Bria said.

Chapter Thirty-two

Sam

I watched as the girl I hated the most, my so-called sister, walked down the aisle with her arm intertwined with my father's. Seeing her smile so brightly and my father look at her like he was the proudest man on earth at this moment made me sick to my stomach. I began to cry because I didn't want my father to love her like he did. I felt like he should love only my family and me. *Doesn't he realize that Sharon and Monique don't matter? Doesn't he understand how crazy it makes me when I see how happy they make him? They don't deserve his love. I should blow her brains out right now*, I thought.

I had to compose myself before I went off and did something crazy. I should have sent her that video of Corey and me fucking. Yes, I had recorded him and me fucking the last time he came over and called himself giving me what I wanted. I had held on to the video for all this time, and I still hadn't used it. Thinking back on that day made me horny. . . .

"Why the fuck did you pull that stupid-ass stunt? Why did you have to fuck up everything with my girl? What has she ever done to you besides be a good-ass friend to your ho ass?" he asked.

"Corey, I'm sorry. I love you, and I want to be with you. She doesn't deserve you," I told him.

He let me go and just stared at me.

"She doesn't fuck you like I do, baby. I know she's not sucking your dick. Do you want Mama to make you feel good? You know I know exactly what you like," I said as I dropped to my knees and pulled down his jogging pants.

His dick was already hard, and all I had done was talk to him. I took him in my mouth and swallowed him whole. I went down his shaft and took his balls and dick in my mouth at the same time. I stood up to take off my clothes, and he watched me with this dazed look in his eyes. Then he slapped me on my face and told me to bend over. I did what I was told, and he entered me from behind.

"This is all you wanted, huh? You wanted this dick. That's why you're acting all crazy and shit?" he asked while beating the hell out of my pussy.

"Yes, baby, that's what I wanted," I moaned.

"Throw that ass back!" he yelled, slapping my ass.

I threw it back at him, and I felt myself about to cum, but before I could, he pulled out and told me to turn around. He jerked off to finish off his nut and shot his seed all over my face.

"You got what the fuck you wanted. Now stay away from Mo and me." He pulled his pants up and left me sitting by the door, dumbfounded.

I still remembered that day clear as hell, and yes, he left me on some bogus shit, but in reality, I had the last laugh.

Even though I really couldn't stand Mo, I had to admit she looked beautiful walking down the aisle in her summer wedding dress. Their ceremony was small and very cute. There were white flowers everywhere. The place where the ceremony was held was decorated in peach and white, which was the same color scheme as the bridesmaid dresses. I wanted so badly to act a fool and interrupt her wedding, but I didn't want to piss my dad off. He was the only person saving that ass.

They said their "I do's," and we headed to the reception area, which wasn't far from where the ceremony took place. Corey gave Tremaine a few evil stares, but he didn't say anything to us, period. Bria and Kevin both stood up and gave a toast, and then we were all able to eat. I would be lying if I said that Kevin wasn't looking good. He still had some type of effect on me. I started to feel that jealousy arise, and I wanted to snap Zoe's neck for taking him away from me, but this wasn't the time or the place, so I held my composure.

"What the hell is Kendra doing here?" I heard Sharon say. She was trying to whisper to my dad, but she wasn't silent enough.

My mom's head shot up, and I could tell she wanted to say something, but instead, she just looked at Sharon and smirked. You didn't think I was going to fly down here and leave my mom at home, right? That would never happen. We had a mission to accomplish, and we were going to succeed by any means.

Once everyone was done eating, Corey and Mo had their first dance, and that was when the party began. I looked over at my father and Sharon, and I guessed she had decided not to let my mom's presence ruin her night, because they were practically dry fucking on the dance floor. I could tell my dad really loved Sharon by the way he held her and the way he stared into her eyes. I guessed my mom felt the same way about my dad, because, although she was dancing with Kevin's dad, she was staring at them, looking like she was about to cry. I walked over to her and pulled her to the side.

"You need to pull yourself together and toughen up. Don't ever let her see you sweat," I told her while keeping a smile on my face so they wouldn't know what we were talking about.

"You are right. I got this," she said and then walked off in their direction. I didn't know what she had up her sleeve, but I knew some shit was about to go down. She strutted up to my dad and Sharon and grabbed my father by his arm.

"So, you can fuck me every damn day, eat my pussy, sleep and eat at my house, pay all the bills, and take me and your son on business trips with you, but you're here with her," I heard my mom yell. It seemed like everything stopped as soon as my mom opened her mouth. All eyes were on them, and if I had some popcorn, you would have thought I was at the movies. This shit was getting too good. The look on Sharon's face was priceless.

"Kendra, don't start no shit. It's my daughter's wedding day," my father said, looking like he wanted to kill my mom.

"Naw, let the bitch cut up and spill the beans, like she always does. I don't know why you and this ho continue to play with me like I'm some type of punk. This bitch can't do shit right. She doesn't even know how to play her part as the side bitch the right way," Sharon said.

"I'm just tired of him hiding the truth. He ain't never going to stop fucking with me, and I'm not going to ever leave him. I just thought you should know the truth. And I am tired of pretending like we are just coparenting when, in fact, he tells me that he loves me every day. I'm letting you know right here and now that I don't ever plan to leave Tim alone. We come as a package deal. You can either accept it or leave him. The choice is yours. Either way, I'm going to still be in the picture," my mom said, making me proud.

"Baby, she's just trying to ruin what we have. You know I wouldn't go there with her like that again, knowing that she would tell everything," my dad lied.

I had been over my mom's house when they were fucking, so I knew my mother was telling the truth, and although he was acting like he was pissed right now, he would eventually come back to my mom. That seemed to be his pattern.

All of a sudden, all hell broke loose. Sharon ran up on my dad and stabbed him in the arm. Moments later, she was headed right for my mom, who had taken off when she saw Sharon stab my dad. Sharon was just about to plunge the knife in my mother when my dad grabbed her and wrestled the knife from her hand. I guessed she blacked out, because moments later she started to look around the room like she didn't know what she had just done.

"You two fuckers deserve each other, and you know what, Kendra? Even if I leave his sorry ass today, you will never be number one. It will never be you, so why are you trying so hard to take my place? Just know that all you will ever be is a side piece," Sharon said.

"Whatever, bitch. That's what you think. It's been over twenty years, and I'm still fucking him. No matter what you do or say, it's not going to end, so you need to do yourself a favor and walk away now," my mom said.

I was very proud that she had said all that. I couldn't have orchestrated it any better myself. *I see where I get it from*, I thought.

Sharon looked at my mom long and hard before she spat dead in my mom's face. Sharon turned on her heels and walked in the direction of the doors. My mom stood there, laughing.

"I'm sorry, baby," Sharon said to Mo as she exited the reception area. Some lady, who I later found out was Sharon's best friend and used to work for my dad, followed behind her, as did Mo and my dad, even though he needed medical attention. My mom just stood there with a smirk on her face. Bria walked up to my mother and punched her so hard that she slid into the wall. I tried to run up on Bria, but Tremaine grabbed me before I could.

"You two bitches got to go," Bria said, pointing at my mom and me.

I was heated as hell, and I was trying my hardest to break out of Tremaine's arms to get at Bria, but he held on to me tightly.

"Y'all heard what she said. Bounce," Corey said.

Kevin's father helped my mom out, and Tremaine walked me out of the reception area.

"I knew it was a bad idea to come here. Let's just enjoy the rest of our time here and let them be. I am not trying to beat that nigga Corey's ass again," Tremaine said.

"Naw, fuck that. She hit my mother. She needs her ass beat," I said.

"What the hell did I say, Sam? If you would listen to your man sometimes, you wouldn't get in half of the shit that you get into," Tremaine snapped.

"I'm sorry, baby, but you don't understand what they put me through," I cried.

"Bring your ass! We are not talking about this right now. Let it go, like I told you to do," he said, dragging me toward our room.

I'd let this go for now, but this was far from over.

Bria

It had been a month since Mo's wedding. We hadn't seen Sam or her trifling-ass mama again after they came and tried to ruin my best friend's wedding. I had no regrets about smacking that bitch, and if they hadn't grabbed me, I would have done a lot more. Mrs. Sharon had ended up pulling herself together, and she'd come back out to enjoy the reception. Of course, when Mr. Tim had finally come back out, he'd followed behind Mrs. Sharon like a sad puppy, but she ignored him the entire time we were in Puerto Rico. I knew she was embarrassed, but she wanted to be there for her daughter, so she put her pride to the side and did what she had to do. It was sad to say, but I didn't know if their marriage was going to last any longer.

So, David's mom had invited us over for a barbecue. She and I used to be very close, but for, like, the past six months, she had been coming at me sideways. She would tell me that I needed to stop treating Meka so badly. Or she'd say, "How would you like it if somebody kept saying you need to get Junior tested?" Little slick shit like that. I snapped at David for going back and telling his mom our issues, but he insisted that he hadn't told her anything.

When we arrived at their house, the first thing I noticed was Caiden and David's dad playing on the swing set that they had purchased for the grandkids. Junior immediately ran over to them and began to play. I had no problem with the little boy; it was his ratchet mother that I had an issue with.

"There's some beer and mini wine bottles in that cooler, if y'all want something to drink," Mr. Harris said as he came over and hugged me tightly and shook his son's hand.

I went to the cooler and grabbed David a beer and myself a bottle of wine. I gave David his drink and sat down in a lounge chair next to him. I was just about to ask where Mrs. Harris was when she walked outside, with Meka right behind her. It took everything in me not to run over there and smack that smile right off her face. Now I saw why his mom was acting so damn fake. I knew that she knew of Meka, but I didn't know they were all buddy-buddy. David reached over to grab my hand, because he knew I was pissed. I didn't want to be in the same area as this classless ho. I played everything cool for about thirty minutes, but I was fed up with his mom and Meka whispering to each other and laughing and shit. His mother didn't even acknowledge my presence.

"Mrs. and Mr. Harris, I think I'm going to go, but thanks for having me," I said as I stood up to leave.

"You're leaving already? We were all supposed to spend family time together. You haven't even eaten yet," Mr. Harris said. That heifer was no family of mine.

"I'm fine. I'll grab something later," I said as I prepared to leave.

"You sure?" he said.

I decided to be honest with them. "I really don't feel comfortable with all of this, to be honest, and I would rather remove myself," I said as politely as I could. I noticed David's mom looking at me with disgust, and then she opened her mouth. I prayed that nothing slick came out, because y'all know I had zero tolerance.

"Meka is a part of this family too, and I think you need to learn to get along with her. She tells me how badly you treat her all the time," Mrs. Harris said.

"*I* treat her badly? I don't say anything to her at all unless she says something to me, and she never has anything nice to say, so why should I?" I said.

"What is this I hear about Caiden not being David's, and he needs to get a paternity test?" Mrs. Harris said. The entire time she was questioning me, Meka was sitting next to her with her head on her shoulder, acting like she was so sad.

"I don't think David should be taking care of children that he's not sure are his," I said.

"Well, it seems like you are the only one who believe Caiden is not his. My husband and I believe that he's our grandson, and so does my son," she said. "Isn't that right, sweetie?" she said, looking at David.

David looked like he was about to piss on himself. "Yes, ma'am," he said, and my feelings were so hurt.

"Well, I guess I should go," I said as I turned around to leave.

"Good. We don't need any of that negativity when we are trying to have a good time. And if he gets a test for one, he needs to get a test for the other," I heard his mom say, and I stopped dead in my tracks.

"I know for sure that my son is his, and I don't have to take a test to prove that, because my son looks just like his father—unlike Caiden. David, I can't believe you are letting this go on," I said, hurt as hell.

Before he could reply, his mom said the most shocking shit to me. "Well, from what I hear, you weren't all that faithful to my son, anyway, so he might not be David's," Mrs. Harris said, and Meka burst out laughing.

I took a deep breath, because I was ready to show my ass in this bitch.

"Wanda, now you are out of line," David's dad told his wife. At least somebody had stuck up for me.

"Right, Mom. You have totally overstepped your boundaries," David finally said.

"I'm just telling the truth, and, son, don't you talk to me like that," his mom said and shrugged her shoulders.

"I have only been with one man in my entire life, and that's David—not that I owe you or anybody else an explanation about who I allow myself to be intimate with. You're over here letting this ratchet ho tell you lies, so y'all can have your little family time without my son and me, especially since you doubt he's your grandson. I don't have time for this shit at all. Little David, come on. We are leaving," I said. My son stopped what he was doing and ran over to me.

"Mommy, do we have to go?" my son asked.

I didn't respond. I just picked him up and headed toward the car. After taking ten steps, I stopped and turned around. "Oh, and don't you ever ask to see my child again," I said to his mother. I turned back around and continue my hike to the car.

"Baby, wait," I heard David say as he ran after me. "Don't leave. My mom doesn't mean any of that," he declared when he caught up with me and grabbed my arm. He had this dumb look on his face.

"I don't have anything to say to you. Don't try to run behind me now. You weren't thinking about me when your mother was bashing me and blaming me for everything," I said as I snatched my arm away from him. I stomped away from him.

"Baby, wait," he said, but I kept on walking. When I reached the car, I strapped my baby in his seat. When I tried to get in, David stopped me.

"Move, David. There is nothing left to say. It's obvious that your mom thinks you should be with Meka instead of me. I think it's obvious that we don't need to be with each other. I am not comfortable at all with this situation, which was forced on me, and I feel like you don't care about my feelings. I am tired of arguing and fighting with you and your baby mama all the time. I feel like I have no peace, and I can't take it anymore," I said as tears slid out of my eyes. Out of the corner of my eye, I saw Meka walking toward us. I wiped my eyes and quickly regained my composure.

"Baby, you don't mean all this shit. I love you! You are the only woman I have ever loved, and I can't lose you to this shit. I do care about your feelings. If I could take all this shit back, I would. Just please don't leave me," he said, trying to hug me and plead with me.

"David, why are you out here begging her when your family is back there?" Meka said and smirked.

"Right, David. That bitch is your family, so go and be with her," I said, and then I pushed him off me so hard that he almost fell to the ground.

"I've got your bitch," Meka said, but she wouldn't move any closer. I got in my car and shut and locked my doors so that David couldn't stop me.

"He's all yours," I said, loud enough for both of them to hear me, and then I sped off.

When I looked in my rearview mirror, I saw him pulling his dreads back in frustration and that bitch Meka walking toward him. I started to turn around, intending to run both of their asses over, but they weren't even worth it. The truth was, I was tired of this situation, and I knew I would never be fully happy as long as she was in the picture. So it was best that David and I went our separate ways.

David

When Bria drove off, my heart sank because I knew she was going to be pissed and would not want to deal with me. I knew it was going to be a while before my parents saw Junior again, based on the way my mom had treated her. Bria could be very stubborn sometimes. She didn't take no shit, and that was what I loved most about her—unless her venom was aimed at me.

"David, forget about her. I don't know why you don't see that things with her will never work. I want you to be a family with me and your son," Meka said and then wrapped her arms around me.

I pushed her off me ASAP; I already had enough problems. "I don't know why you don't understand that I am not trying to be with you like that. All I want to do is be there for my son," I said as I headed back to my parents' backyard.

"But, David, I love you, and I know you feel something for me," Meka said.

I didn't feel anything for her ass but resentment. If she had never gotten pregnant and started all this shit, things between Bria and me would be good right now. I knew Bria wanted me to get a paternity test done, but the more time I spent with Caiden, the more I loved that little boy, and it would break my heart if he wasn't mine.

"David, did you hear me?" Meka asked.

"Yeah, I heard you, but I'm not trying to hear your messy ass," I said. I turned and addressed my mother. "Mom, you were wrong for butting in my and Bria's business. It's not your place," I said heatedly. My mom had really overstepped her boundaries.

"Son, I was only telling the truth, and sometimes it hurts. That's why she stormed out of here like that," she said.

"No, it's because you ganged up on her with all those accusations that aren't true. You're letting Meka fill your head with bull," I said.

"You and Bria have hurt this poor girl enough. It's enough that she has to see you prancing some girl around who is forcing you to have a blood test done on your son, especially given that she is still in love with you," my mom said, pissing me off.

"I can't even do this with you, Mom. Stay the hell out of my business," I snapped.

"Son, don't talk to your mom like that. But he's right, honey. You need to mind your own business, and I'm not going to tell you again," my dad said.

I texted Kevin to pick me up so I could go home. My dad pulled me to the side.

"Son, I'll have a nice long talk with your mom about interfering in your business, but Bria is right. I have grown fond of that little boy, but I'm not sure if he's yours. I think you should get a test done too," my father said, but I was sick of everyone's input.

"Now here you go, Dad. I wish everyone would just leave this alone," I said.

"Look, I'm your father, and I want what's best for you. I'm not saying you have to do it, but it doesn't seem like a bad idea if you do. Look, either way, I support you," my pops said.

I chatted with my dad until Kevin picked me up. I had him drop me off at home. I had been calling and texting Bria since she pulled away from my parents' house, but of course, she had been ignoring me. I was happy to see she was at home, but I knew it wasn't about to be pretty. I walked in, and she was sitting on the couch, with a glass of wine in her hand, listening to Tamar's CD *Love and War*, so I knew she was in one of her moods.

"Where is my son?" I asked her.

"Oh, he's your son? I think we should wait on those test results so there will be no doubt," she said and then sipped on her drink.

"Quit playing with me. Where's my fucking baby at, man?" I growled, getting pissed at her dramatic ass.

"He's at his grandparents' house—the ones who have no doubt who my son belongs to," she said with a smirk.

"Baby, are we going to do this all night? I don't want to argue with you. I just want to go to bed next to you," I said, trying to switch the mood.

"David, I need some space. I can't do this with you anymore," she blurted out, and the tears came soon after.

"Baby, I'm sorry about today. I spoke to my mother, and I fixed things. Now, can we move past this please?" I said, sitting next to her on the couch.

"There is nothing left to fix. I can't deal with your baby mama and everything that comes with it. I'm done with this relationship, David, and you should go and be with her," she said.

"Bria, you are tripping. I don't want that girl. The only woman I want is you. Why can't you see that?" I said.

"Look at how you allowed your mom to treat me today. Every time I see Meka, she disrespects me, and you let both of them do it. I am tired of the bullshit, and I am tired of this relationship. I want you to leave, and don't bring you ass back. I can do bad by myself, and I don't need nobody else's help getting there," she said. The more she spoke, the more hurt I felt.

"You don't mean that shit. I treat your ass really good, and I'm faithful to you," I said.

"But you weren't always faithful, and that's why we are in this situation now. You need to leave, before I go in there and pack your shit myself," she said.

"Look, I'll sleep in the guest room, but you and I are not breaking up. I'm not trying to hear that bullshit," I said as I got up. I headed to the guest room. I was dead tired and confused as hell by this point. I shut the door and went to sleep as soon as my head hit the pillow. When I got up the next morning, Bria was gone. She had left a note on the fridge.

> *David,*
>
> *I love you, but I really need some time away from you and this relationship. It's hard for me to accept that you had a baby on me. I have to deal with baby mama drama every damn day, and I am tired. I don't know if this is the end for us, but right now, I'm going to focus on being happy and taking care of my son without all the drama. I honestly don't feel like you are ready to be with someone like me. Maybe we are not made for each other, like I always thought we were. Maybe this relationship has run its course.*
>
> *I'll see you around . . . I guess.*
> *Bria*

I called her phone and discovered she had blocked my number. *Fuck my life!*

Chapter Thirty-three

Zoe

Kevin and I were walking through the mall, talking and shopping for little things we needed to decorate our house, which we had just moved into. Since the mall that Corey's dad had given them to run had been making lots of money, Kevin had decided to upgrade our town house to a four-bedroom house in River Hills. It was a lot for me to handle, but I wasn't complaining, because I loved our place. We were about to go into this store when we were stopped by someone calling Kevin's name. This woman approached us.

"Hey, Kevin. Long time no see. I missed you," Imani said and then hugged him like I wasn't even standing next to him.

"Um, hey, Imani. What are you doing here?" Kevin said nervously, automatically making me feel like he was hiding something.

"Hey, silly. I told you I was coming. I officially moved here about a week ago," she said.

I took a deep breath and exhaled loudly because I wanted both of them to know that I was pissed, and I made sure my facial expression said it all.

"This my girl, Zaria, but we call her Zoe. Zoe, this is Imani, my *friend*," Kevin said. It didn't go unnoticed that he emphasized the word *friend*.

"Oh, um, hey," she said nonchalantly.

I didn't bother to respond to her, because she knew who I was, and she knew I had been standing here the entire time. She had just chosen to ignore me like I wasn't shit. Bitches these days had no respect for you or your relationship, but I refused to let this ho have mine.

"Well, I guess I'll let you two be," she yelled to our backs, because I had pulled Kevin away, and we were now heading to our car.

"Baby, I'm sorry. I had no idea that she was here," Kevin said.

"It doesn't seem that way. Her exact words were, 'Hey, silly. I told you I was coming. I officially moved here,'" I said, wanting to smack the dumb look he was giving me off his face.

"I know what she said, but I have not talked to that girl. I promise. I've been ignoring her calls and text messages for a while now," he said.

"Why does she talk like y'all have more going on than a friendship? I don't have time to play these games with you. I thought we were past all the drama and cheating," I said, fighting back my tears.

"Look, I am not cheating on you. That ain't even my style, and you know that. Ever since you fucked up with that bitch-ass nigga Dontae and we got back together, you've been on some insecure shit. I love your ass, but you better start trusting me," he said as he got in the driver's seat and I got in the front passenger's seat. I had no idea how this situation had ended with me being the bad guy, but I was not having it.

"I tell you what. You better tell that bitch to lose your number and to never contact you again, or you and her are going to meet a side of me that neither one of you is going to like," I said, staring him directly in the eyes.

He started laughing at me like I was some type of joke.

"I'm dead-ass serious, Kevin," I said.

"Okay, baby, I hear you, and that girl means absolutely nothing to me. I like when you talk that shit to me," he said.

I didn't respond; I just nodded my head. I meant every word I had said. I was going to fuck both of them up if I found out anything had happened between them two.

Kevin

It seemed like all I attracted was crazy women. I could not believe Imani had moved her ass down here. What I liked most about her was that she was able to have that sex partner relationship with no strings attached . . . or so I thought. Now, all of a sudden, this girl had done turned crazy on me. After Zoe and I saw her at the mall, she began to text me nonstop about how it was good seeing me and how we should meet up for dinner and things like that. When I wouldn't respond, she started calling my phone. Zoe was getting irritated and was ready to go find the girl and fight her. So I decided to meet up with her in hopes that we could fix this situation and I could move on with my life. I knew I had some good dick, but these bitches had lost their minds. The good thing about all of this was I hadn't heard a peep out of Sam, so I guessed she was really happy with ole dude. I wished her all the best, but I was praying for Tremaine because Sam was definitely not dealing with a full deck.

I had told Imani that I would meet her at her place because I didn't want to have this conversation in public. I walked up to her house and rang the doorbell. My plans were to make this shit as quick as possible; I didn't need any extra problems. When she opened the door with nothing but a red bra and a thong on, I knew I had a fucking problem on my hands.

"Hey, Daddy. I'm happy you finally showed up," she said with a smile on her face. Imani was sexy as hell, and she had the perfect shape, so it was hard for me to stay focused. My dick had got hard as soon as she opened the door. I cleared my throat before I finally spoke.

"Imani, put some clothes on. I didn't come here for all of that," I said.

"Come in," she said.

I walked into her place and stood by the door.

"Make yourself comfortable," she said as she walked toward the back of the house. Moments later, she came back with her body wrapped in this silk robe that matched her underclothes. She sat on the couch, and when she did, I could see her honeypot, and it was clean shaven. I stood there and tried to look elsewhere to avoid looking at her.

"Look, Imani, Zoe is my woman, and she is the only person I want to be with. I need you to stop calling me and texting me, because I'm not trying to go there with you," I said.

She sat on the couch quietly for a while, and then she stood up and walked over to me.

"Your mouth is saying one thing, but your pole is saying something totally different," she said as she grabbed my dick and began to caress it. I was already hard as hell, but just the slightest touch from her made me even harder.

I slowly moved her hand away, and I turned to leave, because I saw this getting bad real fast. I loved Zoe, and I knew it would kill her if I slept with Imani.

"Baby, don't leave. Please give me the chance to show you that I really love you and want to be with you. I can treat you good. You cannot tell me that the time we spent together wasn't good," she said.

I turned back around and faced Imani. "What we had was good, but we both moved on. That was years ago, Imani, and last time we talked, we both agreed that we would just be friends and that was it. If you felt something different, you should have spoken up then. You waited until Zoe and I were back together and years later to express how you feel. That shit ain't cool. I told you what it was before you moved up here, and ain't shit changed, so don't hit me up no more," I said.

"I feel like I deserve to have a chance to prove to you that we can have something good. You just automatically put me into the 'friends with benefits' category, without even seeing if we could actually have a relationship," she said.

It was true, but I hadn't been looking for a woman when we were messing around, and she had known that and had told me that she wasn't looking for a man, either, so it had all worked out.

"Imani, you knew what it was walking into things with me, so don't try to act brand new now. Just let it go, because my feelings for Zoe won't change. So just move on with your life please, and leave me alone," I said. I then walked out the door and ran right into Zoe. I didn't know what to say, because I didn't even know what she was doing here, and I knew this shit looked suspect as hell.

"Baby, let me explain, because it isn't what you think it is," I said.

"Please explain this shit, because from where I'm standing, it looks like you two just got done fucking," she snapped.

When I looked back, Imani was standing in the doorway with her robe open, exposing her bra and panty set. Imani had this dumb-ass smirk on her face, which I wanted to slap clean off.

"Baby, I came here to tell her to stop calling my phone and texting me. I told her I love you and want to be with you, and that was it. I didn't touch the girl," I said.

"Yeah, that's for now, but you will see that I am the one for you. She ain't got nothing on me. You told me I had the best sex ever," Imani said.

I wanted to punch her ass in the gut, but before I could, Zoe was up the stairs and on top of Imani. Zoe was trying to kill that girl, and it took everything in me to pull her off.

"Baby, calm down!" I said to Zoe.

Imani stood up. Her mouth was full of blood, and she was still talking shit.

"Don't tell me to calm down. This ho is too disrespectful," Zoe snapped.

"No, your ass is disrespectful, coming to my house, trying to fight me and shit," Imani spat.

"Bitch, you better stay the hell away from my man, or else it will be a lot worse," Zoe said.

"He's your man for now," Imani said and then laughed.

"We'll see," Zoe said, and then she stormed off to her car, climbed in, and pulled off. I had one last thing to say to Imani's messy ass, because I had seen a side of her that I didn't like.

"Let me make something real clear to you. Even if my girl and I break up, I still wouldn't choose you," I said, and then I walked off. I heard her slam her front door.

I drove home, anticipating the drama that would unfold when I got there.

Chapter Thirty-four

Imani

I wouldn't pretend like it didn't hurt me when he said he would never choose me, but I was still hopeful that I could change his mind. I originally moved here because my grandmother had gotten sick and needed someone to help take care of her, and since my grandmother had practically raised me, I could never not help her out. So I had found a good-paying job in Milwaukee and had moved to there. I had never wanted to end things with Kevin, but I had never been in the business of keeping a nigga who didn't want to be kept.

I had thought I would be able to just move on with my life without thoughts of Kevin, but I'd been wrong. I had thought about him almost every day since he called things off with me, and I knew I had to make things right between us. I was a very sexy and intelligent woman, so I knew I would have no problem finding a man. Hell, men tried to get with me all the time, but my heart was with Kevin. I didn't give a shit if he had a girlfriend; she wouldn't have him once I was done with their asses, and he would be all mine. I had never been in the business of breaking up happy homes, but Kevin was like no other, so he was worth the fight, and I was willing to go all the way to end up with the man.

Tim

My life had been hell over the past few months. Kendra's loudmouthed ass was always starting drama, and I was about sick of her shit. She always picked the wrong time and place to be ignorant too. I had been so pissed when she said all that shit in front of everybody, and my wife had been, too, because she had stabbed my ass and would have done the same to Kendra if I hadn't stopped her. I had thought about just letting my wife kill her ass, but I couldn't live with myself if I knew my wife was in jail behind my mess.

I had cut Kendra's ass completely off. I would be lying to myself if I said that I didn't love Kendra. I would even go as far as to say that I was in love with her. That was why I could sit here and say that I knew that I was not completely done with her right now. I was just teaching her ass a lesson. I had tried to leave her alone, but her ass had me slightly whipped. She did certain things to my body that no other woman had. She was also a lot of fun when we hung out, and she was down for anything. I had allowed myself to feel strongly for another woman besides my wife. For a while I had just ignored the feelings I still had for Kendra, but I had become so reckless and messy that I couldn't keep up with all this shit.

Things with Sharon had taken a turn for the worst, and I really felt deep down in my heart that shit was about to hit the fan. For starters, she hadn't put my ass out when we made it back to the States. Secondly, she was acting like nothing had ever happened. She was acting like she hadn't stabbed my ass and like I hadn't had to get some stitches. In all the years we had been together, years in which I had done some fucked-up shit, she had never responded like this. She normally put my ass out and stopped talking to me for a few days or weeks, but this time, she was acting different. She cooked me dinner every night, and she had even started having sex with me again—with a condom, of course. We had been using those ever since we got back together. The shit felt weird as hell, using condoms with my wife. I didn't know what was going on, but I was going to go along with it.

Since I was not fucking with Kendra right now, I had been fucking around with Madison more lately. Tonight I was meeting her at the Aloft Hotel for a much-needed stress reliever. Madison knew how to use her mouth and tongue to relax your body and make you forget about all your problems. I got something different from all the women I screwed around with and were a part of the Tim Peterson team. Madison knew how to shut up and cater to my every need—unlike Kendra or Sharon. Neither one of them knew how to shut up. I sometimes felt bad about what I was doing to my wife and family, but I couldn't stop, and believe me, I had tried. I almost felt like I had a problem.

"Hey, baby. How was your day?" Madison asked when I entered the room.

"Good. Did you run my bathwater?" I asked as I headed straight for the bathroom.

I needed to relax; I had had a long day at work. I got in the bath and freshened up, and when I stepped out of the bathroom, Madison was lying in bed, playing with herself. Yeah, I couldn't see myself stopping any time soon.

Kendra

Tim had not spent any time with me since we left the island. He had barely spent time with his son, either. I knew it had everything to do with that bitch Sharon. She was probably telling him he couldn't be around his son or me. I knew I was going to have to hurt her ass, because no one would ever come between my kids and their father again. I had done that shit with Sam, but I was definitely not doing it with my son. I would do anything in my power to make sure that didn't happen, and even if I had to hurt a bitch to ensure that, I would.

Since Tim wouldn't return any of my calls, I had decided to stalk his ass to see what he was up to. I was going to get out of my car to confront his ass when he was leaving the office, but I was on my phone when he walked out and got in his car. So, instead, I followed his ass. When I noticed he was going in the direction of his house, I started to turn around and head back, but then he made a turn that was in the opposite direction of his house. I followed him until he parked at the Aloft Hotel and handed his keys to the valet.

What the hell is he doing at this hotel? He better not be with another bitch, I thought. It would be a damn shame if his ass was cheating on me *and* his wife with someone else. Tim could never turn down a pretty bitch, and he wondered why my ass was so insecure when we were officially together. I had caught his ass cheating on me on more than one occasion, and I had had to whip his ass and the girl's ass he had cheated on me with too. I couldn't believe I loved this man when he had caused me so much pain over the past twenty-plus years, but the heart wanted what it wanted.

I had damn near fallen asleep while I waited on Tim to come out of that hotel. I figured he must have a business meeting here. I wouldn't allow myself to think another woman was in the picture. I took one last glance at the front door to the hotel. I had been parked across the street from the front of the hotel for almost two hours, and he hadn't come out yet. I was just about to pull off when I saw him coming out of the hotel, all hugged up with some woman I had never seen before in my life. I was really sent over the edge when they stopped and tongue kissed as if they didn't have a care in the world.

I immediately saw red, and all logic went out the door. I hopped out of my vehicle and darted across the street. Before he knew what was happening, I smacked the dog shit out of him. He was stunned as hell, and the bitch with him looked like she was scared.

"What the hell? Who is she, and why is she putting her hands on you, Tim?" she said, rubbing his face.

I was about to punch her ass, until Tim interfered.

"Kendra, what are you doing here? And your ass better keep your hands to yourself," he snapped.

"What the hell are you doing, coming out of the hotel with another bitch?" I snapped.

"I'm not your bitch," the little ho said.

"Kendra, don't come over here questioning me like you are my wife. I don't owe your ass any explanation. You are my side bitch, not my main one," he said, and my heart instantly broke. He had never spoken to me like this, and I wouldn't let his ass get away with doing so now.

"I don't give a damn if I'm not your fucking wife. Your ass stays fucking me, and you act like I'm your fucking wife. Don't try to act brand new in front of this bitch. So who is she?" I said.

"Like I said, you are not my wife. I don't owe you any-thing," he said.

"But *I'm* your wife, so explain to me why you are out here arguing with two other women, when you should be at home with me," Sharon said from behind me. She had appeared out of nowhere.

We all stared at her, and I could tell all hell was about to break loose.

Sharon

I had had enough of Tim's bullshit, and it was time to let the cat out of the bag. So, about six months ago, I had decided that my and Tim's marriage was finally over. I could no longer stand the cheating and emotional abuse I was suffering while being with him. He had completely turned me into a woman I didn't even recognize. I didn't used to play that cheating shit. I would leave his ass at the drop of a hat if a man decided to cheat on me, but with Tim, it was totally different. He had cheated on me for our entire marriage, and I had just accepted it like a fool.

I had always known deep down in my heart that Kendra would eventually come back in the picture, because even after he married me, the bitch had still been desperate to sleep with him, and although he had stopped for a while, their affair had eventually become a full-fledged one. When she made her announcement at my daughter's wedding, that had sealed the deal for our marriage. This nigga and his side ho had embarrassed me for the very last time. Like I mentioned earlier, she wasn't the only mistress.

I had hired a private investigator six months ago so that I would have all the proof I needed to get this divorce over and done with. A small part of me had hoped that he wouldn't find anything. A small part of me had actually wanted to believe that Tim loved me enough to want to do right by me, but that had been wishful thinking. When I found out that he was cheating with a woman named Madison, who herself was married, and that he was still fucking with Kendra, I'd had my lawyer draw up those divorce papers fast as hell. The private investigator had pictures of Tim kissing and hugging both women and pictures of him wining and dining both women. He also had a picture of Tim and Kendra fucking in his car. I had got all the evidence I needed, and so I had decided it was now time to confront that ass. I was going to personally give him those divorce papers.

I had downloaded the Find My iPhone app to his phone so that I could keep track of what his nasty ass was doing. Imagine my surprise when I had found out he was at the damn hotel. My initial plan had been to get the room number and the room key and to walk in on him and whatever bitch he was with, because he had reserved the room under his name but with our joint bank account, like the messy-ass man he was. I hadn't made it to the hotel in time, though. When I'd walked up to the hotel, he and that chick Madison were arguing with Kendra. I had witnessed the entire argument, and they'd been so deep in the shit that they didn't see me walk up. I'd pulled out my phone and recorded their asses so that I would have even more proof to show the judge.

They'd all had a shocked look on their face when I finally announced my presence. The scene before me hurt me like never before, but I refuse to let them know that. I put on my game face and continued to do what I'd come here for. Tim looked like he wanted to disappear, and that bitch Madison had a lot of balls, because she was still hanging on to my husband's arm, but I didn't care about none of this shit anymore. Tim and I were done, so he was no longer my concern. Kendra was looking like she wanted to take off running. She talked all that shit, but she knew I would beat that ass. Although I was sure Madison knew that Tim was married, because he still wore his ring, Kendra was worse. She'd been at this shit for years, and that was why I hated her ass so much.

"Why is everyone so quiet now? You know what? I don't care to address you two bitches, because my so-called husband is the one to blame," I said.

"Sharon, I'm sorry. I know this looks really bad, but I think I have a problem. I can go get counseling so that we can fix this, baby," he said, finally letting go of Madison and taking a few steps toward me.

"Tim, what about us? You said that once I was officially divorced, we would start a family together," Madison cried.

He ignored her and kept coming toward me.

"Tim, I don't even need you to explain shit to me. I had your ass followed. You've been fucking both of these bitches for at least six months, and it could be longer, for all I know," I said.

"You had me followed? You didn't trust me?" he said when he reached my side.

I looked at him like he had lost his mind. I knew he couldn't possibly believe I could ever trust him. Monique had told me a month ago about all the things that had gone on with her and Sam and about how Sam had slept around a lot, and I saw where she got it from.

"Tim, you can't be dumb enough to think that I would ever trust your ass after all the bullshit you have taken me through. I came here to give you this and to let you know that we are done. You can have these two desperate-ass bitches. I know for sure that you can have Kendra, because she is not going to ever leave your dirty ass alone, and two dirty bitches deserve one another," I said. I handed him the divorce papers and then turned to walk away.

"I'm not going to be one of your bitches anymore," Kendra yelled to my back.

I ignored that bitch, because I had given her enough of my energy. I started walking back to my car.

"Sharon, you can't divorce me! I won't have it," Tim yelled.

I just kept on walking, because even if he didn't sign the papers, I knew a judge would grant me my divorce based on the evidence that I had against him. I was done with Tim's sorry ass, and now it was time to be happy and to let go of all the bullshit he had put me through.

I had already moved all my clothes and everything that was dear to me out of the house that Tim and I shared, so I was ready for a fresh start. There was no need for me to ever return there. I pulled my phone out of my pocket and called Cameron.

"Hey, baby. I'm on my way home," I said to him. *Out with the old and in with the new*, I thought.

Chapter Thirty-five

Monique

Things for me couldn't be any better since I had become Corey's wife. We had moved into a bigger house, and we were already working on having babies. Despite all that, Sam's childish ass had been playing on my phone. I knew it was her silly ass because I had no other enemies. For the life of me, I couldn't understand how we were best friends one minute and then we turned into enemies. I didn't understand why that girl hated me so much when I hadn't done anything but love her. I had taken her in with open arms even after she betrayed me the first time. I couldn't let this bitch ruin my life. I planned to get to the bottom of whatever her issue was with me and handle it accordingly, because I was tired of all the drama, and I just wanted to be happy.

I had never thought in a million years that my parents would be in the place they were in right now. My mom had been out of the house they shared for about four months now. I knew that she was staying with her new boyfriend right now, and I must admit that I really liked him. He treated my mother so good, and for the first time in years, my mom was truly happy. I could see it in her eyes. I could also see that she was still sad about getting the divorce, but my father didn't deserve her. I still loved my father, but to be very frank, he ain't shit.

It seemed like everything was going good in my relationship right now, but I was almost scared to accept that fact. Every time things seemed to be going good for me, Sam would come with her bullshit and rip that happiness right out from under me. I was trying to keep a positive outlook, but it was hard sometimes, and it didn't help that both of my friends were going through relationship problems right now. So I was just waiting for my time to come. I knew it was messed up, but that was how I felt, and as long as Sam's retarded ass was in the picture, I was afraid it might always be that way.

I planned to look deeper into Sam and what was really going on with her. I remembered Bria telling me that Sam had a history of mental illness, which Sam and her mother had tried so hard to hide, and I was almost positive that my father knew what was going on as well. Speaking of Kendra's dirty ass, when I caught her, she had an ass beating coming. One, for what she had done on my wedding day, and two, for how she had hurt my mother. I was sick of letting these two bitches get away with murder, and when I got done with both of them, they were going to wish they had never tried me, because payback was definitely a bitch, and so was karma.

Bria

David and I had been officially separated for about five months now. I'd become so tired of dealing with all the drama that came with his so-called baby mama. I just hadn't been able to deal with it anymore, and he had made clear what he wanted when he refused to get a blood test on that little boy. Not only that, he had allowed his mother to disrespect me in front of Meka's ratchet ass. I was over all of that, and my life had been so much more peaceful since

I left him. I didn't have to worry about none of that shit anymore; my only concern was my son. I could go to sleep now without worrying about how this bitch planned to ruin my day tomorrow.

I would be lying if I said I wasn't hurt and I didn't miss David, but I felt like I had made the right decision. Of course, he called and texted me on the daily, trying to work things out, but I was just not feeling it anymore. I had always been faithful to him, even when I left him the first time. He had cheated on me when things got hard for us, and as a result of that, he may have fathered a baby with an ignorant-ass bitch. Truthfully, every time I saw Caiden, it was a constant reminder of David cheating on me, and no matter how much I loved that man, I just couldn't see myself suffering like that on a daily basis.

I allowed him to see his son, but I had told him that he better not take my child over to his bitch-ass mother's house, as she had had the audacity to say that my son may not be his. I had swabbed David and my son weeks before he and I broke up. David was a hard sleeper, and he slobbered when he slept, so I'd been able to get his DNA without a problem, and the results had come back today. Of course, there was a 99.9 percent probability that he was the father. I had made copies of the results, and I had personally taken those copies over to David's, his mother's, and Meka's bitch-ass house and had put one copy in each of their mailboxes. This way, they would know for sure that he was the father of my son.

I was tired of being cooped up in the house, and I wanted to meet new people and have a little fun, so I had called my girls up and arranged a night out on the town. We had decided to go barhopping on Water Street instead of doing the whole club thing tonight. I had on some high-waist cut-up jeans, a nude crop top, and nude heels. I had my hair in wand curls, and I wore some diamond earrings and a matching bracelet. I was looking and feeling good as hell. My girls and I had met at Mo's house, and we had started turning up before we left there. Corey's ass thought he was slick. He had called David, had told him that I was over their house, and had described what I had on. David had then called me and questioned me. I had ignored his butt and kept it pushing. Tonight was about me, and I wasn't worrying about the drama that I had going on in my life.

We were at this place called Brothers. This handsome guy walked up to me and introduced himself. He was tall and had a caramel complexion and a low haircut. His eyes were the same color as his skin, and he had the sexiest smile. His body was nice and toned, and he had tattoos covering his arms. Miss Kitty start thumping at the sight of him. Zoe and Mo were in their own little world, so that gave me some alone time to see what tall and sexy had going on for himself.

I found out his name was Nathan, and he played basketball for Marquette University. This was his last year, and the NBA was looking to recruit him. He was here tonight with a bunch of his teammates, celebrating a game they had won the night before. What I liked most about this guy was that he wasn't coming on strong and he was very polite. He spoke to me like he had manners, and I must admit, for the first time in a long time, I was not thinking about David and our issues. We sat at the bar and talked all night, until my girls were ready to go. We exchanged numbers and promised each other we would keep in touch.

I had never thought in a million years that I would be this attracted to someone other than David. He was all I knew. But I felt at peace with Nathan, and I had known him for only a few hours. When we left the bar, though, I immediately started thinking about David. All this drinking had made me horny, and I missed him, but I refused to give in. So, I took my lonely ass back to my parents' house and cuddled up with my baby. I thought of how I was going to make a life for my son and me, without his father if things didn't change for us.

Zoe

I was pissed, to say the least, when I walked up to Imani's house and my man was walking out her door. I immediately saw red and wanted to attack both of their asses. I had got Imani's address out of Kevin's phone, and I had intended to confront her myself. Imagine my surprise when I discovered Kevin was already there, and this heifer was standing in the doorway, with nothing on but a bra and panties. When Kevin brought his ass home, he was met by the sight of his clothes burning on our barbecue grill in the backyard. I knew he hadn't slept with her, because she had confirmed that they hadn't gone to bed, but his ass should not have been there. Since I couldn't take my anger out on Imani, I had decided he would have to do.

I had been dealing with crazy bitches since I got with Kevin. First, Sam, and now this bitch Imani. I made Kevin change his number, because Imani had been calling him all night, and I was ready to go over that bitch's house and blow her ass out of her misery. Things calmed down after that, but I knew I was going to have to beat her ass again, because Imani seemed to be the same way Sam was. To make matters worse, I had just found out that I was six weeks pregnant, and I hadn't told Kevin yet. I had held out on him after the Imani situation for about a month, and as soon as I gave him some, his ass had got me knocked up.

I knew I needed to tell him that we had a baby coming soon, but honestly, I didn't know how he was going to feel or if we were even ready to be parents. We had so much drama going on in our lives, I didn't know if this was going to be an added pressure that we really didn't need. Whatever the consequences were, we had to deal with this pregnancy, because I refused to get rid of my baby. The pain I had felt when I lost my baby by Dontae was so excruciating. I had never felt so much pain in my life. Getting hit by a car caused less pain.

I had to get my life in order because I couldn't let stress cause me to have a miscarriage. So, I had to do whatever it took to make sure that I had a healthy baby—even if that meant leaving the man I loved. I loved Kevin, and I did want to be with him, because he was a good guy, but I couldn't keep getting out of character and fighting women who didn't know how to let go. Hopefully, things would get better. If not, then I was going to be forced to make the decision to walk away.

Sam

I was still hurt and pissed off about the events that had taken place at my so-called sister's wedding. I didn't want her to have a happy ending, because she didn't deserve it. She had stolen so many years of my life from me, which I would never get back, and it was time that she finally paid for what she had done. I had been sitting in my bed for the past hour, with my legs pulled up to my chest, rocking back and forth, with tears streaming down my face, thinking about the childhood I had had without my father. As a child, I had cried myself to sleep every night, and I had prayed to God that he would send my father, but he had never come, and that was because Mo had had him all along.

Did she know how bad it hurt not to have your father in your life? Did she understand that feeling you got when you longed for something all your life and you never got it? She was the reason I had done all the fuck-up shit I had done over the years. If I had had my father, none of this would have happened. I started kicking and screaming on top of my bed and yelling, "I hate you. I hate you." Tremaine tried to enter the room when he heard my screams, but I had locked the door.

"Baby, are you okay?" he yelled, but I didn't respond. Instead, I pulled my legs back up to my chest and screamed and cried some more.

"Baby, open the door! Is someone in there with you?" he yelled.

I could hear the panic in his voice, but I couldn't come out of the trance I was in. I started mumbling, "She's dead. She's dead," as I rocked back and forth. I heard a loud crash, and it was Tremaine. He had kicked in the door. He rushed over to me and checked me out.

"Baby, what's wrong? And who's dead?" he asked as he sat down next to me, but I couldn't respond, because all I saw were visions of me getting rid of Mo for good. I didn't see or hear him get up and leave the room, but he came back moments later and held me tight. I was still crying and mumbling things. I didn't know how long we sat there before my dad arrived at our house.

Tremaine threw me over his shoulder and carried me out of the house. When they tried to put me in the car, I began to kick, scream, and shout out all types of things. They were finally able to get me in the car. I didn't remember anything after all of that. All I knew was that I woke up in the mental institution.

Sam

I could not believe my dad had taken me to the mental institution. When he'd arrived at our house, he immediately knew I was having one of my episodes, so he'd brought me here. I had never wanted Tremaine to see this

side of me. I had tried so hard to hide my disorder from
him and everyone else. I had stopped taking my pills long
ago, and every time I felt an episode coming on, I'd been
able to control it and calm myself down, but on that day, I
hadn't been able to. I was released after being held there
for a week. They made sure that they sent me home with
my pills. I had told my dad to come and get me, because
I didn't want to face Tremaine, so I was surprised to see
Tremaine and our son standing out front, waiting for me.
I was pissed with my dad, and I would deal with him later.
I knew that sooner or later I was going to have to face
Tremaine, but I just didn't want to do it so soon.

My son ran to me, and I picked him up and kissed him all
over his face. No matter how medicated they had had me,
I had still missed my son with everything in me. I walked
over to the car, trying to avoid Tremaine. I was so ashamed
and afraid that he was going to leave me, and I wasn't
able to face that right now, either. That would only make
me crazier, and I didn't want that. I wanted to save all my
energy for Mo. Thoughts of her stealing my life were what
had caused my episode. I strapped my son in his seat and
tried to get in the back with him, but Tremaine stopped me.

"Samariah, don't do that," he said, grabbing my arm.

"Do what?" I mumbled.

"Avoid me. Can I please have a hug and a kiss?" he said,
shocking me. I was hesitant at first, but then I fell into his
arms. He lifted my chin so that I was looking into his eyes.
He brought his lips to mine, and I melted into his arms. I
really loved this man, and I hoped I didn't scare him away
with my disorder. We finally finished our kiss and got in the
car.

"Are you hungry?" he asked.

I nodded my head yes.

He took me to IHOP. We sat down, and we placed our
order. We sat in silence for a while, but then our silence
was broken.

"Baby, why didn't you tell me that you have that disorder?" he asked.

"It's not easy to tell someone you have multiple personality disorder. Plus, I didn't need you judging me," I said.

"Sam, I would never judge. I just felt like I should have known so that I could better help you," he said.

"If I had told you, you would have left me, like everyone else who I thought loved me," I said as I began to cry.

"Sam, I love you. As a matter fact, I am in love with you, and at this point, there is no turning back. I am not leaving you. I am going to help you through this," he said.

I looked deep into his eyes, and I could see the love he had for me radiating off him. I began to feel bad for all the bad things I had done over the years. Seeing how much he loved me made me want to get better for him. "Tremaine, I don't deserve you. I have done so many horrible things. Maybe we should separate. I don't want to cause you any more trouble or pain than I already have," I told him.

"Like I said, Samariah, we are in this together. I am not leaving you, and we are going to do whatever it takes so that we can get you better—especially for our son," he said.

"Okay," I said as he pulled me close to him.

I planned to get myself together right after I destroy that bitch Mo. . . .

Chapter Thirty-Six

Sharon

Since the day I walked out on Tim, I had felt nothing but peace and happiness. Cameron treated me so good that I was almost scared to allow myself to feel more for him than I already did. Tim had done a number on my heart, and I was not trying to go back down that road again. As I had originally thought, Tim hadn't signed the divorce papers, but the judge had granted me my divorce, anyway. Now I was finally free from his ass. It had been about three months since the divorce was finalized and about seven months since we had separated.

From what I had heard, he and Kendra had finally made things official, and you know what? I didn't even care. He was now her headache, and he was going to do the same shit to her that he had done to me, but maybe even worse, because Kendra was a dick-sick whore, and she didn't care how she had Tim as long as she had him. You know what? She and Tim were going to get what was coming to them because of the way they had treated me.

Enough about them. They had taken enough of my energy. Things with Cameron were so exciting and brand new. He had taken a month off work just so that I could get things off my mind and focus on a future with him and on letting go of my past. We'd gone to Jamaica for two weeks, and then we'd left there and flown to Italy. That was the best time I had had in a long time, and I couldn't be better.

I had finally let Tim go, and a weight had been lifted off me. I was finally happy and free, and I had God and Cameron to thank for that. Tim had had a good thing, but instead, he wanted these ratchet whores who were not good for anything but a fuck. Even though I was over what he had done to me, I was still looking for an opportunity to get in Kendra's ass for all the hurt and pain she had caused me.

Kendra

Guess what? I finally had my man, and it felt damn good. We hadn't made things official right away. He'd waited until his divorce was final before we said we were officially a couple. I didn't understand why we had even waited that long, because he had practically moved in when he realized that things were really over between him and Sharon. He'd ignored my calls and texts for about two weeks after Sharon gave him those pictures, along with the divorce papers, but after that, he was right back sucking, licking, and long stroking me like nothing had ever happened.

I had made sure to check that bitch Madison, and I had told her to stay away from my man. Now that we were together, I was going to make sure his ass stayed faithful to me. I planned to be on him like white on rice. It had been cool for him to sleep around when we were not official, but now I was not having it. I mean, I wouldn't leave him if I caught him cheating, but I would beat him and whatever ho he had decided he wanted to cheat on me with. I knew it sounded crazy, but I was crazy in love with Tim, so I wouldn't leave him for something as small as cheating.

I had waited twenty-plus years for this moment, and it was finally a reality. Since his house was bigger, we had decided it was best that I gave up my condo and move in with him. I didn't even feel bad about sleeping in the same bed he and Sharon had shared or living in the same house that they had shared. Like I said before, I'd take him however I could get him. However, I did make him get a new comforter set.

Tonight I cooked one of his favorites, which was smothered pork chops with homemade mashed potatoes, corn on the cob, and homemade biscuits. I had his plate ready, along with his favorite drink, because I was expecting him home at any minute now. I poured myself a glass of wine while I waited for my man. Three more glasses of wine and almost two hours later, his ass finally decided to come home.

"So, what took you so long to get home?" I said and then took another sip of my wine.

"I had to stay at the office late to finish up some last-minute paperwork for this case I'm working on," he said as he loosened up his tie and avoided eye contact with me.

"Why weren't you answering my phone calls? And why, when I called your office, did your secretary say that you left the office for lunch and did not return?" I quizzed. I knew his ass was going to come home and lie to my face. When I had realized he was an hour late getting home, I had called his phone and his office. Of course, he had not picked up his phone, and what he didn't know was that his secretary and I were closer than he thought, and she gave me the tea on anything I wanted to know.

"Look, Kendra, she has no idea what's she talking about. And kill all that questioning. Where is my dinner and drink?" he said, irritated.

I didn't push it further, because I knew that all he would do was continue to lie. I got up, heated up his food, and made him another drink. I leaned in to give him a kiss, and I was overwhelmed with the smell of Chanel perfume. My first impulse was to slap his ass and throw the drink I had just made him right in his face, and that was exactly what I did.

"Girl, what the hell is your problem?" he snapped as he stared at me with pissed-off eyes.

"What bitch were you with? I smell her perfume all over your trifling ass," I said.

"I don't know what the hell you're talking about. Your ass is always tripping," he said.

"Your ass ain't nothing but a liar! I know one thing. You and whatever bitch you were with better end that shit right now, before I kill both of your asses!" I yelled, and then I stormed off to our bedroom.

Of course, his ass didn't follow me. I knew one thing. I had been waiting for this moment for too long, and I wouldn't let any other woman steal what belonged to me.

Monique

So I had figured out why Sam was so crazy. My dad had called me when he admitted her to the hospital so that I could support my sister. I had refused to go and see her because all she desired to do was make my life a living hell. I had considered paying her a visit while she was there, just to let her know that I knew her little secret, but I knew I would just be stooping to her level if I did that. I now knew that Sam was capable of anything, and I truly believed she had something to do with Zoe's accident, and she was probably the one who had hurt Bria too.

My thoughts were interrupted by a message that had been left on my phone. I did not recognize the number, but I clicked on the message, and my heart literally stopped in my chest. It was another video of Sam and Corey having sex. I knew shit between us was too good to be true, and I knew Sam was the sender of the video. She refused to let me be happy, and I was sick of her bullying. I didn't know how much more of this I could take.

"I just want to be happy!" I shouted as tears streamed down my face. "Why does this girl want to hurt me?" I shouted again. I fell to the floor and cried my eyes out. My heart hurt so badly, and thoughts of killing myself swirled around in my head. I didn't hear Corey when he came into our house. I just felt him shaking me, and that was when I realized what was going on.

"Baby, what's going on? Why are you lying on the floor, crying?" he asked.

I didn't say a word; I just handed him the phone.

"Baby, I am so sorry you had to see this, but I am glad I told you before she did," he said.

Before Corey and I had got married, we decided to come clean about everything we had done so that there wouldn't be any surprises once we said, "I do." He had told me about Sam, I had told him about Tremaine, and we had moved past it. Even though he had told me about Sam, it still hurt to see him with her. I was more hurt by her actions. She did not care who she hurt, and she didn't care that I was her sister. All she cared about was making sure I was miserable.

"Why does this girl hate me so much?" I cried into my husband's chest.

"I don't know, baby, but you can't let her steal your happiness. You can't let her break you. You have too many people who love you and care about you to let her do this to you," he said, and he was right. I had had enough of her bullying, and it was time to put an end to all this shit. I stopped all that crying and pulled myself together.

It was time to pay Miss Sam a much-needed visit.

Bria

David and I had been broken up for a while now, and I missed him like crazy. I knew he was at his office with Kevin and Corey right now, so I decided to stop by and pay him a visit so we could talk about some things. Last time we spoke, he had cursed me out about the DNA test on him that I had submitted without his knowledge. He was beyond pissed at me. In fact, I had never seen him that mad. I remembered the argument we had had.

I was lying in my bedroom, browsing the Internet for an apartment, when David stormed in. "So, you tested me and my son without my permission?" he shouted.

"Hi to you too, David. And yes, I tested you and your son to prove to your mother and your baby mother that Junior is definitely yours," I said while I continued to browse the Internet.

He slapped my computer on the floor and snatched my ass off my bed. "You don't have shit to prove to either one of them. Your ass is becoming just as ignorant as Meka's dumb ass. You better get your shit together, because I am tired of playing games with you, Bria. You better bring your ass home, or else I'm leaving your ass for good. Think it's a game!" he said and then turned to leave. The way he was talking to me had me wet as hell.

"David, I'm—" I wasn't able to finish my sentence, because he stopped me.

"Don't say shit else to me! You heard what I said," he said, and then he stomped out of the room. I heard him leave the house.

I felt like shit, and he was right. I had not been acting any better than Meka's tired ass. About a week later, I decided that it was time for us to make up and for me to return home. I would figure out a way to accept the baby situation and be happy with the love of my life. I made sure to wear a fitted sundress that hugged my body tightly. I wore my hair bone straight and applied a small amount of makeup to my face. I threw on some summer wedges and headed out the door. I had already packed my baby's items and my stuff and had loaded them in my car.

I got behind the wheel and headed to the mall. I parked my car and walked inside the mall, then headed straight for their office. I was looking and feeling good, and I was ready to see my love. I was about to enter his office when I heard a female's voice on the other side of the door. Whoever she was, their little meeting was about to get broken up. I entered the office just as Meka leaned in and kissed David on the lips. He immediately pushed her away, but I didn't know if it was because he saw me or he was rejecting her advances.

"Meka, what the hell are you doing? Bria, baby, this isn't what it looks like," he said.

Now, I was normally a strong woman, and I ordinarily would never let this bitch see me cry, but today I didn't even care. The tears flowed freely from my ass, and my heart broke in two. I glanced at Meka. She sat back in her chair, with a smirk on her face and her arms crossed on her chest. I turned on my heels to leave the office, and David damn near pushed the desk over trying to get to me.

"David, let that bitch leave. She doesn't deserve you," Meka shouted behind us.

I stopped dead in my tracks. I turned around slowly and ran full speed toward her. I tackled her ass like I was a quarterback, and she went flying to the floor. I jumped on top of her and gave her blow after blow to her face. I felt someone lifting me off her, but I was in my zone. I tried to kill that bitch. When I finally looked up, David and Corey were holding me back, and Kevin was helping Meka off the floor. Her face was bloody, and her right eye had already begun to swell.

"I can't believe you let that ho put her hands on me like that, David!" Meka yelled.

"Man, get that bitch out of here," David said to Kevin.

"Oh, so you are just going to treat me like I'm not shit!" Meka screamed as Kevin practically dragged her out the door.

"You ain't shit," David yelled. He sat me down in a chair. "Baby, I am sorry, but you have to know that I didn't kiss her. She kissed me," he said.

"I don't even care, David. I thought I was going to come here and make everything good between us, but I now see that we just don't belong together," I said as I stood up to leave.

"Baby, that's not true. I will fix all this shit," he said.

"I'm done, David. I can't live my life like this. I have a son to think about, and I can't keep doing this shit," I told him.

"Baby, please."

"I love you and probably always will, but I am done," I declared, then headed toward the door.

"I'm not letting you go, Bria," he said, grabbing my arm.

I gave him the meanest look I could muster up, and he let me go. I ran out of his office and out to my car. Once I got inside the car, I cried like I had never cried before. . . .

Chapter Thirty-seven

Meka

I was so tired of that trick Bria putting her hands on me. This time she had overdone it. I wanted so badly to call the police on her and press charges, but I didn't want to look like a scary bitch. I was terribly hurt about how David had treated me after the fight. I had been trying with everything in me to break them up, but nothing had seemed to work, until I became friends with David's mother. I'd gone crying to her about how Bria was turning David against me and my son and all that bull, and she'd fallen for it. She thought Bria was the worst person in the world.

What she didn't know was that David and I had never really been in a serious relationship. David used to be somebody I would just fuck and get money from, but I had ended up falling deeply in love with him, and when he ended things with me, I had vowed to do whatever it took to get him back. I had been sleeping with his friend Mitch at the time, and when I ended up pregnant, I had had no clue which one fathered my baby, and I still didn't. All I knew was that I wanted David, and I wanted to be a family with him. I also knew that David would take care of his child, like a man should. So, I had told him that he was the father, and I had been working on repairing our relationship.

When I found out that Bria had left him the night his mom confronted her, I'd been as happy as ever. I had just known he would come running back to me, but he hadn't.

Bria had David's ass whipped and lovesick. He didn't want anybody but her. The day Bria and I fought, I had called David and told him we needed to discuss putting our son in day care. He had told me to come to his office to discuss it. I had made sure to put on a matching bra and panty set, and I had worn some tight-ass jeans, a fitted blouse, and some sexy red heels. I strutted into his office and sat down. I was insulted that he never even glanced my way.

Instead of talking about our son, I told him all the things I wanted to do to him. Through the window, I saw Bria walking into the office, so I knew I had to do something right away to piss her off. I knew my presence alone would make her mad, but I wanted to ruin her. That was when I leaned in for the kiss, hoping David would kiss me back. When he pushed me off him and I saw the look on her face, I knew they were over. She began to cry, and I wanted to laugh so hard, but instead, I just sat back and smirked.

After the fight, I drove straight to David's mom's house. I rang her doorbell, and when she opened the door, I fell into her arms and cried hysterically.

"Meka, sweetie, what's wrong?" she asked.

"Bria attacked me, and David just let her," I said as I pulled out of her embrace so that she could see my face. I wanted her to hate Bria and to never want to deal with her again. That was why I lied to her about Bria.

"Why would she do such a thing?" she said.

"She saw David and me kissing, and she just lost her mind after that," I explained and forced myself to cry harder.

"Oh, God. She just can't stand the fact that my son chose to be with you instead of her," she said.

"Everything was fine between David and me until she showed up. Now he acts like he doesn't even know me," I cried.

"You hush now, baby. I'm going to fix all this mess right away," she said as she wrapped her arms around me tightly.

My job was done, and once I got done with Bria, David and his entire family were going to hate her. Wait and see.

Zoe

We hadn't heard anything from Imani since that day I had Kevin change his number, so I guessed that was a good thing. Nonetheless, things between Kevin and me had been very bad. We had been arguing all the time, and now I was even more insecure. I questioned him every time he left our house, and if he was gone too long, that turned into an argument. I still hadn't told him that I was pregnant, but I planned to do so today. Things had to change, because I was under too much stress, and my relationship was suffering to the point that I felt like Kevin was going to leave me at any moment if I didn't get it together.

I cooked a nice dinner for us this evening and created a romantic atmosphere by lighting candles in the dining room and creating a path of rose petals that led to our bedroom and bathroom. Kevin worked all day and took good care of us. The least I could do was make sure he came home to a clean house and a good hot meal. I had decided I was going to let go of every negative thing that had tried to tear us apart, even my foolishness, and would love my man like he deserved to be loved.

He walked in, with this stressed look on his face. It changed once he saw all the lit candles and the rose petals. "To what do I owe this surprise?" he said, with the biggest smile on his face.

"I just wanted to do something nice for you, baby. I miss the once happy relationship we had, and I just want to get that back," I told him.

"Well, since we are on the subject of our relationship, I have something we need to talk about."

"Okay. What's up?" I said. I was very nervous because I automatically thought he was going to break up with me due to all the drama I had been causing in our relationship.

"Listen, Zoe, I love you with all my heart, but I cannot live with all your insecurities and you constantly accusing me of cheating on you. If you want things to work with you and me, that has to end today. Otherwise, we are not going to make it. I'm not giving up on us. I'm just letting you know that if you continue with this mess, you are going to push me away," he said.

"Baby, I am sorry, and I already realize that. That is why I am making efforts to change and be a better girlfriend and mother," I told him.

"What do you mean, mother? You having my baby or something?" he asked, then walked up to me and kissed me on the lips. I hadn't realized I said something about a baby.

"Do you think I'm pregnant?" I said, smiling at him.

"You just said you are going to be a better girlfriend and mother, so what's all that about?" he replied, wrapping his hands around my waist. Then he began to rub my belly. I looked into my man's eyes, and I saw how much love he had for me and how true he really was to me, and at that very moment, all my insecurities left me.

"I am three months now, and our baby will be born in early December," I said, happy to finally tell him the news.

"Baby, I'm so happy. I can't wait to meet my son," he said, now kissing my belly.

I laughed at him, and his excitement made me more excited. "How do you know it's a boy? It could be a girl."

"Whatever we're having, I'll be happy either way," he said.

That night we were finally able to relax, and for the first time in a long time, I felt complete, and I knew everything was going to be good.

Monique

I had decided that today would be the day I confronted Sam about her bull. I parked my car on the street, then walked up to her house and rang the doorbell. Moments later, I heard fumbling, and Tremaine opened the door. He was holding my nephew, and this was the first time I had ever seen him. He looked just like Tremaine and my dad, and he was so handsome.

"Hello, Tremaine. Is this my little nephew?" I said as I walked inside. I reached out to take my nephew.

"Yes, this is him," he said, passing the baby to me.

"I'm here to talk to Sam. Is she here?" I asked as I played with my nephew. I felt a strong connection with this little guy, even though this was my first time meeting him. I wanted to spend more time with him, but we all knew how silly his mother was.

"Yes, she's here. Uh, Mo, I just want to apologize for everything and at least be cordial for my son and Sam's sake," he said.

"I want the same thing, Tremaine, but I am not the one you should be talking to. Sam is the one who seems to have the problem," I told him.

As soon as those words left my mouth, Sam came strutting into the foyer. I could tell she was not expecting to see me. She rushed over to me and grabbed her son out of my arms. "What the hell are you doing here?" she asked with an attitude.

"I need to speak with you," I responded, keeping my cool.

"Well, talk," she said.

"Not in front of my nephew." I already knew things would get heated, because Sam didn't know how to act.

She handed the baby to his father, and Tremaine carried him toward the back of the house.

"Sam, we are sisters, so I can't understand for the life of me why you continue to try to do things that hurt me. I haven't done anything but be good to you and give you chance after chance, and you still find a way to betray me. What is your problem with me?" I said.

"I don't know what you are talking about. I don't have a problem with you,"

"Look, Sam, I am really trying to fix things between you and me," I said seriously.

"You know what? I am going to be real with you. My problem is you take everything that belongs to me," she said.

"What have I ever taken that belonged to you, Samariah?" I asked.

"For starters, you stole Corey from me, and you stole my father from me. You had the childhood I was supposed to have, but I couldn't, because you and your mom took that away from me."

I knew then that things would not get better between us, and that they might even get worse, but I continued to try to work it out. "Sam, you can't blame me for something our dad chose to do. I found out at the same time that you did that we are sisters. I love you, Sam. I don't hate you. And I just want to see you happy," I said. "You need to stop with all this mess and let that shit go. And as far as Corey is concerned, he was never yours. You knew how much I wanted Corey, and you slept with him and didn't tell me until Corey and I were in a relationship. And the way you told me was even worse. You told me the night of my engagement party, in front of everybody. I still forgave you and tried to move on, but you were still playing games. I am trying to fix things now, but you need to let go."

She stood there, quiet, for a while, like she was contemplating what I had said. Finally, she spoke. "Forget what you're talking about. I don't want to hear shit you have to say."

"I have one last thing to say, because I don't have time to go through the long list of bull you have done, but I will start with the shit you just pulled last week," I said, pulling out my phone. I showed her the video.

"So, why do you assume that I sent you this?" she smirked.

I chuckled at her ignorant self. "You sent it, but that shit backfired, because Corey had already told me what went down between you and him," I said.

"Well, if you knew already, then why are you still here?" she asked.

"I'm here because I was hoping that we could end whatever this is that we've got going on, but I now see that you are too ignorant to do that. I'm just going to let you know that I'm on to your ass now, and we are going to have some real problems the next time you come for me, because I am sick of your shit," I yelled.

"Well, I am sick of your existence. You think you are the shit, but I've got something for your ass," she said.

"I am the shit, and I guess that's why your silly ass is mad, but I don't have time for your shit. I said all that I had to say to you," I responded.

Tremaine walked back into the foyer. "Hey, ladies. Keep your voices down. Little Tremaine can hear you."

"Get out of my house. And how the hell did you know where I am staying?" Sam said.

"I'll gladly leave. And I knew where you were because I used to fuck your man, or did you forget that? We fucked all over this house, and the last time we fucked, it was on that very same couch right there," I said and pointed. "The least he could have done was get y'all a new place," I added and then turned to leave.

"Please go," Tremaine said to my back, because I was already heading to the front door.

When I stepped outside and looked back through the open door, I could see them going at it. That was what her ass got. Now she had a taste of her own medicine.

Sam

To say I was pissed would be an understatement, because I was beyond pissed. I was so mad, I could literally kill her and I wouldn't think twice about it, but right now, I had bigger fish to fry.

"I cannot believe you have me staying in the same house you were fuckin' that bitch in!" I snapped.

"Sam, I honestly didn't think it would be a big deal. It's not like you didn't know we had slept together. We were dating for a while," he said.

"I don't give a damn if you were dating for ten years. You should have moved me and your son into a different place."

"Okay, baby, I hear you. I already had plans for us to move, anyway," he said.

"Are you still in love with her? You want her back, don't you?" I said.

"Are you serious?" he asked.

"Dead ass," I said.

"Sam, if you can't see by now that you are the only woman that has my heart, I don't know what to tell you."

"I don't believe your ass, especially since I caught y'all in here talking alone, and you're taking her side," I snapped.

"Sam, you have lost your mind. I was not taking up for her. And you know what? I'm done with this conversation." He was about to take off.

"Baby, wait. I know you love me, and it better stay that way. I don't want to have to hurt you too," I threatened. I was so serious, because, like I had said many times before, if I couldn't have him, no one else would. I had decided that Tremaine was the only man for me.

"Don't threaten me, Sam. I have a surprise for you, but you two may have ruined it. Sam, I don't understand why you won't just let go of whatever it is that you are holding on to with Mo."

"I have let it go," I lied.

"I heard everything y'all talked about, and my question to you is, do you have feelings for Corey?" he asked.

"No, I don't have feelings for him, the only man I love is you," I replied, and I was telling the truth.

"Well, if that's the case, baby, I need you to stop with all this mess and focus on our family. Oh, and since y'all ruined my surprise, I bought us a house, so get to packing," he said and then smiled at me. I ran over to him and jumped in his arms. He picked me up and wrapped my legs firmly around his waist. I began to kiss him all over his face to show my appreciation.

"Baby, thank you for everything you do for me and our son," I said.

"You are welcome, but promise me you are going to do better, Sam. If you don't change, I am going to leave you, because I'm trying to do great things, and I need you on board with what I'm doing," he said.

I answered him by kissing him on the lips and then trailing my lips down his neck. I dropped to my knees and pulled down his basketball shorts. I took his balls and pole in my mouth and sucked on both of them softly, with a hint of roughness. His head tilted back, so I knew he was enjoying the feeling of my warm mouth going up and down his shaft.

Once I was done, and I knew he was about to cum, I took off all my clothes, and I bent over in front of him and touched my toes. I took my middle finger, licked it, and then began to play with Miss Kitty. He stood there with his pole hard as hell, watching me bring myself to an orgasm. I used my finger to tell him to come to me, and he did what he was told. He entered me while I was bent over, touching my toes. I played with my clit while he continued to stroke me really good. Moments later, we had both cum, and we fell on the couch and cuddled.

Once I got rid of Mo, my life would be perfect, but I could no longer wait. Something had to be done now.

Chapter Thirty-eight

Sharon

Things between Cameron and me had been perfect, but today I had an agenda. My daughter had told me that Kendra and Tim had made things official. I texted Tim and told him I wanted to talk, and of course, his ass was all too eager to do so. I hadn't seen him since the day I left his sorry ass, but today I had something to prove. He asked me to come to the house we had once shared so we could have this so-called conversation. I drank a whole bottle of wine before I went there because I had to be tipsy to do what I had in mind.

I pulled up to the house, and the front door flew open before I had even parked my car good. Tim was at the door, with the biggest smile I had ever seen on his face, but this visit wasn't for pleasure. It was just business. I walked up to him and gave him a tight hug and a kiss on the cheek. Don't get me wrong. Tim was one of the finest men I had ever laid eyes on, but now the sight of him made me sick to my stomach, and his touch was just as bad. I pulled myself together because I had an agenda, and I was going to accomplish it.

I walked inside the house, and everything was totally different. There was new furniture and pictures of little Tim and Kendra all over the place. The house was still clean, and to be honest, it looked good. Tim and I sat down on the couch, and I made small talk with him.

"Do you mind if I use the powder room?" I asked.

"Sure, baby. This is still your house too," he said.

I gave him a weak smile and headed in the direction of the powder room. I skipped the powder room and went into the bedroom we had once shared. All types of memories flooded my mind. Once upon a time, this man had made me so happy. He had made love to my body like no other, but now it was over, and I had moved on with my life. I took my camera out of my purse, cut it on, and then placed it back in my purse. I went back to where Tim was sitting. It was time to put on a show. I walked over to him and sat on his lap.

"You know, I miss the way you touch me and make love to me. You think we can make love one more time for old times' sake?" I said and then brushed my lips across his.

His pole instantly got hard. It never took much for me to turn him on. I grabbed his hand and led him to the bedroom. Once inside the room, I pushed him on the bed and then turned to examine the camera in my purse to make sure it was still on. Blocking Tim's view with my body, I placed the purse on the dresser, pulled out the camera so that only the lens was showing, and pointed the lens at the bed. Then I slowly took off my clothes to give him a striptease. I had the perfect body for my age, and I knew Tim loved every inch of it. I told him to take all his clothes off, and he did as he was told.

"Come over here and lick Miss Kitty," I told him once he had undressed.

He picked me up, put both of my legs over his shoulders, and dove head first into my honeypot. I came in his mouth twice, and I almost forgot whom I was with. I pushed him on the bed and put a condom on his pole.

"Sharon, do we really have to use one of these?" he said, pointing at his condom-wrapped penis.

"Um, yes, if you want some of Miss Kitty," I purred.

I fucked Tim in every position imaginable until we had both come twice. Once we were done, I immediately got up and got dressed. Then I pushed the camera back inside my purse, picked up the purse, and headed to the bedroom door.

"Sharon, where are you going?" Tim asked, with a panicked look on his face.

I stopped and turned to look at him. "I'm going home," I said nonchalantly.

"What do you mean, you're going home? We just made love. I thought that meant you wanted to work on us," he said, and I burst out laughing.

"You couldn't have thought that. I would never be with you again, and trust me, this was the last time we will ever sleep together," I said.

"Sharon, please. I don't love Kendra like I love you. I would leave her in a heartbeat for you. You have my heart, not her," he said, practically in tears.

"Well, what can I say . . . ? You should have thought about that before you cheated on me with several women and ruined our marriage. This was fun, but it will never happen again, and there will never be a you and me again," I said, then turned to leave once again.

He turned his back to me, and I used that as an opportunity to cut the camera off.

"Well, I've got to go," I said with a big-ass grin on my face. And with that, I left my old house. I had got what I had come there for. Now I was going to send the video I had shot to Kendra so that she could get a taste of what she had given me.

Payback is a bitch!

Bria

I hadn't talked to David since the day I left his office, but his mother had called me, trying to check me for beating

Meka's ass. When she said Meka's name, I hung up in her face, because I already knew that Meka had told her a bunch of lies, which she had obviously fallen for. She called back several times, but I didn't answer. When she realized I wasn't going to pick up my phone, she sent me a few text messages, telling me how wrong I was for hurting Meka and how I needed to accept the fact that she and David were trying to work on their relationship. I blocked all their asses and kept it moving.

Nathan and I had been spending a lot of time together. I had told him all about David, and he had been keeping my mind off all my problems. At first, it was just something to do to help get over the pain I felt from this situation with David, but now I thought it was turning into something more. I liked spending time with him, and when we were not together, I found myself thinking about him a lot. Not to mention, I hadn't had sex since the day David and I broke up, and I was horny as hell, but Nathan had been the perfect gentleman. He hadn't tried one time to have sex with me, and I really appreciated him for that.

Today Nathan and I decided to go to this place named Chops. It was one of my favorite places to eat. We were about to head inside when I felt someone snatch my arm. I was about to snap at whoever the hell it was, until I looked into David's eyes and saw nothing but anger and hurt. I got scared because I didn't think I had ever seen him look this pissed.

"We have been broken up for all of two weeks, and you have already moved on to the next nigga," he said.

"Man, hold up. Don't be grabbing on her like that. And I am not your nigga," Nathan said.

Before things escalated, I put an end to it all. "Nathan, can you please give us a minute?" I asked him.

Nathan looked hesitant at first, but he eventually walked off.

"First of all, David, we have been broken up for months now, and second, you should have thought about what I was going to be doing before you let this ho of a baby mama of yours ruin our relationship," I snapped.

"I don't want to hear none of that shit. Despite her being messy, I was faithful to your ass, and I took good care of you and my son. Just because things got a little hard, you are ready to give up on me," he said.

"Isn't that what you did? When you found out I was pregnant, you turned into a different person and cheated on me with that rat who has made both of our lives a living hell, and you refuse to do anything about it. You won't get a paternity test to even see if the child is really yours," I snapped.

"Bria, baby, I am trying to fix all this mess. I love you, and I can't do this without you. You are my rib, Bria. I need you by my side," he said. At that moment, I wanted to run in his arms and take him back, but I had to be strong.

"If you want me back, your actions would show that, but I am not going to wait around for you to do that. I gave you almost ten years of my life, and you put this woman you barely even know before me. As of now, I am done with you, David. I've got to go," I told him, and then I walked off. He ran behind me and grabbed me.

"Just give me some time. I will fix all of this," he pleaded.

I nodded at him, then walked inside the restaurant and left him standing outside. It took everything I had in me to walk away from him, because, truth be told, he had my heart, but I refused to go back to that messy situation. If he got a blood test, only then would I consider taking him back, but if he didn't, David and I were over for good. I found Nathan at one of the tables, but I was no longer in the mood to eat.

"Hey, you," I said to Nathan.

"Hey, you ready to eat?" he asked, smiling at me.

"I'm not really in the mood to be here. Maybe we can grab some fast food and go back to your place," I suggested.

"Cool," he said, and then we left the restaurant. We stopped at KFC for some chicken and at the liquor store for some Patrón.

When we got to his place, we ate our food and took shot after shot. I was past drunk. I wanted to drink away my feelings. I wasn't thinking about David, but my ass was still horny, and the liquor only seemed to increase this. Nathan was sitting next to me, looking and smelling good as hell. I straddled him and just stared in his eyes for a second before I placed my lips on his. His lips felt good against mine, and I was so wrapped up in our kiss, until an image of David popped in my head. I slowly pulled away from the kiss and sat back down next to Nathan.

All of a sudden, he laid me down on the couch and hiked my dress up. He didn't bother taking my panties off; he just pushed them to the side and dove headfirst with his tongue into my honeypot. I wanted so badly to stop him, because I had begun to feel bad, but his head game was something serious, and he immediately brought me to an orgasm. Once he was finished, he went into the bathroom and brushed his teeth, then came back with a wet cloth and wiped me off. He pulled me close to him on the couch, and we both drifted off to sleep.

When I woke up the next morning, I had a major headache, and my stomach was growling. Nathan was no longer next to me, and I realized he had moved me into the bedroom. I was so glad I didn't have sex with him, because I now realized I would have regretted it. Truth was, I really missed David, and he was really the one I wanted. I just couldn't deal with all the drama anymore. A few minutes later. Nathan walked into the bedroom with some breakfast, which smelled and looked awesome.

"Hey, sleepyhead," he said.

"Hey, handsome," I said, then kissed him on the lips and took the breakfast from him.

We ate breakfast in bed and talked about miscellaneous stuff. Then he dropped me off at my mom's house, and he went to basketball practice. I was so confused because I was actually feeling Nathan, but I knew my heart belonged to David. I just didn't know if David deserved it or if we were really meant to be together, like I had always thought. I had to figure out something, because I didn't want to break anyone's heart.

Kendra

I was sitting on the floor, playing with my son, when I got an e-mail from Sharon. *What the hell does this bitch want?* I thought.

From: Sharon

Subject: Payback is a Bitch

After watching this video, I hope you feel as hurt as you have made me feel over the years. You do know karma is a bitch, and you reap what you sow!

I was hesitant at first to even click on the e-mail, but my curiosity got the best of me. As I began to watch the video, I was filled with hurt and rage. When I heard Tim say that he would leave me for Sharon and that he loved her more, I really began to bawl. Karma had hit me, but unlike Sharon, this shit didn't faze me, because I was not leaving Tim. But I would check him and Sharon about what he had done. I dropped my son off at Sam's new house and headed straight to Tim's office.

"Hey, girl. I was just about to call you. That ho Madison is in there," his receptionist told me, pointing at Tim's office.

"Oh, really? Thanks for the update, girl," I said, and then I walked toward his office. When I opened the door, I got the shock of my life. Madison was bouncing up and down on my man's dick, and I could tell that he was in pure heaven. She was buck ass naked, and so was he. I stepped into the office. They were so into the sex that they didn't even realize that I was inside the office. I was so hurt and lost in what was going on that I wasn't able to open my mouth.

"Yes, Daddy. Cum for Mama," Madison said as Tim gripped her hips and began to pump inside of her harder. I knew he was about to cum, because he made the same face every time I made him cum. Hearing her speak brought me back to reality.

"Ain't neither one of y'all about to be coming in this bitch," I said as I threw the picture of Sharon that Tim still had on his desk. Madison jumped off Tim, and when she did, you could see the cum squirt from his pole. This nigga did not have the decency to wear a condom, which pissed me off even more.

"So, not only are you still sleeping with her, but you're fucking her without a condom too?" I snarled, walking closer to Madison. But before I could put my hands on her, Tim jumped in the middle of us.

"What are you doing here, Kendra?" he said, clearly exhausted.

"That's all you can say to me when I just caught you cheating on me?" I asked.

"Madison, get your things on and please leave," he ordered.

Madison threw her clothes on, but she didn't leave the office.

"You're still fucking Sharon too, I see. She sent me the little video you two made," I said and then slapped the shit out of him.

"Kendra, keep your hands off me! And I have no idea what you are talking about. I never made any video with my wife. I mean, ex-wife," he told me.

I pulled out my phone and played the video. "What the hell is this, then? Please don't try to lie to me, because those are the same sheets we just picked out when we moved in together," I growled.

He took the phone from my hand and began to watch the video.

"Wait. You moved in with her, when you just told me that you were going to get a place with me and our baby?" Madison said and burst into tears.

"She's pregnant? Oh, hell naw!" I screeched, and then I repeatedly punched Tim all over his body. The only reason Madison didn't get a few punches was that she was pregnant, and I wasn't trying to go to jail. Tim was finally able to gain control of my arms, and then I burst into tears.

"How could you do this to me? I stood by your side after all these years, after I watched you marry and have a baby with someone else. I still wanted you after you treated me and your daughter like we didn't exist for all those years, and you still had the nerves to cheat on me and have another baby on me," I cried, not believing my own words as they left my mouth.

"Kendra, please go home. We will fix this as soon as I get there," Tim said.

I didn't say another word; I just left his office. I drove around for about thirty minutes before I called the only person I knew who would be there for me.

"Hey, can you get away?" I asked when he picked up the phone.

"You know I can for you," he answered.

"Meet me at our spot," I said.

We said our good-byes, and I headed to the Residence Inn downtown.

I know you are probably thinking, *Who is this mystery man she is calling to meet up with*? Well, let me explain. Let me be clear. Tim had always been my top priority as far as men were concerned, but for the past five or six years, I had been seeing someone else on the down low. We had started as just friends, but then, about a year after we met, we became secret lovers. The interesting part was we both had someone. He was married, but their marriage had been messed up long before I stepped into the picture, and, well, I had Tim. Whenever Tim was acting a fool, my lover was there to pick me up. He really wanted to be with me, but I could not see past the love I had for Tim.

I walked into the hotel suite, and when I saw my lover, I fell into his arms, and I instantly felt better. I wouldn't be returning home tonight. Hell, who knew? I might stay gone for a few nights. Tim needed to know that two could play that game.

Zoe

I had loved every bit of our relationship since I apologized for my behavior and chose to have a happy relationship. I was six months pregnant now, and my man treated me like a queen. Tonight he took me to dinner and a movie, and I ate too much, so now I was tired and ready to take my chubby self home. I had gained a few pounds with my pregnancy, but of course, it was mostly my stomach. We pulled up in our driveway, and I saw a woman leaning against Kevin's car. Once we got out, we realized it was Imani's snake ass.

"What the hell is she doing at our house?" Kevin said heatedly.

"I don't know, but you better fix it before I beat this girl's ass—pregnant and all," I warned loud and clear so that she could hear me.

"Baby, chill. I've got this," he said. He walked over to Imani, and I walked closer so I could hear what the hell they were talking about.

"What are you doing at my house? And how did you even know where we live?" he asked.

"Kevin, I am sorry to show up here like this, but I really need you right now," she said as she began to cry. I almost felt bad for her, but it was my man she was trying to steal, and I couldn't have that.

"Imani, I am not your man, so I am asking you as nicely as I can to please leave my property," he said and pointed in the direction of her car.

"Please, Kevin, I miss you, and you are all I can think about. You changed your number, so I had no way of contacting you," she cried. It was time for me to step in, because she had gone beyond disrespectful.

"Imani, I am trying to be peaceful, but you are taking things too far. You come to my home and beg my man to be with you, like I'm not even standing right here. The only reason I haven't beat your ass yet is that I am pregnant. You need to go right now, before I lose my damn mind and hurt your silly ass," I said after stepping up to her.

"Baby, I said to chill. I've got this," Kevin said.

"You ain't got shit. This bitch is standing here, disrespecting me, like I'm not even here," I said, pointing at her.

"I don't give a damn if you are pregnant," Imani muttered. "You left him to be with another nigga. I would never do that to him, and I was the one who helped make him feel better once your ho ass left him with a broken heart. Now you think I am supposed to back down because y'all are back together and now you're pregnant. You probably got pregnant on purpose, just to try to keep him."

I was so pissed that I couldn't even say anything, so I did the next best thing: I punched that bitch right in her mouth, and her ass hit the ground.

"Baby, get your ass in the house before I hurt you. If anything happens to my baby, we are going to have some problems," Kevin snapped.

I did as I was told, but not before I spit on that bitch.

"You're just going to let her do this to me?" she squealed, now on her feet. She tried to get to me, but Kevin held her back. I dashed to the front door and stood in our doorway with a smirk on my face. Kevin grabbed her by her shirt and began to snap on her.

"Look, I tried to be nice to your ass a long time ago, but you are taking things too far. Leave my house, and don't bring your ass back. I don't want you. I would never be with you. You and I will never be. I don't know how many ways to say it," he said as he let her go.

She dropped to her knees and began to wrap her arms around his ankles so he couldn't walk properly. She was crying hysterically and acting a damn fool. "Kevin, please. My grandma is sick. I have no one else."

"That is not my problem," he said as he pried her arms off him.

Just then, a few police cars swarmed our house. The officers got out of their cars and immediately tried to arrest Kevin. I ran up to two of the officers and tried to explain to them what had happened. They didn't believe me until the neighbors came over to verify my story. They couldn't arrest me or Kevin, because Imani was on our property. The next morning we went down to the courthouse and got a restraining order put on that crazy bitch. Hopefully, that ass beating and this paperwork would keep her ass away. Otherwise, I was going to end up hurting her silly self.

Chapter Thirty-nine

Tim

My life had been a living hell ever since my wife handed me those pictures and the divorce papers. I had become reckless with these females, and it had cost me my marriage and had gained me two more children. I didn't regret having kids; I just wished I had remained faithful to my wife. I was missing her like crazy, but after seeing how she had played me to get back at Kendra, I knew she was done with me. Even if she weren't, I knew that finding out that I had another baby on the way would seal the deal.

The day Kendra had discovered that Madison was pregnant, I told Madison that we needed to cool it for a while, and I sent her ass home. I assured her that I would take care of my child, but she was already threatening that if we were not together, I wouldn't be seeing my child. I told her crazy ass I would see her in court if she tried to pull that shit. She ignored me and told me I would be knocking at her door in a few days for some more pussy, but she couldn't be further from the truth. The truth was, I was done playing games with these women. I decided that day that I would be faithful to Kendra and would focus on getting my law firm in order. Since all this shit went down, I had been slacking on my cases, and my partners had had to pick up the slack for me.

Kendra deserved to have me all to herself; she had put up with my shit for all these years, and her love for me had never wavered—unlike Sharon. That is, if the paternity test I had taken for my son came back that he was indeed mine. So, the night I told Kendra to take her ass home and I would meet her there, she never showed. I called Sam, and Kendra wasn't there, so I figured she would come home at any moment. Imagine my surprise when I woke up the next day and Kendra still hadn't shown up. I went everywhere, looking for her, and I couldn't find her anywhere.

She finally brought her slick ass home two days later. We argued about it for a few hours, because she couldn't seem to keep her story straight. Somehow, our fight turned into us making love, and I left it alone as far as she was concerned, but I couldn't get the thought out of my mind that she could have possibly been with another man. When I sat and thought about it, I realized that over the years, her ass would disappear for a couple of days every time she got mad at me. So, to ease all the negative thoughts that were swirling around in my head, I decided that if everything turned out great with the paternity test, I would propose to her.

To get things off my mind, I decided to take Kendra out to the Capital Grille for dinner. When we got there, the first person I spotted was Sharon, sitting in a booth by herself. It wasn't a big surprise to see her there, because it was her favorite place to eat. We walked past her; it was the only way to get to where the hostess was taking us. Of course, when we walked past her, Kendra gripped my arm tighter and smirked at Sharon. Sharon didn't even let our presence faze her. I was hoping to see a little hint of jealousy or some type of love still there for me, but there wasn't any.

I saw some white guy walk up to Sharon's table, and she got up and hugged him tightly. I figured he must be someone she was doing business with, until she French-kissed the hell out of him. I wanted so badly to go over there and act a fool, but I kept my composure.

"I had no clue she was into white men," Kendra said.

"Who?" I asked, acting clueless. I didn't want Kendra to know that I was paying Sharon any attention.

"Don't act dumb, Tim. I know you were looking over there just like I was," she said, now facing me.

"Who cares? We have both moved on," I said, then kissed her on the lips.

About ten minutes later, I watched Sharon get up and head to the bathroom. I excused myself and headed there too. . . .

Sharon

I wasn't fazed at all by seeing Kendra and Tim together. It wasn't like it was something new. He and I were the past, and Cameron was my future. I know y'all might think this is crazy, but Cam and I had gone to Vegas and tied the knot. I knew it probably seemed so soon, but I was not getting any younger, and I knew that Cam was the one for me. I hadn't told anyone yet, but I planned on doing so soon because I couldn't hide this big rock he had got me. I washed my hands and headed out of the bathroom, and of course, Tim's dumb ass was there, waiting for me.

"Tim, what do you want? I really don't have time for any drama today," I said.

"So, you found you a new man. I'm sure he's no better than me," he smirked.

"You're right. I have found me a new man, and he is nothing like you. He knows how to treat and respect women—unlike you," I said, trying to push past him.

"What about the night we shared?" he asked.

"That was just business, not personal." I laughed.

"Sharon, feelings don't just conveniently go away. I was with you for over twenty years. You mean to tell me that you don't love me or think about me?"

"I will always love you, because you are the father of my child, but I am not in love with you. I am in love with Cameron," I said.

"Oh, so his name is Cameron? Well, does Cameron kiss you like this?" he said, then tried to kiss me, but I put my hand up and stopped him right in his tracks. He snatched my hand and stared down at my ring finger. "What is this? Is this some type of joke? Are you wearing this ring for decoration or something?" I hated that he had seen my ring, and I hated that I was about to burst his bubble, but he needed to know what reality was.

"It's not a joke, Tim. Cameron is my husband, so now it should be clear to you that it's over between us and you need to move on with your life," I said.

"You married that nigga!" he shouted, loud enough for everyone in the restaurant to hear.

"Tim, I am done with this conversation. I don't owe you any explanation," I said, and then I tried to walk away, but he grabbed my arm and pinned me against the wall.

"What the fuck? We haven't even been divorced a year, and your no-good ass has already married someone else. You mean to tell me I mean absolutely nothing to you now?" he shouted.

Moments later, Kendra and Cam came running over to us. Cam grabbed Tim and pulled him off me, then rushed over to me.

"You must want your ass beat by putting your hands on me," Tim said to Cam.

"If you ever disrespect my wife by putting your hands on her again, yes, we will be fighting," Cam said.

Kendra and I grabbed our men and pulled them in separate directions. Cam and I returned to our table, but we did not sit down. Cam left a hundred-dollar bill on the table, and we left the restaurant.

"Sorry about all that, honey," I said once we were back in the car and on our way home.

"You have nothing to be sorry about. It wasn't your fault," he said, grabbing my hand as he drove. "What was all that about, anyway?"

"He got mad because I told him I was married to you. That was my ex-husband," I explained.

"Well, he needs to get over himself and realize you have a real man now, and you don't have time for his little games," Cam said.

"I'm sure he realizes it now," I said, smiling at him. I put Tim out of my mind because he no longer deserved to occupy space in my thoughts.

When Cam and I got home, I made love to my man, and we put what had just happened out of our minds for good.

Chapter Forty

Monique

Like I mentioned before, I was going to get everything I needed to know about my so-called sister, and today was the day. I was meeting up with my father. I had a list of questions I was going to ask him, and he would give me the answers.

Around noon, I knocked on his door, and moments later, he answered.

"Hey, Daddy. You look rough," I said as I stepped inside the house. I hugged my father, and the overwhelming stench of alcohol hit me like a ton of bricks.

"Hey, baby," he slurred.

"Dad, it is twelve noon. It's too early to be drinking."

"Don't worry about me, honey. What made you come over? I've been trying to get you over for months now," he said as he sat on the couch.

"I need to talk to you about Sam, and I need some real answers," I told him as I took a seat on the living-room couch.

"What about her?" he asked.

"What is wrong with Sam? You told me she was in a mental institution, but you really didn't go into any detail as to why," I said.

"Baby girl, why is that important? You two act like you can't stand each other, when you used to be best friends."

"Daddy, I need to know so I can better understand how to be there for her, and I want to understand her so that we can rebuild our relationship," I lied. I had no intention of building anything with her, because I had tried several times, and each time, I had been bit in the ass.

"She has multiple personality disorder," he said.

I tried my best to hide my shock. "How did y'all discover this?"

"When she was twelve years old, she beat up some boy and his girlfriend because she had a crush on him, and she didn't want to see him with another girl. When the police found out that she did it, she was arrested, but she had no recollection of what she did," he explained. "During the interview process, she started screaming at herself, and basically, she went crazy, so they sent her to be evaluated, and that's when she was diagnosed."

I couldn't believe my ears. I had heard rumors about her doing that, but I had never thought it was true. "I think Sam really needs help, Dad. She could be responsible for a lot of the things that have been happening to everybody around here."

"My daughter is fine. She doesn't need any help," Kendra said, suddenly making an appearance. My dad and I both looked at her. I had had no clue she was here. This was the first time I had seen her since she pulled that stunt at my wedding. And I still hadn't checked her for ruining my wedding, either.

"She obviously does, and you two are not helping her by hiding the fact the something is seriously wrong with her," I said.

"Mo, she will be fine. She is taking her meds," my dad insisted.

"She is trying to hurt me. Who knows who else she is trying to hurt? You two won't be satisfied until she kills someone," I muttered.

"Baby girl, I think you are taking things too far. She is not capable of killing anyone," my dad said.

"Right. Sam wouldn't hurt a fly," Kendra said, pissing me off.

"Well, let me go, Dad. I'll leave you here with your home-wrecking-ass girlfriend." I stood up to leave.

"Little girl, I won't be disrespected in my own home," Kendra snapped.

"You mean my mama's house. My father bought this house for my mother," I said through my laughter.

She couldn't say anything. She just stood there, looking stupid. I kissed my dad good-bye and left that house. As soon as the front door shut, I heard them arguing. I absolutely could not believe Sam had actually hurt people. Now I knew for sure that she could have hurt Bria and Zoe, and Lord knows who else. For now, I was going to hold on to this little tidbit of information, but if she came at me again, we were going to have some problems.

Bria

Nathan and I had been spending a lot more time together since the day he went down on me. We still hadn't had sex, because I wasn't ready. I was horny as hell, but the only man who had ever been inside of me was David. To be honest, he was the only person I had ever wanted to be with on that level. Nathan was sexy as hell, and I loved how we were together, but the more time I spent with him, the more I realized that I really wanted to be with David. So, I invited Nathan over to my parents' house to let him know how I felt, because I did not want to lead him on. I greeted him at the door with a tight hug, and when I pulled back, he kissed me on the lips. I didn't resist, because this would probably be the last time we ever shared a kiss.

"Hey, Nathan. I really need to talk to you," I said as I ushered him inside the house.

"Okay. What's up?" he said as he sat down on the couch next to me.

I felt nervous all of a sudden, but I knew what I was about to do was right. "Listen, I love being around you and spending all the time we spend together, but my heart is still with David, and I don't want to hurt you or lead you on," I said. He looked crushed, and I started feeling really bad.

"It's okay, Bria. I respect you even more for being honest with me and going about things the right way," he said, and then he smiled at me.

"Nathan, I love everything about you, and under different circumstances, I would definitely be your woman."

"I know you would, but if that nigga acts up, you know how to get in touch with me," he said. Then he grabbed my face and gave me one last kiss.

We walked outside hand in hand, and I gave him one last hug when we made it to his car. Just as we were releasing each other, David pulled up in front of my parents' house, hopped out of his car, and walked over to us.

"I thought I told you to stay away from my girl," David said, sizing Nathan up.

"Bria, remember what I told you," Nathan said as he ignored David and got into his car.

When Nathan pulled off, I looked at David, shook my head, and turned to walk in the house, and he was right on my heels. I had had plans to call his crazy ass when I got back in the house, but he had already beat me to the punch by just showing up.

"Bria, I need to talk to you," he said once we were inside.

"You're right, David. We do need to talk," I said calmly.

"I took the blood test," he blurted out.

I tried my hardest to hide the smile that had spread across my face, but I couldn't.

"Your ass can't even try to fake like you aren't happy," he said.

"When did you take the test?" I asked.

"Well, you know I had to sneak and do it, because she doesn't let me see him without her being around, so I took Caiden and Junior to the bounce house, and when Caiden said he had to use the bathroom, I used that as an opportunity to swab him," David said.

"So, how long before you get the results back?" I said, trying to hide how excited I was.

"I got them back today, but I haven't opened them yet. I wanted to do this with you."

"Okay, but before you open them, there is something I want to tell you," I said.

"What's that? Please don't tell me that you're pregnant by that nigga or you're really trying to be with him. I don't want to have to murder his ass," he said.

I had started to play on his emotions, but I decided against it. "No, I am not pregnant, boy, and I have never had sex with him or anybody else—unlike you," I said with an attitude.

"Sorry, baby. Just say what you got to say," he urged.

"Well, I ended things with Nathan today because I couldn't stop thinking about you. I love you, and I want us to be together, but you have to put your mother and Meka in check. Otherwise, we can't be together."

"Baby, I am so glad you said that, and as you can see, I love your ass, because I got the test done. I just want us to be happy," he said.

"Me too." I kissed his lips.

"I have one more thing I want to ask you," he said.

"What's that?" I responded.

All of sudden, he dropped down on one knee and pulled out a little black box. My heart began to beat out of my chest, and my legs felt like they were about to give out.

"Bria, I love you with every inch of my being. I would never love anyone the way that I love you, so can you please make me the happiest man on Earth and be my wife?" he said, with tears of joy coming out of his eyes. I had started crying when his knee hit the floor. He opened the box and pulled out a fourteen-karat gold, heart-shaped diamond ring.

"Yes, I will marry you, David," I said as more tears streamed down my face. He placed the ring on my finger, and it was a perfect fit. He picked me up, and I wrapped my legs around his waist as I planted kiss after kiss on his face.

"Okay, baby, I know you're excited, but there are some things that we have to take care of tonight, because after today, all the games end," he said.

"Okay," I said, wiping away both of our tears.

"First things first. Open this envelope," he said.

I snatched the envelope out of his hands and opened it. I stood next to him so that we could see the results at the same time. I couldn't believe my eyes; I almost broke down in tears again.

"Let's go to this bitch's house and nip shit in the bud right now," he said as he snatched my arm and led me out of the house. . . .

Meka

"Yes, baby, right there," I said to Mitch as he was beating Miss Kitty from the back. Mitch and I had never stopped sleeping together, and personally, I wouldn't mind being in a relationship with him, but I felt like I loved David just a little bit more. He pulled his pole out and began eating my kitty from the back. I loved when he did shit like that; he had me ready to climb up the walls.

Mitch had been trying for months now to be with me, but I had kept stringing him along because I felt like there was still hope for David and me. Mitch had money but not on the level that David did. As far as sex went, Mitch had David beat, but that was only because David refused to eat Miss Kitty, no matter how many times I suck his pole. Now, don't get me wrong. David had a big dick, and he knew how to use it, and if he ate pussy as well, he would be the perfect man when it came to that area. He said he had never gone down on any woman.

Mitch had just flipped me over on my back and entered me again when my doorbell rang. I ignored it, until they started beating on my door.

"What the hell?" I said as I slid out from under Mitch.

"Baby, what are you doing? I was just about to cum," he said in a whiny voice.

"Me too, baby, but I have to get the door. Someone is beating on it like they are the police," I said, pissed as hell that I couldn't finish my orgasm. "You stay right there. I'll be back to take care of him, so keep him nice and hard for me," I told Mitch as I got up and put my robe and house shoes on.

I went to my front door and snatched it open without even looking to see who it was, and I didn't even bother asking. I was shocked to see David and Bria standing there together, holding hands. I had just known when we had the last fight that they would be over, but I guessed I was wrong once again.

"What the hell are you two doing at my door this time of the night?" I snapped as I tightened my robe.

"We have something we need to talk to you about," David said.

"Me and her don't have shit to talk about. Now, if you want to talk, that is fine," I said and rolled my eyes at that stupid bitch. I really hated her with everything in me. She thought she was the shit.

"Look, Bria is about to be my wife, and whatever concerns me concerns her. Show her that ring, baby," he said, knocking all the breath out of my body.

"Wife?" I said, fighting back tears.

"Yes, wife," Bria said, flashing a big-ass heart-shaped ring in my face.

"What's up, man?" Mitch said, startling me. I hadn't even heard him walk up. I felt like shit, knowing that two men I had slept with were friends. Bria looked at me with a smirk on her face and shook her head.

"Look, what are you here to talk to me about? I don't have all day to deal with this shit. If you came here to tell me y'all are about to get married, you could have kept that shit to yourself, because, trust me, I don't give a fuck," I lied. Truth was, I was hurt as hell to know that he had chosen her and not me.

David handed me a piece of paper.

"What the hell is this?" I asked before opening it up.

"Oh, that's just paperwork stating that Caiden is not my son," he said, with this dumb-ass look on his face.

"What do you mean, he isn't your son?" I said as my heart began to beat out of my chest. My hands were trembling so badly that I could barely unfold the paper he'd given me.

"Just like I said, Caiden is not mine, so you stay the fuck away from me and my family," David said and then turned to leave.

"You let this bitch talk you into testing my son. You are all Caiden knows," I screamed after them.

"Well, you better introduce him to his real father, because I am not him, and if your ass texts me or comes around me or my family again, your ass will be going to jail," David said.

"David, don't do this to our son," I begged as I tried to run after him, but Mitch grabbed me and held me tight.

"He's not my son, but I know whose son he might be," David said, nodding at Mitch. He and Bria then got in his car, and he pulled off.

I collapsed in Mitch's arms and cried my eyes out right there on my porch.

"Meka, is there a possibility that Caiden is mine?" Mitch asked me.

Instead of lying, I decided to tell the truth, because at that moment, I was sick of all the drama and the lies, and I knew I needed to get my shit together. "Yes, Mitch, there is a strong possibility that he is yours. I just thought that David would be a better fit, and I was in love with him, so I never told you," I said, now scared to look into his eyes.

He lifted my head up and looked me in the eye. "We will get a test done to make sure. Either way, I am here for you and little man," he said, shocking me. I had never taken Mitch as a stand-up guy. He lifted me up off the porch, and we went inside the house.

Maybe this was all for the best. . . .

Monique

My dad had invited all of us over for a small get-together. At first, I wasn't going to go, but he said it was okay if my friends came with me. I hated being around Kendra, especially knowing how she and my father had hurt my mother. Also, they had been acting like shit never happened and like I was supposed to be okay with their relationship. I definitely could not stand being around Sam's silly ass for too long, either.

"Baby, please loosen up and try to at least act like you want to be here," Corey whispered in my ear as we stood in my dad's backyard, where everyone had gathered.

"But, baby, I really don't want to be here," I pouted.

"Well, act like it, anyway," my husband said as if his was the final word on the matter. "Besides, you are doing this for your father, not Kendra," he said.

I plastered a fake smile on my face and continued to mingle. Sam kept stealing glances at me. Her condition had me feeling slightly scared, because I didn't know what her crazy ass was thinking.

"Hey, everybody. I want y'all to gather around and come closer to the dance floor," my dad said.

He had gone all out for this little event he was having. He had the backyard decorated really nicely. He had also hired a DJ and had had a dance floor erected. He had had Foodtique's Urban Cuisine cater the party, and he also had had a bar set up.

"Kendra, come stand next to me," my dad said. Just the mention of her name had me pissed the hell off. "Also, can I have my son and daughters come up here?"

Sam and my little brother walked up front, but I just stood there.

"Baby, get your ass up there," Corey said through clenched teeth, then pushed me forward slightly. I dragged my ass up front and put a fake smile on my face.

Kendra, Sam, and my little brother stood on the opposite side of my father, with big-ass smiles on their faces, and I was on the other side, feeling like an outsider.

"Well, I called you all here because I wanted you to be here to share this special moment with me," my dad said and then dug in his pocket, looking for something. I was staring at my husband when I thought I heard my father say, "Kendra, will you marry me?"

My head snapped in their direction, and when I saw my father on one knee, about to put a ring on Kendra's finger, I nearly lost my damn mind. I rushed over to my dad and snatched the ring out of his hand before he could get it on her finger well enough.

"What the hell are you doing?" Kendra screamed.

"Bitch, you will not ruin this for my mother," Sam said and then ran toward me. Before she could get a lick in, I punched her ass right in the mouth. I tried to knock her teeth out of her mouth, but I didn't hit her ass hard enough. Corey and Tremaine grabbed us and held us apart.

"Monique, what the hell is your problem?" my dad shouted.

Bria and Kevin were taking everyone at the party inside the house, so we could be alone, I guessed. Sam was trying to get to me, and Kendra was screaming at my daddy.

"How in the hell are you going to marry somebody who destroyed your marriage and broke up your family?" I said.

"No, you and you whore of a mother stole our family. He was with my mother first," Sam said.

"Tim, I want her out of our backyard and away from our house right now!" Kendra cried.

"Bitch, what about all the parties you and your stupid-ass daughter ruined for me and my mother?" I said.

"Kendra, I would never put my daughter out of my house. Mo, you were totally out of line with what you did, and you and your sister are out here fighting like y'all don't even know each other. If I ever see you two fighting again, we are going to have some major problems," my dad said.

"Dad, how are you going to marry her when you and mom haven't been separated for a year? That's wrong," I said.

"Your damn mother is already married!" Kendra screamed.

"Bitch, you don't know what the hell you are talking about," I snapped.

"Oh, but I do, and your mom is married to Cameron." I knew she had to be telling the truth, because that was my mom's man's name.

"I don't give a damn if she is. He still has no business marrying your ho ass," I said as I tried to get out of Corey's arms and choke Kendra. Sam tried to come for me again, but Tremaine held on to her tightly.

"Corey, get her out of here so that she can calm down," my dad said.

"You better get a blood test for your so-called son, because if Kendra is anything like her daughter, then she has probably slept with half of Milwaukee. Like mother like daughter," I shouted.

Corey led me to the driveway. I got in the car, pissed as hell.

"Baby, how could you do that to your father on his big day?" Corey said once he was behind the wheel.

"Fuck all of them. Look at how many times they ruined our engagement party and our wedding. Don't take up for them," I said.

"Sweetie, two wrongs don't make shit right. You need to at least apologize to your dad," he said, and he was right. I'd apologize later. Right now, I was ready to go home and forget about the bullshit that had happened tonight.

Chapter Forty-one

Monique

A few weeks had passed since everything went down at the engagement party for my dad and Kendra. I had called the next day to apologize, and all had been forgiven. I had also called my mother and given her a piece of my mind for not telling me that she got married. I wanted to be mad at her, but I couldn't be. Even though my dad had said that all was forgiven, I really wanted to make up for ruining his party, so I had put together a birthday party slash engagement party for the two of them. Even though I couldn't stand Kendra, if that was who he desired to be with, then I just had to accept her

I had hired a DJ, and Bria and I had cooked all the food for the party. We had rented out a beautiful hall that was decorated very nicely. I had been running around like crazy, trying to make sure that this party would be a success. I had got two banners, which said HAPPY BIRTHDAY, TIM and CONGRATULATIONS, TIM AND KENDRA. I had had pictures of him and her set up throughout the venue, as well as pictures of my dad with his friends and his children. The setup was really nice, and I was satisfied with the outcome.

Kendra walked in with one of her friends, and I decided to be the bigger person and apologize for everything that had ever happened between us. I decided I would give her a second chance and start again with a clean slate.

"Kendra, can I speak to you for a moment?" I said just as Sam walked in with Tremaine.

Kendra looked hesitant for a moment, but she eventually came with me.

"Listen, I want to apologize for ruining your engagement party. I also want to apologize for disrespecting you," I said sincerely. I wasn't expecting anything from her, so I was about to walk away when she began to speak.

"I am sorry too for everything I did to hurt you and your mom. I just really love your father, and although I went about things the wrong way, I am glad that we are finally in a good space," she said sincerely.

I gave her a hug, and I felt someone's eyes burning a hole through us. When we released each other, I saw Sam staring at us like we had boils on our face or something. I ignored her and went to mingle with my friends.

The party had been in full swing for about two hours, and my dad still hadn't shown up. I called him several times, but he didn't answer. I walked over to Kendra and told her to call him. Just when she got her phone out of her purse, my dad walked in with a big bottle of Hennessy in his hand. He looked like he was drunk already, so I knew this was about to be a long night, but nothing could have prepared me for how this night really ended. . . .

Tim

It was my forty-second birthday, and you would think that today would be a good day, but it was far from good. I had been drinking all day, and I had nothing to celebrate. I walked into my birthday party and second engagement party drunk and mad as hell.

"What the hell are y'all in here celebrating for? There ain't shit to celebrate," I slurred.

"Daddy, where have you been, and what do you have on?" Monique said and snatched the bottle out of my hand. I snatched that shit back because I needed it.

"Look, I am the father, and you are the child. Don't question me," I said, pointing my finger in her face.

"Daddy, let me talk to you outside please," she said just above a whisper.

Out of the corner of my eye, I saw Kendra and Sam walking my way.

"Daddy, come on," Mo said, grabbing my arm, but I snatched it away, because I had some shit I needed to get off my chest.

"Honey, why are you here, dressed in your pajamas?" Kendra asked.

"Daddy, we have been calling you all night. What's going on with you?" Sam asked.

"Ask your trifling-ass mother what's wrong with me," I slurred.

"Tim, what is going on with you? And why are you talking about me like that?" Kendra said.

"No, the question is, who else have you been fucking?" I said.

"Are you crazy? Daddy, don't do this here," Sam said.

"Right. Whatever y'all need to talk about, do it outside," Mo said.

"Naw, fuck that. I want to know who else this bitch has been fucking!" I yelled at the top of my lungs. All eyes were on me, and that was exactly how I wanted it to be.

"Tim, I haven't been with anyone but you," Kendra said just above a whisper.

"Oh, you haven't been with anyone but me, huh?" I said, getting in her face.

"No, Tim. I haven't. You are embarrassing me and your-self. Can we please do this at home?" she said through tears.

People were trying to mind their own business, but I could tell they were still being nosy.

"Girls, leave me and your father alone and let us talk please," Kendra said.

The girls walked away hesitantly.

"Listen, I done gave you the best of me, and you come in here and try to dog me like I'm some type of slut bitch. You need to pull yourself together and act like the man I said yes to," she said.

I looked in her eyes and burst out laughing, because she really didn't have a clue. She slapped the shit out of me and tried to walk off, but I wasn't finished with her ass. I grabbed her arm and spun her around so that we were face-to-face.

"Kendra, do you know I actually thought your ass was a loyal woman up until today?" I said.

"Tim, what are you talking about? I have always been loyal to you," she cried.

"Well, then, please help me understand, because, baby, I am really trying to understand this. Please tell me why I got the results from a DNA test that I got done on me and my son, and they are saying that there is a zero percent chance that Timothy Peterson Jr. is mine," I said through tears.

"You did what?" she said.

"That's all you have to say to me after I just told you that my fucking son is not mine, you silly bitch!" I screamed and then grabbed her by her neck. I was about to kill the lying bitch.

Everybody ran over to us, and they tried to pry my hands off her neck, to no avail.

"I lost my wife and family because of your lying ass," I said as I shook her. Her eyes were rolling to the back of her head, and I felt the life leaving her body. A moment later Kevin Sr. was finally able to get my hands off her.

"Man, what the hell is wrong with you? Choking on a woman like that," he said as he helped Kendra up from the floor. She fell into his arms and cried on his shoulder.

"You stay the hell out of my business, man. This bitch is a no-good, lying whore," I said, trying to reach for her again, but I was held back by Kevin Jr.

"Hey, man. Stop calling her out of her name," Kevin Sr. said, getting in my face. Now, this nigga had gone too far, trying to protect a bitch he barely even knew.

"Pop, chill out, man. This is his business," Kevin Jr. said to his father.

"Right. That's my woman. Don't tell me how to treat her, unless you know something I don't know," I snapped.

"Yeah, nigga, I do know something you don't. When you're dogging her out and treating her like shit, I am the one who picks up the pieces and makes her feel better," Kevin Sr. said, getting in my face.

"What are you trying to tell me, man? Are you trying to tell me that you're fucking my woman behind my back?" I growled, getting in his face. I could not believe my ears. I knew he wasn't saying what I thought he was saying.

"Kevin, please don't do this. Just leave it alone. I can handle him," Kendra said.

"That's exactly what I'm telling you, nigga," Kevin Sr. spat.

I looked over, and Kendra had a look of fear and defeat written all over her face. "So, this is how you do a nigga? You sleep with my best friend behind my back?" I said, on the verge of tears.

"Tim, I am sorry. I didn't mean to," Kendra said.

"You don't owe him an apology. I told you to leave his sorry ass alone," Kevin Sr. said.

That was all I needed to hear. I punched that nigga right in the lips that he was talking all that shit from. He punched me back, and we ended up on the floor, beating the shit out of each other. It took a while for the others to separate us.

"You better find somewhere else to stay, because we're over," I told Kendra.

"No, you can't leave my mother, Dad. We are supposed to be a family," Sam said and then walked over and grabbed my arms.

"Her ass should have thought about that before she slept with my best friend," I said.

"She can fix it, Daddy. Can't you, Mom? You can fix it," Sam said, looking from me to her mother.

"Sam, it's not that easy, baby. Just let it go," Kendra said through sniffles. I couldn't help but notice that she was now in Kevin Sr.'s arms, but that shit didn't even faze me anymore, because I was definitely through with her tired ass.

"No, I'm not letting shit go. I have waited all my life to have my daddy, and I refuse to let him walk out of my life again," Sam shouted.

"Baby girl, just because your mom and I are not together doesn't mean you won't be a part of my life. I know for sure you are my child," I said.

She started shaking her head back and forth, and I knew things were about to go from bad to worse.

Sam

I had had no idea that my mom and Kevin's dad were sleeping around, period. I was pissed at my mom for not telling me what was going on and for not being faithful to my dad. Her ass had one job, and she couldn't even do that right. It really wasn't her fault, though. Monique and her mom were the ones to blame.

"No, you are just going to go back with Sharon and forget about me, like you did for all those years," I said.

"Baby, I will never forget about you," my dad said, slowly walking toward me. I began to cry.

"Dad, how could you leave me and Mom to start another family? Do you know how hurt I was when I found out you were my dad and Monique had the chance to grow up with you?" I said.

"Baby, let's go talk about this in private," he said.

"Yes, Sam. Calm down, baby," my mom said.

"No, I won't calm down. This bitch got the life I always dreamed of. She gets whatever she wants. She had the perfect little life, while I had to live in hell without my father," I screamed.

"Sam, we made mistakes, but you still had a good life," my dad said.

"I hate Monique, and I hate her black-ass mother. And you know what? They don't deserve to walk this earth," I said. I slowly pulled out the knife I had had in my purse this entire time. I didn't take it out completely yet.

"That's your sister, honey. Don't say that," my mom said.

"Well, I mean it. I hate her," I said, looking Monique dead in the eyes. She looked like she wanted to say something, but she remained quiet.

"Baby, you can't blame them for the choices we made," my dad said.

"I mean every word I am speaking. I hate her, and I blame her for my growing up without my father. I love you, Daddy. I can never blame you. I know that if you hadn't been busy trying to make her happy, you would have been with me and Mama," I said.

"I don't hate you, Sam. I love you. You are my sister," Mo said, finally speaking up. She stepped through the crowd so that she would be closer to me.

"No you don't. You are jealous of me, and you took my daddy away from me," I said, getting angrier.

"Sam, I really do love you," Mo said through tears.

"Bitch, no you don't," I said as I snatched the knife all the way out of my purse and plunged it in her chest.

"Ah!" Mo screamed.

"She stabbed her!" Bria screamed.

I lifted my arm to stab her again. Corey tackled me to the floor and started choking me. I lifted my hand and plunged the knife in his arm.

"Ah!" he howled and rolled on the floor.

I was about to get up, but Bria kicked the knife out of my hand and jumped on top of me. She hit my head on the floor several times. I felt myself about to black out, until someone grabbed her and pulled her off me. I tried to get up, but they had me pinned to the floor. I began to kick and scream, but no matter how much I did, I couldn't get out of their grasp.

"Call an ambulance!" someone shouted.

"I think she is dead," I heard someone scream. I hoped that bitch was dead. She deserved to be for what she had done to me.

"Sam, baby, I'm right here," I heard Tremaine say.

About ten minutes later, the police rushed in and tried to handcuff me, but I wouldn't let them. I scratched, kicked, and screamed, until I felt a sharp pain in my arm. My eyes got heavy, and I could no longer feel my legs. I collapsed on the floor, and moments later, my eyes closed.

Monique

I had woken up in so much pain, but I had woken up. I could not believe that years of drama with Sam had boiled down to my husband and me being stabbed. She had really tried to kill me, though, and if she had stabbed me two inches to the left, she would have succeeded. I had lost a lot of blood, but I was going to live. So, I thanked God for that.

It had been a few months since everything went down, and we all were just trying to pick up the pieces. However, it was really hard for me to move on, because all I could think about was how this girl whom I had grown up with and who had turned out to be my sister could hate me so much. I had a pretty good idea why now, but I really needed some closure. So, against my husband's wishes, I drove up to the hospital to pay Sam a visit. I know you must think that I am crazy, but I understood more about the sickness she had and how she was capable of anything if she was not taking her meds. She was my only sister, and even though it might take some time, I planned to help her every step of the way . . . if she allowed me.

I walked into the hospital and stopped at the reception desk. "I'm here to see Samariah Peterson please," I said to the nurse.

"Can I have your ID?" the nurse said. I gave her my ID, and she made copies of it. Moments later, she gave me a visitor's pass and escorted me to the visiting area. I sat and texted my husband to let him know where I was. It seemed like forever, but Sam finally came out. She still looked beautiful, but she also had this tired look in her eyes. She sat in front of me, but she couldn't look me in the eye.

"Hey, Sam. How are you?" I said.

"Hey," she said.

I was quiet for a moment because I was trying to find the right words to say. "Sam, I need some answers. I need to understand why you hate me so much," I said.

She was quiet for a while. She was quiet for so long that I thought she wasn't going to speak. She finally looked up and stared into my eyes. "Mo, I really don't hate you. I think it was the fact that I tried to hate you so much that drove me to do what I did. It all started when you got with Corey. My relationship with Kevin had started falling apart, and it seemed like things for you started to get better. I started wishing I was you, because everybody loved you. When I found out that you were my sister and that you got to grow up with our dad, I was really hurt and jealous. You know how much I wanted my dad in my life. I would cry on your shoulder all the time about that. I don't know. Something took over, and I could no longer fight the disorder, and I just went crazy," she said as tears fell out of both of our eyes.

I reached over the table to wipe her tears away, and she flinched at first, but then she allowed me to do it.

"How can you be here when I have done nothing but cause you hell?" she said.

"Sam, I love you. You are my sister, and I understand you are sick. If you allow me, I want to help you get better," I said.

"But why? I don't deserve you in my life," she cried.

"You do. Sam, you have to let go of the past and focus on your future. If I am willing to let go of everything you have done, then you should be willing to accept that and move forward. No matter how you feel, you are my sister, and despite how scary this is for me, I choose to be by your side and help you," I said.

"You are right. I'm letting it all go," she said, and I knew that she was telling the truth. "Just please don't leave me, sis," she added, and for the first time, I saw how vulnerable she really was.

"I won't," I said truthfully.

We hugged and sat and talked for a few more minutes, and when I left after that visit, it felt good. I finally felt like I was able to live my life without fear of something bad happening to me. It was crazy how life was sometimes. The same person who had caused me so much hell, I forgave, and I would be there for her.

Bria

I could not believe a night of celebration had turned into *A Nightmare on Elm Street* Milwaukee style. Sam had gone completely fucking crazy and had tried to stab everyone at the party. I was just happy my best friend had survived, and I hadn't had to bury her. I didn't know if I could have forgiven Sam like Monique did, but I applauded her for it. She visited Sam once a week, and she had said that Sam was making really good progress. As for Sam's and my relationship, it would definitely take me some time to get over what she had done to me. She admitted that she was the person who had attacked me and had caused me to have my baby early. I wanted to go up to that damn hospital and do some reckless shit, but I decided to just let it go.

Things between David and me couldn't be better. We had got that crazy bitch Meka out of our lives, so that was a blessing. We had later found out that Mitch was the father of her son. I was pissed that we had had to go through all that bullshit, only to find out that my man wasn't the father. I had heard she and Mitch were in a relationship. I was happy for her ass. Even though she had caused me so much hell, I was just happy that I didn't have to deal with her messy self anymore. It was even better that she had got her own man. Now she wouldn't be coming for mine anymore.

The relationship I had once had with David's mom was gone. I mean, we spoke to each other when we saw each other, and she had tried to resurrect that relationship, but it just wasn't there anymore. She had turned on me so fast, and I now knew that if I did something she didn't agree with, she would turn on me, and for that reason, I would never try to connect with her like that again.

Kevin and Zoe were doing great. They had had a little private wedding ceremony after the birth of the twins. Yes, I said twins. Zoe had gone through her entire pregnancy thinking she was pregnant with only one child, but when she went into labor, they'd found a second heartbeat. She had had a boy and a girl. From what I had heard, Kevin was still pissed at his dad—he wasn't on speaking terms with him—but knowing Kevin, he would forgive him soon.

Besides the little minor things, life was good for me. We had had to postpone our wedding because we were having a little girl. At the time, I'd been six months pregnant and as big as hell. After I gave birth to my son, I'd sworn that I wouldn't get pregnant again, but when David and I got back together, I hadn't been able to keep my hands off him and he hadn't been able to keep his off me, and that was how we had ended up with baby number two. Life was great, and I guessed there was a thing called a happy ending.

Tim

I regretted the day I ever laid eyes on Kendra. She had come in, turned my life upside down, and ripped my heart out of my chest while she was doing it. I could not believe I had actually thought I would marry her and live happily ever after. I couldn't just blame her for what had happened to me, because I had made the decision to lie down with her and every other woman I had cheated on Sharon with.

Sharon would always have a part of my heart, but she had moved on with her life, and I had to do the same.

After the party, Kendra and I had gone our separate ways. We had both realized that we just were not good for each other. Our relationship had been full of turmoil and drama, and that was no way to live. Even though she hadn't tried to get back with me after that night, if she had, I would not have taken her back, because I couldn't get over the fact that my son wasn't mine. She and Kevin were together. He had left his wife and had got together with Kendra. I had also found out that the little boy was Kevin's, and although I was pissed that they'd been sleeping around behind my back, I knew he was a good man for her, and they deserved each other.

I had decided to really throw in my player card and settle down. I didn't cheat anymore, and Madison and I had decided to work on our relationship and raise our son together. I had got a test done, and he was indeed mine. Madison was a little whiny, but I did love her, and she was a good woman to me. We barely argued, and my life was much more peaceful now. My firm was doing well, and right now, I was just enjoying life. I visited my daughter Sam every week, and Mo and I had repaired our broken relationship. I planned on spending the rest of my life with Madison, but I was not rushing to get married. I was just going to let things flow naturally. I had wanted to rush and marry Kendra because Sharon had married her dude, but I was a changed man now. I was doing things the right way this time around.

Sam

Life up until this point had been a living hell for me, but I could finally say that I was a better person now. I had admitted to every bad thing I had ever done to the people I loved, and that had started the healing process for me. They had wanted to give me life in prison for what I did, but because of my disorder, I had ended up doing only a year in the mental institution. I had been taking my meds faithfully, and I didn't think any evil thoughts anymore. They had signed my release papers, and today I would be able to go home.

I would be so happy to see my son. Tremaine hadn't allowed my baby to see me that often at the mental institution. When I walked outside, I was saddened that my mom was the only person there to pick me up. I was disappointed that my sister was not there. We had grown close over this past year, so I just knew she would be there for my release, but she wasn't.

"Where is my son?" I asked my mom as soon as I got in her car.

"Um, hello, and I missed you too. He's at my house," she said. She kissed me on the forehead and drove off. I hated that I was going to have to start over completely, but I would no longer play the victim. I was going to find a job, get a place for my son and me, and do what I had to do to stay healthy for him.

"I thought we were going to your house," I said when my mom pulled up in front of this beautiful house.

"We are, but we have to make a quick stop," she said.

I didn't feel like making any stops; I just wanted to cuddle up with my son. We got out of the car and went inside the house. As soon as we shut the door and my mom cut on the lights, everyone jumped out and shouted, "Surprise!" I was shocked, to say the least. Everyone was there—Bria and David, Kevin and Zoe, Mo and Corey, my dad and his new woman, and my son. Tremaine Jr. ran up to me and hugged me tightly. My sister wobbled over to me and hugged me tightly.

"I see you and Corey have been having fun," I said as I rubbed her belly.

"Yeah, I'm five months," Mo said, smiling that beautiful smile she had.

"Mommy, I missed you," my son said.

"I missed you too," I told him as I planted kiss after kiss on his face. I was so in tune with my son that I didn't see Tremaine walk up to me.

"We missed you so much," Tremaine said, startling me.

"You missed me?" I said as my lips trembled. I had just known he would be done with me once he found out about all the grimy shit that I did.

"Yes, I missed you, and I told you that I would never leave you," he said as he bent down to kiss me on my lips.

"You still want to be with me after all the things I did to the people who love me? I don't deserve you," I cried.

"Baby, that was your past. You just needed a little help, and if they can forgive you, then so can I," he said and then wiped my tears away.

"I love you so much, Tremaine, and I promise to make you proud," I said.

"I know you will." He smiled. "Welcome home, baby. This is all for you."

"You got us another house, baby?" I said excitedly.

He nodded his head yes, and at that very moment, I felt whole. I knew that from this moment forward, things would be good for me. I thanked God for second chances.

The End